Learning Late

also by Chelsey Blue Spicer

Paramour Promise
Requited Rivalry
Optimistic Oath

The 4th Collection of Colorful Choices

Learning Late

Chelsey Blue Spicer

To the women who found themselves later in life.
and
To the single moms who try to make it look easy.

1

Victoria's finger circled the rosy bulb, pinching and twisting occasionally. Her body melded against the cushion that complied to her will. The woman across from her couldn't hear the drumming in her head. A smooth tongue peeked out as the woman's speckled star-blue eyes gazed downward. Victoria's lip pulled back between her teeth as her fingers traced the delicate details surrounding the bulb.

"So, you've been out as a lesbian for approximately six months. You've established your new life in Scottsdale. You got the new job as an Assistant Principal," the woman's eyes wandered back up to Victoria. "How do you feel now?"

The pillow in Victoria's arms shielded her from the therapist. She hated that she loved how the maroon, rose, and pink stitching felt like the pillows on her mother's couch. Still, she leaned back with it still clutched against her chest.

"Lonely," she confessed.

"So, you still haven't had any contact from your family?" Dr. Rose probed, even though they both knew it was the case.

Victoria sighed and looked up at the ceiling tiles. The dim lighting of the room made it seem as though the stars had all combusted in the panels of universes. She searched the divots of the panels looking for constellations, another reminder of the small-town life she'd left the year prior.

"Victoria." Dr. Rose's voice pulled her back from the blankets covering the Utah lawn. Tore her from the childhood memory surrounded by giggling sisters and cousins as they gazed at the heavens. The promised land was now dark at her defiance of the words and her place.

"No. And I won't." Manicured fingers dug into the cloth-covered cotton. "I knew that it would be like this."

The flesh on the inside of Victoria's lower lip bled from her constant chewing. She'd been working at the same spot since she'd arrived at the office. She scraped the metallic taste off her tongue with her teeth, then swallowed the evidence of regret. "It doesn't make it easier though."

A fan burred on the Ikea desk, fluffing Dr. Rose's mane with each oscillation. Her hand ran over the notes page on her obnoxious yellow pad. She scratched another line to the weekly confession. Then, she looked over the 1980s nerd glasses that had fallen toward the tip of her nose.

"How have you been managing loneliness?"

Victoria's eyes rolled as her head fell back against the wood-paneled wall behind her. "How does one manage being lonely?"

"What do you do to distract yourself from feeling lonely?"

Victoria sucked her teeth and connected six divots into the little dipper. "I downloaded the TikTok app because I wanted to be prepared for the new school challenges I would potentially be seeing when I start next week. That was a rabbit hole that started with a lot of lumberjacks and somehow, I am now on lesbian TikTok."

"Do you enjoy social media apps?"

"No. I closed down most of my accounts after I saw the wedding photos of my niece. We'd been close her whole life, and I didn't even know the wedding was happening."

"What else have you done?"

"I signed up for one of the meet-up adventure days with other gay people, but then... I chickened out and just stayed home. I couldn't fit into my work clothes, so I joined a CrossFit gym. I haven't really spoken to anyone other than basic greetings. I also started to sign up for a dating app, but I had to fill out the 'about me' section and I couldn't think of anything to say."

"Why not try the basics? Things you like to do. The food you like to eat," Dr. Rose suggested.

"I tried." She put the pillow down, then leaned forward. "I don't know what I like anymore. Every part of my life has been flipped upside down. I never used to have time to just do things. There was always church. Some niece or nephew or brother or sister's birthday party to attend. After work, I had to cook dinner, or go to the store, or clean the house. I never realized how much time I spent cleaning up after Michael, until it was just me and now dinner is leftovers for three nights and laundry goes into the actual bin, so I don't have to tidy anything."

"Is it nice not having to clean up after your ex-husband?"

Victoria's lips turned up slightly at the corners. "I had spent every Saturday morning scrubbing pee off the floor and the toilet since I was nineteen. Can I just tell you how amazing it is not to choke on shaving cream stench every time I use the toilet?"

Dr. Rose reciprocated the smile. With a nod, she said, "I can imagine that must feel very liberating."

"Yes." Then Victoria shrugged. "I mean, I guess it is."

Dr. Rose made another note. Victoria wondered what type of archive someone could read someday about the mundane details of her life Dr. Rose found interesting enough to write down.

"So, you mentioned starting the dating profile. How do you feel about dating a woman?"

"Terrified." The word had catapulted from her lips before she'd even had the opportunity to weigh the confession. Shaking her head, Victoria said, "I bet that sounds stupid."

"Does being terrified of something new seem like something that should be deemed stupid?"

"No." She thought about how many times she'd listened to a student justify their actions with fear. "It's just... I mean... I left my husband because of my feelings for women. Now, I'm too scared to date a woman."

"Let's talk about the aspects of dating a woman that you find scary. Is there something in particular?"

Victoria's hand pressed against her eyes and down her face. "Who asks who out?"

"Can you explain?"

Victoria looked up with only her eyes at the therapist. She didn't know how to explain the obvious. The more options her brain provided her tongue, the more she realized though, it wasn't obvious. Not to the therapist who had known she was a lesbian since she was a teenager.

"I guess it is stupid. I know women are equal and blah blah blah. But girls wait for boys to ask them out. It's not something girls do."

Dr. Rose set her pen down. "I can assure you I have been asked out by women before."

Victoria's hand shot up. "Yeah, but you are very clearly a feminine female."

She hated the way Dr. Rose's eyebrows crinkled in the middle. Hated how she tilted her head when the therapist looked at Victoria. Hated how it felt like she was a picture hanging just enough off-center to draw attention to her lack of straightness.

"Do you feel masculine?"

"I'm not the sundress-wearing Barbie, but I am not about to cut all my hair off and start wearing baggy clothes," Victoria spat.

"Then, is that the type of woman you find attractive? Someone more masculine?"

Twisting her head to the side, then back, then the other side, her neck popped twice. "No."

Dr. Rose's pen was between her teeth. "Do you feel a feminine woman would not ask you out?"

Victoria's empty stomach fluttered, the air pushing its way into her throat. She swallowed the excess saliva hoping to sedate the hunger at having again forgotten to eat before her dinnertime session.

"I don't know if she would ask me out. I don't know if I could gather the courage to ask someone out myself." She took a deep breath, clenching her stomach to stop the flutters.

Pen scratched to paper. "You said *she*. Is there a woman you are interested in, but you are worried about asking her out?"

"No. Well. No, but yes." Victoria leaned back once more. She didn't have to close her eyes to see the smooth biceps of the brunette woman deadlift. The thick thighs bound only in the thin spandex stretching as the woman's muscles flexed.

"There's this woman at my gym. She has the rainbow lanyard and the "Lexa Deserved Better" sticker on her water bottle. I know she's gay. I mean I guess she could be more on the masculine side but that's because she is tall and thicker framed and I know she's beautiful, but if I ask her out then I don't know what to do. I have never planned a date in my life. And if I did plan a date, and it went well, and we kept dating, then we would get to the point of... you know."

She looked up at Dr. Rose. The blue eyes didn't suggest knowing anything, and Victoria wondered briefly if the woman took a class on appearing flat and clueless.

"You know," Victoria lowered her voice to a whisper, "the sex part."

Victoria sucked her teeth, then shut her mouth. She didn't want to watch the pen detail another shred of her incompetence as evidence.

"So, what I hear you saying is you are attracted to an identifiably gay woman at the gym. You would like to possibly go on a date with her, but you are nervous about planning a date and if the time came having a sexual relationship with her."

"Yes."

"What type of experiences can you think of that you have had planning other outings?"

"You mean like dinner?" Victoria asked.

Dr. Rose nodded.

Victoria studied the wall above Dr. Rose's head.

"I used to choose the restaurant for my monthly outing with Micheal. Sometimes, I would suggest we see a movie. Simple things. I would inform Michael of the dress code of the venue. That's about it."

"So, you are comfortable choosing a place to eat for yourself and a companion. You have previously chosen movies to see. Possibly even arranged to attend one of those small-town festivals or something. You were able to communicate attire suggestions, so your companion at the time would not feel under or overdressed."

Victoria huffed. "You're saying I know how to plan a date."

"Technically, you said so." Dr. Rose scribbled another note on the paper and Victoria found herself leaning forward with the hope she'd be able to make out what was on the page. "Since you are capable, then possibly the real fear is what happens when you plan an amazing date, and she would like to take the evening to the bedroom."

The pillow pressed against the front of Victoria again. Her fingers found the bulb on the pillow, and as she twisted it, she realized how pornographic the whole thing must look. She slapped her hand over the nipple-shaped protrusion.

"I don't know what to do with a woman's body," she practically shouted.

Victoria bit into the same spot on her lip, extracting another dose of sobering corporeality. She closed her eyes.

"It's like I'm walking through the temple again and no one ever said anything about what was about to happen. Yes, I'd heard about sex in high school, but I didn't know how it worked and good sisters did not ask those kinds of questions."

"Victoria, have you explored your own body?"

Victoria's eyes shot open. "You mean like masturbated?"

Dr. Rose's lips smooshed together, and then she nodded. "That is one method, yes."

"No. I wouldn't even know what to do."

The therapist got up from her chair, letting the pages of the notepad flop against the fading leather. She rifled through the folders on her desk until she held up a pamphlet. "I would like to refer you to a colleague."

Victoria scanned the familiar laminate boards chaotically shoved together. The familiarity of the pillow felt like it too was being torn from her grasp and the stiff couch seemed to tilt, sliding her off it.

"Victoria, come back to me," Dr. Rose called through the tunnel of another place no longer safe. Dr. Rose held the shiny trifold out to her. "I am not saying I want to stop our weekly sessions. The referral is not for a therapist, but rather a coach."

A single eyebrow rose on Victoria's face. "Like a life coach?"

"Sort of, but no."

Victoria took the thick page. The glossy texture felt good between her fingers. She looked at the front, then flipped it over.

"An intimacy coach," she read aloud.

She'd never heard of intimacy coaching, but when she opened the pamphlet, her eyes grew.

"Is she a prostitute?"

Dr. Rose laughed. "No. Sarah is not a prostitute. Consider her like a health teacher at a high school but instead of STDs and abstinence lectures, she teaches anatomy and how to successfully pleasure a partner."

Victoria looked at the woman settling back into her chair. "She can teach me how to give a woman an orgasm?"

The smile on Dr. Rose's lips spread up her cheeks to her eyes. "She can teach you how to give a woman or even yourself an orgasm. And her service is completely tax deductible as a medical expense since she is being referred by a medical professional. I would like you to reach out to her. Next week, we can talk about how you felt about the conversation and go from there."

"I don't have to do it if I don't like the conversation," Victoria checked.

"You don't have to reach out to her at all. However, I have worked with Sarah for a long time. She is very professional and very, very good at helping individuals and couples improve their confidence in sexual intimacy."

Dr. Rose checked the watch on her wrist before she pulled the pages on the pad down until all the details of Victoria's life were lost in the pile.

"Our time is up."

2

"What is with the influx of ass-licking clients? Like there is only so many times I can explain how to wash an asshole properly for oral stimulation." Sarah rubbed her fingers to her temples.

Monica's choked laughter tried to rupture the speakers of the car as Sarah rested her forehead against the steering wheel.

"*Maybe 50 Shades of Abuse has a new sequel,*" Monica offered.

She turned and watched the clock on the Navigator's digital display move from 8:10 to 8:20 PM. Her brain totaled the number of hours she'd spent at the library and meeting with Monica's referrals. She chewed on the number 28 and then counted the number of appointments she had scheduled in the evenings for the rest of the week.

"*Where are you headed to now?*"

"The Whites, and I'm already here. It's a one-hour session, so start a timer at exactly 8:30. I will check in by 9:40," Sarah yawned as she answered. "After, I have an initial with the baby gay. What's her name, again? It was something royal sounding."

"*Victoria. You're doing an intake interview?*"

"Yeah, she seemed skittish when she called yesterday, so I suggested a meeting to go over what to expect." Sarah sighed. "Tell me about the Whites."

"*Married since high school. Kids are mostly grown. He cheated on her a year ago. Good news for you, they are not ass lickers... yet.*"

The audible groan erupting from Sarah's throat caused the speakers to rattle again. Sarah hoped Monica was choking this time.

"*Maybe you should take the ass licking off the list so people will stop getting new ideas.*"

"I can't do that. Even though it sounds appealing, it's one of the highest requests for follow-up sessions. Especially since the baby gay and the Whites are the only new clients you've recommended in over two months." Sarah flipped down the visor and checked her make-up in the mirror. "Anything else I need to know about the wifey White?

"*Well... I have been working with Karen for—*"

"Her name is Karen?" Sarah pressed her fingers to her temples. "Is she a middle-aged white lady?"

"*Yeah, but she doesn't live up to the name. So, Kirk cheated, and the shitty part is—*"

"Don't say shit." Sarah shook her head as her best friend laughed at her expense once more. She opened her eyes to see the clock move from 27 to 28. "I have to go."

"Okay, but Sarah, be gentle with this one. Karen has a lot of body dysmorphia."

"Thanks for the heads up. I'll make her feel beautiful, promise."

Sarah hung up and then opened the messenger app. She quickly sent a text to Karen White she'd arrived and left the familiarity of the SUV. She pulled the suitcase from the backseat. The wheels slapped the asphalt and then fought their way to the sidewalk.

The cardigan sweater was overkill for the late Arizona summer, but people's houses tended to be too cold. The otherwise silent street attempted to swallow the sounds of her presence. Sarah walked under the flickering streetlight toward her second client of the night that swallowed her in pitch as it turned off. The black suitcase glided alongside her as she made quicker steps up the driveway to stand in the hue of the soft yellow porch light.

When the door opened, Sarah pushed the unnecessary large-framed glasses up her nose. She watched Karen White's eyes move over her face, down her throat to her chest, and settle on the silver buckles of her Goodwill loafers. As the new client appraised Sarah, Sarah studied the freshly curled blonde locks hanging around the round face of the woman. The woman's eyeliner had begun migrating to the inner corner of her red-rimmed chocolate eyes. Straight white teeth bit into the painted pink lips.

Karen looked over Sarah's shoulder at the vacant street. Sarah watched the dark eyes scan the entryways and sidewalks in the houses across from her own before, ushering Sarah within. As the door shut behind Sarah, the woman said, "Thank you for coming."

The door to the house was left unlocked, which allowed Sarah to breathe a little lighter.

She briefly scanned the family photos hanging over the pale sofa. Everything coordinated in the muted vanilla room that screamed at Sarah not to disturb the parallel vacuum lines. She liked the efficiency of the arrangement and made a mental note to recreate the setup in the living room of a house she'd own one day.

"I thought you would be taller for some reason." Karen's statement pulled Sarah's mind out of Pinterest mode. The corners of her lips lifted into a smile, but Sarah took note it never reached her eyes. "I also for some reason thought you would be wearing one of those black jackets that ties in the front to cover a whole lot of leather."

Sarah's chest rose and fell with a quiet chortle. She forced the smile to reach her eyes as she pushed the glasses once more up her nose, then tucked her brown hair behind her ear. With a choreographed awkward shrug, she said, "I can refer you to someone that dresses like that."

Sarah glanced toward the back of the house. "Is Mr. White home?" she asked as she cataloged the rear sliding glass window as a potential exit, then checked the front door once more for any questionable locking mechanisms.

Karen raised a hand in the direction of the stairs. "He's just putting the dog in the kennel upstairs. I actually don't know what is taking so long."

Sarah looked at the White children in twelve years of school photos lining the walls of the staircase. When she turned back to the middle-aged mother pulling at the floral top, she understood what Monica had meant when she said to be careful.

"Your children are not home, correct?"

"Oh no. Our youngest is the only one who still lives at home, but she is at a friend's house." Karen's arms closed over her chest as her eyes danced around the floor.

Sarah reached out, resting her hand on Karen's bicep. She used the first contact to pretend to soothe Karen's worries. Then she offered, "You would be surprised how many couples seek out intimacy coaching. It is nothing to be ashamed of."

"Dr. Rose said that this has worked with her other clients."

With a nod, Sarah tried to reassure the woman. "I have worked with Dr. Rose for a long time. I can promise you that if she didn't think this service would be of use to you, she never would have referred you to me. Are you aware of what I do?"

"I read the brochure, but I have never heard of an intimacy coach before. I don't really know what to expect. I mean we have kids. We know how to have sex. Is this like a Karma Sutra thing?"

"No," Sarah squeezed the woman's arm lightly. "I work with couples to explore various types of sexual activity. There are other sessions I offer when partners are seeking more adventurous activities, but things like Karma Sutra are not things that I would coach. Tonight, we will be going over more basic aspects of pleasure."

"So, you're going to show us how to have better sex." Karen's gaze wandered to the top of the still-vacant stairs. "Like, teach me how to keep him happy."

Sarah kneaded the woman's arm, waiting for the brown eyes to meet hers once more. "No. I'm not going to teach you how to please him tonight."

Karen's eyebrows scrunched in the middle. Sarah could tell Karen was trying to separate what she thought was going to happen from what Sarah was trying to explain.

Carefully, Sarah said, "I'm here to show him how to have sex with you. How to become the god of sex with you."

The woman's eyes widened. "I thought you were going to say you were going to teach me how to give a blow job."

Sarah didn't laugh because four years of coaching had made her very aware of the internalized inadequacy. She fixed the smile in her eyes once more.

"Men don't need sex to stay. They need to feel good at sex, and women need to feel good when having sex, so they want to do it more often. I'm here to teach your husband how to master the art of your climax."

Sarah watched as a fever moved up Karen's chest and settled in her round cheeks. "I've never... I mean I don't think I have... you know?"

She didn't have to fake the smile this time. She patted the woman's arm as she said, "Well, let's change that for you."

Brown eyes fell to the ground. Shaking her head, Karen said, "I just want to be better for him. I don't want him to leave me or go off with another woman again. I mean look at me."

Thick hands gesture up and down the curves of her pillowed frame.

Even though Sarah didn't have permission, she pulled the woman into a secure hug. She squeezed the soft flesh that melded around her embrace. She held the woman close, recognizing the Redkin conditioner wafting from her hair. Her fingers carded the curls from the woman's face as she said, "Look at me."

The brown eyes rose until they met Sarah's green. "I understand that me being here feels like you failed."

The woman nodded.

"I promise by the end of the hour this moment will be replaced with a happier memory."

The stairs creaked as Mr. White descended. Sarah watched as the soccer ball-shaped head bobbed with each step. He cast her a cheeky grin, rubbing his hands together as he reached the bottom of the stairs.

"Mr. White," Sarah greeted him.

"Hello. You must be the sex lady."

"Yes. I am."

"So, what do we do to get started," he asked.

His disregard for the woman under Sarah's arm told Sarah everything she needed to know about why they were all standing in the living room. She squeezed Karen in a side hug and led her toward the light at the back of the house. "Let's go get the contract finalized so you can get the most out of your hour."

The Whites signed the multiple pages of the confidentiality contract while

Sarah sat at their dining room table. As the pens clicked closed, Sarah watched Karen's chest barely rise and fall. She reached across the table, placing her hand on Karen's since she now had in writing the woman's consent for physical contact. She squeezed the woman's hand until she felt the fingers curl under and reciprocate the contact.

Sarah turned to the man. "Can you please retrieve my case?"

As the plastic shell slapped against the table, Sarah smiled and gave Karen one final squeeze before releasing her. Then she stood and opened the case.

"Karen, your husband has run you a bath upstairs. While you relax, your husband and I are going to go through the information in this section of the binder."

From within the case, Sarah retrieved a three-ring binder that she placed on the table before Karen. She thumbed through the tabs, opening the section to an anatomically correct image of a woman's vagina. She pointed to the image with numbered labels.

"The objective is for him to be able to identify the key areas of a woman's sex that create the most pleasure. Then he will practice his technique on a silicon model with instruction. Once I am satisfied with his progress, we will come upstairs so that you can assess his proficiency."

Karen looked up at her husband, and the smile playing on her lips deepened the wrinkles at the corners of her eyes. He matched the look and held up his hands. "I promise I won't fail."

"I won't allow him to fail," Sarah assured.

As Karen made her way upstairs, Sarah moved the open notebook to the man. "Take note of the various parts. The labia are the outer folds. The vulva vestibule is the outer area of the vaginal opening."

Leaning against the table, Sarah tapped the clitoris at the center of the page. "This is the most critical area of a woman's sex. Touching this spot will cause the muscles in her vaginal canal to tighten. You will experience substantial pleasure when you apply the correct amount of pressure."

"I know what the clit is," he said, leaning back in his chair.

Sarah matched his position, then waited for him to meet her eyes. When he did, she asked, "Are you familiar with your wife's?"

"Of course."

"What does your wife's taste like?"

Mr. White shifted in his seat. He placed a hand on the binder, then leaned toward it. His eyes scanned the page as though the answer was printed there, and then the table and the kitchen counter passed it.

"You mean..." he started but stopped.

"Yes, describe to me what your wife tastes like. Every woman is unique."

"She...Well, it's like a... Are you talking about like what a vagina tastes like?" Sarah nodded.

"Uh... its—"

Shaking her head, Sarah moved the glasses off her face and rested them on her head. "Please, don't waste your money by wasting our time making up a story. If you do not know, then say you do not know. It will not make me think less of you."

"I haven't..." His hand rubbed the cropped hair at the base of his neck. "I haven't eaten her out since high school. It never got anywhere, so I stopped trying."

"I understand."

Sarah got up from the table. She patted the broad shoulder, then placed her finger just below the hooded bean in the picture. "As you look at the clit, I want you to imagine it as a clock."

Sarah moved her finger to the top of the clit, drawing a steadily slow circle around the area. "I want you to think of the twelve hours. Each hour will bring your wife different sensations. When you touch them in combinations, it will cause her to at times moan, cant her hips, and even squirm."

She placed a hand between his shoulders as she leaned in closer. "Nothing is more exciting than watching a woman unravel in your hands."

Mr. White touched the image just as Sarah had.

"Good," she praised his participation. "Now imagine the clock and picture your wife's face as you run from six to one." She placed her hand atop his. "The first contact will undoubtedly cause her to tremble. Her head will fall back into the pillows as she exhales. At one, you trace a circle, connecting the hours. She shutters, maybe a hand comes up, scratching your head."

He licked his lips. "Does it only work if I use my tongue?"

"No," she said. "If you remember the clock, then you can use your fingers while lying alongside her, standing up in the shower, or while sheathed within."

She felt his breath catch in his chest. He moved his finger up, down, and diagonally. He whispered the numbers of his clock, then paused.

"You said something about pressure. How do I know how much to use?"

Sarah moved behind him. Her fingers pressed lightly against the muscles of his shoulder blades. His body relaxed under her touch. Slowly she increased the pressure working at the knots in the muscles. When a sigh slipped through his lips, she leaned closer to his ear.

"I don't know you. I don't need to know you. I just need to apply more pressure until your eyes start to roll back. I can feel your body relax to my touch. Karen's clitoris is a muscle with more nerves than your shoulders. As you touch her, her body will respond. You just have to observe the changes."

He nodded, and she withdrew contact from him. He tapped the two-dimensional magic button. "Is there a combination that works every time?"

"There is a specific number that will be more sensitive than others. Every woman's number is different. If you study the clock, take your time if you will, then you will find the one that sends her to the edge of oblivion."

Placing her hand back on his shoulder, she added, "You know the edge you leap over when you feel the tightening in your stomach. When you lose the ability to control your thrust, and your abdominal muscles contract wildly but the only thing that is completely clear is the fireworks display playing on the inside of your eyelids."

"Yeah," he choked.

"If you massage the clock, manipulate the time. She will see a show that you created for her. Is that something you would like to do?"

"Yes."

"Good." Sarah left him with the binder. She flipped the interior canvas cover of the suitcase over and retrieved a silicone female torso. It was heavy, and the slapped against the table alongside the image as Mr. White's eyes bulged.

"Is that...?"

"Yes." She chuckled, then admitted, "This is a very expensive sex doll."

"Does it have a name?"

Her eyes rolled this time. Why men always wanted to name the headless thing was beyond her.

"It does not."

He looked from the doll to Sarah. "What am I supposed to do with it?"

"It is one thing to look at a picture and trace patterns. It is another thing to touch a three-dimensional model."

"You want me to play with that?" he asked.

"Not play, practice."

She took his hand in hers. Pulling the index finger out from the rest, she placed it on the clit. "Feel how it shifts its position?" she asked.

"Yeah." He pulled his hand back. "This is weird."

"Things are only weird if you make them weird," she stated.

He sucked his teeth and side-eyed her. With a sigh, he put his finger back on the silicon vagina and prodded it. "It doesn't look the same," he said.

"Because the image shows an exposed and excited clit. The doll's clit is hooded."

"Like Assassin's Creed."

Sarah chuckled. "Exactly. You can't catch the Assassin if their hood is up, they blend in. So, you have to coax the clit out of its hood."

He pinched the hood.

"Ouch," Sarah said loudly, causing the man to jump away from the fucktoy. He stared at her, then back at the doll.

She furrowed her brows and set her lips in a tight line. "Don't pinch the clit."

He nodded.

"Say it."

He rubbed the back of his neck once more. Then cleared his throat. "Don't pinch the clit."

"Good. Try again." Then added, "Gently."

Karen's hug lasted longer than Sarah would have liked as the nighttime heat caused a droplet of sweat to run down her spine. The woman had been a trembling mess by the end of the hour, but it had been worth it for Sarah to watch the excitement spread over Kirk White's face.

"I don't know how I can thank you." Karen wiped the tears from her cheeks.

"The trust you gave me, the agreed upon fee, and a good review with Dr. Rose is thanks enough," Sarah stated simply.

"Oh," Karen fumbled with her robe, retrieved an envelope from the pocket, and handed it to Sarah.

Sarah carded through the eight twenty-dollar bills. She tucked the cash into her pocket. "Would you like me to email you a receipt? You can write the session off as a therapeutic medical expense."

Karen laughed. Shaking her head, she said, "Sure."

"I will have it for you first thing in the morning."

Sarah allowed Karen to hug her once more before she turned toward the street. The light had resumed its flickering as though to warn her against making any excessive noises.

"One more question," Karen said. When Sarah turned around, Karen made her way closer. "The binder. It had a lot of tabs within. Are there other... uh... lessons you teach?"

Monica's laughter broke free from a cobweb in Sarah's mind. Sarah nodded with her fixed smile. "I will send you a list of other *lessons* I offer with your receipt tomorrow. If any are something you find interesting, then we can arrange for a follow-up."

"Thank you, Sarah."

"You're welcome. Now if I may suggest, you have a very eager husband upstairs who would like to further practice the application of his developing skills, so go enjoy it."

As Sarah retreated, Karen stood on the porch. The mother of three daughters watched Sarah secure the suitcase and herself within the spacious SUV before she closed the front door and turned off the porch light.

Sarah quickly sent Monica a text to let her know she was in the car, then pulled up the map to the last client of the night. It was a thirty-minute drive to the Scottsdale townhouse. She set the destination and pulled away from the curb toward the freshly out, divorcee.

3

Victoria stared at the hanging clock with its unmoving arms. She rolled two AAA batteries between her fingers, debating if the analog time was worth every lonely moment being measured. The batteries clunked into the kitchen drawer.

She swirled the glass of wine, sniffing the liquid like she'd learned on the trip to further separate herself from the path chosen for her. The wine legs flowed like rivers to a maroon lake. The glass almost tumbled out of Victoria's hand when the phone vibrated on the granite countertop. She set it down carefully, making her way toward the front door.

Stopping at the entry table, she carded her fingers through the roots of her hair and checked her reflection in the mirror. She pressed at the extra skin under her chin, then the crow's feet at the corners of her eyes, wishing it was that easy to make it disappear.

The door protested as knuckles struck it on the opposite side. With a hand to her chest, Victoria took a deep breath and exhaled.

"Coming," she said quietly, so as not to let the woman think she was standing right next to the door. Closing her eyes, she told herself she was in control, then straightened her shoulders. She raised a single eyebrow at her reflection and practiced a half smile.

Victoria nodded to herself. This was nothing compared to coming out. Just another step toward being who she wanted to be, instead of who she was supposed to be.

Pulling open the door, she was met with the most complex eyes looking up at her through bulky glasses perched on a perfectly symmetrical nose for booping. The outer rims of the woman's eyes were green with warm brown spires extending outward like a forest. They left tracks on Victoria's flushing skin as they trekked down her body and back up.

The woman tilted her head. Then she said, "I bet you thought I'd be taller." The modulated voice soothed the tremors running over Victoria's face. The coach tapped a short, manicured nail to her scrunched lips. "Or dressed as a dominatrix."

Victoria barely heard the words exiting the plump pink lips. She swallowed the excess saliva threatening to choke her and raised a single eyebrow she'd practiced. "I don't know what I expected honestly. But I'm glad you're not dressed like a dominatrix."

"That is refreshing," Sarah stated. She pushed the glasses up her nose.

Victoria's chest locked as the smile spread up the woman's narrow-shaped face. Licking her lips, Victoria said, "I bet."

"I'm Sarah."

"Victoria."

Sarah glanced down the hallway, shifting her weight from side to side. "Do you have someplace we can go over the contract and limits?"

"I'm sorry. Yes." Victoria moved out of the doorway, giving Sarah the space to enter the room with her large black purse.

Blackberries and vanilla wafted over Victoria as Sarah passed her. Her mouth opened, swallowing more of the dessert-flavored woman. Victoria savored the smell as all images of the thick-thighed weightlifter purged her memories, replaced with nude lace peeking out from the partially unbuttoned white dress shirt.

Sarah stood just beyond the door as Victoria closed it behind her. Victoria watched as Sarah examined the painted finish of the door. She glanced back at the door, then at Sarah.

"Are you expecting someone else?"

The almond-shaped eyes looked at her over the rims of the glasses. "No." Sarah pushed the straps of her purse farther up her shoulder. "I checked that the door did not have any locks that could stop me from being able to exit. Hazards of the job."

Victoria looked at the door and back at the professionally dressed woman. "Has that... happened before?"

"There was once a house that had a deadbolt that required a key on the inside."

Victoria felt the wrinkle in her forehead deepen. "That's terrifying."

"Yes, but like I said, it's a hazard of the job," Sara stated. She looked down the entryway toward the kitchen. "Is there a back door?"

Victoria nodded. She pointed to the rear of the townhouse. "It's a set of French doors. No weird locks, I promise. But there is a wooden stick in the bottom."

"Thank you."

Victoria watched the woman scan the hallway decor like she was perusing an Ikea showroom. She bit her lip wondering what the wall hangings would tell Sarah about her. Unsure of what else to do, Victoria moved to divert the woman's assessment. Her low heels clicked against the wooden floorboards as she made her way toward the well-lit kitchen. She checked just briefly, breathing easier with Sarah following her.

"Can I get you something to drink?" Victoria offered. She gestured to the bar stools at the kitchen island.

"Water, please." Sarah set her bag on the counter and withdrew a black leather folio before taking a seat. "Were you able to read through the contract I emailed you?"

Victoria pressed the computer panel on the refrigerator door. As the ice ground in the maker and clinked against the glass, Victoria was pulled back to the house. Her house. The house she owned, and she didn't need to worry when she was in her house.

She felt heat spread up her arm when her finger brushed against Sarah's hand. Her eyes danced around the room, searching for an answer to a question that she wasn't even able to process. She willed her lungs to breathe normally but every fruity breath made her heart race a little faster.

She looked at the source of her confusion and realized Sarah hadn't taken a drink. Those eyes were watching her in the same way they'd studied her tri-panel painting.

Victoria checked the glass wondering if something was wrong, then realized she hadn't answered the question. And Sarah was waiting for an answer.

"I'm sorry. Yes. I read the contract." Then Victoria added, "I found the cheating clause to be quite interesting."

Sarah raised the glass and sipped the water. Wiping the corner of her lips with her fingers, Sarah looked up with a smile. "I work with many couples, and some have had prior issues with infidelity. I never want my services to add to the falling apart of a marriage."

"That's thoughtful of you."

Taking her seat, Victoria adjusted her top, then folded her hands on the counter. She considered finishing off the wine but found herself chewing on the inside of her lip. She shifted again when Sarah opened the folio.

"I have a physical copy of the contract I will need you to sign before we can get started with the expectations regarding privacy. Please understand if we were to meet outside of an appointment, I would pretend to not know you, and the same is expected of you. I do not accept referrals from clients, so it is written into the contract that you will not discuss our appointments with anyone besides Dr. Rose."

Victoria looked over the paperwork, ensuring it was the same contract she'd viewed electronically. She glanced over the counter until she saw the pen held out by Sarah. She signed the contract and slid the pages back to Sarah, who scooped them up and placed them within the folio.

"Now that's done, can you please share with me what you wish to learn?" Sarah took another sip of water.

Victoria ran her fingers over the cool granite before she tapped the pads against the solid surface. She looked everywhere but at the woman next to her. "Dr. Rose said you could help me learn techniques to help a woman reach a sexual climax."

"Have you ever climaxed?"

Victoria choked on the abruptness of the question. An alarm went off in her ears as the muscles in her arms and legs tightened. She ran her tongue over her teeth, then closed her eyes. She tasted the familiar lie, but it was sour instead of bland. She'd left bland in Utah. Left in search of something fruity sweet, not sour.

"No," didn't taste sweet but it wasn't bland either.

"Would you like me to assist you in learning that skill as well?"

Turning to the woman, Victoria raised her eyebrow once more. "Do they not go hand in hand?"

Chocolate locks tumbled freely across Sarah's face as the professionalism softened to familiar humanity. Sarah nodded, then said, "In a sense yes, however, it will shift the path of the instruction. I will say that if you become comfortable in managing your own climax, you will earn a form of instant gratification that spurs confidence in your ability to do so to a woman in the future."

"Basically, you're saying if I can make myself..." Victoria swallowed. "If I can climax, then I will be able to do it to someone else."

"Yes."

"For you to teach me how to..." Victoria shook her head, tossing the rest of her sentence back to her brain for a redraft. She tried the next that was sent out on the conveyor belt. "Does that mean—" but she cut that one off with her teeth. She started the next, "Are you going to..." but the terror and hope of what was implied was too much so she smothered it between her lips.

Sarah's brows cinched in the middle. Victoria could feel the hazel eyes gathering information from her face. Humanity vanished as Sarah fixed the lightness back into the steady stare of a professional. "Am I going to participate?"

Victoria nodded to stop the non-verbal interrogation, then looked Sarah directly in the eye.

"No," and Sarah's gazes confirmed her honesty.

Victoria watched a slightly crooked front tooth peek out and bite into the lower lip. Sarah looked up over the top of her glasses with her chin angled toward her chest. "Please don't take this as condescending. I know you reached out to me because Dr. Rose asked you to. You have never been with a woman before, and it would be inappropriate of me not to provide you insight into the lesbian world."

Victoria nodded, not trusting herself to speak.

"A woman's first climax at the hands of another person is not only an incredible moment in her life but also forms a kind of imprint," Sarah explained.

Victoria studied the dark cabinets of the kitchen before turning back to Sarah. She tried to fit the concept into her working knowledge of a relationship, but it was like putting a triangle into a circular hole. She looked at Sarah. "Imprint?"

Sarah nodded. "Like baby ducks on the first creature they see when hatching."

Shaking her head, she still couldn't find a way to make the piece fit. "How so?"

"I won't pretend to know why it happens, but I guess…" Sarah stopped in the middle of her sentence. Her jaw shifted as though she was chewing on each phrase, breaking it into easier-to-digest pieces. Her eyes popped up, and she raised a hand. "So, I think of it like this. The first time a woman climaxes with another woman that is coming into her own as a lesbian… it's like a woman's first fully euphoric state of being. The association with the person involved creates a lasting impression on them."

Victoria embraced the professional situation, swallowing the remnants of Sarah's scent that still lingered on her tongue and wondering how she would ever wash her mind of those eyes.

Cooly, she stated. "And you don't want that to be with you."

"As an instructor, it would be unethical for an attachment to be formed with me. I also feel the need to warn you to take care not to 'U-Haul' into bed."

Victoria closed her eyes and shook away the desire she'd initially had to U-Haul Sarah into bed. She forced a half smile, then looked up at the confused guest. "I was trying to convince myself that was just a stereotype."

Sarah's face twisted amusingly, and Victoria wondered how many sessions she'd have to pay for to learn each expression. But Sarah's chuckle pulled Victoria back to the reality she'd just tried to accept.

"So, how do you do help me—" Sarah held up her hand, silencing Victoria. "Teach you."

"How do you teach me to climax without any participation?"

Sarah leaned back in her chair, taking a sip from the water glass. "That is up to you."

"So, I choose what you teach me?"

"I have diagrams and models to teach you everything about female anatomy." Sarah took another drink. "I can expose you to a variety of stimulants that will increase your desire, like the pheromone perfume I am currently wearing. From there, I can leave you to practice what you learned, or I can stay and provide oral instructions as you perform personal practice."

Sentences swirled around Victoria's head, mixing together as the room started to tilt around her. Sarah's subtle sweetness twisted into recognizable manipulation, circling quickly. The tip of the whirlpool pushed out a single option of Sarah being in the room as she had her first orgasm.

"You're saying... you would stay and watch me touch myself."

Sarah carded her hair back from her face. "I would prefer not to watch because if you were to make eye contact with me that could cause you to potentially associate me with your first time."

"You don't want to be my mommy duck."

Victoria's heart fluttered at Sarah's laugh bouncing playfully off the walls. "While that is an active kink in some circles... sorry. No, I do not wish to be your mommy duck."

They shared the momentary familiarity of humor. While the echoes settled around them, Victoria tried to put all the pieces together.

"So, you're going to show me pictures. Then what do you do for stimulation?"

"There are a variety of options. I can run you a bath with pheromone-enhanced candles. I possess a library of erotic films that range from heavy petting to more intense sexual intercourse. I am also willing to aid in relaxation in the form of back or head massages."

"So, I pay you to watch porn with me?"

"If you wish," Sarah stated. Then she added, "If you strictly wish for suggestions and what physical reactions to look for that will indicate you are ready to move into the next stage of practice, then I do not have to sit and watch porn with you."

"This seems like I could have done it on my own."

Sarah folded her hands on the counter. "I don't pretend that anything I am providing is incapable of being learned with self-study. My services are more of an all-in-one package, which eliminates the searching and reading phases."

"How much does this all cost?"

"I need to know if you would prefer me to stay for your release or if you would like to schedule a follow up call the next day to discuss next steps."

"I think I would prefer to practice on my own."

Sarah exhaled. "Thank god." Shaking her head, she followed up with, "I'm sorry that is so unprofessional."

"Honestly, it is a relief you want to leave," Victoria said even though the words tasted sour.

Sarah rummaged through her purse, then slid a menu in front of Victoria.

"So, basic book work is $30. We will go over your parts and how to make them work for you. I will provide you a list of resources that could aid in getting you in the mood, then I leave. You contact me if you require further assistance."

Victoria tapped the second menu option. "The $50 option is the book work with the use of your 'resources'?"

"Yes. We will again go through the book work. I will provide you with silicon models to practice with while I aid in your hand placement. We will complete the stimulating activities you want, and then I will leave you to your own hands."

"Just for my own information, how much do you charge to watch?"

"I don't watch." Sarah's lips straightened into a line that told Victoria she was very serious about the difference between watching and being present. "However, my presence during your practice is $100 per hour for all prior described activities and to stay until you have managed at least one successful climax. I will provide guidance for after care, and then I will leave."

"Do you have to stay a lot?"

Victoria watched the blush spread over the smooth cheeks. "Not typically for individuals, but there is always that voyeuristic person that insists. Couples often request guidance in process."

"You make $100 an hour to wa—" Sarah's chin raised ready to correct her. "Sorry. To provide narration while a couple has sex?"

"Yes."

"How long does it normally take?"

"For simple calibration is an hour. However, most bedroom instruction is typically 2 hours or more."

Victoria pulled up a mental calculator and started working through complex formulas. Shaking her head, she said, "I went into the wrong profession."

"I still work a day job, so you probably didn't because I'm here working while you make enough to pay me to be here."

Victoria felt the wavering insecurity solidify in the change in control. Sarah was nothing more than a new employee. Beautiful, professional, and at times playful, but still there to complete the tasks she requested.

"I would like the $50 option," she stated flatly. But before she could stop herself, the fear slithered past her teeth and into the open, "Does that make you think less of me?"

Warm fingers wrapped around her tired hand. She looked up, lost in the green forest eyes. Her soft lips pulled up revealing a single dimple on her left cheek.

"If you understood how many different types of candles, I have had to smell to find ones that work, or how many hours of porn I had to watch to create the collection I have on my computer, you would understand that I have the goods."

Victoria's stomach rolled as the chuckles turned into hearty laughter. She closed her hand around the fingers, realizing this was the most physical contact she'd had in close to a year.

"Thank you," she whispered as what was left of the laughter threatened to turn into crocodile tears.

"Of course." Sarah didn't pull away until Victoria released the woman's fingertips.

Victoria swallowed, her eyes looking over the light fixture she'd chosen to match the modern feel of her new life. She traced the metal base down the poles to the twisted iridescent light bulbs.

"So, now I schedule another appointment?"

"Let's set a block of time that is comfortable for you." Sarah dug through her purse, withdrawing a physical date book. She looked up when Victoria raised a single eyebrow. "I prefer not to list my clients in a digital calendar."

"Appreciated."

Sarah flipped through the pages of her book. "So, it's Wednesday. I am booked for the rest of the weekdays. Would Sunday work for you?"

"Uh... yes. That's fine. I start my new job on Monday so if we could not make it too late."

Sarah bit down on the pen in her hand, then withdrew it, "Would you like to begin at six or seven?"

"How about seven?"

"Seven it is," she said. The pen scratched against the paper. Folding the date book closed, Sarah placed the pen atop. "I would suggest eating a meal before our meeting and drinking plenty of water throughout the day."

"I will. Thank you."

Sarah gathered the menu and her belongings. Victoria stood on wobbly knees. She straightened her shoulders before leading Sarah to the door.

Victoria followed Sarah out of the entry into the driveway. Before Sarah could leave, she said, "Thank you. I mean, I was very uncomfortable with the whole thing when Dr. Rose brought it up but I'm not feeling so nervous now."

"You're welcome, Victoria."

Victoria turned when Sarah did, heading back into the house. Sarah's scent lingered in the facade of comfort. Kicking off her shoes, she stretched on her toes and held her breath as she moved up the stairs and shut the trailing scent away from her. She fell onto the bed.

Her face collided with the cotton-covered duvet. Crawling on the bed still dressed in an outfit she'd spent hours selecting for this late-night meeting, she built a cocoon around herself with the heavy blanket and three pillows. She willed herself to sleep, but blackberry custard still lingered on her tongue. When rest finally came, she found herself lost in a forest, searching for the brunette with a single dimple.

4

The seductive earthy aroma and the whir of the handheld frother lured Sarah from Monica's stiff couch to the kitchen. She twisted her brown hair into a messy bun atop her head before breaching the entrance and dropping her body onto the barstool. Monica didn't look up from her Kindle as she slid a cup of coffee across the granite countertop.

Sarah wrapped both hands around the cup, praying to the coffee god that this would give her the energy needed to get through the day. She sipped the caramel-colored liquid and moaned as the warmth spread down her chest settling the grumbling in her stomach.

"I didn't even hear you come in last night," Monica said. Her finger flicked up the screen she was fixated on as she took a drink.

"The 101 was closed again," Sarah grumbled. "Surface streets from Phoenix took me an hour to get back. I just crashed on the couch since Tris was out cold and you were busy brushing your teeth for forty-five minutes."

Monica looked up at Sarah over her glasses. Sarah licked her teeth as she watched her best friend's eyebrows scrunch in the middle.

"Brushing my teeth?" Monica asked.

"Your toothbrush is *really* loud. I think you need a new one," the nine-year-old whined from the living room. Sarah listened to the slapping of bare feet against the hardwood floors. She took another drink of coffee as the girl slumped onto the stool next to Sarah.

"Morning, Mom," Tris said to Sarah. The child looked around the kitchen then grabbed the plate of half-eaten pancakes from Monica's side of the counter and stuffed as much as she could into her mouth at once.

"Morning, creature," Sarah said over the rim of her cup. Her eyes were still on Monica's now flushed face. The therapist opened her mouth, closed it, and then tried again.

Sarah licked the froth from her lip, then laughed.

"I was—" Monica tried but stopped herself.

With a shrug, Sarah set her cup down. "Everyone needs to practice self-care. Though we should talk about your technique because it shouldn't take that long to finish."

Monica's wide eyes narrowed at Sarah. "There is nothing wrong with my technique." She set the Kindle on the counter and grabbed the empty plate Tris was dragging her finger across to gather the last of the syrup.

Sarah chuckled. "Sure." Turning to the child busy licking her sticky fingers, Sarah added, "Speaking of teeth brushing, go brush yours because you have a dentist appointment today."

The middle finger popped from Tris's mouth. "It's vacation," she stated.

"Which is why we are doing it now," Sarah stated. "Wash your hands and face too."

Tris's mouth twisted in disgust as she slid out of the chair. She stomped out of the room hissing, "This sucks."

Only when the foot stomping retreated behind the slam of the bathroom door did Monica lean back across the counter.

"How'd it go last night with Victoria?"

Sarah pulled the cup back up to her lips. "Not as I would have preferred," she said, then covered half of her face with the cup to hide the blood she felt rushing to her cheeks.

"Did she freak out?"

"No." Sarah set the cup down. "When we were going through the different options, I said something stupid."

"That's not like you." Monica leaned in closer with a sideways smile. "What did you say?"

Sarah ran her hands over her face. She peeked through her fingers "I said 'thank God' when she said she didn't want me to stay after instruction."

"And that's stupid because...?"

"Besides the fact that it's double the money?" Sarah picked up her cup.

"Okay, but really, from someone who knows Victoria, it probably made her feel more comfortable."

"It was just so me... and not..." Sarah glanced over her shoulder toward the empty hallway before whispering, "Not sexy Sarah. Plus, I don't want her to think that someone wouldn't want to be, you know, with her."

Monica stared at Sarah blankly. Slowly a smile crept from the corners of her lips to crease in the corners of her eyes. "You didn't believe me when I said she was attractive."

Sarah's head fell backward as her teeth held her bottom lip so she couldn't provide Monica any more ammunition. With a heavy sigh, she looked back at her best friend. "I thought you were fucking with me." With a roll of her eyes, Sarah added, "But seriously what is with the woman's eyebrow?"

"What?"

Sarah tried to raise a single eyebrow. When she failed, she pushed her left eyebrow up her forehead. "You know... when she raises a single eyebrow."

Monica shook her head. "Never in my life have I ever heard someone say they were attracted to someone because of their eyebrow. There's even this

Scottish father that does a whole thing on Youtube about it."

"It's not that her eyebrow is hot," Sarah protested. It's the look in her eyes when it raises. It's this look like... shit, I don't even know."

"You're ridiculous."

Sarah picked up her cup once more. "I know."

"Did she schedule an appointment?"

"Yeah."

Monica returned her attention to her Kindle. "But you don't get to watch."

"I don't watch," Sarah stated, rolling her eyes.

"You'd watch her." Monica flicked her finger up the screen once more.

"Why are we friends?"

Monica peeked over her glasses again. "Because we never tried dating."

"Don't start," Sarah warned. She tipped the cup to drain the remainder of the contents into her mouth then stared at the bottom, waiting for it to automatically refill.

"You don't want to spend the rest of your life alone."

"Says the single woman." Sarah got up from her stool and made her way to the coffee pot. She didn't bother with the cream frother, just swallowed the steaming bitter liquid, washing away the other equally bitter comebacks.

Monica held up her finger as she swallowed another swig of her own coffee. "Temporarily single. I have to go to my cousin's kid's birthday party in a few weeks, and I'm going to see that redhead stripper again. Not going to date her, but at least I can get laid." The therapist wiped at the corners of her mouth, then flicked up the screen again. "It wouldn't kill you to try to date."

"I've dated," Sarah stated.

"Once and she was too old for you."

Sarah rolled her eyes again. "Clearly, wasn't too old."

"Also, wasn't single," Monica reminded her. "Plus, my cousin is an asshole. I told you that before she tried her, 'oh, poor me' bullshit on you."

Sarah chugged the remainder of the second cup, then set it down. She held onto the sink and waited.

"I know a woman."

She knew the wait would be short. "No."

"Please."

"What's happening?" Tris asked as she made her way to the pantry and pulled out a container of Pringles. Before she could pop the top, Sarah took the container and put it back.

"Trying to get your mom to go on a date," Monica stated.

The glare from being denied the chips left the girl's eyes. She looked Sarah dead in the eyes. "You should do it."

Sarah fluffed the back of Tris's natural afro. "And why should I do that?"

Tris wiggled away from Sarah's grooming. "Because it's almost my birthday. If you get a girlfriend, then she will buy me presents too."

"I'm sorry, what?"

The missing-toothed smile spread as her shoulders shrugged. "You get a girlfriend and I get more presents."

Monica glanced momentarily over her glasses. "See, the crotch goblin agrees. I am setting it up."

"No," Sarah stated.

"Yes," the other two said in unison.

"No." Sarah gave Tris a slight push. "Go get your shoes on, we're leaving."

Monica raised the glasses from her nose and set them on top of her head. She tilted her head and Sarah watched her best friend's eyes run up and down her body. She rested a finger on her lips.

Sarah glanced down at the t-shirt she'd found in her rundown Civic the night before. The detergent stains mocked her, so she folded her arms to cover them.

"You know it's only, like, seven years until you're 35," Monica reminded her.

Straightening her shoulders, Sarah stared Monica down. "So."

Monica moved toward Sarah. She tucked a lock of Sarah's straight hair behind her ear. Resting the smooth hand on Sarah's cheek, a smug grin spread over Monica's face. "Don't tell me you forgot the marriage pact."

"What about it?"

"You're almost 35."

Sarah stepped closer to Monica. She studied the way her best friend's eyes dilated, and her nostrils flared. Satisfied the pheromone lotion was still strong enough to cause her best friend's blackmail to backfire. Close enough to be within kissing distance, Sarah adjusted the clasp of the necklace chain to the back of Monica's neck. Raising her eyes from the subtle hint of cleavage to Monica's painted lips, then up seductively to Monica's eyes, she whispered. "Maybe that's my big plan."

Monica's gaze flitted to Sarah's lips. "I can't tell if you are being sarcastic or serious."

"I'm not going on a date with a woman you know."

"You were lying." Monica searched Sarah's straight face.

Sarah thought about her sister's postnatal body, laying the flailing newborn, Tris into her arms before walking out the door in search of her next fix, wiping away any hint of amusement from her expression.

Monica took a step backward. Her arms folded over her chest, as she glanced back to the Kindle on the counter. When she looked up through squinted eyes, she shook her head. "You said kissing me was like kissing your sister."

Sarah shrugged, a smile only creeping up her face when she made her way back to the living room to get anything Tris left behind in Monica's posh home. Confident she'd left her best friend to stew enough to abandon any idea of setting her up, Sarah returned to the kitchen. She pulled her phone from the charger Monica left there the night before.

She opened the messenger app to Victoria's text message: "I look forward to seeing you Sunday."

5

Victoria's legs wobbled like jelly under her as she hobbled to the car after her hour at the gym. As she put her bag into the trunk, she noticed the woman she'd been drooling over the past few months stop at the vehicle parked next to hers.

"You did great today," the woman stated as she wiped the sweat from her forehead and then neck with a towel before tossing it into her trunk.

"Thanks." Victoria leaned against her car, chugging half the bottle of water in her hand. As she screwed the cap on, she said, "I'm Victoria."

The woman held out her large hand. "Echo."

Victoria took the calloused hand in her own. "Nice to meet you."

"Yeah, you too."

"So, how long have you been coming here," Victoria asked.

Echo looked at the sky as though she was measuring the time by the sun. "Uhhh... about a year now. I took some time when Henrie was born to figure out how to manage being a mom and work and stuff, but I've been back full time for about six months."

"That's awesome." Victoria glanced back at the gym trying to come up with something else to say.

Echo closed the trunk. Her olive-toned skin shined as the sun beat down on them. She popped the top of a supplement cup and took a drink.

Victoria turned as Echo asked, "What about you?"

"Two months now," Victoria answered. "I... uh.. moved to Arizona at the start of summer and figured this was a better place to meet new people than at a bar."

Echo snorted slightly. Her drink dribbled from her mouth to her shirt. While cleaning herself up, she said, "I mean the gym is great but don't knock the bar."

Victoria played with the edge of her tank top. "I've never actually been to a bar."

"Really?" When Victoria looked at the taller woman, she noticed her wide chocolate eyes and gaping mouth.

Victoria bit her lip. "I was Mormon."

Echo's mouth shut. She bobbed her head in a nod, and scanned Victoria head to toe. "Well, I own a bar if you ever wanted to tread down the path of sin."

"Really?" Victoria's thoughts spilled from her mouth. "I don't know why but I honestly never thought of someone owning a bar in today's society. It's just something I think I only placed in old westerns."

A muffled laugh quaked Echo's chest. "Well, it definitely looks country. When I bought it, it was a failing country-themed lesbian bar, but it still has its rustic feel. Plus, we still have line dancing classes once a week."

Victoria scanned the entrance to the gym once more, then looked back at the woman. "Echo's Escape?"

Echo's mouth spread into a crooked toothed smile. "Well, you've heard of it at least, so it's not failing so much now, even though Phoenix now has two lesbian nightclubs that might put me under."

Victoria nodded. "Yeah. I googled gay bars when I moved here."

Echo rested a hand on her hip, and the tattooed bicep on her arm displayed pleasantly. "Ex-Mormon and lesbian. Sounds like you've got stories."

Victoria laughed and shook her head in denial. "Not really."

"So, you moved to Arizona... alone?"

"Yeah."

"Make many friends yet?"

"Uh...one." Victoria sighed. "This place is a lot different than back home."

"Where was home?"

"Salt Lake."

"Yeah. People aren't very friendly around here." Echo's phone beeped. She checked the screen, then typed a response to whoever was texting her. She closed her eyes momentarily, then let out a slow breath. "Sorry. My wife. She wants to know how much longer I am going to be."

"Oh." Victoria swallowed thickly and straightened her shoulders, overcompensating for the disappointment. "I can let you go."

"Naw, it's cool. She works all week, so she can chill with the kid for a little more than an hour by herself. You got kids?"

"No."

The phone in Echo's hand went off again. The woman didn't look at it this time, so Victoria asked, "How many kids do you have?"

"One. Henrie is about to turn one."

Victoria's eyebrow raised. "That is the age of need. It's good you get out for some breathing time."

"Yeah." Echo ran her hand over the undercut. "So, what do you do?"

"I am starting a new job as an Assistant Principal at an elementary school."

"New state. New job. It's a whole new world for you." Echo's hands clapped together, startling Victoria. "Hey, do you play darts?"

"No."

"Would you be interested in playing darts?" Echo raised her eyebrows a few times.

Victoria bit her lip. Then twisted them back and forth as she chewed on the 'no' she was about to provide. Echo's eyes changed her mind.

"Would I have to be good at darts?" Victoria asked.

A snort came from Echo's nose. "No, my sister from another mister sucks and she still plays with me. But I'm trying to get the little sister to work for me since the job market sucks, she won't be able to play anymore."

"I have never shot a dart in my life."

"It's okay. I'll teach you."

Victoria shrugged. "Okay, I can try."

"Cool." Echo handed her phone to Victoria. "Put your number in."

As Victoria typed, a text flashed across the screen, "*You can't seriously expect me to work all week and then be home all day with this kid on Saturday. I did my time babysitting, so come home.*"

She didn't mean to read it. But it was there. Her mind ran over the message again and again to the point that she mistyped the number twice. She wondered what type of woman Echo was married to if her wife thought spending time with their kid was babysitting.

Echo took the phone back.

Victoria watched the woman's chest rise, but it didn't fall in a normal breathing pattern. Instead, the warm eyes closed.

When she looked back up at Victoria, the smile no longer reached her eyes. Victoria heard her phone vibrate, and she checked.

"That's my number."

"Thank you."

"Okay, well Thursday is our next match and if you can't make it this week, then let's shoot for the next week. I'll introduce you to my sister because she'll be working that night if I have anything to say about it."

Victoria nodded. "Okay. I'll be there."

Echo's phone began to ring. She stared at the screen and shook her head. "Okay... Yeah. Sweet. Well, I have to go but I'll see you Thursday."

"See you then," Victoria said with a half wave to the back of Echo's head already ducking into the car.

Victoria tossed the empty water bottle into the passenger seat and plugged her phone into the charging port. With the air conditioner blasting, the chilled sweat clinging to her body reminded her of home.

The leaves around Salt Lake could be changing around her if she'd stayed. She'd be shopping for new flannel shirts with her sister, unaware of the apparel ties to the lesbian community.

Her stomach grumbled. She pulled the Kind bar from her bag but nothing about the colorful package made her want to eat it. She wanted real food, like she'd find at the Latter-Day Cafe.

After a quick search, she plugged the address to the Original Breakfast House. Following the navigational cues, Victoria's mind wandered to what it would be like to be at a bar with a bunch of people like her. With a right turn, her mind shifted to the possibility of meeting someone at said bar.

As she waited for a parking spot outside of the diner, she contemplated asking Dr. Rose's guidance. The woman's over sugared voice would ask her to explain her own feelings about each one. Dr. Rose would smile, and even though she had a perfectly well-maintained smile, it would feel like she was laughing at Victoria as she'd make Victoria describe her insecurity about being around so many gay women.

Victoria reached for the phone, deciding that she'd dined alone enough this week. Just as she pulled up her favorites, the screen changed to the face of the person she intended to call.

"Jen, I was just going to—" but the sound of Jen's daughter screaming in the background cut her off.

"*Are you busy?*" Jen asked. Then, "*Jackie, I hear that you are upset but stop yelling at me. Mommy can't just not go to work.*"

Victoria watched as a space opened up and determined if she was busy enough to not be the last-minute babysitter. Shaking her head, she followed the car out of the parking lot.

"I'm on my way."

"*I'm sorry.*" Jen's exhausted sigh came through the line as the screaming continued. "*I don't know how I forgot that I was on call today, and Jackie's nanny is out of town for the weekend.*"

"It's fine. I just need to stop at the gas station really quickly, and I'll be right there. I was actually down the street."

"*Jackie, honey, Victoria is coming to see you.*"

Something in the background shattered. Then Victoria heard the child scream, "*I don't like Victoria!*"

Victoria pulled into the QT parking lot.

"*I'm sorry. She's just mad at me.*"

"It's fine," Victoria said. It wasn't like the feeling wasn't mutual. "I'll see you in a minute."

Victoria didn't knock at the front door of the giant house. Setting her purse down, she palmed the king-sized Cookies and Cream bar in her pocket. She made her way toward the screaming at the back of the house.

When she turned the corner, the five-year-old's red rimmed eyes narrowed at her. The tiny feet ceased jumping on the indoor trampoline with the plastic lightsaber in her hand.

Victoria pulled the top of the forbidden candy bar from her pocket of her hoodie, revealing to the child the bribe. She dropped it back within as Jen's sneakers squeaked down the hall.

Jen jumped, her hand coming up to her chest as she turned the corner. "You scared the shit out of me."

"You said a bad word," Jackie chanted. "You owe me a dollar! Ha! Ha! You owe me a dollar!"

Victoria raised an eyebrow at her friend. "Last time I was here, it was a quarter."

Jen rolled her eyes and dug her hospital badge from the bowl on the built-in bookshelf.

"I never have change," Jen growled. She grabbed her purse and rummaged through the mom-bag until she pulled out her wallet.

The dollar bill dangling from Jen's fingers was enough to shut the little girl up and send her running to her mother. She wrapped the child in a hug as the child fingered the prize with her undoubtedly sticky hand.

"I should be back by ten."

"As in ten tonight?" Victoria raised her eyebrow, unaware that she'd committed her entire day to the momentarily pacified spawn.

"Be good for Victoria, Jackie. Mommy loves you." Without answering Victoria's question, Jen slung the purse over her shoulder. "There's vegan lasagna in the fridge and ramen in the cabinet," Jen called back to them as she made her way to the garage.

The door slammed closed and the silence that had fallen around them was interrupted by the rumbling garage door.

Jackie held her hand out to Victoria. The woman placed the candy bar on the tiny marker-covered palm. But pulled it back before she said, "No more screaming."

"No more screaming," the child confirmed.

Victoria started to give it to the girl, then stopped again. "And no telling Mommy."

"No telling Mommy."

Before Victoria could think of any more conditions, the candy was torn from her grasp and the girl was running toward the tiny table of artificial sweets and stuffed friends.

"What do you want to do today?" Victoria asked, pulling her phone from her pocket. She glanced up to the child's mouth stuffed with half of the chocolate and the other two crunching the remainder between the fingers of both hands.

Instantly regretting her life choices, she returned her attention to her phone. She sent a message to Dr. Rose that she needed to cancel her session. When she looked up, Jackie was gone, and the house was silent.

"Jackie?" Victoria called.

A muffled giggle came from the hallway. Tiny feet slapped against the floor before the child jumped out. Jackie cried, "I found you!"

"Was I lost?" Victoria asked as she looked at her feet that hadn't moved.

The head of blonde curls bounced as the child doubled over in laughter. "You're funny. We playin' hide and seek."

Victoria glanced around the room. "So, that means it's your turn to hide and my turn to seek then, right?"

The toddler bounced on her toes nodding.

"Okay, you go hide somewhere in the house and I'll come find you." Victoria expected the girl to run off. Instead, she just continued to bounce.

"Go hide," Victoria said.

"You have to count," Jackie stated.

Victoria sighed. "One... Two..."

Jackie laughed and clapped. She bounced as Victoria reached seven. Victoria shooed the girl away, who finally took her cue and scampered out of the room and up the stairs.

Victoria pressed her hands to her face, rubbing away the frustration.

As the youngest child of her seven siblings, caring for children had never been her responsibility. Learning she'd never carry a child in her twenties had lessened her family's expectations of her to take interest in their offspring. Yet, in her new life, she'd only managed to make friends with Jen; the single mom always being called into work.

Briefly, Victoria wondered how long she'd get away without searching for the chocolate-covered child.

Two minutes was the answer to her query.

The child was screaming from atop the stairs, "It's alive!"

Victoria ran to the bottom of the stairs and gazed up at Jackie. Her body was still bouncing and pointing. "Hurry. Hurry. It's alive."

Taking the stairs two at a time, Victoria swore off ever coming back to this house. She followed the girl to Jen's bedroom where the child stood over something rumbling against the rug.

"What is—" the next word froze on the tip of Victoria's tongue.

Jackie reached out with her innocent little hand toward the vibrating, silicon cylinder. The jelly rabbit figurine's ears moved so quickly that they were practically invisible.

"NOOOOO!!!!" Victoria screamed, scooping up the vibrator. The sticky surface startled Victoria into chucking it on the bed where it continued to jut around on the comforter.

Quickly, she tore the corner of the bedspread over the still-moving toy. Victoria turned to Jackie as the child withdrew two more wiggling womb weasels from the drawer alongside Jen's bed. The child waggled them in the air, and cried out, "Swords! Fight me!"

With the vibrator still alive and searching for a way out of its cozy cave, Victoria ripped the plastic penises from the child and yelled, "Out!"

But Jackie didn't move. She looked up at Victoria. Bits of white chocolate and black cookies speckled the lip that trembled, then opened wide. The wail covered the sound of the sinful schlong.

Dropping the dicks, Victoria scooped the child up and closed the door to Jen's bedroom of playthings. She carried Jackie down the stairs and into the backyard where the princess castle playhouse provided a much-needed distraction.

Flopping into a patio chair, Victoria fished out her phone. She calculated the eleven hours left in Dante's first circle of hell. She decided not to text Jen about the pack of peckers on her bed.

Instead, she demanded: "Where is the spare carseat? We are going to the zoo."

6

Sarah lay listening to Tina, the terrorist cat, rip fresh gouges into the arm of the dilapidated couch. Her finger traced over the purple marker left by the young Picasso, who was typing away on Monica's inappropriate Christmas gift at the other end.

She studied the intensity of Tris's eyes locked on the Chromebook screen. The child's index fingers poked chaotically but intently, slamming against each key.

The constant tapping irked her, and she yearned for the child to go into the only bedroom within the apartment, so Sarah could curl up under her comforter and get some sleep. Working every night this week had worn her out and being on the tail end of summer break meant Tris was with her every moment of every day that she wasn't meeting clients.

Without looking up from the screen, Tris asked, "What's your favorite color?"

"Black, like my soul," Sarah stated. Her eyes drifted away from the child to the frayed edge of the NU t-shirt. The material separated at the hem between her fingers as she poked along the tattered stitches.

"You work at my school," the nine-going-on-ninety-year-old retorted.

Sarah dropped her arm over her face. As she willed herself to think of a color, the frustratingly beautiful client's face popped into her head with that annoyingly attractive eyebrow arched over the challenging iris.

"Brown," she said. Sarah's stomach twisted and she reached for her phone.

She glanced over at Tris staring at her from just over the screen. The middle of her unibrow scrunched in the middle. "Whose favorite color is brown?"

"Mine," Sarah stated.

As the girl went back to typing, Sarah opened her messages. She scrolled through the numerous clients she'd seen since Wednesday until she reached Victoria's name. She typed out a confirmation text for Sunday's visit, unsure if the fluttering in her gut was nervousness or excitement as the word delivered displayed in tiny print below her message.

"Would you rather watch a movie, go on a hike, or visit a museum?"

Sarah looked out the first-floor window at the dark sky then back at her phone. "It's, like, seven o'clock. We're not going anywhere."

Tris's eyes rolled, and Sarah recognized Monica's influence. "But if you could, what would you do?" the girl whined.

"Uhh..." A yawn ripped through Sarah's thought process. She wiped the exhaustion from her eyes and then down her cheeks. "I guess... I don't know... Go on a hike."

"You don't hike," Tris stated.

"I used to, smart ass." Sarah's head fell to the side as she looked over the lanky arms and legs that had outgrown all her school uniforms from last year. "Before you ripped your way into this world." Then Sarah held up a finger. "Actually, I tried that one time when you were like four. The Greysons invited us to go. We made it halfway up the mountain and you laid down in the middle of the trail and said the sun was eating you alive. That ended our hiking adventures."

Tris narrowed her eyes before returning to slamming her fingers against the keys. "I don't think that is true," she stated as she abused the keyboard.

"What are you doing?" Sarah asked. Her attention had shifted back to her phone as she checked to see if the message to Victoria had changed from delivered to read.

The child hummed a single note to herself. "Just writing things I know about you."

Sarah's unused abdominal muscles quaked as she tried to hold herself up and peer over at the computer screen. Tris twisted so the screen in front of her was completely out of view. Unable to hold the crunch, Sarah's tired body flopped back onto the cushion that squeaked under her weight.

As the terrorist feline started to claw at the material again, Tris hissed loudly.

The scratching ceased. Sarah and the cat stared at the tightly wound curls wiggling on their ends over the top of the computer screen.

"What was that?" Sarah asked as Tina scampered away.

"It makes her stop," Tris stated. "What's your favorite food?"

"Chicken Marsala."

Shaking her head, Tris typed and asked, "Is that the runny brown sauce chicken?"

A chortle broke free from Sarah's lips. Her chest shook as she said, "Yes, the one with mushrooms."

"You know mushrooms are a fungus?"

"Yep." Sarah opened the Best Fiends app and picked up on the level she'd started earlier. "Delicious fungus."

"Gross."

While gliding her finger over the screen to connect the colored dots, Sarah added, "You love them too."

"I do not," Tris challenged

"You eat them all the time."

"No, I don't." But the statement had lost the tone of confidence.

"I put them in every meal." Sarah twisted around the trail of yellow flowers, winning the level.

"No." The single word pulled Sarah's eyes from the screen.

She felt the smile rise. "I chop them really, really small, so you never see them, but they are in spaghetti and gravy and even in your eggs."

The computer slid down the girl's lap. "Why would you do that to me? Do you want me to die?"

It was Sarah's turn to roll her eyes. "Obviously, they won't kill you since you have been eating them your entire life."

"My whole life is a lie!"

Sarah's phone dropped to her chest. She stared at the child whose hands hung in the air dramatically over her head.

"Where did you hear that from?" Sarah asked.

"Aunt Monica," the girl said with a shrug. She resumed her focus on the computer screen. "She lets me watch the grown-up shows when you're working."

"Does she now?"

"Yeah. Yesterday, we watched *The Hunger Games.*" Tris slammed a few more keys down. "She lets me watch SpongeBob too."

Sarah pinched the bridge of her nose. "I'm gonna kill her."

"She said when you said that to remind you that you're too pretty for prison."

Breathing in deeply, Sarah tried to remember why she was friends with Monica.

Tris's head popped up over the screen. Her crooked front teeth were on full display when she looked at Sarah. "What does that mean? To be too pretty for prison."

Before Sarah could even contemplate the answer Tris launched questions from her mouth like a slingshot. "Can only ugly people go to prison? And... and... who decides on how ugly you have to be?"

Sarah sucked her teeth as each question pelted her unshielded body.

"If you are only a little ugly, do you go to prison for a little? Am I too pretty for prison?"

Sarah held up her hand and waited for the girl to cease fire.

Shaking her head, Sarah said, "Ask your uncensored aunt."

Tris tilted her head. The gears in her still-developing frontal lobe turned until the moment passed. With a simple nod, she said, "Okay. But I'm going to add that to the bio."

Sarah sat up. "Excuse me, what?"

Tris ignored her. Her hickory-colored fingers resumed their attack.

"What are you writing?"

Tris held up a single digit, her right hand sliding along the trackpad and smacking the lower right side. "Shh. I'm working."

Sarah reached across the couch and ripped the computer out from under the child's hands. She scanned the screen, looked at Tris's eyes looking around the room, then back to the dating profile the girl had just submitted.

"You..." Sarah started but the remainder of the sentence got lost in the cavern of her mouth hanging open.

She pointed to the screen, then at Tris. "How did..."

She scrolled up and down the screen. Shaking her head, she said, "Why would you..."

Unable to complete simple sentences, Sarah stopped trying to speak. She stopped at the bio section and silently read: I went to collage. I am smart. I have a daughter. She's going to be the coolest kid in the fourth grade. She really wants her mom who is me to have a girlfriend by Christmas. I want to go hiking. My favorite color is brown but it is not. It is blue because I buy a lot of blue. I like chicken masila and gross mushrooms. I am too pretty for prisom.

"You spelled college and prison wrong," is the first sentence that made it over Sarah's tongue and through her gritted teeth.

Tris's shoulder shrugged. "I'm nine."

Sarah scrolled back to the top of the screen. Her upper lip curled as she stared at every freckle on her face present and accounted for in the unflattering photo. Her tongue was hanging out of her mouth as the very photogenic child matched her expression.

Every fiber of her wanted to be mad, but as she scrolled through the profile, she could tell the kid had put in a lot of work. More effort than she'd put into any school assignment, ever.

Sarah took a deep breath and exhaled slowly. Still staring at the screen, Sarah asked, "Why did you do this?"

Tris moved from the corner of the couch to Sarah's side. She smacked her lips together. After a huff, the child explained, "I heard you and Aunt Monica talking. She said that you promised to get married when you're thirty-five. But you don't like her like that."

Sarah closed her eyes. "She was just messing with me."

"Yeah but..." Tris started; the rest of the sentence inaudible as her lips moved.

"But what?" Sarah asked.

"But you haven't been on a date since stupid Simone." Tris looked up at Sarah from where her head lay on Sarah's shoulder. "You know Voldemort's sister."

Sarah laughed even though she knew she shouldn't encourage the name-calling.

"I don't need to date," Sarah stated.

"You used to smile all the time." Tris wrapped the ashy arm over Sarah. "You smiled at your phone and when you talked to her on the phone. You used to get dressed up and put on your red lipstick. But since she stopped calling, you stopped smiling."

"I still smile," Sarah argued weakly.

"But it's different. It's like you smile because you have to."

Sarah bit into her bottom lip until the pain in her chest manifested into reality. She bit harder to chase away the memory of empty promises and hidden kisses.

"Okay," Sarah whispered.

"Okay?"

"Okay," Sarah repeated. "I'll try it for a week."

The weak half-hug turned into a full embrace as the girl squealed. Then she sat back and countered. "Two months."

"Two months?" Sarah choked out. "I said a week."

Tris's lips scrunched into an expression reserved for hormonal teenage girls. "Aunt Monica says always start higher than you want."

"Aunt Monica and I are going to have a chat." Sarah grabbed the girl and pulled her back into a hug. "Two weeks."

"A month and two weeks." Tris's curls tickled Sarah's nose and lips. The coconut curling cream rubbed off on Sarah's face.

"A month," Sarah conceded. "And not a day longer."

The girl broke the embrace. "And you'll go on a date. At least one." She held up the thin finger. "And... And you... and you wear your red lipstick."

"I promise within the month I will go on a date," Sarah repeated.

"And wear the red lipstick."

Sarah sighed. Shaking her head at the computer screen, she said, "And wear the red lipstick."

"And the high heels with straps and the black dress," Tris added.

"I said I would wear the lipstick."

Tris crossed her arms over her chest and threw herself back against the couch. "Okay. Fine."

"Okay," Sarah held the computer out to the child. "But we have to fix the spelling of both prison and college. Oh, you spelled Marsala wrong also. I don't want people to think I write like a nine-year-old."

Tris took the computer back from Sarah. She navigated the website better than Sarah would have expected, returning to the edit feature. Sarah spelled the words for her and allowed the girl to repost the profile.

"Can we watch the second Hunger Games movie?" Tris asked with her begging smile.

"How about *Raya and the Last Dragon*?" Sarah matched the girl's face.

The smile dropped from the kid's eyes as they narrowed at Sarah. "I'm not a baby."

"I love Raya and I'm not a baby."

Tris's eyes rolled back into her head. "I have to know what happens to Katniss."

Sarah chanted the words *pick your battles* silently. Then said, "Fine."

Springing from the couch, the girl bounced to the cinder block and plank shelf. She grabbed the Roku remote and pressed her finger to the panel across the bottom of the TV. She prodded the panel, searching for the spot that would turn the whole thing on while issuing commands. "You make popcorn. I'll get the movie."

Sarah took the computer with her to the kitchen. As popcorn erupted in the microwavable bag, she downloaded the dating app to her phone. Her head began to pound as she watched the faded icon brighten.

The microwave chirped the successful completion of its task, just as Sarah opened the app.

She called to the girl who'd run down the narrow dark hallway to her bedroom. "What's the username?"

"MomSarah."

Sarah shook her head in disgust at the inaccurate and lame descriptor. "Password?"

Tris skipped back from her room with her Princess and the Frog Blanket in skeleton pajamas. The cuffs on the arms and legs were at least five inches too short. "Huh?"

"What's the password?"

Tris launched herself onto the couch, sending the cat, about to scratch the side, running toward the kitchen.

"My lunch number. T. O. dollar sign."

Sarah tapped the code into the box. "Didn't work."

Tris looked at the ceiling, then at Sarah. "Did you make the T big?"

"No."

"It's a big T," she stated.

Successful with the correct capitalization, Sarah opened the app and allowed the alerts to be activated. As she sprinkled Tajín over the popcorn, the first alert hit her phone.

"Did you get a date?" Tris's entire body had shot up and she stood on the couch.

Sarah carried the bowl around the tiny counter. "Get off the couch like that, and it's not a date. It's an alert."

"What are you waiting for?" The girl bounced. "Read it."

"Later."

"WHY?!"

Sarah tilted her head and said in her most annoying voice, "Because I have to know what happened to Katniss."

7

Victoria's eyes popped open as the fan whirling above the bed chilled the sweat coating her skin. She blinked trying to process the dream. She could still see the smirk on the sex coach's face as she had hovered above Victoria and disappeared below the sheet that was now twisted around Victoria's ankle.

The pulsing in her sex only grew stronger when she pressed her legs together, then abruptly disappeared. She wondered if that was what an orgasm felt like and if she'd had her first while dreaming about the woman who'd warned her about the power of imprinting.

Running her hands down her face, she tried to process the sensation that had vanished. She lay dissatisfied with the experience, considering that people seemed to be making a big fuss over something not that impressive.

Victoria bit her lip.

But if it *was...* and she'd done it by thinking about that woman... Her thoughts ran in circles, rounding them up with a thread of possibility. Maybe she could do it again. And again.

Even though the sun peeked through the blinds, her alarm had yet to go off. She didn't know how much time was left before she'd be called from her bed to head to the gym or worse babysit again, but what was the harm in trying again?

She closed her eyes. She focused on the plump lower lip tucked between Sarah's teeth that she wasn't supposed to imprint on. The way the corners turned up as it popped free. The smile rose to the almond-shaped eyes.

Just take it slow, Sarah told herself.

The imaginary woman's delicate hand guided her own under the elastic band of Victoria's pajama bottoms to the dark curls covering her sex. Victoria carded her fingers through the hair, then spread herself open.

Her middle finger slid against the slick bead. She passed the bundle of nerves coating the digit in her essence as she pressed it repeatedly against the opening. She circled the canal enjoying the new sensation. Slowly she entered herself with a single finger, clenching her muscles around it.

The palm of her hand pressed against the bud as she picked up the pace in the slick channel. The single digit made her body yearn for more, so she added another and tried again. She explored different angles as she dipped repeatedly within, spreading the two fingers and stroking the sides of the velvety passage. Again, she pressed faster within herself, until she realized the sensations within were less pronounced than the fire she felt as her palm pushed against the bead.

Removing the digits from within, she prodded the bead. A momentary shot of electricity rippled through the nerve of her groin. She rubbed it up and down, then side to side, concentrating on making the sensation repeat.

Begging the pulse to return, to vibrate against the pads of her finger, Victoria pressed on it harder. The bead grew against her touch, but just as the rippling sensation returned, it disappeared.

The image of Sarah gone as she scrunched her eyes together and willed the exhaustion in her forearm to hold out just a little bit longer.

With each failed attempt to replicate the pulsing she'd felt when she'd awoken, her movements became more erratic. Her fingers wildly slid back and forth as she pressed her cunt into them.

When she couldn't keep up the pace, she switched hands. Her left hand picked up exactly where she'd left off, only lasting a fourth of the time.

Switching back, she tried again. She willed Sarah to come back to her. Tried to see the smiling eyes looking down at her. Listened for the voice telling her she was almost there.

But Sarah wasn't there.

The slickness of her fingers had dried. Her calloused finger scratched the sensitive flesh. The bead practically vanished as her sex became raw from the brutal attack she'd given it. Unable to continue, Victoria bit her lip as she screamed internally at the tears threatening to spill from her eyes.

Her chest felt hollow. The nails on her fingers dug into her balled fists. She tried to fill it with air, but the damned tears had found an escape route from the corners of her eyes and the mucous blocked her nose. She gasped for air as the guttural cry of incompetence roared from her open mouth.

Victoria sobbed until the alarm on her phone screamed for attention. Wiping the snot from her face on the back of her hand, she shut off the alert.

Holding her breath, she prayed today would be a leg day at the gym.

She wasn't certain who she was praying to, since she knew the god she'd been taught to honor had abandoned her for the desire she had for the thick-thighed woman she'd watched doing deadlifts and the mouthwatering sex instructor.

She opened the text from Sarah she'd received while folding tiny socks in Jen's living room. "*Victoria, I wanted to confirm our meeting Sunday at 7pm.*"

She stared at the words, not realizing she was holding her breath until it rushed out of her nostrils in protest. Her teeth dug into her lower lip. She considered declining the meeting. She knew it would be hypocritical after she'd sent a follow-up the day after their initial meeting stating she was excited to meet. But that was Thursday when she'd just woken up after the first full night's sleep since the tiny voice in her head suggested she was gay.

Sarah had said that nothing she was going to tell Victoria, Victoria couldn't find herself. Closing the unanswered message, Victoria opened the Safari app. She typed lesbian porn into the search bar. Before she could even read the options, she closed the app. After being confronted with Jen's assortment of anatomically engorged toys and chasing a questionable orgasm, she knew she needed Sarah.

"This is so stupid," she said to no one.

The shower couldn't wash away the words Victoria's mind used in its calculated attack. She pressed her head against the cool tiles as the water turned her skin red.

She shut off the tap. Droplets of water sliced through the steam on the glass door. Her skin was still too hot, and her stomach twisted until she had to swallow the bile that had risen in the back of her throat.

Getting out of the shower, she stood in front of the mirror. She waited for the coating on the mirror to clear and her reflection to appear from the shadow world on the other side. Pressing a hand to the mirror, she wondered if the woman looking back at her was able to make herself climax. If she lived in another universe that made knowing her own body less sinful.

She looked at herself, staring back. The edges of her hair line speckled with gray strands a fourth of an inch long. She pressed at the bag under her eyes the nighttime eye cream didn't seem to touch. Pushed at the cheeks that had rounded out from bored-binge eating. Then she looked at the breasts with perky nipples staring back at her.

Straightening her shoulders, she raised a single eyebrow at the woman in the mirror. The same eyebrow that had made the cheeks of the attractive sex teacher blossom into a rosy pink. And she reminded herself that she lived in a universe where her body wasn't sinful, and she could do anything with a little practice.

Victoria made her way back into the bedroom where she'd abandoned her phone. Still completely nude, she looked over the bed that Sarah had visited her in the dream. The hairs on her arms prickled under the fan as her confidence wavered.

Before she could change her mind, she sent Sarah the reply: "Yes. I will see you tomorrow."

8

Victoria held the front door open for Sarah as the coach pushed a large black suitcase into her home. The wheels glided over the laminate floorboards, breaking the silence of the house.

Sarah glanced back as she made it past the entry table to Victoria. A warmth spread through Victoria's body as the other woman's eyes scanned down to her navel. Victoria opened her mouth, then remembered. She moved out of the path of the door to show Sarah her exit path was free of terrifying locking mechanisms.

Sarah's eyes ran over the door and the frame, then she smiled at Victoria. "Thank you."

"Of course," Victoria said with a slight shrug of her shoulder.

When Sarah turned back around, Victoria admired the way the woman's blouse clung snuggly to her torso and tucked neatly into the form-fitted slacks. She followed the material down Sarah's back to the pleasant curve of her ass. As her eyes made their way back up, she felt the burn of embarrassment rush up her chest to her cheeks.

Sarah's lip had found its way between her teeth as she tilted her head and smiled back at Victoria. Sarah nodded toward the dimly lit living room. "Would you like me to set up in here, the kitchen, or your bedroom?"

Victoria glanced at the stairs, never having considered that Sarah would be in the bedroom she'd neglected to clean. The possibility of Sarah in her bedroom made her heartbeat loud enough to block out the ticking of the clock. She stared at the brunette as the beating turned to pounding and the rich aroma wafting from the woman made her momentarily wish this was something different.

Victoria swallowed, then pointed to the spotless living room. "There... living room... I have a TV."

Instantly, Victoria felt the heat rush into her face again. She stared at the ceiling as she replayed the stammering and the statement about owning a television. She reminded herself it would have been more interesting to say she didn't own a television.

"Have you ever heard of gay panic?" Sarah asked.

Victoria's gaze dropped back to the woman still standing with her hand on the handle of the suitcase. She raised a single eyebrow, then licked her lower lip.

"No," she admitted.

"It's a term used to describe when a person experiences a panicked sensation at the possibility of romantic interaction with someone of the same sex. It's very normal in the beginning chapters of their gay life as they are still developing a sense of confidence in their ability to speak to someone they find attractive."

Victoria rubbed the tips of her fingers together. Her arms hung at her sides pulling her shoulders to the ground. She scrunched her face up. "So, I shouldn't feel ridiculous right now."

"No feeling shouldn't be felt." Sarah rested her hand on the suitcase. "I just want you to know that it's something that happens so that when you start to feel it, you can identify it."

"You sound like Dr. Rose," Victoria half whispered. She was grateful Sarah didn't further indicate her knowledge of Victoria's attraction.

"Yeah. Sorry about that." Sarah tucked a strand of hair that had come loose from the low ponytail behind her ear. "I tend to be very clinical about terminology when I am meeting with a client."

She pointed to the living room. "I'm going to get set up."

The suitcase was opened, but the contents were all neatly secured. Her fingers ran over several items, withdrawing two black cylinders that looked a little too much like the swords Jackie wanted to play with a few days ago. If having an orgasm required plastic penises, Victoria decided she wasn't interested. She'd had enough experience with penis to know that wasn't going to work.

"Would a glass of wine make you feel more comfortable right now?" Sarah asked.

Victoria shook her head. "I'm not sure anything can make me comfortable."

She leaned against the threshold of the living room, trying to gather the courage to enter. Shaking her head, she explained, "I just feel like I should sit down and listen to what you have to tell me, so you don't have to waste your time."

Sarah set the items in her hands on each end table before moving into Victoria's bubble. The sound of glass connecting with wood made Victoria feel just a tiny bit better, but stupid at the same time for not knowing the items weren't sex toys.

She took Victoria's hand, the warm thumb tracing a circle over her flesh. "Don't worry about the time. You're not paying by the hour, and I did not schedule any appointments following yours."

Sarah looked up at Victoria with just her eyes. A knowing and patient gaze seemed to look directly into Victoria's soul.

"We can take as much time as we need to make sure you feel safe and comfortable as we go through the materials."

"Sounds like a poor business plan," Victoria said. She regretted the statement when Sarah's soothing caress ceased, and the contact was severed.

Sarah's innocent eyes rose with her chin. A smug smirk spread over her lips, while her eyes hardened into a well-practiced 'fuck around and find out' stare.

"Experience has taught me that clients who feel comfortable and safe are more likely to schedule follow-up sessions and provide positive reviews for continued business." Sarah tilted her head, "Also if I charged by the hour, it would probably be cheaper to hire a prostitute. However, if you would like to pay me a prostitute's wage without any sexual return, I am sure we can come up with a number that can make you feel well fucked."

Victoria's lips parted. The idea of being well fucked by the sex coach caused the heat to spread through her body as the pulsing in her crotch took away her breath. She was having an orgasm now. Right there in her entryway with just the woman's verbal offer to fuck her well financially. She swallowed as her thighs pressed together. It only lasted a moment, but Victoria was practically shaking.

"I'll get the wine," Victoria was able to choke out.

"And I'll get set up."

When Victoria returned to the room with the two glasses, she froze in the doorway. Sarah had lit several candles and taken a seat on the couch. The scent that had permeated her dreams wrapped around her. A flesh-colored, silicon torso lay on her coffee table rooted Victoria in place.

Sarah patted the seat next to where she sat. "It won't hurt you; I promise."

Shaking her head, Victoria broke through the threshold. "It just feels weird," she said.

Sarah took the glass from Victoria's extended hand. She held it up when Victoria was seated next to her, waiting.

A soft chuckle rumbled Victoria's hollow chest as the glasses clinked together. The hair had fallen in Sarah's face again, and Victoria couldn't fight the urge to push it behind the woman's ear.

"Thanks," the coach whispered from the pink tantalizing lips. Victoria's eyes flitted between them and the woman's dark eyes.

Sarah turned away from Victoria, leaning against the couch from her place on the floor. "How has your week been?" she asked between sips of her wine.

Victoria pulled her leg up to rest her arm on. "I made a friend at the gym. She owns Echo's Escape."

"I know the place," Sarah said, taking another drink.

"Have you been there?"

"I let your therapist take me once in college. It was fun. Dancing. Women.

Booze. I think it will be a good experience for you."

"Do you like to do those things?"

"Do I like to do dancing, women, and booze?" Sarah asked into her glass.

Victoria stared at the way the woman's jaw moved with each swallow. "Yeah."

Sarah looked at her with that same damn smirk. "Yes. I have enjoyed doing the dancing, women, and booze before."

"What does that look mean?" Victoria asked.

Sarah's brows scrunched together. "What look?"

"The smirk you are giving me. Don't get me wrong, it's very attractive in a playful way, but what does it mean?"

Pale delicate fingers ran over the rim of the glass. Sarah made five complete turns before, she said, "I guess it's my way of not laughing."

"What did I say that was funny?"

"Your not-so-subtle way of asking me if I was interested in women. I'll be honest, you are the first single woman that I have worked with that is my age. It's just different, I guess because I want to make sure that I don't mess up by letting you fixate on me, but I also want to make sure you know that you are attractive, and your subtle questions will have an effect on a woman someday."

"But not you." Victoria swallowed an eighth of her glass.

Sarah bit her lip. "Whether they have an effect or not doesn't honestly matter. We signed a contract stating I would teach you how to please a woman that is not me. If we were to ever flirt or let's just say it, have sex, then I would walk away feeling like a prostitute. And I have worked very hard to make sure clients understand that I am not a prostitute."

"What if I canceled the session right now?" Victoria watched Sarah from the corner of her eyes.

Sarah leaned her head back against the seat cushion letting it fall against the material. She turned to Victoria. "When I leave your house, I have a life. It's chaotic and busy and is not conducive to romantic dinners or candle-lit escapades. And tearing up that contract puts that life at an unacceptable risk."

Victoria nodded. "I understand. I'm sorry. I should have...."

Sarah took Victoria's hand in hers. She entangled their fingers together. "You'll hear this in your time with women, and I hope you hear the honesty in what I am going to tell you. Not every woman is in a place for a relationship. If she is open enough to tell you that, then it has nothing to do with you. It's where she's at."

"So, if I survive this lesson..." She swallowed. "And I met a woman that's not you at the bar, then I would be able to... satisfy her?"

Sarah set her half-empty glass on the table and released Victoria's hand. "If you don't blow her mind, then I'll give you your money back."

"Okay."

Victoria took another drink, finishing her wine. It was just enough liquid courage to stop torturing herself with what-ifs.

"So, what do I do?" Victoria asked, getting to her knees before the female facade.

Moving down alongside Victoria, Sarah asked, "Have you begun to explore your own body since we last spoke."

"Yes," Victoria whispered barely audibly. Sarah took Victoria's hand in hers and brought it to the model.

"Good." Sarah positioned Victoria's hand above the vagina. "Where did you touch yourself?"

Victoria glanced at Sarah from the corner of her eye, then back to the model. She first touched the vaginal opening and then moved to the clit.

"And what brought you pleasure?"

"Both." Victoria tapped the clit lightly. "This more so. But it felt... different."

"This little bud is hooded," Sarah purred.

"Hooded?"

"What you felt on your body was what is called presented. The more stimulation you give it, the more it presents into a little bulb." Sarah spread Victoria's fingers around the clit and the vulva. "The clit presents in the bud but extends down the walls and has an internal pressure point within the vaginal canal."

"The g-spot," Victoria croaked.

"Yes."

"I did some homework," she admitted.

Sarah chuckled softly. "It's like you don't even need me."

"Which is more sensitive?" Victoria asked.

"The external portion tends to be more reactive. Depending on the woman, there is an area where the nerves will be particularly sensitive."

Sarah ran Victoria's finger around the clit. "Circle it with your fingers first. When you are comfortable you can use your tongue, but you don't have to until you are ready."

Victoria's eyes snapped to Sarah. "Like now?"

Sarah shook her head. Her hand came off of Victoria's as she held it up. The sultry whisper faded into the playful candor. "I'm sorry. I meant when you're with a woman. I clean this but I would prefer you don't lick my instructional materials."

Victoria laughed, pulling her hand away. "Thank goodness."

They smiled at one another. The lock of hair had fallen from behind Sarah's ear. "You have a hair." Victoria reached over and pushed it from the woman's face.

Victoria's eyes fell to Sarah's lips. She wanted to throw caution to the wind as Sarah pulled her lower lip between her teeth. But she turned back to the model as she thought of the extent the woman went to keep herself safe.

She reached back to the model and demonstrated.

"So, circling increases the stimulation. I instruct clients to think of it like a clock. Run around all twelve hours then twelve to six. Then around again. Get more creative with the number sequence until you find one that causes the woman to cant her hips toward you. Then keep going until she cries out and her legs lock around you. And that's it."

"That's it," Victoria stated. Her brow raised in question.

Sarah laughed. "I mean, afterward hold her. Tell her she's safe. Snuggles." She held up her hand. "Don't expect her to roll over and go to work on you. When the climax is intense it may take a while for the woman to be physically capable of reciprocating sex."

"Okay."

"So, you have the instruction. Now you just need to practice."

Sarah leaned back against the couch. She raised the glass to her lips and finished what was left.

Victoria stared at the model, comparing her memory of self-exploration to what Sarah had told her to do. She'd done a lot of it and her clit had changed when she was touching it, but it didn't work. Didn't make her pulse like moments before.

"You know how you asked if I had explored myself?" Victoria asked.

"Yes."

Victoria licked her dry lips. "It didn't go well."

"Would you be willing to share what happened?" Sarah asked.

"I don't know."

"You don't know if you want to share, or you don't know what happened?"

With a huffed breath, Victoria leaned away from the model. She fingered the empty glass. "I don't know what happened."

She shook her head. "I know I didn't do the clock thing, I guess. But it was like the more I tried the less I felt."

Victoria sighed. "Look, I know you were relieved that I said I didn't want... you know... you to be there."

"Victoria, look at me," Sarah instructed.

But Victoria didn't want to look at the sex expert. She didn't want to see the pitiful stare.

Sarah's fingers wrapped around Victoria's hand. The chill in Victoria's soul warmed in the simplistic embrace.

Victoria looked up.

"Would you like me to stay?" Sarah asked.

"Please."

"Here or in your room?"

9

The floorboards creaked under Victoria and Sarah's feet as they walked up the narrow staircase. Sarah peeked at an open door as her head breached the second floor. The light from the hallway illuminated a decently sized bedroom, complete with a made-up bed and subtle decor.

Victoria led Sarah by the hand down the hallway and passed a second bedroom complete with another bed set toward the final door at the back of the house. Sarah didn't ask why a single woman chose a place with so much space. She'd reminded her wandering mind that it wasn't any of her business, but the reminder didn't stop the wishful part of her from feeding her images of Tris living in a place like this.

As she looked past Victoria to the final room, her eyes began to scan the pathway. She'd let her fantasies get the best of her and had forgotten to catalog a safe exit if Victoria was not as innocent as she appeared.

Victoria left Sarah at the threshold of the bedroom door. She followed Victoria's movement across the room until the bedside light flipped on.

Glancing back down the hallway, she identified six picture frames she could use as projectiles on her way back to the stairs. Then, she ran her fingers along the doorway searching for any latches. When she turned back around, Victoria was watching her.

Victoria nodded to the door. "You should check that too."

Sarah forced a smile on her face before returning to her safety check. She tested the lock by pushing it into the lock position and turning the handle to release it. She closed it partially and checked the back of the door for anything on the other side.

With the door check done, Sarah breathed for the first time since entering the room. Her eyes scanned over the teal and purple accents. As she took in the space, Victoria gathered discarded clothes and shoes, before shutting them behind another door.

A part of Sarah wanted to check that door too, to ensure she wouldn't end up tethered within. But she didn't. Instead, Sarah stepped further into the room.

Sarah placed her hand on the foot of the bed and asked, "May I sit here?"

She followed Victoria's eyes to the floor. Finding nothing of particular interest, she looked back at the bed and around the space. Where every other room contained walls of family photos, the space was void of any reminder of who Victoria had once been.

Victoria wrapped her arms around her middle, one playing with the hem of her shirt. "Yes," she practically whispered.

Turning back to the woman still staring at the floor, Sarah's mind raced to put the pieces of the puzzle before her together. She swallowed as the realization hit her. The lines of the contract rules blurred with the knowledge that she was the first woman in Victoria's bedroom, let alone on her bed.

Sarah sighed and straightened her back. She was here to do a job, not play lover to a client.

"Would you prefer to have your clothes on or off?" Sarah asked.

Victoria shifted her feet as though she was teetering between the two options. When her body stopped moving, she said, "On... but can I change into something else?"

Sarah nodded. "Of course."

Victoria quickly disappeared into another door Sarah should have checked before taking a seat on the bed. She looked back at the still-open door.

The hallway called Sarah back to the space where she'd been more comfortable drawing hard lines of what to do and what not to do in.

From behind the closed door, she could hear Victoria chastising herself in the bathroom. Sarah recognized the words of self-deprecation, she too told herself in the mirror too many nights a week.

When Victoria stepped out of the bathroom, Sarah tasted the words as she took in the skimpy scarlet satin nightgown. Victoria's arm wrapped around her middle again. Sarah wondered if the woman was attempting to hide the curves of her figure.

Getting up from the bed, Sarah moved toward Victoria. She stopped halfway and extended her hand to the woman, waiting for the temptress to step into the lesson.

A pink tongue peeked out, stroking Victoria's bottom lip. Her chest rose and her shoulders straightened. Sarah watched the resolve settle in the woman's eyes that looked directly into her own. She closed the gap between Sarah and the bathroom, resting her hand in Sarah's.

With Victoria committed to the lesson, Sarah moved alongside her. She guided Victoria to bed.

Victoria sat on the edge. Her fingers tugged the edge of the camisole toward her knees.

Standing before her, Sarah coaxed Victoria's chin up until the warm brown eyes were looking up at her.

"I'm going to turn the light off."

Only when Victoria nodded did Sarah step toward the nightstand. With the light out, Sarah blinked several times. As she turned back, the glow from the hallway left Sarah enough visibility to make her way back to Victoria.

Once more, she stood before the woman. This was all new to her. The older lesbians she'd worked with never wanted her to stay, and she wasn't sure what to do for the first time in all her years of coaching. With a couple this was easy, she guided them into position and let their instincts do most of the work for her. She couldn't exactly do that with Victoria, who looked ready to flee from the room.

"I'm going to help you relax," Sarah said softly. "Lay back."

Victoria took the cue and leaned back against the bed, but she propped herself up on her elbows and continued to watch Sarah closely.

She still had no idea what to do, but once upon a time, Simone had rubbed her feet. It had relaxed Sarah so much that she didn't fight her then-boss when the woman spread her thighs and pressed against her. Obviously, she would not use a foot rub to crawl on top of Victoria.

Shaking her head, she tried to toss away how the woman would feel under her sharp angles. Sarah got to her knees and took Victoria's foot in her hand. The woman fell back against the bed, so she wouldn't be able to see the amount of times Sarah had to swallow with the woman's shorts too short to hide anything.

At least it was dark. She couldn't directly see the other woman's sex. Just smell it while she pressed against the soft sole, massaging the ball of the woman's foot.

"Tell me about what you were thinking last time you were touching yourself," Sarah instructed, trying to refocus on the woman as a client.

"I... uh..." A soft sigh broke from Victoria's lips, and then she said, "I was thinking about this girl that I met."

Sarah pressed against each toe, then ran her thumb down the arch. "What do you find attractive about her?"

"Her eyes at first. I got lost in them when we met, then I dreamed about them later. Then the way she smelled. It reminded me of home. I know I left, but I had good memories and family. The way she smells reminds me of late spring. And she has this smirk. It's playful... and sexy."

Sarah's chest froze. The air in her lungs was trapped as she remembered what Victoria had said about her.

"I have to hold myself back from trying to kiss her because... because.... I just want to see if I can stop her from laughing at me."

Her fingers paused momentarily. She swallowed the lump in her throat, trying to gather the courage it would take to walk out of the room.

She was focusing so hard on breaking the contact that the question falling from her lips caught her by surprise. "And what did you picture her doing to you?"

That shouldn't matter. Sarah knew she needed to leave because this was only going to lead to--

"She was on top of me," Victoria admitted. "Her mouth was kissing my neck, then my breasts. And when she touched me, it didn't make me want space. It made me want her closer."

Heat spread over Sarah as the knot in her stomach twisted. She should have demanded a chair. Shouldn't have put herself at eye level with the woman's pussy, especially when her hands had moved to Victoria's calves without her even realizing it. At least in a chair, she could have been facing the opposite direction. Dictated the actions like a phone sex operator and avoided Victoria seeing her.

But she'd already screwed up. She knew by asking Victoria to go back to that place, she would not avoid the reality that what was about to happen would involve getting deeper than she was comfortable with.

"Put your hand on your chest just under your breast and press a little. Feel your heart beating. Feel the way your chest rises and falls."

Sarah couldn't see if Victoria had followed her instructions, but she continued. Comforted in the thought that once this was done, she could leave with the knowledge Victoria wouldn't need her anymore. Justify she'd done what she was paid to do, and no more.

"What do I do next?" Victoria asked.

Sarah knew she needed to get Victoria further on the bed. She stood up, her hand still touching the other woman. "Move farther up on the bed."

Victoria didn't break eye contact as she scooted toward the center of the mattress. Coaxing Victoria's feet, Sarah guided her until Victoria's knees were bent and legs were open for when the time came to touch herself.

Sarah moved onto the bed and lay alongside Victoria. Leaning against her hand, she instructed, "Close your eyes."

Victoria didn't do it immediately. Her eyes studied Sarah, causing Sarah to chew her lower lip. She wasn't sure what Victoria's eyes were telling her, so she tried to reassure the woman of the two fears Sarah thought could be the meaning of the look.

"I'm not going to leave you," Sarah promised. "And I'm not going to watch you. I'll roll over in just a second to give you as much privacy as possible with me being in the room."

Victoria reached over to where Sarah lay on her bent arm. She brushed the stray hair from Sarah's face, then ran a finger down Sarah's chin.

Sarah took the hand that had ignited the alcohol into her system, setting her body a blaze. She placed it back on Victoria's chest and held it.

"Are you ready?" Sarah asked.

Victoria closed her eyes and exhaled the breath she'd been holding.

Without moving, Sarah said, "Imagine the woman leaning over you. Her hand is on your breast."

Sarah closed her eyes, picturing Victoria under her. "Can you see her?"

"Yes."

Sarah pulled her hand back and rested it alongside Victoria's bicep.

"Good. Place your hand on your breast and knead it gently."

Sarah didn't open her eyes. She simply controlled her breathing, ensuring every exhale was steady. She counted to ten between five breaths to allow Victoria time to explore.

"Now, touch your nipple. Run your finger around it, then gently twist it until it's pert."

Victoria's musky rich scent reached Sarah's nose once more. She breathed it in, separating the components in her head as the bed shifted slightly under Victoria's movements.

"Do I... Do I take my shirt off?"

"Would you feel more comfortable without it on?"

Victoria's hand took Sarah's in her own. She squeezed tightly, drawing Sarah's eyes open to the woman twisting her perked nipple. "I don't think... I'm ready," Victoria whispered.

"Then you should not take it off," Sarah stated warmly.

She licked her lips as Victoria pressed her ass into the bed and her legs clenched together tightly. "It's... It's... pulsing. I think... I think I'm having an orgasm."

"That's not quite it yet," Sarah explained.

She hoped Victoria didn't hear the smile she was wearing at Victoria's innocence. She remembered being very young and thinking a pulse was the same as a climax.

"Picture this dream girl kissing you," Sarah whispered. "Move with her."

Victoria's fingers left her nipple and raised to her lips. She caressed them softly, then returned to her breast.

"When you're ready, run your fingers through your vagina."

The digits stilled on Victoria's nipple. Slowly, her hand moved down her stomach to where the satin of the shirt had risen.

The index finger of Victoria's hand disappeared between her legs in the shallow light as Sarah watched carefully. Her own wetness grew between her legs.

Sarah closed her eyes as the hypocritical knot twisted tighter in her chest.

She'd assured Victoria that she didn't watch during lessons, and she chastised herself for breaking her word.

Her body eased backward to erase the ease of access. "What do you feel?" Sarah asked blindly.

"I'm really... uh... moist."

And Sarah couldn't stop the 'me too' that crossed her mind.

"Coat your fingers, and this time practice the movements we went over downstairs."

The bed under them began to move slightly. The woman's breathing beside her became more labored.

"Think about..." Sarah had to stop herself before the word 'me' almost fell from her lips. "The girl," she finished.

A sex-rich scent filled the room. Sarah had to swallow repeatedly as the seductive aroma filled her lungs.

"Just think about the girl as though it is her hand instead of yours. Not the numbers."

Victoria's breathing became more erratic. The bed moved with each cant of the woman's hips, gyrating Sarah's pulsing sex.

"Keep going," Sarah encouraged. She stared at the blades of the oscillating ceiling fan.

"Imagine her telling you how good you feel. How beautiful you are. How lucky she is to be with you right now." The words tasted sweet on her lips, and for a moment too long she savored the flavor.

"Tell me how it feels," Sarah instructed.

Sarah pressed her thighs together when Victoria pulled her arm up and held Sarah's hand against her heaving chest.

"So, good," Victoria gasped. "Yes... there... like fire that tickles."

"Don't stop," Sarah told her.

Victoria's knees fell open, her leg resting on Sarah as the sounds of her fingers slid vigorously against her sex.

"I can feel..." the words tapered off into a loud moan. "It's... oh my god!"

Sara balled the comforter in her fist.

"Oh my god! Oh my god!"

Victoria's body erupted as her thighs clamped around the hand between her legs. She rode out the waves of her first orgasm until she fell back into the bed. Her chest rose and fell, and her arm rose to clasp over her face.

Sara pulled the spent woman into her arms when Victoria went from pleasure to tears instantaneously.

"You're safe," Sarah whispered. "It's okay. You're safe. I got you."

Victoria clung to Sarah's arms against her chest. Her body pressed back so

Sarah could hold her closer. The emotional release, as demanding as the orgasm, shook the woman.

"Thank you," Victoria whispered hoarsely. Then, "I'm sorry I made you stay when you didn't want to."

"No place I would rather be," Sarah said, wishing it wasn't true.

Sarah held Victoria tightly, then ghosted her fingers over the woman's arm. This was the thing she'd missed over the last year of celibacy. And the contact was immediately missed when Victoria pushed herself up.

Victoria looked back shyly. "I have to go to the restroom."

"That's normal," Sarah offered. "Go ahead."

With Victoria gone, the shameful arousal in Sarah's crotch made her skin crawl. She got up from the bed she never should have been on.

The hair Victoria had pushed from her eyes was back. The reminder of the woman's touch made her stomach churn until bile rose in the back of her throat. She wrapped her hair up into a new ponytail.

"Thank you," Victoria said from the doorway of the bathroom Sarah hadn't realized had opened.

"You're welcome," Sarah stated cordially. She pointed at the door. "I'll just get my things and get out of your hair."

"Okay." Victoria wrapped her arm around her middle once more. "I'll help you get your things."

Sarah didn't wait for Victoria. She felt the woman trailing her as she descended the stairs quickly and went straight to the candles still burning in the living room.

The first blew out easily, but the second took three tries to get the flame to extinguish.

"Sarah," Victoria said.

Sarah stared at the still-melted wax in the candle before she looked up. "Yes," she said coolly.

"Are you okay?"

Sarah smiled broadly, showing all her teeth. "Yes. I'm great." She stood awkwardly with the candles in her hand, waiting for the wax to settle. She should have blown them out before they went upstairs.

Looking back at the woman leaning against the threshold to the space, Sarah knew she was fucking up. She bit her lip, allowing the pain to bring her back to her reality.

"So..." She tried to come up with something. Her mind ran through everything she'd learned about Victoria. "Uh... you said you start a new job tomorrow?"

Victoria stood up straighter. She nodded and smiled. "It's a pretty big change for me. I am moving into leadership, but it's exciting nonetheless."

"Cool," Sarah offered.

Even though the candles weren't ready, Sarah decided she'd rather deal with the mess later than participate in awkward small talk.

She put the candles in their space, the wax sliding out of the top into the suitcase. Once zipped up, she lugged the torso to the suitcase and secured it in the other zipper compartment. The zippers screeched in protest and the floor swore at her as she slapped the wheels against it.

"Okay, well I think I have everything."

As they made their way to the entryway, Victoria picked up an envelope from the table and held it out to Sarah. Sarah stared at it. The acid in her throat was a promise, not a threat.

Shaking her head, Sarah said, "I would just rather not take your money."

"Why?"

Sarah licked her lips repeatedly, then shrugged. "I just don't feel right taking your money."

"Does this mean... I shouldn't schedule a follow-up?"

Sarah opened the front door and pushed the suitcase over the entryway.

Once she was safely outside, she turned back to the woman. "Uh... I think. I think it would be better if you practice some more and then we can touch base and discuss from there."

"Okay," Victoria said to the back of Sarah's head.

Sarah looked back only once she'd hefted the suitcase into the back of Monica's SUV. She waved to the woman standing in the doorway watching her, then ducked into the car.

10

The plastic cushion obscenely grunted each time Victoria shifted while in her new boss's office. Grateful the principal hadn't come in from playground supervision, Victoria tried to find a position she could stay still in. The last thing her nerves could handle would be a question of if the chair had farted or her as she had her first real meeting with the woman.

Through the window, she watched tiny humans in maroon and navy polos trudge alongside their parents through the large metal gate to the playground. Boisterous middle schoolers bumped into each other with their backpacks slung over one shoulder as they practiced the art of creating social chaos amongst their peers.

Victoria heard the bell ring as the herd of primarily parents and kids flooded through the single-entry point. Having never worked at an elementary school nor dropped off a child of her own, Victoria found the scene fascinating. It was following another bell that the flow of traffic shifted as the adults vacated the area free for the day of their older offspring. They chatted amongst each other as toddlers in pajamas slouched in strollers on their way back home.

The sound of the door opening pulled Victoria to her feet. Her carefully selected position was lost as she smiled at a small Latin woman bursting into the room. With a clap of her hands, Principal Maria Velaquez sent out the energy she'd accumulated from the morning tasks in waves over the still office.

Instead of shaking Victoria's hand, Principal Velaquez wrapped her in a tight embrace. Victoria patted the woman's back from a hunched position.

"Oh mija, I am so happy you're here." The principal held Victoria's arms as she stood back and looked up at her. The smile faded, but the warm chocolate eyes remained wide. "Aye Dios mío! We have been in a tough spot without someone to handle discipline for half of last year."

"I'm happy to be here," Victoria stated.

"Siente," Principal Velasquez said.

Victoria's brow scrunched in the middle. Her mind sorted through every memory from college Spanish trying to figure out when she'd heard that word before. With her memory failing her, she said the word in her head multiple times trying to see if it sounded like its English counterpart.

"¿Hablas Español?"

She smiled weakly, recognizing this one. "No, but I did sign up for an online course."

The woman took a seat behind the vintage teacher's desk. "Good. You'll need it."

When Victoria continued to stand, Principal Velasquez explained, "Siente means to sit."

The heat of embarrassment settled in Victoria's cheeks before her brain chastised her for not remembering the word. She prayed for silence as she lowered herself carefully into the chair, and the god she'd forsaken punished her.

Principal Velasquez leaned back, her fingers rolling a cheap gel pen. She looked Victoria over as though for the first time she saw the new person in her employment.

"So, tell me about yourself," the principal requested.

Victoria's fingers found the hem of her shirt and rubbed the material between them. She hadn't expected the question post-hiring and wasn't sure what it was she was meant to share.

"Uh... I'm from Salt Lake. I have been in Arizona since the beginning of summer."

"What brought you to Phoenix?"

"I was just looking for a change."

"Did you move here with your family?"

"No. Uh... my divorce finalized, and I needed a change of scenery." Victoria's eyes flitted to the family photo in the small silver frame. Unable to come up with anything else, she asked, "Are you married?"

"Aye, yes. Married my childhood crush. I told him when I was eight that he was going to marry me, and he said, 'Okay.' We have seven children. Do you have children?"

"No... it's just me."

Principal Velasquez set the pen she'd been playing with down on her desk. "You used to teach high school, correct?"

"Yes". Victoria sat up straighter in her seat. "I taught Economics for twelve years."

"And this is your first time in leadership."

"Yes. I finished my admin program over the summer, and I was very excited when I learned of this opportunity. I know that it will be different from what I am used to, but I am confident in my ability to adjust to the new surroundings."

The smile returned to the principal's face, her cheeks rising until her eyes crinkled in the corners. "I do not doubt that you are. We use a PBIS system. Are you familiar?"

"Yes." Uncomfortable with the short answer, Victoria's mouth began to shoot off anything it could come up with as relevant to earn some trust with her new boss. "We had an entire course on it in my program. Most of my peers were elementary school teachers, so I gathered a lot of insight into some of the differences in the programs between the two levels."

"Bueno," the principal stated. "It will be different. Teenagers can tell you what is happening, while younger children are still learning to process their emotions. Patience will be critical in building relationships, and even though you are responsible for discipline, the relationship is going to be what the child needs."

Victoria nodded along with the words of wisdom. As she prepared her response, the door to the office banged open.

"Hey Maria, sorry I'm late. The alarm didn't go off, and then I hit every red light"

The air in Victoria's lungs got stuck behind the lump that had formed in her throat. She turned at the familiar voice rambling behind her to the last human she expected to see at her new job.

The pressed business attire from Sarah's side hustle was replaced with the pair of black jeans that clung to her slender thighs. The hint of cleavage Victoria had engrained in her memory was cloaked in the oversized royal blue knit shirt.

"First-day traffic is always so terrible, and I know that, which is why I set the alarm for early but then it turns out I set it for PM instead of AM. But I brought you coffee and—"

The intimacy coach's forest eyes landed on Victoria as the pale hand held out a paper cup.

"Oh, Sarah. I'm glad you're here." Principal Velaquez rose to her feet, pulling Victoria up with her. She moved around the desk and pulled Sarah into a tight hug.

Sarah squeezed the woman without breaking eye contact with Victoria.

Once the hug was complete, Principal Velasquez held out a hand to Victoria. "This is Victoria Brenten. She's our new AP. Victoria, this is Sarah O'Keefe and she's our guardian angel."

"Social worker," Sarah corrected quietly.

The office didn't fill with the fruity scent of the woman, but Victoria could still taste it. She clenched her thighs together as the pleasant pulse reminded her of Sarah's arms around her less than twelve hours ago. Swallowing the sweetness of her memory, she stared into the wide eyes.

"Do you two know each other?" Principal Velaquez asked.

"No," Sarah spat out quickly.

The single-syllable word hit Victoria in the chest. The trapped air rushed from her lungs as she tried to understand why Sarah would deny knowing her. But she didn't correct the brunette still clutching two paper coffee cups.

Victoria held out her hand, then dropped it when she realized her stupidity. "Ms. O'Keefe, it's a pleasure to meet you."

"Just call me Sarah, and yeah you too." Sarah looked at the coffee in her hand. "Sorry, I didn't realize we were getting a new AP, or I would have brought you coffee too."

"That's kind," Victoria stated weakly. "Thank you but I don't drink coffee."

Both of the women looked Victoria up and down like she'd grown another head. Principal Velasquez took the coffee from Sarah's hand. They sipped the drinks in unison.

Victoria fumbled through options of phrases she could use to break up the silence in the room. Every one of them felt funny in her mouth.

Her stomach fluttered as a thought crossed her mind with Sarah's eyes roaming over her body. Their paths had crossed in the real world, which meant now Sarah would have to see her. See her as a woman and not a client.

Victoria raised her eyebrow at Sarah. "So... we will be working closely then."

"I... I'm going...." Sarah looked at her purse, then patted her side. "I think I left my keys in my car."

Without another word, Sarah left the office as quickly as she'd entered. The air fled with her.

"Sarah is amazing," Principal Velaquez praised moving back to her chair. "You will love her and if you ever need help with a kid... Let's just say she has a gift."

Victoria couldn't pull her eyes from the door to where her new boss had just taken a seat. "That's good to know. I... uh..." She turned back to her new boss. "Sorry. Um... Is there any way I can get a list of all disciplinary issues from last year? I would like to familiarize myself with who has done what to whom and what action was taken."

"Of course." Principal Velasquez took another sip of her coffee before getting back to her feet. "I'm sure you want to get yourself settled in your office."

"Yes. Thanks."

Principal Velaquez led Victoria through the corridor of offices until she reached a miniature lobby. Victoria felt like a giant as another petite woman stood behind an L-shaped desk and introduced herself as Letica Mitchel, Victoria's assistant. Victoria smiled at the woman, shook the outstretched hand, and bid farewell to her new boss.

Once behind the closed door, Victoria's smile fell. She leaned against the back of the door, hiding from the window open to the lobby. She sucked in as big a breath as possible to fill the emptiness in her chest.

When Sarah had left the night before without accepting her money, Victoria had laid in bed content with the change in circumstances. Her dreams had come easy, and when she woke Sarah's scent had intertwined with her own.

Victoria told herself it wasn't her imagination. There was no possible way Sarah didn't feel it. But the woman's denial of knowing her cracked the fragile confidence building within Victoria.

She moved away from the door and settled into her chair. It squealed as she leaned back, her eyes roaming over the lobby until they landed on the woman in the office across from hers.

Sarah's hair lay half dry around her face. Dark circles hung under the tired eyes as she pressed her hands over the mouth that had promised Victoria she was safe with her.

The vacant stare narrowed as their eyes met through the glass. Sarah's hands dropped from her mouth. She straightened her slumped shoulders, hardening like stone.

Sarah was the first to break eye contact. She disappeared from view, but Victoria waited for her return.

The phone rang, dragging Victoria's attention from the window to the caller ID. Sarah's name appeared on the small screen.

Victoria looked up to find Sarah back in view, this time holding the phone to her ear. When Victoria made no move to answer, Sarah's head tilted and brows scrunched, challenging Victoria not to answer.

On the fourth ring, Victoria picked up the phone. Before Sarah could say anything, Victoria said, "This is Victoria Brenten. How can I help you?"

"I feel the need to remind you of the confidentiality contract you signed."

Victoria wasn't sure what she expected when she answered the phone. But that wasn't it. She searched Sarah's face for any hint of a smirk. Anything to tell her this was a joke.

"Is that what you *really* want? To pretend you don't know me?"

"*Yes.*" The word was so final and cold, it burned.

"Last night..." Victoria started. She shook her head. It didn't make sense. She decided Sarah must be in denial, so she tried to remind the woman. "The connection... between us."

"There was no connection," Sarah stated curtly. *"You contacted me to provide a service, and I provided said service."*

"That's not true."

Sarah's lips were set in a straight line. *"How so?"*

With a furrowed brow, Victoria searched Sarah's face again. Still not finding what she was looking for, she argued, "You didn't take my money. At that point, I stopped being a client."

"I know the woman you were dreaming about was me."

Victoria's heart went into overdrive.

"Your comment about the smirk. You'd asked me what mine had meant earlier in the evening."

Victoria's fingers played with the rough material of her top. She replayed the conversation in her head and realized the mistake. There was no taking it back now, and the fact Sarah stayed meant something.

"So, you know. I didn't mean for you to find out like that. I mean yes, it's embarrassing that you know that I was dreaming about you, but I'm not sorry. I made it pretty clear I was interested in you before that."

"Well, I am. I am sorry." Sarah sighed into the phone. She looked away from Victoria as she confessed, *"That is why I didn't take your money. I crossed a professional boundary, and I just didn't feel right about taking your money. But that doesn't change the contract."*

Victoria's shoulders rose. "Actually, I think it voids the contract. Since you knowingly crossed a boundary, what happened stopped being about business and started being about pleasure."

Sarah scoffed and the smirk that spread across her lips wasn't playful. *"What pleasure?"* she spat. The woman leaned back in her chair. Her fingers strummed against the papers on her desk. *"I didn't do anything besides lay next to you while you fucked yourself. Is that what you want people to know? Because if you want to void that contract, that is what they will know."*

Victoria raised an eyebrow at Sarah.

"If you weren't going to take my money, then you stayed for a reason. You stayed because you wanted to be there with me."

The toxic smile fell from Sarah's face. The social worker whispered her quiet confession, *"I can't have that world collide with this world. I have everything to lose."*

"As do I."

Sara ran her finger through the long straight locks, pushing it back from her face. She bit her lip, and the tired eyes looked down.

After a heavy exhale, Sarah stated, *"Look, we already lied and said we didn't know each other so that's the reality now. You don't know me. I don't know you. It was designed specifically for no one to know me."*

There was a power she realized she held in the situation. Victoria weighed the consequences of pressing Sarah to acknowledge her. Hiring Sarah wasn't a threat to her career. She'd broken no law. However, Sarah's nightly activities could threaten Sarah's job.

Had Victoria found out and not been a client, she would probably be the first to request Sarah's dismissal. A part of her felt guilty for even admitting it to herself.

"I won't tell anyone," Victoria promised.

Victoria watched the relief wash over Sarah. The thin frame melded into the chair.

"*Thank you*," Sarah said.

Victoria forced herself to smile. "So... we are going to be working together."

With a slightly familiar chuckle, the woman from Victoria's living room reappeared. "*Yes, which means keep your mind out of the gutter and stop imagining me naked.*"

Victoria rolled her eyes, then looked back at the woman. "Same."

Sarah's head tilted. The single dimple in her cheek deepened as she stared at Victoria. "*Why do you think I imagine you naked?*"

Victoria raised a single eyebrow at Sarah and watched the slight blush rise in her cheeks.

"*We are professionals*," Sarah stated.

"Yes. Professionals who work together," Victoria agreed.

"*That's it.*"

"Mmmhmmm," Victoria answered. Unsure what else to say, she set the phone back on the receiver and looked away from the window.

She smiled at the desk. Her cheeks burned as an image of Sarah naked on the surface invaded her mind.

She tried to find something else to think about, so she looked out the window. The temptation was just across the hall though. The sexy social worker chewed on a pen while Sarah stared down at some papers.

A part of Victoria wondered if Sarah was thinking about her. The familiar pulsing returned once more and caused Victoria to shift in her seat and squeeze her thighs together.

The fear of asking a woman out had been wiped from Victoria's mind as she created scenarios in her head leading her to an opportune moment to ask her co-worker on a date.

A light rapping on the door sobered her mood, bringing her shamefully back to the present.

"Come in," Victoria beckoned.

Ms. Mitchel stepped into the office with a single sheet of paper. "Maria asked me to give this to you." She held out a page of instructions. "It's how you look up past discipline reports in the student information system. IT said they would be here within the hour with your computer."

"Thank you, Ms. Mitchell," Victoria said as her assistant took her leave, shutting the door behind her.

Victoria took the paper from her assistant and scanned over the instructions. Without a computer, she was unable to accomplish anything. She set it on the empty desk and scanned the equally empty office.

With nothing to do, Victoria looked up once to the open door across from her window. Within the tiny office, Sarah was watching her. Victoria raised her eyebrow once more at the woman. Instead of the desired smirk, Victoria received a dramatic eye roll.

Sarah got up from her desk and closed the door to her office.

With only a postered door to look at, Victoria returned her attention to the space surrounding her. She made a list of things to get at the office supply store as she waited for IT to arrive with something for her to do.

11

By the second week of working with Victoria, Sarah was counting down the days until Fall Break. Every day had begun with a phone conversation with a social worker at the Department of Child Services, and today was no different.

The hollow walls of Sarah's storage closet office offered no soundproofing, so screaming was not an option. She swallowed the pain as she listened to the DCS worker on the other end of the phone explain she was coming to do an immediate removal of a first grader from campus.

"I understand," Sarah said. Her tears threatened to flood the dam she had built over the years. She typed the student's name into the computer. "I have no contact information for Dad."

Sarah navigated through a couple of screens until she could see the child's enrollment documents. "Birth certificate says Dad's name is Miguel Ramirez. Yes, it was issued in Arizona. She's a citizen."

She leaned back in her chair. "Do we know where ICE took Mom?"

A knock on the door brought Sarah's eyes to the ceiling. She willed the tears to go away as the door opened, even though she hadn't called the visitor in.

She glared at Victoria standing in the doorway for the hundredth time in fourteen days. The first couple of times had been cute the way Victoria would bring her everything to make sure she was handling issues at an age-appropriate level. It was the first time a newly hired AP acknowledged her competence, which forced Sarah to see the woman, and not the client. However, the cuteness faded with every interruption until Sarah began to doubt her new boss's competence to the point the sight of the woman in her doorway drew a heavy sigh from Sarah's lips.

She did her best to ignore Victoria waving at her like whatever she wanted was more important than the phone call she was on.

"Can we hold off pulling her out of class until the end of the day?" Sarah asked the DCS worker.

"I need your help," Victoria interrupted.

Sarah placed her hand over the mouthpiece of the phone. "Can you not see that I am on the phone?"

She didn't wait for a response, just spun her chair away from the woman still standing in her space.

"I'm sorry, I missed that. Can you tell me again what time you will be here?"

She listened to the instructions the DCS worker gave her. She sucked her teeth and nodded. "Okay. I will have her ready for pick up at 1:45. Thank you."

When she turned around, she rolled her eyes at Victoria still standing in the doorway. The phone hit the receiver with more force than she intended, missing the latch point to tumble on the desk.

"What do you want?" Sarah asked, trying to hang up the phone again.

"I have a kid in my office, and I can't get a hold of his parent."

Sarah waited for the rest of the information that would justify barging into her office. When Victoria didn't say anything else, Sarah probed, "Okay... did you try calling again?"

"I called twice."

Sarah stared at her. She waited but when Victoria continued to expect her to solve a problem that wasn't a problem, she said, "So, call again."

"But no one is answering, so do we call DCS?"

Sarah's brows scrunched in the middle. Slowly, she said, "No."

"But I can't get in touch with his mom."

Glancing back at the picture of the child whose world had been torn apart this morning caused a fire to burn in her chest. "Keep trying."

Victoria scoffed. "That's it? I just keep trying?"

"Yes. Mom is probably at work."

Sarah watched Victoria turn back to her office, pulling the social worker's attention to the preteen sitting across the hall from her. Recognizing the boy immediately, Sarah got up from her chair.

Diego Horna wasn't a troubled kid, but he'd seen more than his share of trauma. Sarah thought of the time she'd held him against her as he gripped the steak knife he'd been asked to turn over after his brother had been shot walking home from the high school by a rival gang the night before.

"What did Diego do?"

"He told his teacher to calm the f down."

Sarah's eyes shot from the boy with the man bun to the woman. She had to shut her mouth to keep from echoing the boy's words to Victoria.

She dragged her tongue over her teeth, trying to scrape away Victoria's floral perfume.

"You're joking about calling his mom, right?" Sarah snapped.

Victoria's shoulders rose, and she raised her chin until the height difference between them was more noticeable.

"Why would I joke about this?" Victoria asked.

Sarah's head dropped to her shoulder. She searched Victoria's face for the slightest crack in the bitch mask she was wearing. When she found no hint of a jest, Sarah raised her chin and narrowed her eyes at the woman.

"Because you're being ridiculous," she stated coldly.

Victoria's upper lip curled just slightly. "Excuse me?"

Taking a step into the bubble Victoria had brought into Sarah's office, Sarah reclaimed the space as her own. Her hands quaked as she said, "You heard me."

"What is your problem?" Victoria asked.

Shaking her head, Sarah heard the disgusted laugh before she realized she was even laughing.

"My problem is you," Sarah wasped. With mouth open, a swarm of hornets flew out to attack the invader. "Your inability to do anything on your own. Your constant need for approval. And your downright pettiness. The overall package is just outright unattractive."

The last word meant to do worse than sting. She knew it was the wrong word for the situation, but the way Victoria's eyes fell to her own body only fueled the fire already burning through Sarah.

She took in another heavy supply of oxygen and let the fire spill from her mouth. "I just got off the phone with DCS because one of our kids' mom just got picked up by ICE. The kid is a US citizen so she's going into foster care. Gone never to be seen from again. And you barge in here wanting to steal a kid from school because he said calm the fuck down."

"Kids can't talk like that at school," Victoria defended meekly.

"Don't confuse ability with desired conformity. They are humans and they come from places that it might be exactly what they hear. Did you even ask him why he said it?"

Victoria swallowed. Her pink tongue peeked out from her mouth as she licked whatever she had thought about saying from her teeth once more. Then she shook her head and set the mask of indifference back on her perfectly made-up face.

"It doesn't matter why he did it. We have rules," she stated.

Sarah pushed past Victoria and her indifference. Each step smacked against the dingy tile as she walked straight past the assistant through Victoria's office door.

"Diego," Sarah said to the eighth grader, still hanging his head. She kneeled in front of the boy, so he didn't have to move much to look at her. The light brown eyes rose to meet hers when she rested a hand on his. "Why did you tell Mrs. Branche to calm the f down?"

The skin on his lips was chapped and red as the crooked teeth chewed at it. He sucked up his snot, then said. "She lost her mind, miss."

"How?"

He closed his eyes, then shook his head. "She was laying into Darius because he lost his pencil. Calling him irresponsible and told him she not giving him no more pencils until his mom replace the one he lost. Then she said that if his mom don't replace his pencil that she going to give him zeros and he gonna be in her class again next year."

"Is that when you told her to calm down?"

"Yeah, miss."

Sarah nodded. "What happened then?"

"She told me to get out her class. So, I came to the office to tell her." his finger rose and pointed to the doorway. "But *she* don't care. She said I'm disrespecting the class. I didn't disrespect no one but the bitch doing the disrespecting."

The boy rocked in his seat. The fear fled from his eyes as he met Sarah's gaze. She squeezed his hand, pulling him back from the space of non-communication. She breathed loudly. Her hand on her stomach pushing out, then in. When Diego put his own hand on his stomach and followed her, she repeated the action and counted aloud to five for them.

The jagged edges on Diego's words were sanded away as they exited his mouth this time. "Someone got to check her, miss. She always yelling at Darius and he ain't done nothing to her."

Sarah looked back at Victoria, then at the boy.

"Diego. I can tell you want to protect Darius, and I appreciate your passion for standing up for others. How could you have told Ms. Branche to calm down in your school vocabulary?"

"I coulda just said calm down. But I was mad, miss. Every fucking day she at him."

Sarah waited for Diego to take two deep breaths. She waited not because she needed him to calm down again, but so he knew she thought about what he said. Then she told him, "Diego. I hear you but your message is getting lost in your anger."

The boy's fingers gripped the material of his khaki pants until the tanned fingers were ash. He closed his eyes, his hand coming to his stomach as he breathed like Sarah had breathed.

Sarah waited for him.

"You right, miss," he stated. Then he opened his eyes and smiled. "Just cause she a bitch don't mean I gots to be mean."

Sarah laughed. "Exactly. Now say that again in your school vocabulary."

Diego nodded. "I got you. I don't have to be mean because she is."

Sarah patted the hand she hadn't released. "Great job."

They shared the moment, but the rest of the situation caught up to them when Victoria cleared her throat.

"This lady saying I got to go to ISS because I said the f word but she ain't gonna do nothing about that bi... Ms. Branche always picking on Darius."

The boy looked over at Victoria, his nostrils flaring like he'd just stepped in dog shit.

When he turned back to Sarah, the snarl vanished. "Miss, do I really have ISS because I stood up to a bully?"

"Yes," Victoria stated from her position. She stepped out of the doorway. "Please wait outside while I speak with Ms. O'Keeffe."

"She serious?" Diego balked.

"Yes, I am serious, Diego."

Diego's chair hit the wall. He got up, almost toppling Sarah over from where she was still kneeling in front of him, before he slammed past Victoria, who'd rushed to keep Sarah from hitting the ground. A single hand had found its way under Sarah's arm and pulled her to her feet.

Without a thought, Sarah pulled herself from the woman's grip. Her fingers yanked pulled at the roots of her hair as she took three steps deeper into the office.

As soon as Victoria shut the door, Sarah spun around. Her hands shot out in front of her. "You can't be serious?"

Victoria sniffed and her chin rose once more. Sarah's body lit ablaze again at Victoria's meager attempt to dominate her.

"I can be. And I am," Victoria stated.

"I swear every fucking admin that walks into this office thinks they got this shit all figured out." Sarah's fists balled at her sides. She tried her own breathing exercises but the more oxygen she inhaled the angrier she got.

Spittle flew from her lips as she hissed at the woman, "He is telling you he was standing up for another kid against someone he was perceiving as a bully, and you don't care."

"It's not about caring, Sarah," Victoria stated. "It's about following through with the consequences for behavior. It is the only way these kids will learn to follow the rules."

The half laugh exited Sarah like a puff of smoke. She looked at the water stained ceiling tiles, shaking her head.

"So, the f-word is more important to you than the teacher yelling at a student?"

"No, that is a different issue." Victoria stepped closer to Sarah. She started to reach toward Sarah causing Sarah's neck to practically snap as she shot her laser eyes at the hand.

"Look, you don't have to agree with me. But I'm following the rules. I can't start choosing who can follow rules and who can break them. That is a slippery slope that I don't want to slide down."

"You want to talk about slippery slopes," Sarah stated. "How about the ones these kids are already sliding down? The slope they are trudging up every day coming to school unprepared with less resources in a society that sees their skin color before anything else."

Victoria's eyebrows practically met in the middle. "Are you calling me racist?"

"No, I'm calling you clueless," Sarah spat. She rubbed her hands over her face.

"What would you have me do? Send him back to class?"

"Yes!" Sarah raised her hands in the air, praising whatever deity was getting Victoria to understand.

"I can't do that," Victoria stated.

"You can't do that?" Sarah repeated, her arms falling to her sides. She stepped closer to Victoria. "You can't send him to the one place he needs to be."

Sarah took another step forward, her body now fully within Victoria's bubble.

"No," Victoria whispered.

The eyes of the woman roamed over Sarah's face pausing at her lips. Sarah watched the painted lip of the assistant principal smoosh between the white teeth.

"That young man had an option not to come today. He also had an option to not say a word and let a kid that is not even his friend get belittled in front of his peers. But he showed up and he stood up," Sarah stated. She watched as Victoria's dilated eyes rose from her lips.

"And next time he can do that without the profanity."

Sarah searched for the baby administrator who'd sought her guidance on everything. But she wasn't there.

"Or... he could just stop coming at all. Just like everyone else in his family did." Sarah placed her hand on Victoria's chest just below her collar bone. She dropped her chin and played a card from her other life. "I bet you never saw the inside of an office like this as a kid. I'm sure it's hard to relate to kids who come from a world that isn't as sheltered."

"No, I didn't." Victoria stated. "My parents taught me how to behave. Parents play a vital influence on their children's lives. It's clear his did not teach him how to behave at school."

Sarah patted Victoria's chest. She leaned in closer to Victoria, feeling the woman's hand find a resting place on Sarah's hip. As Victoria inhaled, Sarah could smell the effect her proximity was having on the woman.

She leaned back just enough to meet Victoria's eyes. Then she let the acid flow off her tongue onto the other woman. "I bet where you come from, someone is saying it's your parents' fault that you turned out gay."

Sarah didn't move. She stared into Victoria's eyes that widened, then welled with unwanted tears.

"Get. Out. Of. My. Office." Each word splashed against Sarah's face.

Victoria's fingers tightened on Sarah's hip as Sarah leaned forward and brought her lips closer to Victoria's ear. "Never wanted to be here in the first place."

The door to the office shut quietly behind Sarah.

"Don't send him to ISS," she told Leticia, gesturing to the boy. "I need a minute and then I'm going to take him up to a buddy class."

"Ms. Brenton said..."

"I don't care what she said. She doesn't even know where ISS is."

Sarah walked back to her office and kicked the door closed. Her whole body shook as she dug her cellphone out from under a pile of files.

The phone rang three times before Monica asked, " *What did the baby gay do now?"*

Sarah threw herself down in her duct taped chair. "I fucking hate her. I hate her and you for putting her in my life."

"She apparently would have been in your life with or without me," Monica stated dryly. *"What'd she do now?"*

Sarah picked up the plastic ballpoint pen and chucked it against the wall. It clattered to the floor.

"She fucking just suspended a kid because he said fuck when standing up for another kid."

"She sounds frustrated."

Sarah glared at the door as she processed Monica's statement. Shaking her head, Sarah groaned.

"How is that your answer?"

"Well, you said she finally came. I bet she hasn't cum again, so she is a walking ball of rage. Maybe you should coach her a little and let her know that now that door has been opened she's going to need to handle her situation or the frustration will build up."

Monica's laughter flowed through the phone like a spring. The sounds washed away the flames that had turned Sarah's tanned skin scarlet.

"I can't," Sarah stated.

" *Why?"*

Sarah pinched the bridge of her nose.

"Did you fuck her?"

"NO!" Sarah yelled, then remembered her office walls were made of paper.

She sat up and hit her head on the desk.

"I let her imprint on me."

"*What?!*" Sarah pulled the phone away from her ear. "*How?*"

Sarah let her head fall repeatedly to the desk. "She told me basically she had a dream about me fucking her in the middle of our session and I was too close when it happened."

"*How close?*"

"She was holding my hand."

"*Did you hold her?*"

"Yes."

Monica's louder laughter wasn't soothing as it came through the phone this time. It pounded against her skull that already throbbed from her own self-inflicted pain.

"*No wonder she's so pissy.*"

Sarah sat up. "What the fuck does that mean?"

"*It means that you fucked with her baby gay heart and knowing you when you found out she's now your boss, you're acting like you always do when someone is interested in you.*"

While the words made perfect sense, there was still a boy in the lobby being punished for doing the right thing.

"Well, I still hate her."

"*No, you don't,*" Monica countered. "*If you hated her, you would ignore her.*"

"I can't ignore her," Sarah argued.

"*You can. You don't want to because you held her hand for a reason. You don't want to admit it, but you knew the rules and what would happen, and you did it anyway. You wanted to be her first. I bet you didn't even take payment.*"

"I couldn't," Sarah said quietly.

The door to her office cried out as someone rapped against the other side. She waited for Victoria to burst through it. When her boss didn't, Sarah knew it wasn't the last person she wanted to see.

"I have to go," she told Monica. Then yelled at the door that cried out again. "Just a minute."

"*Yeah. Go fuck your boss so she stops being mean to kids.*"

"I'm not going to fuck her," Sarah growled.

"*We'll see,*" Monica sang from the other end of line.

"You're an asshole."

"*Buh-BYE!*"

Sarah didn't say goodbye before she hung up. She just set the phone down and said, "Come in."

Victoria's assistant slid into the office and shut the door behind her. She sat down in the chair across from Sarah and breathed out deeply.

"I hate her," Leticia whispered. "She just tried to take Diego to ISS, but Maria came to get her for some meeting, so he is still waiting for you. Do you want me to try to get Xio Horna on the phone?"

She checked the time, then sighed. "She's probably in class. I'll text her to let her know what's going on, and not to call Victoria back."

Leticia's smile grew. "How you going to avoid the date this time?"

"Xio doesn't date," Sarah reminded Leticia. "She's just a Hey Mamas lesbian trying to get laid."

"Too bad she didn't answer the bitch's call. Maybe Xio could have fucked the bitch out of her."

She chewed on the idea of getting Victoria and Diego's mom to cross paths. If anyone could sweet talk a woman into bed for some release it was Xiomara Horna. The strap in Xio's pants would probably terrify the baby gay though.

"Or is someone else interested in the hot mama?" Leticia probed.

Sarah tried to smile, but the fire Monica had extinguished left a distinctive path of pain. The shame festered within her as her words about Victoria's parents replayed over and over again. Made her think about the world she'd come from.

"I don't date," Sarah said, getting up from her seat. "And even if I did, sleeping with a student's mom would be asking to get fired. And that was not on my bingo card of bad ideas this year."

12

Even though it was an early Thursday evening, every table at Culinary Dropout was filled. Victoria arrived earlier than planned and still had to put her name down on the thirty-minute waitlist. While she waited at the bar for a glass of Merlot, she sent a text to Jen that there was no need to rush.

She watched the bartenders dance around each other, seeming to never get in the other's way. While the long-haired blonde reached into the bin with a scoop for ice, the spikey-haired pixie leaned over to pull a bottle of vodka from the silver tray. Their hands never touched, and the two drinks were made and served. Victoria wondered how long it had taken them to learn each other, and if she would ever be able to coexist so seamlessly with the other half of her team.

The glass in her hand was half empty when Jen arrived. She slapped her clutch on top of the wooden bar before sliding into the seat beside Victoria.

"I didn't expect it to be this busy on a Thursday," Jen stated. She held a finger in the air until the spiky-haired woman approached them. The black vest barely contained the lacy camisole beneath. Victoria's eyes wandered over the woman's body, then back to her glass.

With her order placed, Jen turned back to Victoria. "So, it's been a few weeks. Tell me about the new job?"

Victoria huffed out the imaginary candle over her glass. "Today sucked."

The bartender slid a martini across the metal surface to Jen. Jen entered the dance routine with the bartender by sliding over her credit card.

"What happened?" Jen asked.

"I got into it with this woman."

"Parents suck." Jen smiled over the rim of her glass. "I should know I'm a parent. Hell, I'm *that* parent."

"Wasn't a parent. It was the social worker." Victoria glanced over at Jen. "The amazing social worker, who has a gift with children, and blah blah blah that everyone constantly raves about."

Jen's eyebrows rose as she sipped from the frosted glass. "You like her."

Victoria's phone buzzed against the wood. She held the screen up to show Jen the alert that their table was ready. They gathered their purses and drinks, making their way to the hostess stand.

Once at the table, Victoria perused the menu. Nothing on it made her mouth water, so she looked to her friend. But Jen wasn't holding her menu, just her drink. The blue eyes were studying her.

"What?" Victoria asked. She looked down at her shirt, worried she may have gotten something on it.

"You didn't deny liking the sexy social worker."

Victoria's eyes rolled, and then her head fell back against the booth. She sucked her teeth before meeting her friend's eyes once more. "I met the sexy social worker before I learned she worked with me. And... I thought there was a connection and the last couple of weeks were going fine, but after today..."

Victoria tapped her fingers against the table, then pressed the tips to the wood. "Now she hates me. I mean, she was less than thrilled when she found out we were going to be working together, and today, I think sealed the deal for her hating me."

"So..." Jen took another sip of her drink. "You met this girl and had a connection with her. But she didn't like that you two were working with each other. Where'd you meet her?"

Victoria heard Sarah's voice in her head say the word 'contract.' She used the menu as a shield before telling Jen, "I'm not allowed to talk about it?"

The menu slipped through Victoria's hands and smacked against the tabletop. Jen's breasts lay atop the surface as her hand held the cardstock against the wood. She whispered, with wide eyes, "Is she a prostitute?"

"No!" Victoria barked. She stared at her friend who hadn't moved.

"Then where did you meet her?"

Victoria pushed Jen's hand off the menu. She didn't try to block her face this time. "I hired her as a coach."

Jen's fake boobs came off the table as her face twisted in displeasure. "Like a life coach?"

"Yeah. I mean... kind of."

Victoria glanced back at the menu weighing what amount of suffering she was willing to put up with after this meal. The spicy Korean skirt steak was bound to give her heartburn and the butternut squash lasagna would undoubtedly make her bloated.

"So, she's a life coach that is annoyed that you have a life?" Jen shook her head and took another drink. "You're not telling me the whole story."

"She doesn't like to mix her day job with her night job," Victoria stated simply. "I was a client, and now, I'm kinda her boss."

The server approached the table with a tablet in hand. "Thanks for your patience, ladies. Have you had a chance to look over the menu?"

"I have," Victoria stated.

Jen rolled her eyes. "I checked the menu before I got here. I would like the spicy vegan curry."

"That's a great choice," the server stated. Then she turned to Victoria. "And for you?"

"The lasagna, please."

"You got it." The server typed into the tablet. She glanced at the table. "Would you like another round of drinks?"

"She needs a bottle of whatever she is already drinking. She's got a story. And I need her to finish at least two more glasses before she tells me the truth."

"There's no story," Victoria lied.

Jen's finger wagged in the air. "You see the way her cheeks just turned that rosy shade of pink. That's how I know she's lying."

The server chuckled softly. "I'll get that bottle, and would you like another martini?"

"No, just another wine glass."

"Of course."

Victoria raised her glass to her lips, but before she took a drink she said, "This wine is going to make your food taste terrible."

"It's vegan. It's going to taste like shit anyways."

"Then why be a vegan?" Victoria asked.

Then she wished she hadn't.

She wasn't sure how long she'd listened to Jen's lecture on factory farms. It was long enough for the wine to be dropped off and half of the bottle finished between the two of them. It only ended when their meatless meals were placed before them.

Jen scooped up a fork full of eggplant and sweet potatoes. She stopped just before it entered her mouth. "So, the sexy social worker is a nighttime coach. What is she coaching you on?"

Victoria choked on her wine. The acidic liquid burned her esophagus as she sputtered into the napkin that barely caught the wine pouring back out of her mouth. The other patrons stopped what they were doing.

Jen waved her fork in the air. "Don't worry. She's fine." She held up her hospital badge. "I'm a doctor. She's not dying. Just being dramatic."

"Why are we friends?" Victoria asked between her gasps. Her lungs burned as they attempted to relearn the art of breathing. "And does installing metal joints count as being a doctor."

"Because being lonely sucks," Jen stated. She shoved a heaping pile of vegetables into her loudmouth. As she chewed, Victoria gathered her composure. "And yes, it says MD. Doesn't matter if the humans come in and leave as cyborgs."

"So..." Jen probed again.

"She was coaching me how to have sex," Victoria spit out.

Jen's fork dropped to the table. "That's a job? Like, she just tells you how to..." Jen holds up her hand. "Wait, does she demonstrate on herself... or do you let her touch—"

Victoria glanced at the table of four staring at them from across the walkway. She leaned closer to Jen and hissed, "Stop."

Jen looked at the table. "Can I help you?" she asked the gawkers. "What haven't you ever seen two people talking before? Go back to your phones and pretend being out in public means you are socializing."

The group didn't answer Jen, but they did turn away. Their conversation picked up in hushed tones with too many side glances for Victoria's comfort. She got up from her seat in the booth and moved alongside Jen.

"To answer your question, it apparently is a real job because my therapist referred me to her. It's not supposed to be public knowledge because I had to sign a confidentiality contract... and Sarah is adamant about the contract."

Victoria cut the lasagna on her plate into smaller chunks with the side of her fork.

"I thought..." the rest of the sentence dissolved on Victoria's tongue. She tried out the next sentence, but it too was missing pieces. "I thought we could get past it, but I guess, I asked too many questions. I mean. I'm new. But...."

"Damn. You like, like her."

"I did... I mean I do. But she hates me now." Victoria's chin dropped to her chest when Jen's arms wrapped around her shoulders. Pushing the plate away, Victoria shook her head. "I'm so stupid. She told me not to imprint on her, but—"

"Imprint?"

Victoria sniffed. "Yeah. Like a baby duck."

Jen leaned into Victoria's eyeline.

With a sigh, Victoria explained, "Baby ducks form a bond with the first creature they see when they are born."

"I don't get it."

Victoria twisted the hem of her shirt between her fingers, then tugged the bunches down.

"She said that the first person I have sex with will leave a lasting impact on me."

Jen's finger guided Victoria's eyes to hers. "Did you have sex with her?"

Pulling away from the touch, Victoria said, "No." Then, "Kind of?"

"What is *kind of* sleeping with her?"

Victoria turned away from the restaurant. Her voice was barely above a whisper when she confessed, "I had my first orgasm thinking about her while she was with me."

Jen opened her mouth, closed it, and then tried the process all over again.

She looked away, then back at Victoria. "You have never had an orgasm before?"

"No."

"How long were you married?"

"12 years."

Jen scanned the table. "And never?"

"No."

"Shit."

Victoria stared at her full plate of food.

"So, she got you... there. Without touching you, and then it turns out she works where you work?

"Yes."

"And you have feelings for her, but you think she hates you?"

"Yes."

Jen pushed Victoria's plate back in front of her. She used her curry-covered fork to scoop out some lasagna and took a bite. "Eat that. It's good."

"It's not vegan," Victoria stated.

"Neither are you. So, eat the fucking food before the booze hits you and you have to be carried out of here." Jen took a drink of wine, twisting her face in displeasure. She slapped her hand to the table as she swallowed the wine. She gagged slightly, then returned to her rant. "I changed four lives today. I am too tired to carry your gay ass to an Uber."

Victoria picked up her fork. She avoided the side of the plate that had been tainted with Jen's hospital germs. As the sauce coated her mouth, she smiled. It was good.

"So, do you think she hates you because you all work together?"

Victoria finished the food in her mouth before she answered. A skill she wished her friend would learn.

"No. It's because we disagreed about a kid, and I said something stupid about the kid's parents not teaching him how to behave." Victoria flipped the next section of lasagna over. "Then she said that someone was probably saying the same thing about me being gay."

"Damn. You did piss her off."

Jen took another bite of Victoria's food. The warmth of the surgeon's body pressed against her side made Victoria look over the woman she'd befriended after the fender bender in the Trader Joe's parking lot. She briefly wondered why she'd never seen Jen the way she looked at other women, but the thought faded as the food rolled around in her open mouth.

"I kicked her out of my office."

"Well, you should have after what she said. But really, you need to get on a working level relationship with her and drop the rest," Jen stated.

"I was going for the: just be nice to her until she sees me approach. I mean, we are not always going to agree but what couple ever always agrees?"

"That is some toxic bullshit," Jen stated.

"How is being nice to her until she sees me toxic? If I become her friend and show her, I care about her, then one day she'll see me. I mean, I waited twelve years before coming out. I can wait for her to see me."

"First thing you need to know about girls is that shit does not work. Second, don't do that."

Victoria leaned back into the seat. Her shoulders drooped as she chewed on the bitter words.

Jen set her fork down. "Look, I know that wasn't what you wanted to hear. But I need you to listen to it from someone who has lived through the other side of this. I was friends with this woman. Like close friends. So close that Jackie called this woman auntie. She was there when I caught Jackie's dad cheating on me. She was there when my mom died. And then, when I joined a dating app and listed that I was bi, she lost her shit. It turned out that she was there waiting. She was waiting for me to notice her feelings for me. She only wanted to fuck me and when it became clear to her that I didn't have feelings for her, she just left. I thought I had a friend, but she was never actually my friend."

Jen finished the wine in her glass without grimacing this time. While Victoria felt the guilt bubble in her throat for casting her eyes on her friend only minutes before, she processed Jen's story.

"This sexy social worker is already fragile. She's terrified of losing her job, terrified of people knowing what she does as a side gig. Don't be another asshole that ends up hurting her because at some point she is going to find out that you were never really her friend."

Victoria considered if she could just lock away her attraction to Sarah. "So... I just back off."

"Yes. And apologize."

Victoria scoffed. "But she—"

"Apologize and move on." Jen waved the fork in the air. "You can't control how other people behave. Just you. So, apologize for sounding like a cunty administrator."

Victoria reached across the table and pulled her phone from her purse. She opened the short messages from Sarah and stared at the empty message box.

Swallowing her pride, she typed: "I'm sorry I told you to get out of my office. I shouldn't have spoken to you like that. You are wonderful and you are great at your job."

Shaking her head after she hit send, Victoria sent a follow-up text, reading: "Both of your jobs."

Victoria didn't have time to put the phone down before it vibrated in her hand.

"*Are you drunk?*"

Jen leaned over. "You text her now?"

"Yes."

"What did she say?"

Victoria held the phone so Jen could see it, then said, "She asked if I was drunk."

Jen's chuckle brought a smile to Victoria's face. "Well, you have had half a bottle of wine."

Victoria's plate of food slid out from in front of her as Jen began to finish off the rest of the meal. Being vegan wasn't suiting the other woman for the evening.

Refocusing her attention on her phone, she read through the messages again. This crass and blunt version of Sarah wasn't what she expected when she followed Jen's advice. Plus, the wine had made her arms feel a little looser and her blood a little hotter.

Since she was asked a question, she would need to answer it. Denying being intoxicated felt wrong because she didn't want to be someone who lied to Sarah if the woman was fragile as Jen stated. The truth might get her in trouble though. Still, it was the truth, and Sarah had always told her the truth. Even truths Victoria didn't want to hear. So, she replied, "Probably. But it doesn't change that I am sorry."

The three dots waved as Sarah wrote her back. "*Sorry about what I said about your parents.*"

"It hurt but you made your point," Victoria replied.

"*Still shouldn't have said it. Your parents didn't do anything wrong in raising you. You just had the privilege of stability that most of us at the school didn't. Maybe we can talk about ways to build relationships rather than just by-the-book punishments. And please take Diego off suspension.*"

"What did Diego do?" Jen asked. She waved at the server. Then gestured in the air a check mark.

Victoria explained the situation with the kid. She expected Jen to back her up, but her best friend said, "Take the kid off suspension."

"Seriously?"

Jen rolled her eyes. "Yes. That was extreme."

"I was following the rules," Victoria defended.

"The rules sound dumb."

"Says the woman that won't let her kid have a candy bar."

Jen's smile rose. She waved her finger at Victoria once more. "But I do. I just let other people give her one so that babysitting is easier."

Victoria found the restaurant's decor very interesting. Particularly the bar in the opposite direction of Jen's shit-eating grin.

When Victoria looked back, she tried to hide the blush that had risen on her cheeks. "How did you know?"

"I'm a single mom. I know everything." Jen picked up the check that had her credit card already tucked into the folio from the bar. "And I take out the trash."

"Oh."

"Text the sexy social worker back and tell her you'll take the kid off suspension."

Victoria ground her teeth together. She didn't like it, but she followed Jen's instructions. She sent Sarah, "i have a lot to learn so I will take your advice and Diego can go back to class if he agrees to spend some time with me and you to come up with a way that kids could report when they feel a teacher is bullying them or one of their peers."

"*K. He'll do it. Thank you.*" Then the three dots appeared for a fraction of a second before disappearing. "*night.*"

Victoria responded with her own good night and turned the phone for Jen to see the remainder of the conversation.

The surgeon hummed in approval. "Now comes the hard part. Leave her alone and go find some other woman to fantasize about."

Jen scribbled at the top of the receipt until the ink flowed. Victoria started to reach for her wallet, but Jen stopped her. "Tonight's on me. Now let's get out of here before the nanny invites her boyfriend over. Being a single parent really sucks sometimes."

Victoria made her way to the car. She felt the silence wrap around her once within, her new normal. After a heavy sigh, she turned the car on only to see a text message alert on the car computer panel.

With a deep swallow, she couldn't help but wonder what else Sarah could have to say to her.

She hit the play button, allowing Sarah's words to be read aloud.

"*Some unpaid for advice for another situation at hand. Now that you learned how to satisfy yourself it's like releasing the floodgates. Going days or weeks without release can cause you to become very frustrated. I'm not saying you are frustrated but when I ran out, I forgot to tell you that pent-up sexual frustration can cause a change in mood or someone to be more snappy.*"

Before Victoria could come up with a reply another response another message came through. She hit play again, wishing her car sounded more like the woman who rarely spoke to her.

"Probably why I'm a bitch so often... anyways, have a better night and tomorrow let's try not to tear each other down."

Victoria stared at the restaurant she'd just left wondering if Sarah was the drunk one. The confession was welcomed but also confusing.

The brunette knew she affected Sarah. She knew the woman was attracted to her, but she and Jen had said back off. The woman had too much going on for romantic dinners.

But Sarah... Sarah admitted to being sexually frustrated to her. To someone she knew not only was also interested in women but was knowingly interested in her. She admitted it to Victoria, knowing she hadn't been practicing as often as she should have because she too was frustrated.

Sarah didn't want her as a friend because she wanted more from Victoria, but she couldn't ask for it. She was too busy to give Victoria more time in her day with already working days and nights.

So, Victoria wouldn't ask more of the woman. She buried Jen's instructions alongside her newly plotted path. Time could be found in the day. She'd bring the woman the coffee that made her eyes shine with the hope of surviving the day. She'd make the woman, who never brought lunch, a real meal. Hold doors open for her. All those things she was taught to expect to do and have done when she was married.

The drive home made Victoria consider if she didn't need Dr. Rose anymore. She stopped at every red light along the way, not considering that it may have been a sign to slow down. Instead, she congratulated herself on coming up with ways to woo the woman who'd said no to her more than once.

13

August had faded into September and the heat had chilled some into October bringing with it Tris's extracurriculars and the much-needed Fall Break. With Tris away on a Girl Scout hike for the first day of break, Sarah had four hours to get coffee, grocery shop, and shower alone.

She realized she was still listening to the soundtrack to *Descendants 3* as she traveled down the 25mph road toward her new favorite addiction, Badass Coffee.

The addiction brought on by the bossy blonde who delivered her coffee at least once a week claiming it was "a badass latte for a badass social worker," or "for putting together an amazing intervention plan," or the more typical, "You popped into my head as I was about to pass it so I stopped."

If it wasn't coffee, then it was a home-cooked meal that Victoria had mistakenly packed two of or more than she could eat alone. Sarah wasn't naive, but she also wasn't in a position to pass up free food. And her body had become accustomed to the daily meal. At least the week-long break would force her to adjust to the midday emptiness once more. But today she'd make an exception and visit the coffee shop on her own. Splurge even though Monica had only referred her two new clients in the months since school started.

The smell of coffee bolstered her spirits as she sped through the mostly vacant cafe to the counter. Running her finger down the laminated options, she tapped the Toffee Almond Latte picture and ordered.

"Would you like that hot, iced, or blended?" the cashier asked over the bean grinder whirling behind her.

"Blended for a change," Sarah said. Then added, "With whip."

She swiped her card and took a few steps back. Swaying from side to side, she stared at the red notification on the dreaded dating app that she'd kept open when none of the prospects were even worthwhile to go on a simple date with.

"Sarah?"

Sarah closed her eyes wishing the voice was just in her imagination. But the hairs standing on her arm made it very real. She turned around and felt the epoxy she'd used to put herself back together crack.

"Hi," Sarah said to the woman who had ended their relationship in a text message.

The woman tucked the thick lock of hair behind her ear. The years hadn't changed her the way Sarah hoped. When Sarah had become a parent overnight, she'd felt the days and nights blend until the exhaustion of caring for an infant hung from her eyes and shoulders. But Simone looked the same, and Sarah hated that she still loved her.

"How have you been?" Simone asked.

Sarah nodded, her arms crossing her chest. "Good."

Simone nodded. "Good."

"How's the baby?" Sarah asked.

"She's good. Henrietta... She's great. Great."

"That's great," Sarah repeated with a nod of her head.

"Yeah."

Simone gestured to the counter. "I'm going to order."

"Okay, yeah. Good to see you," Sarah lied.

Simone turned away but before Sarah could breathe the woman was facing her again. "Are you busy, or do you have time for a quick chat?"

Sarah bit at the inside of her cheek. The cashier set her drink on the counter and called her name. She ran through the list of things she wanted to do but nodded. "Yeah. I have some time."

They took a few steps together to the counter where Sarah retrieved her drink and Simone ordered hers.

Sarah nodded to the door. "I'm going to go sit outside."

"Okay. I'll be out in a minute."

Sarah took a seat with her back to the street. A cool breeze picked up the dropped leaves. She watched them play Ring Around the Rosey before falling back to the concrete.

The outside air ceased moving and the few cars that had been on the road found a detour as Simone sat in the chair across from Sarah.

"You look beautiful," Simone said. "I mean... you've always been beautiful, but it's been a year since I've seen you and I just..."

"Thanks." Sarah tucked the overgrown bang back behind her ear, remembering the urge she'd felt to change everything when Simone had pulled the rug out from under her feet.

Sarah stared at the way Simone's lips parted before she took the first drink of her coffee. "How's Tris?" Simone asked, setting the cup on the table. "Did you sign her up for those dance classes she was always begging for?"

"She's good. No dance classes because you know my schedule doesn't allow for many activities, but maybe next year." Sarah raised the straw to her lips and let the sweet coffee slush chill the flush rising in her chest. Twisting the cup in her hand, she added. "Monica is teaching her to be a smart ass, though so that's keeping me on my toes."

Simone laughed. Raising the cup to Sarah, she said, "Pretty sure she got that from you."

Sarah chewed at her cheek again. Biting off small pieces of flesh until it hurt, and she switched sides. She tried to think of something to say. An assortment of questions about work made it to her tongue, but before she could string any of the words together, a few fell out.

"Still married to Marissa? I heard her bar is really taking off."

Simone set the cup down and leaned back in her seat. She didn't look up from the table as she said, "Yes."

"That's good." Sarah nodded and looked around at the deserted patio and parking lot. "I'm... um... glad you were able to come back together."

Sarah's leg started to vigorously bounce. She shifted in her seat, then back to the original position. Simone continued to stare at the table, taking sips of coffee every so often.

"Well, I should get going. Tris is on a hike with her Girl Scout troop, so I get to go grocery shopping without her asking for everything she sees."

She picked up her phone and prepared to get up.

"I never meant to hurt you," Simone blurted out.

"I doubt that," Sarah whispered.

"It wasn't an easy choice."

Sarah's eyes shot up to the woman searching her face. The hollowness in her chest filled with air. Enough air to cause the words to hiss from her open lips. "It never should have been a choice."

She sat up straighter as Simone's shoulders hunched from their perfectly poised position. "And if you hadn't lied to me, Tris wouldn't have gotten hurt and I wouldn't have gotten my heart broken. I could have kept my job where I was happy and made more money, but breaking up with me wasn't enough was it?"

"I didn't mean for all of that to happen."

"You told Folson I was a prostitute and showed him my sister's arrest photo, so I was fired and had to find a new job. Tris had to change schools and we had to move again. And don't pretend you didn't do it so that I would have to leave."

Sarah's fingers tightened around her baggy sweatpants. She licked the bitterness from her teeth and shook her head. "Did you ever tell her the truth? I mean, I know you got me fired so I wouldn't tell her, but did you?"

"No." Simone sighed. The last shred of confidence fell from her body as she shook her head. "I'm just trying to hold it together, but every day gets harder. It's like she could do it all without me."

Sarah recognized the calculated play in the new game of chess Simone was attempting to begin. The same sob story of her relationship falling apart, looking for a sympathetic ear. Emotionally cheating on her wife once more, in search of the next heart to break. But Sarah's heart had already broken, and the waterproof glue had never fully stopped the bleeding, so she had no fucks left for her ex.

She tasted the toxicity of the words as the venom spewed from her lips. "So, you're just walking around looking for where to go next?"

"I just... I saw you and..."

"And... what?" Sarah's head moved slowly from side to side. "Thought that I was stupid enough to fall in love with you again?"

Sarah didn't wait for Simone's answer. She gathered her phone, keys, and drink from the table. The chair screamed as she pushed back from the table.

"Go back to your wife. To your kid. Your house. And do what you said you needed to do. Keep the promises you made to her, because you already broke the ones you made me."

As soon as Sarah entered the store, she bypassed the necessities for the holiday section. Nothing she picked up would end up purchased, but the hope she'd have an expendable income one day to splurge on a pointless Happy Harvest sign made her dream. She put the burnt orange fox mug back on the shelf when her phone beeped. The lock screen told her she had a message from LawyerLady waiting for her.

She bit her lip thinking about how Simone's proximity had reminded her of less bland days. Then Tris's comment about her smile being lost replayed in her head. She'd never considered the possibility of holding out for Simone to come back to her until it was in her face and a part of her yearned for the woman to kiss her just once more.

Any rendezvous with LawyerLady didn't have to be a relationship. She could, maybe, just be the distraction Sarah needed to finally heal.

Sarah opened the message and read: *"I am not sure if I should be writing this to MomSarah or MomSarah's daughter. My name is Zoe, and my mother made this account for me. It sounds like we both have ladies in our lives who care a lot about us, and I like to be outdoors. That makes two things in common. Okay, I am going to send this and hope you answer."*

Sarah smiled at the message. She'd hoped whoever chose to message her knew that she had not written it herself. Most of the messages she'd received thus far read like Tris was pranking her though. At least Zoe or Zoe's mom had basic writing skills.

She pushed the cart with her elbows past the greeting cards and religious candles. Her fingers made words that she didn't hear in her head, but she read them aloud to make sure her fingers didn't make her sound like a fifth grader.

"I'm not sure if I should be writing this to Zoe or Zoe's mom but you made me laugh. My kid made this account for me, and I didn't have the heart to just delete it. -Sarah, not the kid."

A check mark appeared just under the message, then another. She didn't know what any of that meant until three dots wiggled in a dialogue box under her message.

"Oh okay. I'll leave you alone. -Zoe, not Zoe's mom."

Sarah stopped pushing the cart. She realized the callousness of her first response but as she plotted a second message, the three dots appeared again.

"Zoe's mom here. I will cook you a platter of chicken marsala if you let my daughter take you to dinner? And I'm Italian, so it won't be any of that fake gravy nonsense. You'll taste the wine."

A soft chuckle rumbled Sarah's chest. She licked her lips, and typed: "Basically you're saying that I will get two dinners for the price of one?"

Turning the corner, Sarah grabbed a box of single-serving chips and put it into the basket. Then she glanced back at the phone that had repeatedly beeped.

"My daughter is an assistant district attorney. She will pay for dinner."

"Also your daughter is adorable."

"I would be an amazing NaNa."

"Hold on my daughter is chasing me."

Sarah stopped pushing the cart. She sucked in her bottom lip to stop the laughter from tumbling out. Pressing her fingers to her mouth, she tried to stifle the escaped giggles as she waited for the message that was coming through.

"I'm so sorry. I didn't think she would actually take the phone. Then she ran away with it and when I chased her she pulled out a nerf gun and shot me."

Nerf gun wars Sarah could get on board with. She clicked the photo icon at the top of the messaging app and navigated to Zoe's profile. Zoe was fit and incredibly attractive in the button-up and tie as she coolly stared at the camera. She scrolled through the other seventeen photos of the lawyer, ranging from a child version of the woman dressed as Pink Power Ranger to a well-built high schooler taking a jump shot from the three-point line. Sarah stopped on the photo of the mother and daughter in a bar. There was no denying the family had good genes.

Sarah scrolled through the lengthy bio that had been written by the chef of the family rather than the legal counsel. Every accolade Zoe won in her life was cataloged chronologically. As well as admissions of being a partial recluse, a promise that she was not in fact raised in a post-apocalyptic war zone, and ending with the woman's obsession with seeking justice for victims of violence.

"So, about this chicken marsala..." Sarah sent, her stomach already grumbling for the potential meal.

Immediately, she received a response.

"She didn't scare you away."

"Is she going to jump out of the bushes and shoot me with a nerf gun also" Sarah asked.

"no i wouldn't tell her where we would be going"

Sarah realized she was still standing in the same spot. She resumed pushing her cart down the snack aisle. She grabbed two boxes of Gushers and three boxes of granola bars.

Making her way down the aisle, she slouched over the cart and typed: "Something tells me she probably has a gps app installed on your phone"

She smiled as she added: "Or she microchipped you at birth. Any strange bumps on the back of your neck?"

"Great. now i need to go see a vet to get scanned."

Sarah navigated the cart to the pasta supplies. Staring at the abundance of options, she thought of the promised dish. She'd never had homemade chicken marsala before.

Picking up the phone, she said, "Okay, I'll make you a deal."

Immediately, she received: *"I'm a lawyer. Deals are my specialty."*

"But capitalization is not? Don't you have to write reports."

"Okay, that burned a little."

"I promise I can type well with a real keyboard. I have been been published."

"I read that in your autobiography."

"Hey, you missed some periods. Also, Nerf is a proper now. It has to be capitalized."

"now"

"NOUN"

It wasn't like Sarah hadn't laughed in a long time. Tris had almost made her pee her pants that morning. But this felt different. Felt nice even.

"Okay, that was Karma," Zoe sent. *"Can we pretend that didn't happen and talk about this deal?"*

She moved her cart out of the center of the aisle and leaned against it.

"Sure."

She chewed on her lip for a moment. Honesty was probably the best policy.

"I promised the kid that I would go on one date and wear red lipstick. Your mom promised me if that date was with you, you would be delivering me a platter of chicken marsala. So if you bring the food, I will wear the red lipstick and we can eat the free meal your mom made so you're not out any money."

Holding the phone, she watched the dots wiggle over and over again.

A little wrinkled man cleared his throat. Sarah looked around and then at him. He nodded toward the shelf she was blocking. She mumbled a quick apology and moved to the next shelf before turning back around to look at the pasta sauce she'd forgotten to put in her cart.

The phone beeped though, and she abandoned going back for the time being.

"Interesting proposition. However, I have a different offer. I provided the platter as promised in a sealed container. You wear the lipstick and allow me to buy you a cup of coffee that you can drink while we take a walk through the Desert Botanical Gardens."

Coffee wasn't really a date. It was just meeting someone. Walking would also be less weird than sitting at a table with a total stranger. She could part ways at any point in time. But she had promised Tris she would go on a date.

"Do I get to tell the kid it's a date?" she asked.

"If I can tell my mother the same thing," Zoe responded.

"Isn't she just going to read the messages?"

"Isn't your kid?"

Sarah nodded her head as she scanned the ceiling tiles above her. She'd never noticed how high the roof of the store was before.

When she looked down, the ten-digit phone number lay in a line by itself. She stared at it. Then at the dots that hypnotically held her attention.

"If you text me, then neither of them can read the messages."

Sarah didn't give herself a chance to overanalyze it. She pressed the number until it gave her multiple options. Then she selected the 'call' option.

The phone only rang once, when a cautious voice answered, "Hello?"

"Hi." Sarah closed her eyes and said, "This is Sarah."

"Uh... hi."

In the background, a sing-song voice called out, *"Is that her? Give me the phone!"*

Sarah pulled the phone away from her ear as the phone rubbed against something.

"Mom, get off of me." There was a distinct umph, and Zoe's voice sounded farther away. *"Why are you the way you are?"*

"Hi Sarah!" the new voice called out from a distance.

Sarah laughed, putting the phone back to her ear.

"I'm sorry," Sarah said. "I know you said text, but I figured I should actually talk to the person I was going to meet in person."

"Yeah. No, I get it." Zoe's breathing was slightly ragged.

"Put it on facetype!" Her mother demanded.

"It's called Facetime and no!"

"Zoe Marie, I brought you into the world and I will take you out of it."

*"It's a nerf gun. It's not going to kill—"*Pop! *"Ow! Are you fucking serious! That's it. I'm going to file a petition to have you committed to an old folks home."*

"Don't yell at your mother. She'll think you're a heathen."

"Well, she already is going to think you're a psycho!" There was another distinct dart pop, and then more wrestling on the other end. Sarah heard Zoe cry out, *"Stop it."* Then, *"GIVE IT BACK!"*

Sarah pulled the phone from her ear as it started to drum the Facetime tune at her. She bit into her lip, but she couldn't stop the smile on her face, and she realized this was the smile that Tris had said she'd lost.

Her finger accepted the call.

After a processing moment, Sarah was face to face with Zoe's mother.

"Hi, Sarah!" the woman cried out. Her body lunged some, but the woman never broke eye contact. *"Oh my, you are prettier than your photos."*

"Thank you. Mrs..." Sarah realized she had no idea how to address the woman. "Mrs. Zoe's mom."

The mother smiled and flipped her hand in front of the screen. *"Oh, sweetie, you can call me Cassandra or Cassie or Mom. I'm good with all of those."*

"You're ruining my life," Zoe groaned from the other side of the camera.

The camera flipped to Zoe holding her hand over her face, then immediately back to the mother who was smiling broadly. *"That's my Zoe."*

"She's very pretty," Sarah said, her hand coming up to shade her face from the couple smiling at her as they passed.

"So, Sarah, your daughter is just the cutest little queen. If you need a sitter so my daughter can sweep you off your feet, I am free any day of the week. I am a pediatric nurse in the NICU, so I know all of the safety things. Any day, you name it. Zoe works days and she's so successful. She is also beautiful. Just look at her."

The camera flipped back around, and Sarah got a view of the distinctive orange muzzle of a Nerf gun.

"You wouldn't shoot your own mother, Zoe Ma—"

The gun went off and the phone screen went dark.

Sarah put her hand over her mouth, clapping it shut. She stared wide-eyed at the dark screen until the phone was picked back up.

Zoe's tanned cheeks were flushed. She was backed against a door, holding the phone out. An awkward smile was plastered on the lawyer's face as she said, *"I understand if you want to back out now."*

Sarah giggled, then smiled. "You two seem close... and fun," she said.

"*I'm the fun one,*" her mother called out, the voice muffled behind the door.

"*That's true,*" Zoe admitted in a whisper. "*But I can't let her know that. So, about our date.*"

"Well, I can't give you a day right now. I have to check in with my friend and make sure she's available to babysit and will agree to not letting the kid watch anymore Spongebob."

Zoe's face scrunched in displeasure. "*I hate that show. One night I went to sleep watching the Ms Pat Show and I woke up to these like ghosts crawling out of Spongebob's eyeballs and it was definitely one of the worst moments of my life.*"

"Your life sounds pretty pleasant," Sarah stated.

"*So, wait, you're still willing to go out with me? After her crazy? What if it's genetic?*"

Looking up at the boxes of Macaroni and Cheese, Sarah nodded to herself. She turned back to Zoe.

"If at her age you have strategically placed Nerf guns in your house to shoot your adult children, then I think you are doing something right."

Zoe rolled her eyes. "*She watches too much TikTok.*" With a straighter posture, Zoe asked, "*But really, you'll go out with me?*"

"Yes. I will go on a date with you."

A broad smile spread over the woman's face. "*I would really like that.*"

"Me too," Sarah confessed.

Zoe held the screen up closer to her face, searching for something. "*Are you at the grocery store?*" she asked.

"Yeah." Sarah flipped the screen to show Zoe the aisle she was on. When it was back on her face, she felt the need to explain. "The kid is at Girl Scouts, so it was the perfect time to get some shopping done."

"*Awesome. I'm hiding in the bathroom.*" Zoe laughed and lolled her head. "*I swear, I have my own apartment. That my mother does not have a key to.*"

"Me too," Sarah stated.

"*Cool. So, what do you do? I mean, you know I'm a lawyer.*"

Sarah tucked a loose strand of hair behind her ear. "I'm a social worker. I work at a school."

"*Oh okay. Sweet. That's awesome.*" Zoe nodded as the conversation stalled. "*I'm sorry about my mom taking the phone and everything. She's kind of all up in my business and since my dad died, I spend a lot more time here. The plus side is that she really is a good cook, and I have finally graduated from professional strainer to onion chopper.*"

Sarah shrugged. "I live with a nine-year-old. There's clearly no such thing as privacy, and I will admit I could use an onion chopper in my life. I tried to teach

Tris, and she put a glass pot lid in a hoodie to block out the smell. Said she saw it on a video."

Zoe's eyes grew wide. "*She's only nine?*"

"Yes." Sarah's brows scrunched in the middle. "Why?"

Zoe ran her hand over the back of her neck. She shrugged a little. "*Just didn't think a nine-year-old would be so... articulate. On your profile, I mean. But the lid thing sounds genius. I'm going to have to try that tonight.*"

"She's pretty brilliant."

"*That's cool.*"

Sarah grabbed a box of rotini and put it into the cart. "Well, I should..."

"*Yeah... uh sorry. I will let you shop.*" Zoe's finger pulled a lock of hair from the back of her head and twirled it between her fingers. "*Can I text you, you know, about the date?*"

"Yeah, of course," Sarah said.

"*Okay. Sweet... I'll... uh... talk to you later.*"

Zoe smiled, her finger reaching toward the red button.

"Hey Zoe," Sarah spit out quickly.

"*Yeah?*"

Sarah felt the blush rise in her freckled face. "Thanks for messaging me."

Zoe's smile spread from her mouth to her eyes. "*Thanks for answering.*"

"Okay. Bye."

"*Bye.*"

Sarah pressed the red button. She sent a silent thank you to the kid who was miserably trailing somewhere up the side of Estrella Mountain.

14

A week away from work should have been relaxing. 'It should have been...' seemed a constant issue in Victoria's life. Like, she should have been able to recognize her lack of desire for Michael before she married him. And she should have had an orgasm before thirty. Also, she should have been able to woo the woman of her dreams in three months, but she didn't.

What she had managed to do was to stay out of Sarah's way for close to two months. Well, not out of her way. It was more out of Sarah's frustrated zone of fire. She placed herself in Sarah's way practically daily as she offered the woman caffeine or Tupperware filled with what she claimed to be leftovers. Sarah's cinched eyebrows told Victoria the woman knew it was a lie. However, the woman never turned down the food or beverage.

With each calorie, their interactions had become less hate-filled. And each time Sarah's eyes didn't narrow at the sight of her provided enough oxygen for Victoria's desire to remain flickering.

When fall break came, the nights she'd spent cooking enough for two were no longer needed. The smile that pulled up the corners of Sarah's lips when she ate the food over the paperwork on her desk was unable to be seen. Victoria's thoughts didn't focus on what to cook next; they swirled around worries if Sarah had eaten at all. Worrying got her to the point of trying to type out a non-flirty message Thursday morning to ask the woman if she wanted to get lunch.

She didn't send it when her typing was interrupted by the weekly text from Echo. Another request to come to the bar, she'd yet to walk into.

She'd run out of work excuses since she was on vacation and Jen had taken Jackie to Disneyland for her fall break from preschool. With zero communication for six days— besides the ramblings within her head of things to do and recipes Sarah may like— Victoria knew she needed to get out of the house.

Music pounded into her chest as soon as she entered the building. Victoria didn't know what to expect from the bar, but Echo hadn't lied when she'd described it as a Western throwback.

Her eyes wandered, taking in her first experience in a real bar. Women of all shapes and forms were already pulling the plastic-tipped darts from zippered containers. Others held each other on the dance floor. Victoria couldn't tear her gaze away when her eyes zeroed in on two women against a darkened wall in a heated make-out session. Seeing something like that on television was different than in real life, and Victoria was unprepared for seeing lesbians out with each other, doing lesbian things like kissing and grinding against each other. And there was definitely some groping that had Victoria feeling that thing Sarah called gay panic because she wasn't sure if that was normal for just hanging out in a bar.

Her eyes fell to her chest, then rose to the dance floor. She eyed the various lesbians as she questioned if someone would be touching her breast by the end of the night.

"You came!" a voice bellowed from behind the bar.

Victoria searched until she found Echo pointing at her. The woman's hand slapped against the bar top and grabbed another woman nearby.

"See!" Echo told the woman carrying a tray. "I told you I made a new friend."

Victoria's smile spread over her face. For the first time since coming out, someone was genuinely happy to see her.

Echo made her way over with a bottle of beer in one hand and her arm draped over the scarcely covered redhead she'd declared their friendship to. It took a moment, but Victoria recalled the detail of Echo's best friend working with her. She swallowed as her eyes ran down the practically bare body of the woman's torso with the generous amount of cleavage heaving from the corset top.

With a deep laugh, Echo said, "Victoria, this is Parker. She's my sister from another mister. Well, not really, but we grew up in juvie together and so you know blood is thicker than water."

Victoria sucked in her lips and shook her head. "I think that means you're supposed to be related by blood."

"Naw," Echo said with a wave of her beer. "The phrase is the blood of the coven is thicker than the water of the womb, so all those people that use it are wrong. And Parker and I may not be witches-witches but we're a coven for sure."

Parker smiled with her chin turned down slightly. Her eyes studied Victoria momentarily, almost as though she could learn everything she needed to know with just one stare down.

"Hey," Parker said once her assessment was complete. "What can I get you to drink?"

"Uh... I don't know. This is my first time in a bar."

"She used to be Mormon," Echo said, pulling on Parker's arm.

Parker looked Victoria up and down once more and nodded. "So, no beer then. How about something that doesn't taste like alcohol?"

"Would it be okay, if I just stuck with water?" Victoria asked. She fiddled with the buttons at the bottom of her shirt.

"Of course," Parker stated. She elbowed Echo harshly in the ribs. "Be nice to her. She looks fragile."

Watching the woman walk away, Victoria wondered how fragile Parker could honestly think she was if she said that loud enough to be heard.

"You really got a thing for taken women, don't you?" Echo stated with a roll of her eyes.

Eyes snapping back to Echo, she answered before she processed the question. "Huh?"

"No drooling over my sister," Echo stated. "She's taken."

Victoria pulled at the hem of her shirt once more. She tried to defend herself with, "I wasn't."

"Uhhh-huh," Echo said into the mouth of her bottle.

Words tumbled out of Victoria's mouth. "I wouldn't... I mean... I'm not just..."

"Breathe. I was fucking with you. Everyone drools over Parker." Echo clasped her arm over Victoria. "That's why I begged her to come work with me even though she has a real job."

"Oh."

"Yeah. She's pretty amazing." Echo pointed to the bar. "And that broody Latina glaring at you is Parker's very jealous girlfriend, so keep your eyes off her ass."

Because Echo said not to look, Victoria's eyes immediately took in the plump rear framed perfectly in a pair of tight-fitting jeans leaning almost completely over the bar.

"I said don't look at her ass," Echo said again with a bit of a whine.

With a shrug, Victoria answered, "You tell someone not to look at something, they are going to look."

Echo grabbed a black case already on the table where she led Victoria. She withdrew two sets of darts and handed one set to Victoria.

"You're not going to hate me if I suck?" Victoria asked.

"She will yell at you the whole night and make you feel like an idiot, but she doesn't honestly care if she wins or loses," Parker stated. She set a bucket of beers on the table for Echo and a bottle of water in front of Victoria.

"Don't tell her that or she isn't going to want to play with me," Echo whined. She turned back to Victoria. "I don't yell the whole time."

With a dramatic eye roll, Parker corrected the other woman. "She does yell. The. Whole. Time. Which is why she never has a partner."

"Don't you have work to do, Princess?" Echo spat. "Or did I put you on the schedule just to give me shit and give your girlfriend free drinks?"

Parker picked up a beer from her tray and smacked it against the top of the one in Echo's hand. The liquid within erupted from the top.

"Every fucking time," Echo protested and then chugged the remainder of the bottle. She coughed as she dangled the bottle at Parker.

"Asshole," Echo choked out hoarsely.

"Be nice to her, or I will fuck up every one of your drinks," Parker warned.

Echo's arms crossed her chest. "Then I'll have to fire you."

"Bitch, please! Fire me?" Parker's hands gestured down her body. "I fucking dare you to."

With a wave of her hand, Echo surrendered. "Go do something to make me money."

Parker winked at Victoria. "Let me know if she is being mean. I'll make her regret it."

"Okay. I will," Victoria said, afraid of what else the woman could do.

"Don't take her side," Echo stated. "You're my friend, not hers."

Victoria didn't say anything about how nice it felt that someone besides Jen wanted to be her friend. Especially, since she managed to bulldoze through any possibility of making friends at work. Even Sarah chose to eat the home-cooked meals alone in her office.

Momentarily, she wondered if Sarah had eaten lunch that day. She didn't have time to dwell on it when the digital machine came to life and the match began. Victoria put away the fear of what Sarah's life was like when she didn't have Victoria to keep her stomach full and her blood caffeinated.

Echo's approach to teaching was trial by fire. She placed the darts in Victoria's hand and explained she had three shots at a time. The goal of the game was to reach 501 points first. She just had to hit the board was what Echo promised.

That was how Victoria learned her new friend was a liar.

She didn't just have to hit the board. She had to hit it on the higher numbers or Echo would shout out that a three didn't help one damn bit. That was after she'd missed the board completely and snapped the plastic tip off one of the darts.

After the second losing match, Echo's jabs got the better of Victoria. She succumbed to her peer's pressure to get a drink and loosen up. With the soda mixed with some form of alcohol she could barely taste, Victoria's darts still hit low numbers but her concern over it became less.

Their opponents took a smoke break between the second and third match, giving Echo time to talk about something other than how to shoot a dart.

"So, it's good to see you. You haven't been to the gym in, like, a month. I was getting used to you staring at me," Echo said, her second bucket of beers now in front of her.

Victoria practically choked on the drink.

"I... I didn't realize I was so obvious. I'm sorry. I didn't know you were married when we first... I just..."

"It's all good," Echo said. She crinkled the wrapper of her beer in her hand. "Made me feel good. Someone noticing me for a change."

"How are things with your wife?" Victoria asked.

"Well, I know you saw the text she sent me a while ago. So things are as good as they can be. Just trying to keep everyone alive and hold the house together." Echo took another drink. "She was all on board when we got the phone call from DCS for Henrie. It was like she wasn't too busy at work for a change but then... Henrie's got a lot of special needs. She was born addicted to a lot of drugs and before you hate on the bio mom, turns out the kid was part of a sex traffic ring. She's only 15 and been through hell so the drugs weren't a choice; they were pushed into her."

"That's horrible," Victoria whispered. She'd learned a lot about trauma from the kids in her school. Most of the kids she saw regularly disrupting classes were foster kids, and Sarah was their safe place.

Victoria's mind wandered just briefly to a thought she'd never considered. Maybe Sarah was in the system.

"Yeah. Parker works at the school and is the kid's therapist. We are thinking about taking her in too, Simone was all in... but something seemed to get under her skin last weekend, so she's been out basically all week even though on breaks she's supposed to take care of Henrie so I can get some sleep. So, I'm tired."

Victoria nodded. "Well, you're doing a great job."

"Thanks." Echo took a drink. Her eyes scanned the dart match they were bound to lose again. "What about you? What's been going on?"

"Just working." Victoria set down the drink she'd been nursing. "Actually, it's been pretty rough. Pretty sure everyone hates me except the woman that I bring lunch and coffee to."

"What makes you think that?" Echo carded her short hair back, then returned her backward baseball cap atop it.

"Besides the fact that no one talks to me unless they have to?" Victoria scanned the space once more, realizing being here didn't feel much different than being at work. "I just get the feeling that I don't really fit in. But I don't feel like I fit in here either. Like, I don't know what to wear or how to talk to anyone. And apparently, I make it very clear to anyone I see attractive that I am... thirsty."

The word felt foreign on Victoria's tongue. Something she'd picked up from her lesbian culture immersion on Netflix.

Echo looked Victoria over. The dark eyes moved from the top of her shirt to her shoes. She didn't say anything besides beckoning Parker back to the table with a wave in the redhead's direction.

"What are you looking at?" Victoria looked down at her shoes.

"I'm not the right person to give you fashion advice."

Parker was making her way back to the bar. Since trying to flag Parker down didn't work, Echo grabbed her by the crook of the arm and yanked her back to the table. The redhead smacked Echo's hand away with the tray, but the bigger woman didn't seem phased by the assault.

With a wave of her hand, Echo said, "Babygay here needs some fashion advice so she can meet a girl."

"I..." The rest of Victoria's sentence dissolved on her tongue as the other woman's eyes ran up and down her body once more.

With a slight nod, Parker's eyebrows rose. "You kinda look like you're goin' to church."

Victoria looked down at what she considered her gayest outfit. Wearing a flannel shirt in Salt Lake meant gay, so it had been one of the first things Victoria had purchased once her divorce was finalized. And she'd heard her assistant call her shoes lesbian loafers once. She wasn't sure what type of church Parker attended because everything about her said lesbian in the wild by her book.

"You okay if I touch you so I can make some adjustments?" Parker asked.

"Uh... okay."

After setting her tray down, Parker single-handedly unbuttoned the entire front of Victoria's flannel. Then, she pulled at the slimming tank top underneath until it was free from her jeans. Before Victoria could move, Parker squatted before her and began to cuff the ends of her pants. After another quick evaluation, Parker stepped even further into Victoria's bubble, her hands coming up to Victoria's hair. The clip that was holding the top half of her hair from her face was removed, then fingers massaged her scalp. Victoria fought back the smile and the moan as Parker fluffed her hair and flipped it side to side until she was satisfied.

"Better, but you need different shoes. Vans or boots. Loafers are for work or if you're wearing a suit. Not for the bar."

There wasn't a mirror for her to see what Parker had done to her, but as two women passed by one of them met her gaze and offered a warm smile. Her heart fluttered and her cheeks flushed at the possibility of the woman finding her new look attractive.

"Thank you," Victoria whispered. She looked down once more to memorize how she should dress if she came back to the bar again.

"Your girlfriend is glaring at us," Echo said with a roll of her eyes. "Does she have to be here every shift you work?"

"She heard Zoe and Evie are coming in," Parker stated.

Victoria asked, "Whose Evie and Zoe?"

"Evie was this girl I was in juvie with."

Echo leaned over the table. "She kicked Parker's ass and then ten years later, Parker got back at her by hooking up with her sister."

"It's not a hook-up if her sister is literally my girlfriend now."

Echo's smile was nothing less than devilish. "And Evie's sister is the broody bitch at the bar who also dated Zoe. And Zoe is now best friends with Evie, even though Zoe and Princess Parker used to be secret lovers."

"It's your fault," Parker said, swiping Echo's elbow with her tray. "You had to introduce me to Evie's mom."

"Who gave you a job."

"And a whole lot of anxiety," Parke countered.

Echo pointed at Parker, but turned her attention back to Victoria. "Don't let this one fool you. She says she doesn't want drama but her demon ass if a magnet for it."

"Obviously. I'm friends with you."

"Family, bitch," Echo corrected. "I'm your fucking family. So tell your girl there is no fighting with you two's mutual ex or her sister."

"I'll do that if you stop making me pose for pictures with Xio," Parker stated.

"That's the only reason I hired you," Echo stated. She met Victoria's gaze, then searched the crowd until she found who she was looking for. "See that masc Latina with the plastic bin. That's Xio, and she is what we call a Hey Mama's Lesbian. Basically, a masc like me, only a whore."

Victoria's lips parted as she tried to figure out how she was supposed to respond to a lesbian being called a whore. Had her sisters said it, she would know it meant steering the husbands away. But now, she wasn't sure if being a lesbian whore was a bad thing or a good thing.

"What's wrong with my photos?" Echo asked Parker.

She held the phone up for Victoria to see that Echo's side interest in photography was good. Really good, because she was definitely a thirsty lesbian who would love to be standing in the doorway between the Hey Mama Whore and the Demon Princess.

"Yeah, that photo," Parker said. "That one has Lyra on edge because she thinks Xio is just waiting for a second chance."

"She doesn't do relationships," Echo stated.

Victoria took that to mean Xio being a whore wasn't a good thing even in the lesbian world.

"I know that. You know that. But Lyra's brain is fucked from all her relationship trauma, so no more photos with Xio."

Echo's head hit the table as she let out and, "Ugh!" When she sat back up, she glared at Parker. "You are always so much drama."

With a shrug, Parker said, "You wanted me to work here."

Victoria cocked an eyebrow at Echo, hoping the woman would understand the signal to share the rest of the story because there were so many pieces of stories but no actual details to help her understand what she thought might be one of those lesbian dating circles. And those sounded like stories she wanted to hear. Way more interesting than pining over a co-worker who detested her. And way better than anything she'd seen on Netflix lately.

"You don't want to know," Echo stated when she noticed Victoria's look. "The thing you will learn is lesbians is you can't meet someone without them having already fucked someone you dated."

"Except Echo!" Parker called out. "That idiot married the first asshole she met at nineteen and refuses to leave her ass."

Parker left them for her girlfriend, not appearing to care that her words were still hanging like a cloud over the table. Rolling the darts between her fingers, Echo seemed to be chewing on her words. She looked up only when her jaw ceased its grinding motion.

"So, I can't tell you how to fix things with your coworkers, but I can tell you that it's always tough being the new boss. No one knows you and no one trusts you," Echo shared as the other team returned from smoking on the patio. "You gotta give it some time, you know. It's a new place for you. You're a new face for everyone."

"I guess." Victoria took a sip of her drink. "I'm not used to being the new face. I mean, I used to teach at the same school as my sisters but now... I didn't think I was this socially awkward."

"I get it. Shit's different when you're not in your element. You kinda have to let them get to know you. You're in this whole reinvention state right now." Echo placed both hands on her hat as though she was trying to keep her head together with the well-worn cap. "Look, you get to decide who you want to be now. Not who you used to be."

"That's what I have been trying to do since I got here. Trying to decide what aspects of my life from before I still want now and what I can leave behind. Like peas. I really don't like peas and since I don't have to see my mother, I'm, like, well I don't have to eat peas anymore."

Echo nodded. "So, I guess that answers the question about contact with your family."

"Yeah. No, I don't talk to them." Victoria's fingers ran over a slice in the tabletop.

"They cut you out?"

Victoria looked up from her glance. "I left before they had a chance too."

"Damn." Echo picked up her beer. "I thought the Mormon church was more accepting of gays now."

"Not really. I mean the kids are forced to meet with the bishop. They can be part of the church, but not really. Even if they decide to live a straight life, any... uh... activity is basically like blacklisting you from any event."

"So, basically you'd get cut out no matter what."

"I mean, I left my husband, which is a big no-no." Victoria looked at her friend. "I was going to be excommunicated for asking for a divorce. My whole family loved him, and I didn't want to listen to how I ruined my life. I mean, I can't have kids, so I was already ruining his life, but this wasn't about him. He's a man so he will get to remarry with someone who can do the things he needs to buy his way into their heaven. And my family... well... they don't have to see me tread down a path they'd have to explain."

They stood at the table where Victoria had vomited her sob story a top. Echo seemed to be swirling the sentences around with the bottom of her beer.

Looking around, Victoria considered if leaving had been worth it. The moderately busy bar had women in it, but none of them had Victoria wanting to stand in the corner with the woman's hand on her boob or her butt.

She briefly considered if Sarah walking through the door would change her uneasiness. The idea was scratched immediately. Sarah didn't want to touch her boob. She didn't want Victoria to even talk to her. Or walk beside her. She probably didn't want Victoria to breathe the same air as her. Each reality brought Victoria back to the point of whether leaving everything behind had truly been worth it.

"I thought coming to the city would help."

She licked her teeth, remembering the fact that she had not once needed to clean urine off the bathroom floor. That was exactly life changing, just a change.

"It has somewhat, I guess. I see gay people everywhere now... but I don't know how to talk to anyone. I mean, if you hadn't introduced yourself to me in the parking lot, I would still be working up the courage to ask if you preferred Lexa or Clarke."

Echo snorted, and then a finger rose as she took another drink.

"First off, the show tanked after they killed Heda. Fucking hot as shit with all her knives and I pledge my fealty to you." Another finger joined the first. "Second, I see people come in and out of this place daily. Everyone has a story. A coming-out story. A work story. A break-up story. You just have to ask them their story."

The two digits moved slowly around the room to remind Victoria of all the queers in the same place at the same time.

"So, I just come to the bar to meet someone?" Victoria asked. She shook her head feeling foolish for even asking. "I don't even know how to order a drink."

"It's an option." Echo adjusted her hat once more. "Look, this isn't New York, so you may want to try one of the singles meetup things. There's an app and everything. I could... I could host a singles night." She scanned the bar once more. "Maybe bring in some business with those other two bars now open."

With a soft shrug, Echo said, "Honestly. I think you're overthinking it. Look at that woman over there."

Echo pointed to a brunette leaning against the bar by herself. A credit card flipped back and forth between polished fingers as the woman's head moved side to side like she was trying to pop her neck.

"She seems agitated," Victoria supplied.

"Why don't you go over there and ask her how her day was? Or what she thinks of the music?" Echo suggested. "Oh, she's wearing a Los Jibbities shirt, so ask her who her favorite TikToker is."

"I don't have TikTok," Victoria stated. "Can't stand it. May even be the death of me with these kids ripping soap dispensers off the bathroom walls."

"Just go talk to her," Echo prodded, taking the drink from Victoria's hand.

Victoria looked down at her freshly gayified outfit and gathered her courage.

Echo gave her a slight nudge. "The worst thing that can happen is she ignores you."

With a raise of her eyebrow, Victoria accepted Echo's truth. The worst thing the woman could do was ignore her, which wouldn't be any different than her normal day.

Victoria's feet dragged against the floor as she made her way to the bar. She licked her lips realizing she forgot her Chapstick. Taking up space an arm's distance away from the woman, she swallowed the fear trapped in her throat. The woman had moved from flipping to tapping her credit card against the wooden surface.

It took several deep breaths before Victoria quickly spat out, "This music is pretty great to dance to, huh?"

When the girl didn't turn to her, Victoria looked back at Echo and the team that they were playing. They were all watching her like she was the latest victim of some gay reality TV show. Echo gestured back to the woman, signaling Victoria to try again.

"How are you doing?" she said louder this time.

The woman turned to her. Her eyebrows were knit together momentarily, and then she put her hand to her chest. "Were you talking to me?"

"Yeah. I was asking..."

"How my day was," the woman finished. "Sorry, I didn't think you were talking to me when you asked about the music."

She smiled warmly, tapping her card once more. "Uh... my day was good. Thanks for asking." She looked Victoria in the eyes. "And listening."

"Do people not usually listen?" Victoria asked.

"No, sorry. That was probably weird." The woman waved toward a table of females across the bar. "My friends asked me to meet them here tonight. They're trying to set me up."

"Oh... that sounds... fun."

The woman smiled but slightly rolled her eyes. "Set-ups are never fun. And the woman they are trying to set me up with is even less fun."

She glanced at the table again. "The one they brought for me is the skinny blonde with the angry eyes. Her name's Stephanie and she's an executive somewhere very important apparently. She's not a bitch, don't get me wrong, but everything I say, she feels the need to correct for accuracy. I don't think I have finished a sentence until now." The woman paused for a moment. "I'm Tanya. Thanks for letting me speak for a whole paragraph."

"Victoria."

Parker swings around the bar. "What can I get for you?"

Tanya tapped her card on the bar. Her eyes wandered over Parker leaning against the other side, then back to Victoria. "Can I buy you a drink?"

Victoria raised her eyebrow at the woman. "What about your friends and the blind date?"

"I have already made it abundantly clear that I am not interested."

"Oh okay. Uh... sure then." Victoria turned back to Parker. She silently pleaded for help.

"Another vodka and coke?" Parker asked with a nod. Victoria took that as her cue.

"Yeah." She turned back to Tanya. "Thank you."

"No, thank you for making this night not a bust. And to answer your first question, yes, this music is great for dancing. Do you like to dance?"

Victoria swallowed.

"Victoria loves to dance," Parker stated, sliding the drink across the bar.

"Yeah. I love to dance." Which wasn't a lie. She did love to dance but didn't know how to dance without embarrassing herself— or wounding someone.

Tanya placed her hand on Victoria's forearm. It had that pesky gay panic rising once more. "Well, I love to dance, and you love to dance, so we should dance."

Victoria took a long drink before Tanya placed her hand in Victoria's. She wasn't sure what ended up happening with the dart match. She didn't have time to worry about it because after Tanya learned that Victoria was extremely uncoordinated, she walked them to a table by the dance floor and they talked. Well, Tanya talked mostly. Her words fell from her lips like she'd been locked in solitary confinement for a week. But Victoria didn't mind because when she contributed to the conversation Tanya didn't cut her off, didn't start her response off with no, and didn't try to explain what she had said back to her like Michael always had.

At the end of the night, Tanya sent herself a text from Victoria's phone.

For the first time in months, she had a text message from a woman who wasn't Sarah. And Victoria felt good about it. However, when Tanya pressed her lips to Victoria's cheek to say goodbye, Victoria didn't feel the heat spread through her body like it did every time her skin came in contact with Sarah's.

She rationalized that she had to figure out how to walk away from Sarah. And even though she hated it, she knew she had to talk to Dr. Rose about it. After all, she paid the therapist to help her deal with walking away with things. So what that she was Sarah's co-worker, friend, or whatever, the woman charged enough to put all that stuff aside.

15

The eight-office strip mall was mostly vacant when Sarah parked alongside Monica's Land Rover. The spot was directly in view of the single glass door to the private office, which offered Sarah peace of mind. She turned to the kid in the backseat engrossed in the latest *Diary of a Wimpy Kid* novel.

"You want to go in with me or wait here?"

"Here," Tris said. She didn't look up as her long thin finger flipped the page.

Sarah nodded to herself, her eyes finding the crooked troop number on Tris's Girl Scout vest. It was a constant reminder of her inability to ever get things done right.

She opened the door without turning the car off. "Lock the doors," she said. But before she shut the door, she stuck her head back inside. "And make sure you actually look up when someone knocks at the window before you unlock them."

"Look up before unlocking," Tris echoed.

"Thank you."

Inside the office, Sarah paced within the small waiting room. The light on the door frame to Monica's session space told Sarah that Monica was in a session, so she'd have to wait to trade the kid for the keys to the Land Rover. She couldn't decide who got the short end of the stick tonight: Monica having to sit through the interrogation from the know-it-all Girl Scout mom or her having to go teach Karen White how to give a great blow job. On her fourth trip towards the door, she decided watching the soccer mom learn to hollow her cheeks as she worked a dildo was less painful than having to listen to how the interrogator's children preferred trips to the Bahamas over Disneyland.

As Sarah paced, she kept an eye on the parking lot. She'd made five more turns around the lobby when the door to the back office opened. She turned abruptly into the body trying to exit.

The force of the client's attempted flight from the office pushed Sarah's half-turned frame sideways. Her feet came off the ground as the room slowly turned on its axis. Two strong arms wrapped around her middle, cradling her against the chest of the client who had knocked her over. She inhaled the familiar floral perfume, not needing to look up to know whose arms she'd been saved by.

Monica snorted from the doorway as Sarah's feet found the ground and the walls returned to the correct angle. Victoria released Sarah like she'd been burned by the flush creeping over Sarah's body.

"Are you okay?" Victoria asked, her hands still hovering in the air around Sarah.

They dropped as Sarah pressed the front of her button-up back into her pants. She looked up at her boss. "Yeah. Sorry... uh... I shouldn't have been standing so close to the door."

"I should have been looking where I was going." Victoria wrapped an arm around the middle of her body, and Sarah briefly wondered if Victoria also imagined carrying an invisible shield that could repel other humans. "Well, I should get going. See you tomorrow."

"Yeah, see you tomorrow," Sarah echoed.

"And I'll see you next week," Monica called after the woman halfway out the door.

Victoria didn't turn back to them or acknowledge the reminder. The door closed with a soft slap.

"She may not come back," Monica stated.

Monica leaned against the doorway. Her heat-induced curls had lost their bounce and the eyeliner under her eyes told Sarah it had been a rough day.

"Bad session?" Sarah asked.

"Eh... no," Monica offered with a shrug. She took a deep breath and met Sarah's eyes. "But the boundaries are now very fuzzy. I tried to ask if she was angry at work about something going on in her personal life. Plus, there is the whole issue with *someone* who had to fuck a client that she works with and now the babygay's all sad because she can't figure out if you like her or hate her."

Sarah folded her arms over her chest. She couldn't help but look at the droplets of disapproval on the floor from Monica's words as they made their way to her.

With a locked jaw, she hissed through her barely parted teeth, "I did not have sex with her."

Monica rolled her eyes. "Honestly, it would have been better if you had at this point."

"How would that have helped anything?" Sarah scanned the parking lot for any threats once more after she located the head of curls in the backseat of the car.

"Had you just fucked her, I would help her through the trauma of women that fuck other women with no strings attached." Monica's head hit the doorframe. "Instead, I have a client that is fucking in love with my best friend, who has paid no fucking mind to the mind games she's playing."

"Mind games? I haven't played a game with her."

Monica's head fell to the side. "Didn't you tell her you're a bitch because you're sexually frustrated?"

Sarah rubbed the irritation from her face. She'd watched Victoria walk away, thankfully not noticing Tris in the back seat.

"That was seriously like two months ago," Sarah growled. "And you were the one who told me to tell her that now she knows how to cum she needs to do it or she's going to be a bitch."

Had Sarah known the woman would read so much into the comment she would have just kept her mouth shut. She just didn't want Victoria to feel like she was calling her a sexually frustrated bitch. Even though she was.

Sarah exhaled slowly before she stated, "I have been very clear with her that I'm not interested in having any sort of relationship or even communication with her beyond that of work, and I mean school stuff not lessons. I'm not giving her any more lessons."

"Well, according to the minuscule amount of info I was able to pull from your client, the only thing you have been clear about is you want your contract upheld."

Sarah's hands shot up. "Yes. I needed her to understand that I will not tolerate her breaching that contract. I can't lose another job."

Monica's head tilted to one side. "Well, could you see how her babygay heart could think a part of you would be interested if it wasn't for your contract? If you told me I'm attractive and I said, 'Well you're a client, so I can't date you.' Can't you see the hint of possibility there?"

Sarah's arms wrapped around her body. She turned around and released herself from her self-embrace. Her hands carded through her hair and pulled at the roots. Then Sarah spun around.

Spittle flew out with her words as she demanded, "Are you seriously saying I teased her?"

"Well, you told her you knew she was dreaming about fucking you, and you didn't tell her to stop." Monica's words sliced through Sarah.

Sarah held her hand over her mouth to contain the dissertation her mind had composed on the toxicity of blaming a woman for someone else's inability to control their urges. The force behind the rant playing out in her head became too strong to hold back, and the words thrust her hands out of the way as they fled their confines.

"I can't control what she thinks about when she's fucking herself and it's fucked up for you to tell me it's my fault she has a crush on me. She's the one obsessing over strangers. And for you to make that my problem is legit shameful on your part. I mean, half the clients you refer me to are imagining fucking me as I tell them how to use their dicks, and you fucking know it. But I don't see you telling me to tell them, 'Hey, fucker don't think about me.'"

Sarah licked her teeth. Shaking her head, she chose violence once more. "It's a good thing you're not a fucking rape counselor."

Monica rolled her eyes. "This was different, and you know it."

Rubbing the back of her neck, Sarah tried to understand but she couldn't. The space between her eyes hurt from the force of her eyebrows trying to meet in the middle. She rubbed at her face, but she couldn't set it straight.

"Are you mad that I didn't fuck her or that I met with her at all?"

Sarah listened to her question bouncing off the walls of the office. She watched as Monica's attention turned upwards, but her lips didn't move in prayer. They didn't move at all, only the blue eyes. Eyes that scanned the popcorn ceiling, then the stiff Ikea couch behind Sarah. They ran around the room until Sarah didn't need an answer.

"You set me up," Sarah hissed.

The blue eyes met hazel once more. "I thought..."

With her shield gripped in one hand, Sarah shot out the other. Her finger held at a dangerous point. "You thought that she's just my type and I would fall for her."

When Monica swallowed, Sarah scoffed, turning away from the therapist. "Well, you nailed it. She is just my type. Tall. Gorgeous eyes. Beautiful tits and ass. Smart. Put together." She turned back as she hollered. "AND MY FUCKING BOSS!"

Monica's body sagged against the frame. Sarah wondered if the woman was trying to hold the wall up or if it was holding her up.

"I didn't know that part at the time," Monica stated. "Even so, she's a better human than my callous cousin, who I told you was never going to leave her wife when you finally told me the truth."

Sarah closed half the distance between them, stopping when she realized she wasn't sure she'd be able to keep from hitting Monica in the face if another sentence of stupid slithered off her snake-shaped tongue.

"You sent me there to set me up and disregarded everything I have done to keep myself safe."

Standing up straight, Monica put herself within arm's reach of Sarah. "Of all the houses you have walked into, she was never a threat."

The molars in Sarah's mouth ached from the pressure of being squeezed shut. Fingernails dug into the flesh of Sarah's palms as she locked her arms at her side.

"She is the biggest threat of all to me," Sarah growled. "She knows I sell sex five nights a week. And since you put me in a position to fuck up, you have her thinking that I probably go to all of my sessions fucking my clients."

"I didn't—"

"Didn't think? Didn't consider that what you decided was best for me couldn't possibly be dangerous for me?" Each word covered in spit splashed against Monica's face as Sarah stepped into the woman's bubble. "Didn't consider if I do throw out the contract and fuck her like you want me to, what then? She won't be okay with the world I live in just like you weren't. Not going to be able to handle the suitcase of trauma I carry from trailer to shelter to one-bedroom apartment after one-bedroom apartment." Sarah's head tilted to the side. "Did you forget where I come from? Do we need to find the article where you told the world how traumatized women will fuck anyone who pretends to like them because they don't have anything else to offer? You know that article you wrote after you tested your theory by pretending to give a fuck about me until I was topless in front of you, and you saw what trauma actually looks like."

The blue stare was broken with a blink. The fight was gone from the woman who had lowered her chin in submission. She inhaled all the air between them, leaving Sarah to spit out the other half of the conversation not offered.

"You were counting on her wanting to swoop in to rescue me from my shitty ass life," Sarah whispered.

The blue irises disappeared behind the caked beige eyeshadow and smudged liner.

Sarah's fingers pressed against her lips, only parting to release what she should have seen coming. "So, you didn't have to anymore."

The therapist's perfectly straight teeth bit into the lower lip that quivered.

"You aren't pushing me on every single person you know because you care about my love life. You are tired of not having a life because of me. Sick of having to show up and play the savior."

Monica's eyes shot open and narrowed at Sarah. "Don't be stupid," she growled.

"Then why do you need me to meet someone so badly?" Sarah demanded.

"After what happened over summer..." Monica reached over. Her soft hand came to rest on Sarah's locked forearm. "I couldn't pretend anymore that this shit is safe. I couldn't be the reason you were in danger. Or if something happened to you having to be the kid's third mommy."

Sarah shook off Monica's hand as she had tried when her hands had been bound above her head. She stepped out of Monica's space to the window. The sun beat through the glass, warming the chill that had spread over her skin, and even in the brightness, she didn't squint her eyes. Unwilling to put herself back in the dark.

"What happened wasn't your fault," Sarah said as she exhaled.

"It was," Monica argued. "You never should have been in that house."

"There was no way you could have known," she told the therapist for the hundredth time.

"I knew when we started this whole thing you could be in danger."

"No more than the trailer I grew up in," Sarah whispered.

"You won't even talk about what happened that night."

"Nothing happened worth talking about," Sarah stated flatly. "And the last time we talked about anything like that you cried. Then broke up with me before we even started anything."

Monica's feet moved about the space that Sarah couldn't turn to. Sarah's eyes were locked on the kid's head thrown back in laughter. The face she'd seen while locked in another closet. Nine years of life flashed through her mind in a matter of minutes. More years of what she could miss if she didn't get out.

"It was my job to protect you," Monica stated. "And I put you there."

Sarah pressed her hand to the glass. "My fucking sister put me there. If we are going to blame anyone for anything, then we blame her."

The phone in Sarah's pocket pinged. She pulled it out and then held it up. "Speaking of Satan."

"What does she want?" Monica asked, wrapping her arms around Sarah.

Sarah read the text with the address to the same Circle K they met at every six months. Her night would be even longer because now she had to travel from Chandler, back to her apartment in Maryvale, then turn around to go downtown Phoenix. At least her sister was predictable.

"I need your keys to go to a session with the Whites, then I have to meet *her* to get the papers signed."

Monica folded her arms over her chest. "Are you giving her money?"

"Only way she'll sign," Sarah reminded her.

Monica left Sarah in the lobby. When she returned, a key fob was folded into Sarah's hand as Monica instructed, "Text me when you get there."

Sarah sighed, looking back at the car once more. "Girl Scouts tonight. She has her cultural project in the trunk. She has to present it, so have her practice on the way there."

"I'll record it," Monica promised.

"Thanks."

A cop car rolled down the street while Sarah sat in the car and watched her twin. The glass offered her a tinted view into the parallel universe she could have lived in. The ghostly pale legs in the short skirt swayed as her sister, Sierra, leaned against a light pole ready to meet her own clients.

Sierra bummed a cigarette off a well-trimmed boy in a State U sweatshirt strolling down the street. She pushed her pointy tits at him and pressed her hand to his chest.

Shaking her head, Sarah whispered, "Bet you're proud that we grew up to be sex workers just like you, Mama."

The carbon copy across the parking lot yelled something at the man as she teetered off balance when his hand dislodged her grip on his sweatshirt. The blackened eyes narrowed at the car, and even though the windows were tinted beyond regulation, Sarah could feel her sister's eyes on her.

The lighter didn't flick to life on the first couple of tries. The path between the pole and where Sarah had gotten out of the car became polluted with profanity. Only when the cigarette was lit and the air hazy around Sierra's head did the twin saunter over.

Sierra held out her hand, fingers curling to herself in expectation. Track marks trailed up the pale skin to ghastly boils in the crease of her arm.

"Lemme see the cash," Sierra demanded.

Sarah held out the five pages of carefully printed legal documents with a pen. "Sign the papers first."

A puff of smoke and the stench of toothrot hit Sarah in the face when Sierra stepped into Sarah's space. "Where's the money, little sis?"

Holding her breath for the smoke to fade from her face, Sarah straightened her shoulders. "You know that's not how this works. You sign the papers, and then I give you the money."

A lanky man walked through the parking lot. He held the pants that had fallen from his frame at the crotch. Sierra smiled and waved just her fingers at him. He nodded but passed by them and disappeared into the store.

Without taking her eyes from the door, Sierra asked with less venom, "How's the kid?"

"Good," Sarah offered. "Getting big. Almost already taller than me."

"She look like me?"

"Yeah."

Sarah thought of how just last week, Tris woke up looking like a younger version of her sister. The softness of her cheeks smoothed just enough to give Sarah a lot of emotions she quickly bottled up with a cork that was currently ready to pop.

Sierra took a shorter drag from the cigarette, then flicked the ashes into the air. "You making sure she's nothing like me?"

"Yes," Sarah promised.

The paperwork was ripped from Sarah's fingers, slicing open her finger. Sierra didn't bother to read them before she signed and shoved them back at Sarah.

Sarah pulled the wad of cash from the front pocket of her slacks. She didn't have time to hold it out before Sierra ripped it from her too.

The twisted twin weighed it in her hand. Sunken eyes raised to Sarah as the cigarette flopped between her lips. "Where's the rest?"

"The rest?" Sarah balked. "This is how much I give you. Same that I gave you last time."

"Shit cost more now." Sierra spat a loogie to the ground.

Sarah's arms dropped to her side. Though she was unsurprised, it didn't hurt any less. They went through this every time. With a heavy sigh, she said, "I don't have any more to give you."

The cigarette hit Sarah in the chest. The white shirt was left singed from the cherry. She swiped at the area, hoping to put out anything that was still lit.

"You just going to steal my kid like you stole my life and you not even going to help me out?" Sierra hissed.

"I just gave you $6000 in cash," Sarah growled. The paperwork crumpled in her fist. "And I never asked for your kid. You dropped her off and just left."

"Well, I'm telling you it's not enough." A nicotine-stained finger poked Sarah in the chest, backing her against the car.

"I'm telling you it's all I have," Sarah barked back.

"Bullshit." The finger pushed Sarah back again. Her spine slapped against the vehicle. "Look at you all dressed up in your fancy work clothes. With your fancy car."

"Not my car," Sarah stated.

A sickly laugh broke from the shattered woman. "Oh! So, you got yourself a rich dick to buy you all the pretty things. Think you're better than me."

"No. It's for work."

"I bet it's for *work*." Sierra's neck snapped as she stood for the first time without swaying. "You're no better than me and you'd be nothing if it weren't for me."

Sarah's eyes fell to the ground as they had every single time Sierra had stepped up so she could stay down. "I know."

"Yeah, you know. You know what I did for you. Everything and everyone I did for you, and you can't even get me enough to live on. Fucking cunt. I should have let them have you."

"You should have," Sarah said, and she believed it.

"Yeah, well I didn't, did I?" Sierra stroked her younger sister's hair. "And I just need a little help now. I need you to help me this time. I got to get him off my neck, you know? Just a little more. You know for all those times I let you hide when Mama passed out. When I kept them entertained so it wouldn't be you, little sister."

"I don't have any more to give you."

Sierra's spit sprayed over Sarah's face as she screamed, "I fucking hate you!"

"I don't have anymore," Sarah whispered again.

The car screamed in protest as Sierra smacked against the pristine silver finish.

"Get it then," Sierra snapped. "Get me more or I'll call the cops and tell them you stole my kid! Kidnapper."

Sierra pulled up her shirt. The stretch marks from Tris's first home lay etched in the skin of the junkie making threats.

"I got the proof she's mine," Sierra said, slapping the evidence she would try to use that would do nothing but end with Tris as a ward of the state.

Sarah clutched the guardianship forms and studied the asphalt that didn't swallow her sister up as she walked away. The reminder to tell Sierra she loved her when she was driving came too late. As the heels clicked away, Sarah wondered if this would be the last time she would ever see her again.

16

Victoria finished Netflix and Amazon Prime. At least the lesbian category of the streaming apps. She clicked through the line of options disappointed that really the category was just a form of trickery because the amount of girl love girl films and series was slim. And most were filled with death.

She had begun to hope with each new show that she'd finally see the women in their elder years enjoying their lives to the point when even the main character was detestable Victoria hoped she'd survive.

With nothing left to watch, she tossed the remote on the coffee table and got up from the couch. Her body cracked and popped as she stretched out her limbs. It was almost noon, and she'd not bothered to get out of her pajamas.

She looked around but found nothing out of place and the dust had been wiped away the day before. The kitchen was clean as her nightly meal prep for hers and Sarah's lunch had ended after fall break when she'd arrived with an extra portion and Sarah had responded with a mostly empty container of her own that looked like a half a serving of old spaghetti.

Future appointments with Dr. Rose were canceled with a text message because she didn't believe in coincidences. That action also took away one of her afternoon commitments, so she searched for something else to do in her silent evenings when the shadows of the house danced around her.

The large bowl of candy lay ready for the sun to set on the table by the entryway, no one ever passed by. All Hallow's Eve had snuck up on her quietly for the first time since her sisters had started multiplying. Arizona didn't offer a change in the leaves nor was there a pumpkin patch anywhere in sight. She'd had no costumes to help sew or paint this year for her nieces or nephews.

She'd meant to offer her seamstress skills to Jen but found herself looking for reasons to avoid their weekly dinners. Feeling guilty for ditching Jen, Victoria found excuses to not play darts with Echo as well. Now, she pretended to be busy reading child psychology books. She'd even signed up for another Master's program through an online university that began that week to convince herself she wasn't depressed.

With each new article she read for the class, her administrator's toolbox was filled with more strategies to work with the tiny humans so she wouldn't have to rely on Sarah. She should have listened to Jen about leaving Sarah alone, maybe then she wouldn't be sulking over the woman's avoidance. She also should have texted Tanya, but after a week of having her number, it felt like she'd missed her chance.

She made her way to the kitchen. The laptop waited for her to log in and start the weekly essay. A stack of research articles rested aside with all the highlights and annotations she'd carefully prepared over the past five days during her solitary lunch breaks and even more isolated dinners. She knew the paper wouldn't take her long, but she'd put it off until tonight. Hoping that if she was focused on improving her life, the trick-or-treaters wouldn't make her yearn for the life that she'd given up wishing for after the last fertility appointment solidified what she'd already suspected.

Sitting down in front of the computer, Victoria did not navigate to the university platform. Instead, she traveled down a rabbit hole of an option Michael dismissed the first and only time it was brought up. With a better understanding of children, Victoria dared a question she'd never verbally spoken. Was she capable of being a mother?

She laughed at the question as quickly as it arrived. But the feeling of ridiculousness quickly caught in her throat. She'd laughed off being a mother whenever someone had asked her because it wasn't a reality.

That was the old her, though. The one who followed her husband's desires despite her own. And the true reality was that she could be a mother. She could be a mother to a child that needed a home. Didn't even have to be a child. She could be good for one of the older ones. She knew of at least ten at the school in a group home. She could even take in a teen. Maybe a queer teen. Make being different easier for them.

Echo fostered not one but two kids, now parenting the teenager who'd dropped Echo's baby off at the hospital after escaping a sex trafficking ring. Victoria could do that, especially with all her new understanding of child psychology.

Instead of writing an essay, Victoria searched for how to become a foster parent in the state of Arizona. She messaged Echo, expecting no response. Instead, she got a link to an agency and a detailed list of why to go to their website and not others. Victoria took Echo's response as confirmation she wasn't crazy and went as far as to fill out a digital form for an orientation on what being a foster parent would take.

She smiled at the sound of the door as the first trick-or-treater arrived. Each step toward the door solidified her will to expand her sights beyond meeting a woman. After all, Netflix had taught her that was not where to seek her happy ending.

17

The weekly Monday night phone call with Sarah's mother had ended so abruptly that Sarah was still staring at the phone screen when it buzzed in her hand. Zoe's name danced on the screen. She wrapped the comforter tighter around her and wiggled in the chair on her patio. Hitting accept, she smiled at the other woman who was barely in the view.

Zoe's body bounced as the gaming headphones held back the untamed curls sticking out around her face. A string of swear words fell from her lips and an Xbox controller came into the screen view.

Sarah smiled at the unfiltered glimpse into Zoe's life. She was about to hang up when the phone caught the woman's attention. Headphones were shucked off, and then Sarah's view momentarily disappeared.

"Uhhh... Hold on!" Zoe cried out. Whatever Zoe used to cover the phone scratched against the microphone, causing Sarah to lower the volume of the call.

When Zoe returned to the camera view, her hair was pulled back into a tight but messy bun, and the room was no longer dark. "Hey," Zoe said, though slightly out of breath.

"Your butt dialed me, I think," Sarah offered.

"I guess it missed you," Zoe stated. A blush crept up Zoe's cheeks as she choked. "Not that... I didn't mean that my butt thinks about you. I mean, it's not that it wouldn't think about you. But really butts can't think, so I just don't want you to think that—"

"Breathe," Sarah said.

Zoe shut her mouth. Long fingers rubbed over her face. Then pale green eyes peeked out through her split fingers. "Sorry," she offered.

"What game were you playing?" Sarah asked.

"Red Dawn Redemption II," Zoe stated. The simple statement bled into an elaborate explanation of the western-themed outlaw. Every detail of the game—from graphics to various types of missions— was provided as Zoe's smile grew wide. But Sarah studied the woman instead of the words.

Zoe's perfectly straight teeth and pristine kitchen in the background made Sarah only smile with her lips to cover the slight overlap of her front teeth. She'd glanced back once to ensure the blinds behind her were still closed, shutting Zoe out of her world.

She chewed on how she could explain in two short days the different worlds they lived in. That she didn't come from the world of moms who cooked dinners from scratch and orthodontics appointments. And that was two days too soon for the social worker who was being won over by the wonderful woman on the other end of the camera. She put off the date for as long as possible. Weeks of flirty texts and half-made plans had come to a point where they had to meet face to face.

"Earth to Sarah." Zoe's hand waved in front of the camera.

Sarah shook her head. "Sorry, my mind wandered as you were talking about the Wild West."

"It's okay. I guess you don't game," Zoe said.

"No. I don't have the coordination for the buttons." Sarah didn't include that she'd never had a gaming system. No one in the trailer park she grew up in had one. "Uh, I grew up in a small town that felt like the Wild West outside of Flagstaff."

Zoe's eyes crinkled in the corners. "Oh, you're an Arizona native?"

"Yeah."

"Me too." Zoe patted her chest. "When I was a kid, it was like no one was actually from here but my friend Ari."

Sarah shrugged. "Quite the opposite in the place I grew up. Everyone was from there and no one ever really left."

"What made you leave?"

"College."

"State U?" Zoe held up the Sundevil Pitchfork gang sign.

Sarah matched it with her hatchet hand. "NU my first year. I ended up at ASU because of Tris a year later, but I still claim to be a Lumberjack." She took a moment to laugh at the twisted scowl on Zoe's face, then said, "I mean I left, but I don't feel like I will ever be far enough away."

"You went farther than me," Zoe offered. "I went to State, which was a twenty-minute drive from the house I grew up in."

"And you stayed in Phoenix."

Zoe's body leaned back into the leather couch. The material around her head was faded from the time the woman spent breaking that particular spot in. "I thought about going out of state, even got a scholarship to head to UCLA for Volleyball."

Sarah waited for the rest of the story which didn't come. Zoe's eyes had traveled away from the camera to something in the distance.

"Why'd you stay?" Sarah asked.

Zoe's attention refocused on the screen. Sarah watched as the woman's hand pulled at the back of her neck.

"Full transparency?" Zoe asked.

"Yes."

Zoe pinched her nose, scrunched her eyes, and held her breath.

"You okay?" Sarah asked.

"Sorry fighting off a sneeze," Zoe stated as her face returned to normal. Apparently free from the potential momentary demon possession, Zoe's serious face returned. "So... I didn't leave because the only school my brother got into was State and we were best friends. I actually never even told my parents about the offer from UCLA because I didn't want it to be another thing I had outdone him in. So, I stayed. Then, I met a girl in college who kept me here for law school because she was still working on her undergrad, and when that ended, I was already committed and felt like I needed my brother more than ever. First heartbreak and all."

Sarah wrapped the comforter tighter around her body, wondering if she'd ever considered her sister her best friend. Without the answer, Sarah deflected the dangerous feelings with the question, "Are you still close?"

"No." Zoe sucked her teeth. The tendons in her hand flexed as she massaged her neck once more. "I... uh... I found out he played an intricate role in my relationship falling apart. I mean, since we are being fully honest, the collapse was entirely my fault, but it didn't change what he did."

"He sleep with your girl?"

"No. Tried to." Zoe's hand dropped and she looked into the camera. "She was a stripper, and I didn't know. Turns out he was one of her regulars and when she rejected him... he put his hands on her and exposed the secret she'd been keeping from me."

Sarah searched Zoe's face. "Why did she keep her work a secret from you?"

"I was a judgmental asshole."

Sarah's eyebrows rose. "Was?"

"Yeah... So... funny story, I saw her again when she showed up on my jury a couple of months ago. That's when I learned about what my brother had done, and I was smacked in the face with who I was and who I didn't want to be."

Even though Sarah hadn't met Zoe, and even though they had only spoken face to face like this a few times over the past few weeks, Sarah struggled to construct the woman Zoe described herself to formerly be. But Sarah knew that people could change. She had seen people go from caring to careless to cruel within hours, days, and months.

"Are you friends with her?" Sarah asked, not sure what else to say.

"Not really." Zoe bit her lip. "I don't want you to think that I am still in love with her or anything. We just have mutual friends. Well, not really friends. Why can't I speak right?"

With her hands rubbing at her face again, Sarah wondered if Zoe was always this nervous.

"Okay." Zoe started again. "I am friends with Evie. Evie is the sister of my ex's new girlfriend. Okay, I said full transparency, so Evie's sister is also my ex, and my exes are now together. But we do not hang out. I see them at events."

"Wow."

"Look, I can't say that I will ever really not see them because Evie's pregnant, and I'm going to be the godmother. Also, my mom and her mom are close friends now. The Greysons are like lesbian collectors," Zoe said, rubbing her hand over her face.

"Evie Greyson?" Sarah choked on her laugh. "You're friends with Evie Greyson."

"Yeah." Zoe eyed her suspiciously. "You know Evie?"

Sarah sucked in her lips, thinking of the Greyson girls. They were all in high school when she rented Dilynn Greyson's guest house. At the time, Sarah felt like she was watching how life should have gone for her when she walked through the main house to do laundry. The difference was those girls got to be kids, and she had a kid weighing down one side of her body. But there were those few weekends when the oldest was brave. Lyra would bring over an Xbox.

Lyra's Xbox was why Sarah knew she couldn't play video games. But she had once with Lyra, then the video games became a guise to make out. Then to have sex, because they were both consenting adults at the ripe ages of 19 and 18. They didn't know how to be out, but still had desires that they kept quiet, so the matriarch wouldn't kick either of them out of the house neither felt they belonged in.

Then Zoe's confession barricaded through the memories. She had slept with a Greyson.

. "So, I know Evie. And I know Lyra and Sadie." Closing her eyes, she shook her head. "Please tell me you dated Sadie."

"I did not," Zoe whispered. "Why?"

With a groan, Sarah let out her truth. "Lesbian circles are so fucked."

"Why?" Zoe asked slowly.

"So, once upon a time. A long, long time ago, I lived with the Greysons. I rented the apartment out back of what I think is now Evie's house. I'm not sure because Dilynn buys up houses on that street like she is trying to establish her own monarchy."

"Oh, I've seen that place," Zoe said. "Yeah, Evie lives there now. There's a single mom who...."

"That's how I met Dilynn," Sarah confessed. "And Lyra and I—"

"Yeah. I'm good," Zoe interjected. She was waving her hand in front of the phone. "Too soon to compare dating histories."

"Kinda already did that," Sarah said with a snicker. "So, you made friends with Evie. That's an impressive task to tame that woman into friendship."

"I like to think we are fixing each other," Zoe admitted. "I mean, she keeps me humble."

Sarah snorted. "Humble and Evie do not belong in the same sentence."

"Well, I hope all the work she does to get kids off the street will fix some of her Karma. I don't want my godson coming out looking like a wrinkly old man."

Sarah snorted. "Yeah, most babies are not cute. Evie and Landon are very pretty though, so I bet the kid is cute."

"Was your daughter a cute baby?" Zoe asked.

The image of Tris's thin skeleton-looking skull lay behind her eyelids. The slight twitch in the infant's limbs as she screamed for days on end.

Sarah licked her lips and opened her eyes. "Full transparency?" she asked.

Zoe forced a smile on her uncomfortable face. "Oh god, she was an alien, huh?" she whispered.

Sarah chuckled. "Well, she sure felt like it, but that wasn't what I was going to say."

"Oh okay."

With a deep breath, Sarah allowed the secret to slip from her lips. "Since we're being honest, let's just put the cards on the table. While you were getting your heart broken in college, I was handed an infant by my twin sister. That's how I ended up in Phoenix and at State. I only made it a semester at NU when I got the phone call from the hospital here."

Zoe's eyebrows cinched in the middle. Her eyes darted around the room and then seemed to focus on a corner of her phone before her face became fixed in a more formal expression. She cleared her throat, but still choked as she asked, "Handed?"

"I was a freshman in college, and she was a drug addict living on the street, doing what women do for drug money," Sarah said. Then Sarah glanced over her shoulder to make sure the patio door hadn't opened unbeknownst to her.

"Wow." Zoe opened her mouth a few times until words finally fell out. "Does your daughter know?"

Sarah smiled at how Zoe still referred to Tris as her daughter. It was a stark contrast to the previous phone call of the evening.

"She knows," Sarah said. "We don't do secrets."

The connection went quiet as Sarah provided Zoe with the time she needed to process the information that had been laid before her. The crickets chirped wildly as a souped-up car contributed to the melody down the street on the other side of the crumbling concrete wall around the apartment complex.

"So, you're a twin?" Zoe finally said.

"Yep. Identical in every aspect." Sarah looked down at her face in the bottom corner of the screen, only she saw Sierra looking back at her. She turned back to her view of the street. This is why she hated mirrors. They were a constant reminder of why she was here.

"You know it's amazing that you stepped up."

Sarah looked back at the phone, not realizing she had been avoiding Zoe's judgment.

"I don't think I would have been able to do that for one of my brothers," Zoe stated. She forced a smile on her face and then pointed at it. "You know, judgmental asshole and all."

Before Sarah could respond the screen flashed, and Sarah read a text from Victoria. "Hold on a second."

She read through Victoria's text and tapped out a response. Coming back to the video screen, she explained, "Sorry, that was my boss."

"Your boss texts you this late?" Zoe asked.

"It's only eight, Grandma," Sarah said with a roll of her eyes. "She's our new AP of discipline this year and apparently started this degree program in school psych. She has to do these application projects and had a question about our school."

"By the looks of it, you don't seem to like this new boss very much."

"Eh." Sarah thought about the woman who treated everyone but her like shit. If Victoria could pull the stick out of her ass, maybe Sarah could find some chill when she was around. "We have a tense working relationship. I mean, we argue a little less often now. And she apologizes each time she is too black and white and everything, but we just don't agree on pretty much anything."

"Rules are rules?" Zoe asked.

"Yeah, but with kids it doesn't work that way."

Zoe's eyebrows seemed to disappear into her hairline as she looked away. "I learned that lesson with my last trial as well."

"You had quite a few months, didn't you?" Sarah prodded.

"Yeah, it's kinda crazy. I thought I was at the top of my game and that my life was perfect. But the case I was working on made me realize how narrow-minded I was."

"The case or your ex?" Sarah asked, not sure if she wanted the answer. When Zoe stared at her through the phone like she'd just read her mind, Sarah shrugged. "I'm guessing the case was the jury your ex was on?"

"Uh... yeah." Zoe's hand pulled at her neck once more. "I guess it was both. It was like the past, present, and possible future had caught up to me, and I had a Christmas Carol-like experience without the creepy ghosts in chains."

"Interesting." Sarah stared at the phone. She chewed on her lip until she realized she was showing Zoe her overlapping teeth. "So, do I need to be worried about this ex ruining our fake date? I know you just said not to be, but you seem kinda—"

Zoe popped up straight. "No. No. I mean, I'll always love her, but as my mom said then when I refused to listen: the things that were said and done could never be undone, and anything that would ever grow from that soil would be corrupted with the toxicity that had already been spilt."

"Your mom sounds like a poet," Sarah offered. But she clung to the part that Zoe confessed to not having listened to her mother.

"Well, those weren't her words exactly. It was more along the lines of 'you were a cruel judgmental asshole, and Parker deserves better than you'."

"Ouch."

"It definitely ouched then, but now." Zoe swallowed. "I needed the ouch so that I could be here. On my couch so my ass could butt dial you. And I would rather plant seeds in the fresh soil between us."

"So, you're the poet," Sarah stated.

"I like you."

Zoe's words hung in the air around Sarah. They were simple, one-syllable words that were directed toward anyone else would make sense.

"You haven't even met me," Sarah reminded Zoe.

"Yeah, but still." Zoe leaned into the phone. "I want you to know that even though we are calling Saturday a fake date, I hope that you will want to go on a real one with me."

Sarah's brain sorted through the sentences to find the reason that Zoe would use to take those previous three words back. When she found the one she needed as a reference, she said, "I need to tell you something."

"Uh oh."

Sarah signed. "Probably."

Zoe sat back up straight. She put on a serious face that fell to a smile. She moved her jaw around and then set a new mask on more stoic than the last. "Ok, hit me," she commanded.

"Since you mentioned that your ex was a stripper and that was the fall of your relationship. I think I need to be upfront with you about my side job."

The mask fell off Zoe's face and shattered against the probably perfect flooring. She closed her eyes and words tumbled from the pillow lips. "Please don't say you're a stripper. I mean, I don't care now, but the last woman I flirted with turned out to work with my ex and Evie still hasn't let me live it down that I apparently am only interested in strippers."

Sarah laughed. She laughed a real laugh at the distress of the woman on the other end of the line.

Only when she gathered herself together, she said, "No, but that is an interesting tangent we should discuss later."

"Okay." Zoe swallowed thickly. "So, what do you do on the side?"

"I am an intimacy coach."

Zoe's eyebrows scrunched in the middle again and Sarah made a note that this was Zoe's thinking face.

The thin fingers scratched Zoe's scalp as her face ran through a variety of thoughts and her lips whispered fractions of silenced sentences.

"What does that entail?" she finally asked.

Sarah shook her head and reminded herself that she had already committed to the truth.

"Well, before my sister handed me a baby, I was going to school to be a psychologist. I couldn't pursue it with having to raise a baby at the same time, which is why I ended up going down the social worker path, which allowed me to finish college faster... sorry rabbit hole. Back to the point, I work with my friend who does couples counseling and she will refer clients to me. Basically, I meet with them and provide instruction on how to increase their pleasure and satisfy each other's needs."

"So, you teach people how to have sex... better," Zoe stated.

"Yes."

Zoe's eyes narrowed at the screen. "Which means you're like a sex expert."

"I guess you could say that."

Zoe's pink tongue traced the straight lines of her teeth. She tilted her head. "I'm not going to lie, that is definitely not a turn-off."

"Really?" Sarah whispered.

Zoe stared at her like a sticker was stuck to her forehead.

Slowly, Zoe asked, "Would someone really be like let me pass up on the woman who knows everything about sex?"

"So, it doesn't bother you?"

Zoe fixed her face, then raised her eyebrows suggestively, "Do I get free lessons?"

"Do you want to look at diagrams of vaginas and practice with silicone replicas that I use with middle-aged men?"

The smile on Zoe's lips turned to a grimace.

With a slight shrug, Sarah said, "Then no free lessons. Plus, I would make you sign a confidentiality contract, and then I couldn't even fake date you."

Zoe raised her hand and swatted at the words. "Yeah, no. I'm good. I am familiar with vaginas."

"And she uses the plural," Sarah stated with a chuckle.

Eyes wide, Zoe began to stumble over anything that she tried to say again. "I mean... the vagina. I have one and I have...."

Sarah laughed at Zoe's fumbling.

"I'm not saying that I... I mean, who hasn't.... Stop talking."

The laughter grew harder, but Sarah couldn't help pushing Zoe a little more. "No please, keep talking about the vaginas you have seen and the personal practice."

"Yeah. I'm going to stop talking."

Zoe didn't laugh, her red cheeks of embarrassment only grew darker as Sarah released the swirling of emotions within her. Only when the laughter threatened to turn to tears, did Sarah fix her face and look back at the woman.

"So, you're okay? I mean, it won't hurt my feelings or anything if you want to cancel."

"No. I'm good." Zoe bit her lip. "Is it something you always wanted to do?"

With a shake of her head, Sarah answered, "No. Just helps pay the bills."

"Okay. Yeah, okay."

But Sarah could tell it wasn't okay. It was okay for now but wouldn't be for long. Might not even be okay before the fake date that was promised, which would mean she would have to go back to reading the messages on the dating app.

The door groaned as Tris pushed it open. She stood in the doorway as a moth moved from the patio light into the apartment.

"Mom, you have been out here forever," she whined. Then, she smiled at the phone. "Is that the lady you're going to wear the lipstick for?"

Sarah rolled her eyes. She held up the phone so the girl could see the woman and vice versa.

"Tris, this is Zoe. Zoe, this is Tris."

"Uh... hi, Tris."

"Hi!" the child bounced on her toes. "Are you excited about your date?"

"Yeah. Yeah, I am," Zoe stated stiffly.

"My mom is awesome, and she says that you guys are going to the garden place next to the zoo. Is it like hiking? Mom says you like to hike but just so you know she doesn't hike."

"I used to," Sarah corrected. "You don't hike."

Tris narrowed her eyes at Sarah, who was still holding the phone in her direction. Turning her attention back to the phone, Tris asked, "Do you want kids?"

"Tris!" Sarah choked.

On the other end, Zoe stumbled over her words. "Uhhh... I guess I hadn't... I mean, I never really thought about it."

Sarah searched the girl's scrunched face. Tris looked at Sarah, then back at the phone. "But you're going on a date with my mom."

Sarah looked at the phone but didn't move the screen from the kid. She studied the way Zoe's hand returned to squeezing at her neck.

"You're right," Zoe stated. "And yes... Yeah, I do want kids. I just..." The remainder of Zoe's sentences dissolved in her mouth.

"Hey kiddo," Sarah said, pulling Tris's attention from the phone. She reached over and took Tris's hand. "Can you go inside, and I will be in a minute?"

Tris kicked an imaginary rock off the patio. She grumbled, then said, "You said that an hour ago."

"I promise I will be in, in a minute."

"Fine."

The door didn't close all the way behind Tris as she stomped into the apartment. Sarah got up and shut it the remaining few inches.

Turning back to the phone, she bit her lip. "I'm sorry. I didn't mean for you to be caught off guard like that."

"It's okay. I should have handled that better. I don't have a lot of experience with kids."

"It's okay. I get it. Like you said, it's a lot to handle when someone shows up with a kid and is like here you go."

"Yeah," Zoe said.

Sarah pushed the overgrown bangs from her face. She looked at the woman studying the bottom corner of the screen, which pulled Sarah's attention down to her own reflection. She wasn't prepared for the bags under her eyes or the wrinkle across her forehead.

She tried to tell her mouth to smile, but all it gave her was a yawn. Her hand covered her mouth as her head fell backward. When she looked back at the phone, she said, "I should go before she comes back."

Zoe nodded. "I should get to sleep too."

"You're going to play video games, aren't you?" Sarah stated.

"I'm going to play video games," Zoe admitted with a smile.

"Good night, Zoe."

"Good night."

Once inside the O'Keeffe women moved through the nightly routine of fixing the satin bonnet over Tris's curls and brushing their teeth in silence. Tris didn't say anything about the fact that Zoe hadn't immediately accepted her. Sarah couldn't find the words to explain to the child that expecting the person she went on the date with to want their instant family was unrealistic.

Tris curled up against Sarah as they moved through another chapter of *President of the Whole Fifth Grade*. They took turns reading, Tris read the left page and Sarah took the right. Talk about the date or red lipstick after the chapter was eliminated from the nightly questions of what the week would hold for them.

Sarah returned to her couch with her comforter. She curled up in the well-worked divot to replay the conversations of the night. From her mother's anger spewing through the phone about denying Sarah's twin to come and live with them to Zoe's stumbling over whether or not she even wanted children. Minutes ticked by and episodes of *Gilmore Girls* played on the screen. The bags under her eyes grew puffier as the tears she'd willed away earlier came back with a vengeance.

18

The Kleenex hung between Victoria's two fingers out to a curly-headed boy with a missing front tooth. The first half of the *Rainbow Fish* read-aloud was spent digging for a prize in his nose. The boy looked at the tissue, then his prize.

Victoria's stomach twisted when the green booger popped into his mouth. She gripped the tissue to her mouth as she fought the urge to gag. A mental note was added to the list that she would not be suited to be a parent at this stage in development.

A call on the radio about the Thursday morning fight at the fourth-grade recess reached Victoria while she was observing the first-grade teacher. A fight was substantially better than vomiting on a six-year-old, so she pushed herself up from a tiny human chair, her knees popping on the way.

Victoria made her way to the nurse's office, which hadn't been updated since the 70s. She stood over the red-faced sobbing boy holding the ice and gauze to his bleeding mouth. Even sitting, she could tell he was big for a nine-year-old.

"Hello, I'm Ms. Brenton. What's your name?"

"Caleb."

"Caleb, can you tell me what happened?"

His swollen lip quivered when he pulled the blood-covered gauze from it. "I was getting a drink and Tris hit my water bottle into my mouth and..." The rest of his words washed away with the tears streaming from his face.

"Do you know why Tris hit you with the bottle?"

The boy shook his head, then whined, "I wanna go home."

"Okay. We'll call your mom."

After confirming Caleb's parents had been contacted, Victoria left the child-like nurse with the giant-sized boy.

Victoria stared at Sarah's closed door as she made her way down the hall to where the girl, Tris, was waiting for her. She wanted to ask Sarah for help with this because a girl attacking a boy as big as Caleb seemed like there was more to the story. She wondered if the attack was a little girl crying out for help for someone else's hands hurting her.

She stopped outside Sarah's door, watching the girl in the chair outside her office door. Thin fingers plucked grass from the navy blue jumper, dropping the pieces on the ground. Her head of tight curls was also filled with grass, and Victoria didn't envy the parent who would have to comb it out later that day.

When she reached for Sarah's door handle, she heard the woman slam something on the other side, then the social worker swore at whoever she was talking to within the office. Not wanting to be at the receiving end of Sarah's frustration like last time, Victoria's hand dropped back to her side.

When she looked back at the child, big green eyes studied her. The valley-colored eyes popped against the warm brown skin framed by the curling tendrils around her face.

"Hello, I'm Ms. Brenton," Victoria said to the girl.

"This is Tris," Leticia provided. "Should I call—"

Victoria held up her hand to silence the question. "I won't be needing Ms. O'Keeffe." The girl's eyes looked past Victoria at the closed door.

"Tris, will you come into my office please?"

The girl stood up, arms folding across her chest. Her shoulders didn't slump but rose. "Please, call my mom. I don't have anything to say until she is here."

"I can—" the assistant started but stopped when Victoria held up her hand once more.

"It's fine. I would like the chance to talk with Tris before we call her mother."

Leticia tried again, "Are you—"

"Come with me, Tris." Before the child could protest, Victoria entered her office and stood by the door.

Tris looked back at the office across the hall, and Victoria felt her stomach twist. The child had clearly been here before. Worked with Sarah before. Victoria's resolve settled to be the one to help the girl from the terrors she was experiencing. It would prove her competence and her compassion to the woman already having a bad day.

Once Tris was in the office, Victoria shut the door to stop the girl from staring at Sarah's door.

The desk created a canyon between the child and herself. Victoria preferred it that way until she remembered how Sarah had gotten down on Diego's level, practically sitting on the floor. She wondered if it was a trick to get a kid to talk to her.

She decided it would be weird to get up now that they were both seated. She pulled out an incident form from a file on her desk and then searched the desktop for a pen.

"Tris, I would like you to tell me your side of what happened on the playground," she stated, still turning over other papers to find something to write with.

She clicked the top of the ballpoint she'd managed to locate during her game of hide and seek. Putting the tip to the surface of the white paper, she waited.

And waited.

And waited until the deafening silence ended with the sounds of whistles for the fifth-grade recess being blown.

"Tris, I am asking what happened on the playground with Caleb," she stated again.

Victoria set the pen down and prepared to get up from her chair. To try Sarah's tactics, but the child leaned back and folded her arms over her chest once more.

"Please, call my mom. I don't have anything to say until she is here."

"I will call your mom, Tris," Victoria assured her. "I would like to have something to tell her though when I call her, like what is going on that you felt the need to hit Caleb?"

Tris resumed picking the grass off of her with one hand, while the other stayed wrapped protectively around herself.

"If you don't tell me anything, then I have to take what Caleb said as what happened," Victoria warned.

"No, you don't," Tris half-mumbled.

"Excuse me."

The green eyes rose to Victoria once more. The child sucked her teeth before her jaw ground the words between her them. She must not have liked the way they tasted because she spit them out in a single breath.

"Just because he said something doesn't make it true and my mom says you don't have to believe anything that someone else tells you but you gotta choose to believe it because they don't tell the truth. She says no one really says the whole truth anyways, just tell you what they think you want to hear so that you don't not like them anymore."

Victoria closed her mouth which had fallen open. A mild reprimand flashed in her head, but she paused the way Sarah had. She put her hand on her stomach below the desk and felt it move out as she breathed. With each breath, she dissected a part of what the child had said.

When she looked up from the desk, Tris had slumped back into the chair.

"Did Caleb say something to you? Did he do something to you?" Victoria asked.

Tris's arm smeared away a single tear that had fallen from the corner of her eye. "Doesn't matter," she muttered.

"I want to understand," Victoria said softly.

Those anger-filled eyes rose. "My mom told my aunt that you don't care about anything but being important."

Victoria's brows knit together in the center. She'd had zero engagement with anyone that even slightly resembled the child by her recollection.

The girl sucked back her snot and straightened in her chair again. With a firmer voice, she demanded, "Please, call my mom. I don't have anything else to say until you call my mom."

Victoria sighed and hit the speed dial for Leticia while on speakerphone. "Yes, Ms. Brenton."

"Can you please get Tris's mother on the line?"

Leticia looked at Victoria through the window. "On the line?"

"Yes, as in call her so I can speak to her," Victoria hissed.

"I can just go get her," the assistant offered.

Victoria picked up the phone. "I'm sorry?"

"Sarah's in her office. The door is still closed, but I can get her."

Turning her body away from the child, Victoria attempted to whisper, "As in Sarah O'Keeffe?"

She glanced over at the child, whose lips had curled at the corners into a smirk that must be buried within the O'Keeffe's DNA. She looked at the girl square in the eyes.

"Yes, please go get Ms. O'Keeffe."

Victoria tapped her fingers on the desk waiting as the girl had resumed picking the grass from her shirt and dropping onto the office floor.

There was a knock on the door before Sarah stepped inside and shut it quietly behind her. Victoria breathed easier when the woman didn't immediately start yelling at her.

Sarah appeared to not even notice Victoria was there, moving straight to the child who hopped from her chair and closed the distance between them. The gangly arms wrapped around Sarah's tiny middle.

Pressing the brown hair down against the girl's face, Sarah asked her, "Are you okay?"

"I'm sorry," Tris cried.

Tris's words replayed in Victoria's mind about the conversation between Sarah and her aunt. The fantasy she built in her head about Sarah seeing her, the real her. Not the client. Not the boss. But wanting the mother who had caressed Victoria as she sobbed like the child in the woman's arms was a figment of her imagination. She'd never been more than a client, and now would never be more than a boss who the social worker thought didn't care.

But she did care.

She cared more than she did before because she understood why her very presence threatened Sarah. She understood the depth of the plea when the confidence had fled the woman as she told Victoria she had everything to lose.

Victoria cataloged every aspect of the child who matched the woman she'd not known was a mother.

"What happened?" Sarah asked.

"Yes, Tris, what happened?" Victoria asked. She said a silent prayer that Sarah could hear the concern in her voice.

Sarah glanced over at Victoria before focusing all of her attention back on the child launching into the details she'd previously been unwilling to share.

"Caleb kept taking the ball. It's the only one left since the boys kicked the one we had on Monday on the roof." Tris paused, searching Sarah's face.

When Sarah nodded, Tris continued.

"We were playing, and we asked him to stop. He didn't and he took the ball, and he threw it at Madi's head. It hit her in the face and knocked her glasses off. He laughed at her. I told him to apologize but he said to shut up. I told him he was being mean and that he owed Madi an apology. Then he said if I didn't want to get hit too, I should get out of his face. Then he pushed me and..."

Sarah waited as Victoria held her breath.

Fresh tears crept down the girl's cheeks. "And he called me the n-word."

"So, you hit him," Sarah stated.

"No," the child said, shaking her head. "I was upset but he's scary. He's soooo big."

Sarah's eyebrows met in the middle. "I don't understand. Ms. Mitchell said you hit Caleb in the face with his water bottle."

"I didn't hit him then," Tris mumbled as her chin fell.

Sarah guided Tris back to the chairs across from Victoria and held her hand as they sat.

Tris wiped her other hand under her nose. A trail of mucous shimmered under the humming fluorescent light bars.

"So, what happened after he called you the n-word?"

"He took our ball, and he went over to the boys. When recess was almost done, he was getting a drink of water and I hit the bottle from him, but it hit him in the mouth and his lips started bleeding. I ran away and he ran after me and tackled me. He was trying to hit me, so I kneed him in his boy boobies."

Victoria had to actively fight the smile that threatened to spread across her face.

"And then the teachers came and I told *her*," Tris's thin arm shot up with a single digit pointed at Victoria, "to call you and that I wouldn't tell her what happened until I called you but she said that if I didn't say anything that she would have to believe what Caleb told her even though he lies all the time. So I told her that she didn't have to believe anything."

Tris's chin fell to her chest once more and her shoulders collapsed forward. "I know I broke the rules and that even when we have to defend ourselves, we take our punishment but that it would be okay because I didn't really do anything wrong."

"That's right, honey," Sarah said. She pulled the sleeve of her cardigan over her hand and wiped the tears from her daughter's face.

"I'm sorry, what?" Victoria asked.

"What is the consequence for a first-time offense for fighting?" Sarah asked.

Victoria swallowed around the lump in her throat that wouldn't clear. This was the woman who fought her over every single disciplinary action she'd ever assigned.

"We haven't—"

Sarah turned to Victoria. "I believe the consequence is a three-day service recess, correct?"

"Well, yes but—"

"Do you have a service project in mind? Or can I suggest lunch table clean up and field trash pick-up?"

Victoria clicked the pen she'd not even used closed.

"I don't think—" she tried again, but Sarah turned away from her.

"We understand the rules and we recognize that the rules in place do not account for reasons why events take place. So, rather than her losing instructional time, we would rather you assign her consequence."

The room was hot. No, Victoria was hot, boiling. She pulled at the bottom of her shirt to give her chest more access to the air.

It was a day ago when Sarah had practically cussed her out for assigning a consequence to a kid, and now when it was her kid, she was all rules are rules.

"Tris, can you please wait outside?" Victoria requested.

"Tris, go back to class," Sarah stated.

Victoria stood up. The chair fled from under her and hit the wall. "You do not—" she started.

"Actually, go ask Ms. Mitchell to call Monica. She can come get you."

Tris looked between Victoria and Sarah. Then she got up and left the office.

"Sarah, you cannot come into *my* office—"

Sarah held up her hand, slicing Victoria's sentence off. The gesture made Victoria's heart race, but she closed her mouth.

"I'm going to stop you there. I am not a parent that doesn't understand how this whole thing works. I don't need you or anyone else undoing all of the work that I put into teaching Tris to stand up to bullies or how to survive the real world. This is the school world, and she and I both know the rules and the lessons on how to stop bullies do not align."

"Who do you think you are, coming in here—" Victoria swallowed the rest of her sentence. Remembering their dance of disdain already done, where she'd tripped on her pride and landed on her face.

Victoria looked up at the woman ready for a fight that Victoria didn't want to have.

"Tell Tris she owes no service time." With a shrug, she added. "Like you said, she did what she should have done. The real issue is dealing with the fourth grader using racial slurs."

She smiled as another thought popped into her head. "Next time she needs to go to a teacher before she hits him in the boy boobies."

Sarah's lips curled up at the corners. The smile didn't warm her face, but Victoria felt the room settle around them.

"Thank you," Sarah said. She licked her lips before adding. "Caleb's mom works for DCS. She's in the middle of divorce, so Caled might be... Honestly, I don't care. But Tiffany and I grew up together. You should make that call because I... I may not be able to be professional with the history there. But call her and not Dad. Tiffany will... she's not racist. I know that. Not even one of those fake I'm not racists. Won't stop me from telling her to take her kid back up to the trailer park we came from because he would fit right in."

Sarah's eyes shot up to Victoria. "Sorry. I didn't mean to tell you that. I should go and... uh... take care of things."

Victoria nodded but looked away from the woman who hated her. She listened for the door to click shut before she swallowed the vanilla cookie scent that had come into the office with Sarah. Drank the reminder of home and family until her body felt a little less empty.

19

From behind her desk, Sarah could keep an eye on Tris as she waited for Monica. She needed her friend to talk to the kid because Sarah was too angry. Her blood had reached 214 degrees, and her ears felt like steam was coming out of them.

Never in her life had she wanted to harm a child before. As she watched each piece of grass plucked away, she imagined shoving it down that little shit, Caleb's throat. She wanted revenge and it wasn't okay, but he had forced Tris to defend herself too early. She was still a little girl, and Sarah was so sick of big boys trying to break her family. Even if it was Tiffany's kid. Her first crush, who was on her way to apologize according to Leticia.

Leticia had called Monica for her, so she hadn't bothered to text her best friend who arrived with a wrinkle indented on her forehead and lips cinched shut.

"Hey," Sarah said as she caught sight of Monica about to head into the discipline area waiting room. The heels of Monica's overpriced shoes ceased their clicks against the dingy tile floor as she turned. She twisted from side to side in search of Sarah's voice until she narrowed her eyes at the closet doorway where Sarah sat.

Leaning against the metal doorjamb, Monica looked within the space, not bothering to try and crowd within.

With a furrowed brow, Monica asked, "Is this your office?"

Sarah sighed. "Yeah."

"Did it used to be a closet?"

"Probably."

She tried not to let Monica's disapproval get to her. Tried to remind herself she'd made the best choice for her and Tris by changing majors to social work so she wouldn't have student loans when she graduated. But it didn't stop her shoulders from falling inward.

Tapping her fingers against the door frame, Monica signed. "So... Tris got in a fight."

"A kid called her the n-word, and she hit him in the face with a water bottle."

Monica's arms folded over her chest. The vein in her neck popped out as she growled, "So, why is she being sent home?"

Waving away the warning, Sarah explained, "She wasn't sent home. I asked them to call you to come get her because Victoria and I were... It just wasn't pretty, and I was angry."

Sarah watched Monica's eyes moving from left to right as though she was reading through a list of potential responses. Her tongue ran over her teeth, then her eyes settled back on Sarah's seated form. "So... what's your plan?"

Sarah bit her lip. "I didn't really have one. I just needed to get out of her office, and I had to..."

"Sarah, I have clients coming in at one." Monica's head dropped to the side slightly. The anger of Tris's potential suspension was now redirected at Sarah. "I can't just cancel to stay home and play mommy. That's a you thing, not a me thing. I only said yes to be the emergency contact if you actually had an emergency and you being frustrated with your boss is not an emergency."

Five years prior, Sarah had begged Monica to list her as an emergency contact. Even then, the other woman was annoyed, but Sarah listed her best and only friend first when enrolling Tris in kindergarten. She'd once had the Greysons to fill the remaining spots, but after she had an affair with Greyson's partner's best friend it was safer to avoid them altogether. So, the three remaining friends Sarah didn't have were named out of thin air and their phone numbers were a few digits apart. In all of Tris's years at school, Monica had never been contacted and Sarah hadn't considered the possibility Monica would be pissed about having to come down to the school.

Sarah rubbed her hands over her pants to dry the sweat from them.

"I'm sorry. I wasn't thinking when I had them call you. I will..." Sarah got up and moved the files and papers around, in search of her keys. "... just find my keys. I'll tell my boss... not Victoria. Maria. I'll tell Maria that I need to take Tris home."

"I already came down here," the therapist snapped.

Monica's eyes rose to the ceiling. The way the blonde's hair shook and the cold blue eyes dropped to her made Sarah shrink further into her seat.

"I'm sorry," Sarah said again. "I just reacted because Victoria was arguing with me, and I was so mad at the kid, and I snapped at Victoria even though she wasn't terrible, and it was just so stupid to call you to come down here when I should have just left. Because you're right, this is a me thing. A me problem. None of this is your problem and it never should have been your problem. I just wasn't thinking because I didn't want Tris to see how mad I was because I know she'd try to act like me, so I tried so hard to hold it all together and I'm just sorry. I'm sorry."

When Sarah ran out of breath, Monica asked, "You two are still fighting?"

Sarah's fingers pushed the hair from her face, and she fell back into the chair. "Well, no... I mean I thought I was going to have to fight her, but it was different this time. She was different. Just like she's been different, and I like stopped taking her free food and I did what I shoulda done to begin with, but I got the call, and I was so scared and ready to fight her for Tris."

Monica raised her shoulders in a slight shrug. The frustration at being forced to come to the school seemed to evaporate before Sarah's eyes from her best friend.

"Well, that's good," Monica offered with a half a smile. "Look, I will take the crotch goblin back to your place. Can you get there by 12:30?"

Sarah nodded rapidly. "Yes. I will. I promise"

"Okay." Monica glanced back at where Tris still sat in the chair. "I will try to get her to talk about the fight. But it's time you stopped thinking about getting her into counseling and actually do it. There's a lot she is going through with just your guys' lives and all."

Sarah's chin dropped to her chest. "I know."

Looking back at the kid still covered in dried grass, Sarah sighed. She calculated a minimum of two hours to get it all out of her hair tonight. She added YouTube how to twist hair to her parental list of things to get done.

"I just—" but Sarah stopped the excuse before it had time to finish coming out of her mouth. But then she admitted, "It's so hard trying to balance everything. I'm just so tired of everything being so hard all the time."

"I can talk to this girl I had as an intern last year. She specializes in art therapy with kids. She may be willing to do a school visit and since she is still new, and maybe she won't try to rip you off." Monica looked around the tiny box enclosing Sarah. "I'll even help pay for it."

"I don't need you to do that," Sarah stated. The air returned to her lungs, forcing her shoulders back into place so she could continue holding up the sky.

Monica's lips pursed, but she didn't say a word. They both knew the only reason Tris wasn't already in counseling was because of paying for it.

"I'll figure it out, okay?" Sarah promised. "I got more work at the library so I will be there two nights a week and they gave me 10 hours on weekends."

"Does this mean you're cutting back on clients?"

Sarah shook her head. "No, I have been trying to stack them more into the other five."

Monica shook her head. She shut the door before moving around the desk into Sarah's space. Without asking like she normally did, Monica wrapped her arms around Sarah.

"You are not alone," Monica said.

When the taller woman stood back and looked her best friend over, she let out a displeased breath. Her fingers tugged on the waistband of Sarah's pants. "I'm not sure if you are going to die of starvation, exhaustion, or a heart attack as you try to keep going like you have to support your whole family while they treat you like shit. But you gotta stop."

Sarah shrugged. "I gotta do what I gotta do. The lease is up next month and my rent went up again. The kid grew out of all her fucking clothes again. My mom called and said her meds went up. Sierra wants more money or she won't sign the papers next time."

"Say no," Monica said, wiping the tears sneaking down Sarah's face. "I mean not to the kid's clothes or the rent, but to everyone else. You don't owe any of them anything. Take your sister to court."

"I just can't walk away," Sarah whispered. "But I could legit use some referrals like I would make twice as much as the library so I wouldn't have to be working so much then. I know you're trying to protect me, but please, just trust me to do my job."

"Okay." Monica then added, "I will talk to my friend. And I will talk to a few clients that are all lesbian couples in the mid-life dry spell."

Sarah looked down at the half-completed DCS report on her computer. "Thank you, Monica, for coming. I know this isn't the life you wanted."

Monica hummed as she tucked her hair back behind Sarah's ear. "What started the fight?"

"A bully and a ball. Ask her about what happens to bully's boy boobies," Sarah said quietly as she moved around her desk until the door was reopened to the rest of the world.

"Auntie Monica," Tris cried out. She jumped to her feet when Monica clicked her way back into the hallway. She took the short distance at a run, plowing into the blonde. Her arms wrapped around the woman.

"Hey, goblin," Monica stated. She leaned into the hug and tucked the grass-filled head under her chin.

"I got in a fight," Tris half whispered.

"I heard," Monica stated.

Tris leaned back but still clung to Monica. "Are you mad at me?" she asked.

"No." Monica's finger cradled the girl's chin. "But we are going to sit down when we get back to your house. We are going to talk about what happened."

Tris's chin dropped to her chest and her head pressed back against the woman. "Okay."

The door that had been closed since Sarah had walked out of it opened. Victoria stood in the doorway, not giving the family even a glance. Her lips were set in a straight line, as she glared at her assistant. "Ms. Mitchel, I said I needed that phone number immediately. What is the problem?"

Leticia stared at Victoria, her mouth slightly open. Then her eyes dropped to the desk as she scanned over the surface. She ripped a sticky note from its pad and held it out to Victoria. "I thought you were still on the phone, and I didn't want to—"

Victoria ripped the small note from the woman's outstretched hand. "Doesn't matter if I'm on the phone. When I say I need something immediately, it means I need it immediately."

Sarah watched Monica, studying the interaction. She still cradled the girl's head in her arms, but all attention was on her former client. The blue eyes glanced at Sarah, then back to the woman in a suit and loafers.

Victoria opened her mouth again, but her red-rimmed eyes landed on Monica, then Sarah. The anger previously boiling in the woman slowed to a simmer.

"Oh," Victoria said. Then, softly she said, "Hello."

Sarah watched Monica set her face in a clinical mask of indifference, before she offered a simple, "Hello."

They stood in the office as a cricket crawled across the cold cement floor. Tris didn't release Monica until Victoria silently returned to her office.

"She really is a different person," Monica said quietly to Sarah.

Monica turned to Sarah. "Maybe have some lunch and apologize for being a crazy mama bear. I'll talk to this ninja and we will come up with some better strategies for dealing with our anger."

Sarah nodded. Then she took the kid in her arms and hugged her tightly. She tried not to let it bother her when Tris immediately tried to wiggle out of her embrace.

"Be good," she reminded Tris, earning her an eye roll instead of a response.

When Monica and Tris were gone, Sarah tapped lightly on Victoria's door. She watched the kindergarten lunch recess from the window behind Leticia's head. Victoria didn't answer but it wasn't like there was another exit. Sarah glanced through the somewhat dark window and noticed the phone was not connected. So, Sarah took a play from the admin's book and walked into the room.

"Excuse you," Victoria bit as her hands wiped at her face. The red-rimmed brown eyes rose from the statement Victoria had carefully scripted out. Sarah could see Tris's name at the top. Sarah licked her lips and looked at the woman.

"Let's go eat," Sarah said.

The break room was only slightly bigger than Sarah's office. A vending machine, scratched refrigerator, dented microwave, and table for five were the only things in the room, but it offered Sarah and Victoria a space that wasn't owned by one or the other.

Victoria sat at the table flipping her salad around her plate with her fork. She hadn't said anything after Sarah had mumbled a weak apology. Her cheeks weren't flushed anymore, and the puffiness of her eyes had faded.

"I was so angry," Sarah said.

She also had been unable to enjoy the leftover spaghetti. Not that there was anything to enjoy about it. The dilapidated microwave had only managed to harden the edges of the noodles, while the center remained ice cold. She missed the real food Victoria created in her spacious kitchen, but Monica had been right. She should never have accepted the first meal. If not for leading Victoria on, then for giving her body a glimpse of how life was supposed to be.

"I was trying to make you proud of me." Victoria set her fork down, staring at the rabbit food before her. "I thought, I would handle this one on my own and you would see that I am not incompetent."

"I wasn't mad at you. I'm not mad at you. I just... I couldn't go punch a kid for hurting her, but I wanted to, so I punched the air with my words," Sarah confessed.

A smile spread up Victoria's face. "I almost puked on a kid who ate a booger today. I'm honestly not sure which is worse."

Sarah let her chest rumble with a burst of soft laughter.

"Why didn't you tell me you had a daughter?" Victoria asked.

Sarah's skin itched as Victoria's normally warm eyes stared her down. She tugged at the neck of her sweater, and said, "I mean, I wasn't keeping her a secret or anything. I just... I never planned on, you know, you knowing me."

With a soft nod, Victoria stared at her fork. She pointed at the container of spaghetti in front of Sarah. "Did you do, like, a giant meal prep, this weekend?"

Sarah swirled the crunchy spaghetti on her fork once more but set it down again. She chewed on the words, carefully testing the pH balance of each, until she was confident that they would have the same absorption rate as water. She stroked the words until they were smooth so Victoria wouldn't be cut by any of them.

"I tried. Definitely not as good as yours but... I... I don't know how to handle people doing things for me," Sarah whispered. "So, I mean, I'm the one that takes care of people, and you were so kind to make me food. But over break, I realized I was taking advantage of your kindness when I emptied all our leftovers."

"I actually enjoyed cooking for more than one," Victoria said to the leaf on her fork. "I can't justify cooking a whole meal for just me, so I am left doing stuff like eating salad. And I hate salad."

Sarah smiled, waving her ice-cold spaghetti crisp in Victoria's direction "I'll trade you. I love salad."

Victoria's lips curled up over her teeth. She held up the fork of greens once more. "Um... how about we trash both these and Uber Eats something."

Staring at the spaghetti she wouldn't eat, Sarah knew ordering food wasn't an option. She fixed the smile on her face. "It's okay. I'm not really hungry. I just didn't want you to think I'm mad at you and I wanted to say I'm sorry."

The smile fell from Victoria's face, but she tried to force another in its place. "Thank you."

20

The trail up Camelback Mountain was busier than Victoria had expected for a Sunday morning. She sucked water from the straw of her Camelback strapped to her back, the irony not missed when she first started hiking this particular trail. One foot after the other, she rose above the traffic and never-ending construction.

She passed the small packs of gray- and white-haired humans who gathered together on the casual stroll up the path. As far as she was concerned, this particular trail was a path toward self-punishment. Victoria's internal commentator pointed out a variety of better trails for strolling, which provided more aesthetic landscapes.

At the peak of a particularly steep section, Victoria's progress was slowed by two women around her age. The stream of downward hikers made it impossible to pass, forcing her to follow the women.

Despite Victoria's attempt at self-control, her eyes traced the curves of the woman's honeycomb leggings until they landed on the rainbow tattoo wrapped around her ankle. She smiled at the silent statement.

Getting a tattoo was one of the things she hadn't done on the list of sinful acts when she severed ties to the faith that had shrouded her in community and self-hate.

As her mind wandered between a rainbow-colored butterfly and a dandelion, her feet brought her practically to the heels of the friends.

"So, she didn't tell you she used to be married to a man?" the stout, question-mark-figured woman asked.

Victoria's head abruptly swung upward. Even though her pace had slowed upon reaching them, Victoria's heart pounded against her chest as though she had jogged the majority of the trail.

The tattooed woman sighed. Her fingers ran over the closely cropped undercut.

"No. I mean we were dating for like a month and that is something you tell someone," the tattooed woman stated.

Victoria bit into the silicone mouthpiece connected to the bladder in her backpack, almost choking when the water sprouted into her unexpecting mouth. Recovering without being noticed, she looked out over the Hotwheel-sized cars moving along the city playmat below them. But her ears remained tuned to the frequency of their conversation.

"Well, at least you won't have to put much effort in," the heavier-set woman offered. "I mean, her expectations are probably so low. But like how do you not know you're gay? Or is she bi? You have to get out if she'd bi."

"She said she's not bi."

Victoria noticed an opening to pass. However, she committed to the backseat of their conversation.

"I just don't get how she didn't figure out she'd gay until she was thirty," the short woman stated. "I mean like old women, maybe. They got married right out of high school. But in your thirties... there were already gay people on TV. Like Ellen came out when we were like kids."

Victoria's stomach twisted, wrapping around itself until it tightened into a knot. She hadn't known who Ellen was until she was in her late twenties.

"I don't know. It's just like weird now, you know?"

Victoria knew.

"I don't even want to get to the sex thing. We haven't gone there yet, but she's not going to know how to strap up or anything, which means I'm going to have to be a top and it's just so much work trying to teach a babygay how to be gay. I just wasn't looking for *that* type of relationship at this point in my life."

The breath in Victoria's chest caught under the knot that had migrated to her throat. Her legs shook in protest with each step she took with them.

"So, end it," fell like the blade of a guillotine from the woman's lips.

"I don't want to hurt her."

"You also don't want to have shitty sex for the next year or two while she figures out what we learned in college."

The statement shook the ground below Victoria's sneakers. The complex sentence disintegrated the foundation of the path like a landslide, smashing into Victoria as she stumbled over the loose rocks on the trail. Her worn Nikes slid out from under her. She grabbed the railing, stopping herself from crashing into the ground.

The women in front of her turned quickly to her aide. The one with tattoos took hold of Victoria's free arm and hoisted her back to her feet. "Are you okay?" she asked.

Victoria exhaled deeply. Her feet once more firmly against the well-beaten path. She wiped the sweat from her forehead with the back of her hand. "Sorry. I just lost my footing."

As the brown eyes ran up and down her body, Victoria wrapped her arm around her middle. "You didn't twist your ankle or anything right?"

Victoria shook her head and looked at her shoe. "No. Just hit some loose dirt I think. I'm fine, really. I think I will just head back down."

"Okay," the other woman said. Then added, "Just be careful. Downhill is way more slippery."

"Okay." Then Victoria added, "Thanks."

Just as the women turned back around, an opening presented itself to Victoria in the opposite direction. As she followed the line of people descending from the path, she considered what she was actually thanking the women for. Was she grateful that they cared enough to try and look out for her? Or was she thanking them for verifying all her fears about trying to date?

When she was safe in her vehicle, Victoria flipped the visor down and looked at her reflection. She prodded the crow's feet at the corners of her eyes, then pressed the wiry gray hairs standing proud back into her sweaty hair. Nothing in her reflection could heal the bruises the hikers' words caused.

She couldn't change the fact that she had been married before. But with a little help, she could be sure that no woman doubted her ability to please them.

Her fingers hit the screen as she sent a text to Sarah: "I will pay you double hourly the rate if you will come over tonight at 6. I need your help and there is no one else that I can ask."

Then she sent, "Please."

Then, "I'll triple it."

21

Relief washed over her at the fact she'd checked her lipstick at the last light before pulling into the parking lot. For some odd reason, she thought arriving twenty minutes early to park far enough away from the gate that Zoe wouldn't see her car would be enough. However, Zoe was already standing in the parking lot alongside a red BMW.

'Of course, she's a lawyer and would drive a BMW,' Sarah told herself. She swallowed the inferiority creeping up her throat. She parked the older Civic next to the pristine car.

Zoe lifted her sharp jaw as Sarah's tires ceased crunching the gravel before her. A lizard nearly caused Sarah to choke on her own heart as she leaped from the car. When she looked up at the woman's broad smile Sarah felt like a high schooler trying out for the pros.

"Hey," Zoe said with a raise of her hand over the roof of Sarah's car. She made her way around the Civic and held out the pre-agreed-upon beverage to Sarah.

Condensation coated Sarah's hand, but she held the drink tightly as Zoe and her did an awkward dance avoiding a cheek kiss, leaning into a side hug that also ended in a handshake. Sarah hoped the woman was just as nervous as her because she didn't want this to be another sign she failed to read.

"Thank you," Sarah said. Taking a tentative sip of the drink, she willed the coffee to settle her nerves.

"So, I have never actually been here," Zoe confessed.

Sarah tucked her overgrown bangs behind her ear. "Me either."

"I looked it up and everyone says it's really pretty."

"Cool," Sarah said. She smiled and hoped the red lipstick hadn't spread to her teeth.

"Oh, hold up," Zoe cried out. Wide-eyed, she looked to her hands, then to the shiny car. Returning to her car, and coming back with a large duffle-like bag, Zoe smiled widely. "As promised. My mom made an entire tray. She even let me chop the onions! The lid thing by the way doesn't work if it doesn't have a vent hole."

After a snicker, Sarah said, "She really didn't have to."

With a pull on the back of her neck, Zoe confessed, "She is hoping her cooking will make up for my lack of social grace. That's what she said at least."

Sarah took the tray, almost dropping it under the weight she hadn't expected. With a soft chuckle, she said, "You seem more graceful than me at least."

"Remember that when I trip on air," Zoe offered. Her nose scrunched up as she shrugged.

Sarah laughed. The fear weighing her down gradually lifted with a soft breeze.

They strolled through the park with their iced beverages. It wasn't what everyone made it out to be so the trip was short. A sit-down at a coffee shop probably would have lasted longer. After maybe thirty minutes of looking at a variety of spikey plants, they made their way back to the cars. The cups of ice were disposed of in the trash can at the entrance.

"So, I won't lie, someone said this was a romantic place to take a date, but all the prickly cacti are really not screaming love me," Zoe stated. She shoved her hands in her pockets. "You should probably know that this is the first date I have been on since college. So, I searched for cool places and for some reason this was on the top of the list."

Sarah looked at two saguaro cacti leaning against each other. Their arms had intertwined over the centuries alongside each other.

"Well... maybe you're supposed to look at them and admire their ability to survive. They may not want a hug, but they'll get through the hard times. And I guess it could be more symbolic of 'I'm in it for the long haul, not just the moment.'"

When Sarah turned from the cacti to the woman, she found Zoe staring at her like a crucial piece of evidence for making her latest case.

"What?" Sarah asked, looking down at her shoes.

Zoe's mouth opened, then shut. She seemed to be at a loss for words, until she whispered, "That was just... beautiful."

The sun wasn't hot enough to justify the heat rushing over Sarah's face.

Stepping into Sarah's bubble, Zoe tucked a lock of hair behind Sarah's ear. The smooth thumb from the unlabored hand stroked Sarah's flushed cheek. "You're beautiful."

They stared at each other for a few moments. A tense silence building. Sarah felt the waves of Zoe's nervous energy slapping against her until the woman took a step back instead of forward.

"I feel like I need to talk about the other night," Zoe started. "When we were on the phone... and your daughter asked if I wanted kids."

The beating of Sarah's heart seemed to flat line. She felt her diaphragm give way as her stomach dropped.

"Okay," she whispered.

Sarah watched as Zoe's fingers rubbed against her thumbs. The confidence boiling in the attorney seemed to simmer.

"So...I knew you had a daughter, and I guess... I never really put into place that going on a date with you meant that the future wasn't a matter of if there would be kids but when. I guess... I had blocked it out the zillion times my mom asked about her future granddaughter this week when I told her she finally had to make you food."

"So, is that something you want? Because this is the fake date," Sarah said, offering the woman a quick way out. She lied as she added, "No feelings will be hurt if it is not something you want."

Her feelings would be hurt. Not because the woman wasn't ready for kids. Sarah could accept that. They'd be hurt because the woman had waited until after the fake date to say so, which only meant she wasn't impressed with Sarah.

Zoe's eyes rose from the ground. "I never saw myself as a parent. I think it was like something I thought I would do, you know? In the future, but I know that it's your reality."

"It is," Sarah said with a nod. "Tris is my life. Not the life I imagined, but I wouldn't trade it. So, it's a package deal. You can't have one without the other."

"You're not a possession to be had," Zoe stated. She reached forward and took Sarah's hand. "I want to make that clear. As far as what I want, I... I want to get to know you. But I want us to take our time with that... stuff. I'm really not sure what you would expect from me and I'm not looking to rush into anything."

"I get what you are saying," Sarah promised. "This is why I don't date honestly. Hell, I wasn't even looking to meet someone. Tris is the one that made me a dating profile and I don't think she understands what any of this would mean. She's only ever seen me date once and that ended abruptly and badly. She was all excited because I think that she thought she was getting a new friend who has a debit card. But I won't lie and say that the phone call definitely made it so she is going to be a little more protective and a little less thrilled about you."

Zoe's chin dropped. With a deep exhale, she said, "I deserve that. I mean, I'm an adult and I can't stand the idea of my mom dating, which she totally set up her own profile at the same time she set up mine and she actually found you first."

Sarah laughed. "She is a beautiful woman, but I am glad I'm here with you and not her."

"Me too," Zoe said. "Even if your kid and my mom were the ones that made it happen."

With a deep exhale, Sarah put her cards on the figurative table. "I have been a single parent from the beginning. The last time I dated, it was a mistake. And

I let the woman get too close and involved too fast. Tris didn't like her, but she put on a good show. The thing was when I was with her, I was still a single parent, and with that comes stuff like not being able to do the normal dating stuff... not to mention I work two jobs, so I don't have a lot of time as it is. So, if I am going to do this, it can't be a waste of my kid's time. That's who is losing when I'm out with someone who is just looking for a good time. I mean, I am not above a good time but that isn't what I think you want and if I'm being honest, I don't really want that either. But in the future, I don't want to keep being a single parent if I'm with someone. I need someone that actually wants me and the kid."

"Yeah, I get that," Zoe said. "I don't want that for you either. I just... I need to take things slow."

"Agreed."

Zoe looked around the empty parking lot, before returning her gaze to Sarah.

"Can I ask, where's your sister?"

"Still on the street."

"And your parents?"

Sarah wrapped her arms around her body. Giving herself the hug her creators had never bestowed.

"I... I never knew my father and my mother is not in our lives."

"So... it's just you two?"

"Yep." Sarah let the 'p' pop with the word. Then she nodded to herself. "And we are good that way. Don't feel obligated or think that I need rescuing or anything. I enjoy talking with you and this has been fun. I would be happy to do a real date if it's something you still want, but please know that after that you're going to have to meet meet my kid."

She searched Zoe's face for any reluctance. When she couldn't see through the lawyer's cool mask, she extrapolated.

"I can't just date you on the side and I need to be pretty upfront with the reality that I honestly have no interest in having more kids. I have lived through diapers and tantrums, and I am entering the world of preteen years. So please... before you ask me out, I need you to *really* think about what you want and if you want babies or are just not ready for potentially having an instant family, then you don't have to call me... okay?"

"Okay," Zoe promised.

"Okay," Sarah echoed.

The conversation was stalled when Sarah's phone buzzed. She shrugged and said, "And part of being a parent is checking my phone, even though it's rude on a date."

"No, I get it," Zoe said. Her fingers had found their way into her back pockets as she shifted her weight back and forth.

Sarah read through the text she'd received from Victoria twice. Her mind immediately went to the beeping M-Power box reminding her that morning she only had less than $10 of electricity before she had to refill the card or spend another evening playing Uno by candlelight to disguise how poor they were.

"I'm sorry," Sarah whispered. "My boss has some kind of emergency. I just need a minute."

Zoe nodded as Sarah tapped at the screen. She sent Victoria a text telling her she needed to check her calendar and to give her a minute.

She finished the message and shoved the phone in her back pocket. With a forced smile, she said, "I guess, just think about it."

"Okay." Zoe's feet shifted from side to side. "Do you think... uh... could I maybe... give you like a hug?"

Slowly, Sarah nodded and stepped forward.

She felt the woman inhale as Zoe held her close. Closer than Monica would ever dare, and a part of her hoped Zoe would call. If not tonight, then maybe in a few days when she had time to think.

When the hug ended, they parted ways. Her phone was out of her pocket as soon as she turned on the car.

She looked at Victoria's message again. Triple her fee was something she couldn't turn down. With that kind of money, the electricity would stay on and she could put some away for the Lego set Tris had run her fingers over every time they visited Walmart. With the kid's birthday in just a few weeks, Victoria's money would maybe make it so Monica wasn't the one to make her kid smile the brightest this year.

She looked at the clock. She had to pick Tris up from the Girl Scout sleepover and feed her. There was no way she could get everything done in time to meet with Victoria tonight.

She sent Victoria a text. "I can do tomorrow at seven."

22

With her short hair wrapped in a messy knot atop her head, Victoria threw open the front door when she heard the car alarm chirp. She'd foregone the formal attire and chosen to stay in her gym clothes. This was a decision she regretted now because Sarah looked how she had last time. And Victoria felt the need to tug her shirt from a curve it was clinging too tightly to.

Sarah pushed the suitcase up the drive under the dim streetlamps. Her white button was tucked into her black slacks. Victoria considered if her neighbors thought she was dating a flight attendant, then she realized that was stupid because she rarely saw anyone outside, another reminder that Scottsdale was nothing like Salt Lake.

"You came," Victoria said, not sure why she'd feared Sarah would leave her hanging.

Victoria stepped within so Sarah could run her usual check. She fought back the smile when Sarah shut it behind her without a second glance at the door.

"I feel like I need to tell you I will be taking your money this time," Sarah stated formally. She twisted her hair some, pulling it over her shoulder until the small burn Victoria noticed was hidden.

Victoria followed Sarah to the doorway of the living room. Watched as the woman laid the suitcase gently down.

"So, what are we working on tonight?" Sarah asked as she squatted over the still-closed case.

"Pleasing other women," Victoria spit out quickly. "I... uh... got a handle on what I need to do to... you know. I need to know what to do to someone else. How to make women... uh... climax."

"Women?" Sarah's eyebrows rose pulling the corners of her lips with them. "As in plural?"

Victoria tugged at her t-shirt. Her head fell back, and she noticed the start of a spider web between the ceiling and wall.

"More like women in general," she clarified, unable to look at Sarah.

The suitcase's zipper growled in protest.

"Would you like to do book work only or do you want resources also?" Sarah asked. She ran her fingers over the plastic notebook filled with dividers."

"Hourly," Victoria stated. "Whatever makes it so you feel like you... as you say, properly fucked me over."

Sarah looked up slowly. Her eyes didn't focus on anything in particular, but she shifted the hair from in front of her ear looking to be listening for something. Slowly, she asked, "Is someone else here? Like someone to practice with?"

Victoria shifted her weight. Then she ran her hands over her face.

"No. I just don't know how long it's going to take, and I want to make sure it's worth your time this time."

Sarah licked her lips. "Book work and resources then, which is $50 normally so triple that is $150. And I scheduled you last, so I don't have any more clients tonight. No matter, we'll still be done in time for me to be home at a reasonable hour and $150 should make you feel like you got fucked, I know I would feel that way."

"I forgot about Tris." Victoria shook her head. "I forgot it's Sunday and a school night. I'm sorry. We can... if you want to do this next weekend, then it won't be a school night."

"Victoria, this is your scheduled appointment. I scheduled you purposefully." Sarah looked down at the case. Then she gazed back up at Victoria.

"How about you go pour yourself a glass of wine and take as much time as you need? When you are ready, we will get started."

"Okay." Victoria glanced around the room. "Would you like a glass? I know last time I didn't ask."

Sarah stood up with two black cylinders in her hands. "Would you feel more comfortable if I drank one with you?"

Staring at the floor, Victoria wondered if there was enough wine in the world to make this less awkward. She huffed out a breath. "This isn't how you act at work, so why are you so formal now?"

Fingers ran over the candle wax within the case. Quietly, Sarah said, "Let's play twenty questions after you get us each a glass of wine."

Victoria didn't trust herself not to respond like a fumbling babygay, saying something stupid, so she walked to the kitchen. She sniffed the Merlot before pouring the two glasses full.

"May I use your restroom?" Sarah called from the hallway.

"Yeah, it's the door just across from you."

She raised the bottle to the light, trying to think of what she could ask Sarah. There was less than a glass left, so she tipped the bottle to her lips and downed the remainder of its contents. Twenty questions wasn't nearly enough. She had thousands of questions that she wanted to ask the woman, wondering how much she could get away with for $150.

With both glasses in hand, Victoria made her way back to the living room where the candles had been brought to life. The single flames brightened the space as the cinnamon apples and vanilla wrapped her in a warm familiar embrace.

After months of trying out different scents, Sarah had made her house smell like home. The tension in her shoulders melted away and she wondered if Sarah burned candles in her own home. That could be a question: what scents make Sarah feel like she's home?

She turned when the door to the bathroom opened, her mouth parting as her tongue went dry.

The blouse and slacks that clung to Sarah's narrow frame were replaced with a pair of low-cut jeans and a faded Jimmy Eat World T-shirt. Sarah carded her fingers through the chestnut locks, hanging freely for once. The straight mane hung well past her shoulders, meeting the non-existent curve of her waist.

"You changed," Victoria whispered.

She held out the wine glass to Sarah and took a long drink before she said something else obvious like, 'Your hair is down.' Her eyes ran over the version of the woman she'd wished she'd met through any other means than Dr. Rose.

Sarah shrugged, then reached for the glass. "You wanted a less formal coach."

"I didn't mean to make you change your clothes."

"It's okay." Sarah held up the business attire. "These make me feel like a librarian."

"You make for a very attractive librarian," Victoria confessed.

Victoria heard a slight chuckle from Sarah as the woman tossed the clothes atop the still-open suitcase. It was so natural and reminded Victoria of the chaos within the woman's office.

Moving to the couch, they sat against opposite ends. Sarah pushed herself into the corner of one side and tucked a leg under the other.

"This is a great couch," Sarah praised. Her body sunk into the cushion and her head fell back momentarily.

"One day I'm gonna buy a couch as smooshy as this," Sarah whispered, and Victoria wasn't sure if the comment was for Sarah or her.

Sarah raised the glass to her lips and sipped, then set it alongside the candle.

Running her fingers through her hair once more, Sarah wiggled in the seat. Once settled, she looked over at Victoria's hunched body.

"So, to answer your earlier question: I am always to the point in sessions. I don't like people having to guess what I mean." Sarah held up a finger. "The formality makes dealing with my more questionable and even sometimes sleazy clients easier."

Victoria kicked her lips. "Do you get a lot of those?"

Sarah picked up her glass and took a longer drink this time. She sucked her teeth, before shrugging. "Eh. I work a lot with couples and the heterosexual men often think that I am a dominatrix. The formal librarian look shuts that down some, but even that is fetishized. But let's be real, a part of why I'm able to do this is because I use that fetish or pheromone lotion to entice them into being prepared for the session."

After another drink, Sarah pressed her fingers to her lips. She thought for a moment, tapping the digit against her lips.

"Dr. Rose typically warns me in advance and tries to avoid referring anyone that would make me uncomfortable." Sarah paused, then looked away. "A couple months before your first session there was this guy that set up a session for him and his wife. He... his wife wasn't there and even though I checked the door before I went in, he got the upper hand. I have a strict check-in system though. So, when I missed the check-in, Dr. Rose contacted the police."

Victoria's eyes shot open. She attempted to swallow the lump in her throat, but nothing seemed to clear it, even the wine.

"Were you hurt?"

Sarah sucked her teeth.

"I... I was lucky, honestly. He had... uh... long-term plans rather than... more immediate impulse issues," Sarah explained. "I ended up with a mild concussion from where he hit me over the head, but he didn't have time to do what you are thinking."

"What happened to him?"

"He pled guilty to assault and kidnapping. It's not like he could claim innocence when the police found me tied up in his closet." Sarah's face smooshed into a look of disgust. "I really hate closets. Always have."

"I'm sorry you had to go through that." Victoria ran her finger over the rim of her glass. "Does it ever make you want to, you know, like stop doing... this?"

"Well, I never wanted to do this per se nut you've met the kid," Sarah stated. "She's expensive, so when Monica... I mean, Dr. Rose first asked me to help a few of her clients out, it was a simple solution to making some extra money. I think... really it was her way of helping me get on my feet because I had graduated and lost my public housing with my first job. We were about to head back to the shelter because I couldn't just keep staying in the place we were living. I mean, the woman who rented me the place wouldn't have minded, but... I didn't want to owe her. So, we were going to have to go back to a shelter. Turns out though, my services helped couples recommend her services and we both ended up content with the situation."

At the mention of the therapist, Victoria's mind began to wander about the plausibility of her sessions not being as confidential as she had originally thought. She wondered how much of her life Sarah already knew about. Then a thought crept into the forefront of her mind.

"Are you two...?"

Sarah's brows scrunched in the middle. Then air rushed her lips with the remainder of Victoria's question, "...in a relationship?"

Victoria nodded.

This time Sarah actually laughed. "Yeah, that's a negative. Friends, yes." She took another drink.

"So... are you gay?" Victoria asked, realizing that she'd just assumed Sarah's sexuality when she'd said last time she'd done the dancing, women, and booze.

"No."

Guilt rose in Victoria's throat at the role she'd assigned Sarah in her mind. That was until Sarah gestured to her boobs.

"I'm a female, like you. Therefore, I am a lesbian. Gay refers to men that like other men."

"I didn't mean it like that," Victoria said with an eye roll. She swallowed a large drink. The nutty tones coaxed free the knot in her gut.

Sarah sat up, her body leaning its weight on her knees. She waited for Victoria to look up from her similar position.

"I'm just going to ask this... so we can address it if needed. Was your previous relationship... abusive?"

Victoria ran her finger over the top of the glass as she pictured her ex-husband's face when she told him she was gay. She took a deep breath, and then said, "No."

The glass provided her a momentary shield as she let the memory replay of his slumped shoulders, and the betrayal etched in his brow.

"Michael was... oblivious to anything but himself and the church." She took a sip of wine. "We were both raised LDS with the typical Mormon expectations. We got married in the temple when he returned from his mission like we were supposed to. Lived a pretty boring life. Kids.... they weren't a possibility because I had a very bad case of endometriosis that ended in me having a hysterectomy when I was twenty-four. And I thought it was how it was supposed to be. But he was never abusive or cruel. Just only knew what he knew and didn't care to know more."

Sarah kicked her lips. "What changed?"

Victoria took a deep breath. "It's a very lame story."

"Coming out stories are never lame," Sarah countered.

"I thought twenty questions meant I got to ask you the questions."

"Twenty questions are a back and forth. You ask, then I ask. Fair is fair. Which is rule one about pleasing a woman. You cum, then she cums, or vice-versa. I mean, it's not exactly an even score, but you always return the favor."

Sarah reached her foot across the couch and poked Victoria with her big toe. "Stop stalling. Tell me when the gay panic set in."

"I was looking at a woman in a coffee shop with her rainbow shirt and my stomach fluttered." Victoria glanced over at Sarah. "Literally, like, my tummy got butterflies at this woman with her rainbow lanyard and her fingers holding the hand of the girl next to her. I couldn't focus on the conversation my sisters were having, and it was just like I'm gay."

Victoria leaned back. Opened herself up to Sarah's judgment.

"I left my marriage because my stomach did like flips." She held up her hand. "It was good for him because he is now able to marry someone to give him the kids I couldn't, and I'm here and I know... I know what I didn't know before."

"But you left, like, everything?" Sarah asked.

With a nod, Victoria said, "Yeah. I left my family that was going to disown me anyway. And I moved here. Came where no one knew me or could talk about me."

Sarah sipped her wine quietly.

Glancing over at the woman, Victoria asked, "What about you? Ever married?"

Sarah shook her head, then verbally responded, "No. I had one long-term relationship and well... ever heard the song "Stay" by Sugarland?"

"Yes."

"That about sums it up." Sarah shrugged. "She told me she was finalizing her divorce, and she laid it on thick. We... we worked together, and she was cool and stable and confident until she was hurt and vulnerable and I felt so important. Like someone wanted me and would be there with me."

Sarah wiped her eyes before the welling tears could fall. "Then she adopted a kid with her wife and told me she was sorry via text. Afterward, she told our conservative boss I was a prostitute and showed him a mugshot of my twin sister, so he fired me. Which really meant he told me to resign, or he would make it a governing board problem and I wouldn't be able to find another job."

Victoria stared at the coffee table. "Was she your boss?"

"Yep. The AP of discipline," Sarah whispered. "So, I guess you understand now... why. And the contract and why I lied."

The clock's ticking slowed. Victoria's mind played over the fear in Sarah's eyes that first day. The way the woman wouldn't tell her anything personal and constantly kept her away. The betrayal Victoria had felt was linked to her wants and desires. She'd never considered Sarah in any of it.

"Dr. Rose said I need to put myself out there," Victoria whispered. "Which is terrifying."

She glanced over at Sarah who was mid-eye roll. The coach scrunched her face into an annoyed grimace. "She tells me the same thing. And since you're not her client anymore, you should know she is also just as single and hasn't been on a date in at least a year so take what she says with a grain of salt."

Wine rippled through Victoria's veins as she raised her eyebrow at the woman who swallowed a large gulp of wine.

"So, you're single too."

Sarah set her glass down. The playful energy radiating from the brunette seemed to suck away from Victoria, leaving her floating in a vacuum as the steady green eyes stared at her. Victoria felt like she'd just fucked around and found out in a single sentence.

"I wasn't... I just..." Victoria stammered.

Sarah's stare turned into a smile that spread wickedly up her cheeks to her eyes. "Calm your tits."

"Calm my tits?" Victoria choked on the words as they came out. Her eyes fell, fearing her arousal was poking through her top.

With the glass now half empty, Sarah swirled the maroon liquid. With a slight wrinkle across her brow, Sarah said, "My formality made you uncomfortable, so yes, calm your tits."

The candid vulgarity of the phrase made Victoria smile. She took a deep breath, her body melding into the cushions.

"I am more comfortable with this version of you," Victoria stated.

"Good. What's your next question?"

Victoria calculated the number of hours Sarah could have charged her but didn't. She decided it wasn't fair to the woman or her daughter to keep dragging the session out.

"So... is there a way to get a girl to orgasm?"

Sarah nodded. Then with that blast smirk said, "Many ways."

"Okay, but is there one that works the best?"

Sarah pressed a finger to each place as she said, "Lips, throat, tits, hip, penetrate, clit."

Then she added, "Some women want a strap, but they'll ask for that. You should probably have one though. Also, you want a bullet that you can use because some women can't get off without it because of too much self-care. They make this rose thing also that is more suction."

The wine running from the glass to Victoria's mouth sprayed out over the coffee table. Her teeth hit the edge of the glass as she gagged.

A warm hand patted her back through the hacking.

"You good?" Sarah asked when Victoria's face was fully red and her lungs burned.

Victoria's eyes watered and she prayed that her mascara wasn't running. She wiped her lips and cleared her throat. "So... sorry," she sputtered. "That's like the second time I've heard that term this weekend."

"You cheating on me?" Sarah asked, withdrawing the contact.

Victoria looked over at the woman and down at her glass. It was practically empty, but there was no way she was drunk enough to have started a relationship with Sarah without realizing it. But she remembered the woman had said her last lover had cheated on her, so maybe this is what the lesbians meant when they talked about U-hauling.

"I would never..." but the words didn't sound right, so she stopped mid-sentence.

Victoria looked at the glass again, then back at Sarah staring at her so intently.

"I mean I didn't realize we were..." However, that too sounded stupid.

Huffing out a breath, Victoria fixed her face and looked honestly into the woman's eyes. "I wouldn't cheat on someone like you." Then added, "Ever."

Sarah's flat face broke into a puzzled smile.

"I meant with another coach. Though I don't think Monica actually has another coach to refer you to, but that's good you don't cheat."

Victoria closed her eyes. She'd made a fool of herself. Again.

Sarah tucked her hair behind her ear. "What did you mean, though? Someone like me?"

Victoria bit her lip, then shook her head. She couldn't look at the other woman.

"You have to know you're beautiful," Victoria whispered. "Passionate. So... so smart about so many things. And you fight like a warrior for people. The kids... they just open up to you."

She looked at Sarah. "You're special. Like no one I've ever met."

The smirk had vanished from the woman's face. Her eyes were scanning the room as though she'd never been paid a compliment before.

"I wasn't expecting that," Sarah finally replied.

Tossing all caution to the wind, Victoria said, "Well it's true. And this is stupid, but I wish I had never scheduled these appointments with you."

"Because you found out I'm gay and we would have met at work," Sarah summarized.

"A lesbian" Victoria corrected. "And the work thing... never would have worked out. We both know that everyone at work hates me and if I hadn't already been trying to prove to you I was someone worth looking at, I probably would haven't listened as well, if I'm, like, being honest."

She wasn't sure why she'd expected Sarah to smile or laugh, but when it didn't come, she was back to studying the woman who looked so far way yet was so close.

"I overheard Leticia telling the new counselor to stay out of my way if she doesn't want to be treated like a dog," she admitted.

When the green eyes looked up at Victoria, the breath in Victoria's lungs caught. The confidence that sparkled in the woman's eyes had vanished, and the honest version of work Sarah stared back at her.

Sarah's lower lip popped out from between her teeth. "So, I appreciate that you find me attractive, but I'm not the person you are building me up to be in your head."

"Are any of us who other people see?" Victoria asked. "Like, I don't even know why I'm doing this. No one is going to date me."

"Why do you say that?"

Victoria ran her hands over her face.

"I overheard two lesbians talking yesterday while I was hiking Camelback Mountain. They were talking about not wanting to date women who were previously married to men. One said a person like me wouldn't even know how to strap up. And I am just terrible at trying to talk to a woman. I exchanged numbers with this girl, and she never called me, so clearly after she left, she realized that was a mistake."

Sarah scooched forward on the couch. The coach returned to the room as the glimpse of the woman disappeared.

"Okay, so the strap thing is easy." Sarah took Victoria's hand. "It's a harness that you attach a dildo to. You can purchase one at the adult toy store, Fascinations or Castle. Or you can buy them online at Adam and Eve. Amazon even sells them. And I have several if you want to see it. And I'm sure your mom friend with the drawer filled would even go with you to the store."

"So, you can teach me what strapping you means?"

"Yes, in tonight's lesson, I'll show you how to put it on and a brief tutorial on how to use it. However, before I pull it out, I need you to hear what else I have to say."

Victoria closed her eyes and nodded.

"Please look at me."

It took a minute that felt like a year for Victoria to look at Sarah.

"Victoria, you are beautiful. You do that thing with your eyebrows that is going to drive women crazy. But like I said earlier, you are fascinated by a version of me that you have built in your head. I have a lot of issues, and I'm a single parent who is always at work. I literally went on a fake date yesterday to appease Tris, and I know the woman is never going to call me for a real one. And even if she did, what do I have to offer someone? Instant parenthood as I work three jobs?"

"Three?" Victoria choked.

"Yeah, I usually work at the library during summers but... I needed the money with Tris hitting that growth spurt, her birthday, and the holidays coming up."

"Sarah... that's a lot even for someone with human superhuman powers like you," Victoria whispered. Her eyes ran over the bags under Sarah's eyes.

"It won't always be like this," Sarah said with a certain finality, but her eyes said she didn't honestly think that. "And honestly, I've lived through worse, so this is just a storm, and it'll pass. But my storm shouldn't be your storm. I'm sorry for unloading my stress on you. And I'm sorry again for losing it this week. I mean, that's just a glimpse of my everyday life that you don't want."

"The girl... the one you went on a date with... she's an idiot if she doesn't call you," Victoria stated.

"I want you to think about something."

"Okay."

"You clearly have this idea in your head that you want to date me. I don't honestly get it because I'm not a prize, but okay, let's roll with that. Seriously think about what that means for you. You and I go on a date. Maybe we for once don't end up fighting, and then what? You would have to step into being a parent? Think about that. You don't even like kids, and you have met the sass mouth that is my kid."

Victoria studied the coffee table.

"Take this as a lesson from a single parent." Sarah sucked in a deep breath. "When we date someone, we are not looking at whether or not we work together or if there is chemistry. We care about one thing. We care about if that person is safe to be around our kid. If that person will love our kid or be one of those terrifying step-parents who ostracize them. It's not just a date with a single parent, it's her trusting you not to break her kid's heart. It's a day-one commitment. Does that make sense?"

"Yes." Victoria swallowed. She looked up at Sarah. "I get what you are saying, and you are right about you not being the person that I, likem envisioned in my head when I first met you. I mean, the whole single-parent thing makes sense, but I didn't even know you were a parent until a few days ago."

"Yeah. I don't tell clients about me."

"So, why did you tell me?" Victoria asked.

"Didn't really have a choice since my kid got sent to the office. I mean, in three months you had no idea." Sarah sighed. "But what we are doing here is business. As my boss, it makes sense you know a little about me. That I'm a parent. But as a client, it's not part of the conversation and those lines with you are fuzzy. I don't live or work in the space I would normally run into my clients, but I see you almost every day."

Sarah straightened her shoulders. "Tonight, I'm going to teach you how to strap up, but Monday we might be dealing with my kid beating the shit out of a racist again."

Victoria smiled. "True."

"Victoria, please hear me." Sarah placed her hand on Victoria's. "You're going to meet someone that makes you feel all warm and fuzzy. And when that happens, you will have nothing to worry about when it comes to pleasing her. By the time I'm done with you, she'll never know she was your first."

Shadows danced along the walls as the candles flickered. Victoria wondered if the nightly presence was rooting for her to succeed or laughing at her incompetence.

"Okay," she whispered

"Let me get a few things."

Sarah moved from the couch and pulled out the silicon torso. She placed it on the coffee table in front of Victoria. Then she grabbed two harnesses and a pair of briefs, as well as two dildos.

"That is not a book," Victoria choked out. "And neither are those."

"Fuck the book." Sarah held up the flimsiest option. Dangling it above her waist, Sarah explained, "This is a basic harness, and it has three tightening points. The pad here has what is called an O-ring. The dick goes there, and you put it in before you put the harness on. This one sucks and is cheap, and I am telling you: Do. Not. Buy. It."

She tossed the cheap harness alongside her clothes. The nylon straps slid to the floor as Sarah held up the second one.

"This one is called the Regal Queen harness. It's less likely to come loose. They both work the same. You step into the top, put your legs through these two areas, and then tighten it once it's on."

Holding up the briefs, Sarah said, "These are the easiest to put on and have two O-rings. This one is super comfortable, but you have to strip it off to continue playing, which can be messy and annoying. So as your coach, I am telling you to use this one." Sarah held the regal queen once again and tossed the briefs alongside the cheap one. She pressed the harness to her front and said, "Plus it has the little details that say I'm a boss bitch and I'm going to rock your world."

Victoria's single eyebrow rose as the other woman's cheeks flushed slightly.

"Really, it's perfect for you with your regal name," she said. Then she waved her hand in the air. "Stand up."

"Why?"

Sarah's head rolled. "Because you're paying me $150 to try it on."

When Victoria stood, Sarah lowered herself to her knees and held the top of the regal queen harness open so Victoria just had to step in.

Sarah slid the harness up. She placed it just above Victoria's core and held it in place.

"Tighten it."

Victoria looked over the straps and pulled them until it fit without Sarah's aide.

"Good," Sarah said.

The brunette looked up at Victoria from her knees and Victoria felt oddly powerful.

"So, you know how to strap up now. Let's talk about how to get the toy in."

Sarah retrieved the cheap harness in her hand. She searched the room momentarily, then remembered she'd placed the toys on the tables.

Positioning the tip against the silicone ring, she said, "You can force it through the hole, but a trick is to take a little lube in your hand and rub it over the toy."

Sarah scooped up a bottle of lube from the case and held it up. "Wicked brand is great but use the water-based version."

She squirted some of the liquid into her palm and stroked the head of the toy.

"Then you just," Sarah pushed and twisted the toy against the hole, "work it through the hole. Once the head is through you can pull it the rest of the way and straighten it out."

Victoria watched every action carefully.

"How about you take that harness off?" Sarah held up the other dick. "Put this one in the hole and then get the harness back on."

"Okay."

Victoria followed the instructions, occasionally pausing for Sarah to provide her verbal cues along the way. When the task was done, she stood before the couch, looking down at the silicone rod jutting out from her body.

"How do you feel?" Sarah asked.

Victoria wiggled her hips some. The toy moved in the air, protruding farther than Michael's ever had. With a soft smile, she said, "Less freaked out."

"Good."

"So, what do I do next?"

Sarah tapped the vaginal opening of the model on the table.

"Before you put that," Sarah pointed to the toy, then to the model, "in here, you need to prep her."

Sarah added lube to her fingers and pushed them into the model. "Now this is after the kissing and possibly the licking. You start with one finger and go slow at first. Then move a little faster and hook her clit with your thumb like this."

Sarah's thumb rested atop the hooded clit. She rubbed the same sequence Victoria learned in her first session. After a moment, Sarah added a second finger and spread them out with the model.

"This can be referred to as scissoring, but if a woman asks about scissoring she is talking about rubbing two clits together, not this."

Victoria nodded as she cataloged the information in her mental sex file. Tried not to add a fantasy of what Sarah's clit would feel like against her own, even though she was flushed with the image that popped into her head.

"When you're ready, cover your toy in lube. Hold the tip of your finger at her entrance and use the rest of your hand to guide you in."

Using the toy still attached to the cheap harness, Sarah demonstrated. "The head is the widest part, so take it slow. Push in just the head to start and wait for her to breathe. It's natural for her to hold her breath the entire time you're first putting it in. She will breathe when the tip is fully in. After that move your hips slowly back and forth. You want to give her body time to adjust. Some people wait for the woman to say go. It's considerate, so probably try that until you're comfortable reading your partner's body language."

Looking up at Victoria, Sarah smirked. "This is where your experience with your ex will come in handy. You know what it's like to have one of those in here. Don't just push it all the way in. Take your time with short shallow thrusts that get deeper until you're all the way in. Then the two of you will find a rhythm."

"Okay," Victoria said.

"Would you like to practice?"

Victoria's eyes widened. "Like now?"

"Yes. Now," Sarah laughed. "Unless you have your own female torso to play with when I leave."

"I didn't go buy... I don't..." Sentences failed Victoria. The flush returned to her skin as she looked at the woman still on her knees. "Like while you're watching?"

With a shrug, Sarah said, "I can step out of the room."

"Okay."

Once Victoria was alone, she placed her finger at the entrance and held the head of the cock in the same hand. Just like Sarah had shown her. Then she pushed forward.

As she pushed the model slid against the smooth surface of the table. Victoria tried to self-correct but the model fell off the edge. She barely caught herself before falling on her face.

"Fudge!" she cried out.

Sarah came back around the corner when the model slapped against the floor. She looked between Victoria's grip on the flesh-colored protrusion and the upside-down model. Then back again.

"What happened?" she asked, but she was biting into a fist to keep from laughing.

"It fell off the table, and I tried to catch myself, but..." Victoria shook her head.

"Are you okay?"

"No." Victoria gripped the roots of her hair, not realizing her mistake until her hair was stuck to the lube-covered hand. "I feel stupid."

Sarah picked up the model and put it back on the table.

"Can I help you this time?" Sarah asked.

When Victoria nodded, Sarah took her place behind Victoria. Sarah placed her hand over Victoria's and rested it on the model just under the silicon breast, securing the torso to the table.

"Girls like it when you touch them here usually. It's like a hug. Grounding but also dominant."

Victoria sucked in a breath as Sarah's hand came to rest over of ribs in just the place she'd said to touch. There was no denying the woman's words as a personal truth. She wanted nothing more than to stay just there with the Sarah touching her just like that.

"Okay, hold the cock steady," Sarah whispered. The words ghosted lightly over Victoria's neck.

Sarah's body pressed against Victoria's back, guiding Victoria forward gently with her hips. The hand on Victoria's ribs lowered to her waist, moving her forward.

Victoria felt the resistance Sarah had described, but her hips moved with the woman pressed against her back.

"You're doing great," Sarah praised softly.

They moved in tandem as Victoria pushed and pulled her hips back and forth until the penis was fully within the model.

Sarah's arm wrapped around Victoria's middle. "When you get to this point, you'll start moving together."

The model didn't move, but the two women did. A slow steady dance that caused the flicker of hope Sarah tried to blow out to ignite. The dildo pressed pleasantly against her clit, and she found herself enjoying the lesson more than Sarah probably planned. Sarah's grip tightened around her, each breath a little more raspy until Victoria realized if she didn't stop she was going to cum, and probably send Sarah into panic mode.

"So, that's it?" Victoria croaked, stopping only to feel Sarah's movement behind her to faulter.

Sarah hummed softly, then said, "Not quite."

The arm around her middle vanished and the harness loosened slightly before Sarah adjusted the harness placement to be lower on Victoria's pelvis. As the straps tightened, Victoria felt the pressure of the harness through her stretchy pants on her clit more direct. Then the thin arm wrapped around her once more.

"Press forward, now," Sarah said, guiding Victoria forward with her hips once more.

As Victoria moved, she understood what Sarah had done. She'd made it nearly impossible to avoid the electricity pulsing.

"When you position the base correctly, you can also achieve an orgasm from doing just this."

Victoria pressed back, pushing her ass into Sarah's groin. There was no way to unhear the soft gasp that escaped. She wanted to do it again just to see if she could get Sarah to make that sound again. She didn't move though. Couldn't if she wasn't going to orgasm under the woman's touch once more.

Sarah seemed to understand because she moved away and allowed Victoria the space to get up from the awkward position at the table.

With her back turned, Sarah provided Victoria the privacy she needed to gather her feelings. Victoria cleared her throat once the harness was off, dangling from two fingers that she so desperately now wanted to push within the coach who looked as flushed as she felt.

Sarah smiled and took the toy from Victoria's outstretched hand. She tucked her hair behind her ear once more.

"Are you good with stopping here tonight?" Sarah asked

"Yeah," Victoria whispered. "Let me get your money."

She was grateful when Sarah didn't open the envelope before she left. There was a possibility of Sarah losing her shit when she realized Victoria hadn't paid her the agreed-upon $150. Instead, she'd placed five $100 bills in the envelope before licking it sealed.

The text came later that night. A simple jab at Victoria's inability to multiply fifty by three. But it came with a thank you and a request.

Victoria read it over and over.

"*No more sessions. If you have a question or need help, just ask me like a friend.*"

23

The door to the single bedroom apartment couldn't close because of the shattered jamb. It would have been open all day if Sarah hadn't forgotten to pack clean panties. Technically she had brought a pair, but those were used as she lied to herself about just being turned on by the candles. She'd changed when she found Tris had already been asleep. At the time she'd been irritated the girl was passed out on the couch when Sarah made it from Victoria's to Monica's. Now, she was a mix of emotions, but relief that they hadn't been home when the door was smashed in was at the top of the list.

Sarah stood in the entryway trying to avoid breaking down. Not when Zoe's best friend was the cop dispatched to the take Sarah's report. Avoiding eye contact was easier since every part of the apartment seemed to be in pieces. She traced over foam and cotton from the slashed open cushions of the couch. Then she moved on to the shambling of cinder blocks and salvaged pallet planks. The television and Roku were gone while the YA books with Black protagonists Sarah had collected for Tris lay strewn around the room.

She glanced down at her phone vibrating in her hand. Victoria's name scrolled across the screen, but she ignored it. Maria had already been notified of what was going on, so she didn't need to talk to Victoria as well. The less that woman knew the better in fact.

"So, you and your daughter were out last night?" the young male officer asked.

"Yes."

"And when did you leave the apartment?" the same officer asked.

Evie Greyson stood beside him, hand holding the neck of her vest. It barely fit around her, and she looked more annoyed than usual.

Sarah hit the ignore button when the phone rang again. At some point Victoria would get the message to stop calling.

"I had to work at five last night, so we left here at about four."

The pen scratched on the notepad as Sarah and Evie made eye contact. As annoying as the trainee was, Sarah appreciated his presence for forcing Evie to remain professional.

"And what time did you get back?"

"I came back after dropping my kid off at school at 7:30."

"AM?"

Sarah's head fell to the side as Evie offered Sarah an apologetic smile. The woman's swollen belly protruded from below the vest she continuously tugged on. With a simple shrug and a roll of the eyes, Evie nodded toward him as though to tell her to answer his dumb question.

"Yes." She breathed in and held it for a moment. "I got here thirty minutes later, so 8."

"AM?"

He had to be kidding her. She looked at Evie who was not staring at the ceiling. Barely audible she heard Evie growl, "Stop asking the obvious or you make people think you think they're stupid or guilty. She already said AM multiple times. Move on."

The younger officer's shoulders rose as though he didn't' appreciate being called out publicly for his dumb questions.

"When you got here was the door forced open or was it just open?"

Sarah glanced at the splintered door frame. There were new dents in the exterior as well as a footprint from where it had been kicked in. "Forced," she said.

He scribbled vigorously against the pad, not looking up as he asked another question. "Do you know what is missing?"

"A TV and pressure cooker. Some clothes and pair of diamond earrings." She took a deep breath, preparing herself not to cry when she added, "And two thousand seven hundred and thirty dollars."

"Wow." The childlike man stared at her before schooling his face. "I mean, I'm sorry."

"Yeah." Sarah tried to swallow the lump in her throat. "Me too."

"Can you think of anyone that may be responsible?"

She didn't have to think. She knew. "My sister."

"You have a sister?" Evie asked, then she waved her hand in the air. "Sorry. Pretend I'm not here."

The officer looked up from his notepad. "Why do you think your sister would do this to your apartment?"

"She's a drug addict." Sarah watched the water drip from the open freezer. "When she asked for money last week ago, I told her I didn't have any."

The pen scratched against the pad in the man's hand. "Did your sister know you would be out last night?"

"I don't think so."

He looked over the notes, flipping through her statement.

"Do you have an address for your sister?" the younger cop asked.

Sarah snorted. "No. Last I heard, she was staying with her pimp."

Her phone rang again. She looked at Victoria' name and hit ignore. She'd have been home if Victoria hadn't scheduled a session. Taking a deep breath, she looked at the footprint once more, wondering if Sierra had come alone. Couldn't have. The shoe was definitely bigger than hers, so it was bigger than Sierra's.

Sarah pinched the bridge of her nose, covering the tears welling her eyes. She sucked back the snot and fixed her face.

The officer finished scribbling in his pad. Flipping the pages once more, before he pushed the little spiral pages into his vest pocket.

He fished out a card from his vest and took the one Evie was holding out. He scribbled on the back of one of the cards and handed it to Sarah along with a piss-colored pamphlet.

"This is your incident number and a victim rights pamphlet. If you have any questions, you can reach us at the number on the card."

"Thanks."

Evie cleared her throat, and the twelve-year-old-looking trainee looked at her. She stared at him, probably trying to use some type of witchery she always claimed to know to remember whatever he'd forgotten. He scanned her, then the house looking for the answer. Apparently, Evie still hadn't gotten into Hogwarts or Brakebills.

Evie growled in annoyance before she asked, "Would you like to press charges in the event we locate your sister with your belongings?"

Sarah shook her head and then folded her arms around herself. "What's the point? The money is already in her arm."

The boy cop retrieved his notepad from his pocket and wrote something else down. Probably the answer to Evie's question.

With another tug at her vest, Evie asked, "You have someone to help you clean up, or need someone to get Tris from school? I can call my mom or—"

"No. I'll figure it out." Sarah didn't know how she'd figure it out but at least she knew now where Victoria's tip would be used. "Plus, we both know if you call your mom, she'll Amazon me all new furniture, and I can't...."

"You have someplace to stay until they fix the door?" Evie asked.

Evie looked over the apartment with her nose raised just enough to say she disapproved of Sarah's now even shittier house. Sarah knew Evie was taking in the fact that she hadn't improved her and Tris's situation one iota since leaving her mom's guest house six years ago.

"Yeah." Sarah didn't. She would call Monica though.

Evie looked at the door and then searched Sarah's face. "Do you want us to stay until you get your things?"

Sarah shook her head. What she wanted was for Evie and Officer Oblivious to leave so she could curl up and pray for the ground to swallow her whole.

"No, it's okay."

"Okay," Evie said, but Sarah could tell the woman was not okay with her decision.

"Please, don't tell your mom," Sarah requested. "Just please. Not your mom or your sisters. I... I can handle this, and the less people that know—"

"Understood," Evie interjected with a nod. She held up a finger. "But when you decide you're tired of handling, you're going to call me, understand? I won't tell my mom because you're right she'd rush over here and fix it. But you will call me."

"We both know I'm not going to call you," Sarah stated because she didn't have the energy to lie to the person who used to knock on her door asking to babysit Tris.

Evie licked her teeth and narrowed her eyes. "Then, I'll have to call my mom, who by the way is low-key annoyed that she hasn't seen you or Tris in almost a year."

"Fine," Sarah whispered. "I'll call you if I can't handle it."

"You're not alone, Sarah," Evie said in the same tone her mom used when Sarah handed back her keys.

"Yeah," Sarah said, realizing it would have taken less energy to lie.

The door wouldn't close when the officers left, but Evie did her best to shut it. As they walked down the stairs Sarah heard the woman tell the boy-man to stop asking obvious questions like AM twice again. Then, told him he did a good job on his first B&E, but it didn't sound like she was proud.

Sarah walked through the trashed apartment. The nontaxable savings were gone. The place she laid her head to rest was gone. The fucking pot she used to cook dinner was gone. The food in the freezer was defrosted, and a container of ice cream had melted across the floor. Her thick sweatshirt was missing, along with a couple of pairs of jeans, and all but two T-shirts were taken. Under a pile of work shirts, the little black dress Tris had asked her to wear on a date was sliced into pieces.

That was how she knew it was Sierra. Everything else could have been just thieves, but the dress was a personal statement. Don't be a whore was the message.

She made her way down the hallway to the closed bedroom door. As she pushed it open, the child's bedroom was exactly how they'd left it the day before. Every toy was still in its place. The school-issued laptop was open but dead on the bed. At least the disdain her sister held for her did not extend to the child the woman had birthed.

She fell onto the bed since the couch she'd slept on for the last three years was shredded. She choked as the final blow of the knife slammed into her back by the genetic duplicate running around the street somewhere looking for her next hit.

She didn't know how long she sobbed into the comforter while clutching the worn teddy bear she'd given to Tris as a baby. Her body was tired from the spasmed sobs that choked the air from her lungs, and she was teetering on the edge of sleep.

Even the voice coming from the splintered door sounded too far away to matter. She pulled her legs to her chest knowing the call wasn't for her. No one would be coming to save her because this wasn't a fairy tale and she sure as hell wasn't a princess.

But the voice was for her. Calling out to her from inside the house. A voice she didn't want to hear, from a person she didn't want to be here.

"Sarah," Victoria whispered from the bedroom doorway.

Sarah didn't move. Her grip tightened around the stuffed animal that hid her face from the woman.

"Just go away," she cried out.

Victoria didn't say anything. The door clicked closed, enclosing Sarah from the only unviolated space in her world. Her body tapped into a new well that brought forth more tears.

When the well ran dry, Sarah's body couldn't fight any longer. The darkness welcomed her with nothing and no one to account to or for since she'd already messaged Monica to tell her what happened before the police arrived.

Sarah woke to the orange and purple hue of the fading sun glowing through the bedroom window. She sat up and checked her phone. Monica had called her half a dozen times since Sarah had texted her that morning.

The last text from her friend told her that she'd picked up Tris from school and instructed her to pack a bag to bring to her house.

She didn't want to leave the room. Didn't want to return to the trashed apartment she would have to clean before she explained to Tris that they couldn't come back here. But the urge to pee was too strong.

Sarah closed her eyes before stepping out of the room. She'd spent enough nights walking around in the dark to know the five steps she had to take to cross the hallway to the bathroom. That was the easy part.

The hard part was opening her eyes to the apartment. Stepping around the swallow corner to the destruction of her hard work. But the pieces of her life had to be put back together, so she did it.

Only the pieces had all been put back together.

The tattered cushions were back on the couch, laying weakly against the frame. The cotton and foam on the floor were replaced with crisp lines from precise vacuuming paths. Doors to kitchen cabinets had been closed, as had the refrigerator.

Sarah's heart jumped into her throat when Victoria's head popped up from behind the kitchen counter. With a bandana wrapped around Victoria's head and rubber gloves pulled to her elbows, she looked like an advertisement from 1950.

Victoria wiped her bicep over her forehead. She clutched a sponge in one hand and a bottle of cleaner in the other. A pitiful smile didn't rise on her lips. She didn't even make eye contact.

She simply set the sponge down and stripped off the gloves. Walking around the counter, Victoria moved with purpose to Sarah. Without request or consent, she wrapped her arms over Sarah's quaking body and held her tightly.

Sarah's head fell against Victoria's shoulder and her arms found their way around the woman's waist. Her fingers pulled Victoria closer.

When they released each other, Sarah stepped back. She stared at the floor as she said, "You didn't have to..."

Victoria pulled at the hem of her work shirt. The knees of her black slacks were covered in dust. Softly, she said, "I know, but where I come from, you don't let people face something like this alone."

Sarah glanced at the linen closet where her clothes had been strewn across the floor. The doors were now closed, and she didn't have to open them to know that the shelves within would be organized.

"Where are you and Tris staying tonight?" Victoria asked.

"Monica's." Then Sarah corrected herself. "Dr. Rose's."

"Okay good."

Sarah leaned against the wall.

"What do you need to take with you? I'll help you pack."

With a sigh, Sarah asked, "Why are you here?"

"Because I know what it's like to be alone." Victoria glanced around the cleaned space. "Now where are the bags you're going to take?"

"In Tris's room."

When Victoria stepped toward the hallway, Sarah pulled the woman into another hug. She held on tightly as she memorized the smell of the woman's sweat.

"Thank you," she whispered. "Thank you for putting up with me."

24

The point Victoria's body decided she was old had crept up and pounced on her overnight. She was on day three of recovering from putting Sarah's apartment back together. The pain running from her hips to her knees had made sleeping nearly impossible.

Well, that and the guilt she felt every time she walked past the empty bedrooms in the silent house. She should have offered the rooms to Sarah. It would have been the right thing to do. Fear had stopped her though.

Thankfully, Sarah had a plan, and it didn't involve her.

"Walk away, Victoria," she said aloud.

She even closed the door to the brand-new mattress and empty closet where Sarah could hang her clothes instead of folding them up in a linen closet.

Following her instructions, Victoria moved slowly down the stairs. She wasn't sure if the stairs or her bones creaked more in the descent. She also wasn't sure if she had the energy to pull herself together enough to head to the bar to be Echo's darts partner.

The table provided some relief as she broke one of her mother's many rules by resting her butt atop it. She took a deep breath and vowed to go back to the gym she'd avoided since she'd bailed on the last dart match halfway through to talk to the girl she'd also lost the courage to text.

With the phone in her hand, she crafted several lame excuses as to why she couldn't return to the bar when the three dots appeared at the bottom of the screen in Echo's open message.

'Better not be thinking about bailing, Babygay,' popped up seconds after the three dots disappeared.

Victoria's head fell back, then rolled to the side where the unopened Amazon package still lay. She moved gingerly around the chair to the brown bag and withdrew her first set of darts and a baggy of a hundred plastic tips.

"Get out of the house," she told herself. Then, she sent a text to Echo that she was on her way.

The new darts seemed to find their mark better than the last time, which led to an experience of less yelling from Echo. Parker arrived with another alcohol and coke mixture that she set on the table.

The redhead stopped in front of Victoria. The dark eyes ran up and down Victoria, then she set the tray on the table.

"May I touch you?" Parker asked.

Victoria raised an eyebrow at the woman. "Why?"

With two fingers held up, Parker stated, "First, do that to girls that are not me. Second, I need to adjust you."

"Adjust me?" Victoria asked.

Apparently, Parker didn't care about Victoria's consent to be touched because she didn't wait for it. She tugged the tank top Victoria had dared to wear down a little. Then, she pushed the sides of Victoria's breasts together and said, "Pull your breasts up in your bra."

Victoria did as instructed but felt like the fear she'd had when she first came to the bar had just turned into a reality. She looked down to see the shaded clefs of her cleavage now on display.

Parker hummed in approval, then stated, "The eyebrow thing. It's a brat killer. And sexy as hell."

"A brat killer?"

"Yeah. The single raised brow will stop a brat mid-sentence because it's like a cocky exertion of dominance. It's like a challenge me and I'll own you." Parker stood back and admired her work. "Your shoes are better, now you need a longer necklace with, like, a broach or something bulkier. You have an amazing frame, but you need bulky to break up the straight color."

"Thanks." Victoria glanced at her outfit once more. "I feel like I need you to take me shopping."

Parker laughed without disagreeing. She put the tray under one arm and walked away. Her hips swayed with each step like she knew it would demand Victoria's eyes to watch as each ass cheek rose with each step.

"I told you not to stare at my sister's ass," Echo reprimanded as she raised another beer to her lips.

"Your sister just told me I have a 'brat killer' eyebrow."

"Yeah, right. There ain't nothing dominant about—"

Victoria raised her left eyebrow at Echo. The beer that was making its second trip toward Echo's mouth stopped as the masc swallowed the rest of her sentence.

Victoria bit her lower lip, remembering a time when Echo had been the main character in her fantasies. But this was different. Her imagination had focused on Echo's attention on her, not the other way around. With the tables turned Victoria felt the newly exposed flesh on her chest flush.

Parker chuckled as she passed by. "Told you it was a brat killer."

Echo's shoulders drew back. "I am not a brat."

"Bullshit. We both know you just look like a bad bitch when really you're like 90% an omega in constant heat."

"I am not an omega," Echo barked.

"Do it again," Parker commanded, and Victoria didn't dare disobey. She raised her eyebrow as Echo opened her mouth. Words did not exist as Parker stood alongside Victoria with an 'I told you so' grin plastered across her creaseless face.

Echo broke eye contact and ran her fingers through her shoulder-length layers to the fuzz of her undercut. "I hate you both. This is supposed to be my fun night out and you always gotta ruin it, Lucifer."

Parker shook her head. "It's not my fault you're a big ole softee."

"I'm going to fire you."

"You keep saying that," and Parker walked away as Victoria contemplated her new lesbian superpower.

Echo leaned against the table, staring at her phone. She sent a series of texts before dropping the phone to clatter against the table.

"Everything okay?" Victoria asked.

Echo closed her eyes and sucked in a deep breath. "Yeah. Fine." Her fist balled and knocked against the glossy finish. "It's not fine. Nothing is fine."

"Want to talk about it?"

"I just want to explode. I just... I don't know anymore. I mean we have a life, kids. She was the one that wanted the kids, and it was like once Henrie came and now Henrie's bio mom just moved in like two weeks ago, but Simone just checked out. Well, she was checked out before that. I knew... I knew before Henrie that she had... she'd met someone else. I never told her I knew because then we got the call, and it was like maybe this would fix things. She was home again and not 'working late' all the time."

Victoria reached over and took Echo's hand.

"She sent me a text last week saying she wants a divorce. Said I got to get the kids and my stuff out of *her* house. And so I asked her. I asked her why, and she said she should have left before Henrie. Said she never wanted kids with me. Never wanted me but she just... she just felt sorry for me and she only married for the tax breaks. And she admitted to cheating on me."

Echo ran her hands over her face, then reached down to hold her side like her chest hurt. Her eyes searched the ceiling before they clenched shut.

"She told me in a fucking text message. Told me in a mother fucking text message that she was leaving me and the kids. Well, not leaving me. She wants the house. She wants the house and for me to take the kids and move out. And she wants my car. And I just... the bar isn't doing well. I just barely finished fixing it from the fight that busted the sound railing and stereo. And I just—"

"Fuck her," Parker barked causing Victoria to jump from her skin. She turned to see not only Parker but the brooding girlfriend at her side. "You don't fucking need the bitch. She was never good enough for you and has never for a second been a parent to your girls. So, fuck her. You can live with me and Lyra."

"You and Lyra are just moving into that house," Echo argued. "Me and two kids cannot move into your shiny new house."

"When I got out of juvie, you didn't think twice about letting me move in," Parker stated. "So, yes, you can. You can move your kids into the house, and we will figure it out."

"You can have the house," Parker's girlfriend stated. Then she shrugged slightly. "I mean, you can't have it have it because technically my mom still owns half of it. But Parker doesn't want to live there anyway. And the townhouse I'm in now is honestly enough." Lyra looked at Parker. "You good with staying at there since Evie and Landon moved out? I mean, I know you don't want to live down the street from my family."

"I think I could fall in love with you, Lyra Greyson," Parker said, wrapping her arms around Lyra's neck.

Victoria's eyes grew, but guilt rose in the back of her throat.

"I can't move in with you, let alone take your house," Echo stated.

Lyra's chin rose some. "I know what you're thinking. I've been there. Everything for a trade, right?"

Echo nodded.

"So, you move into the house with the girls, and I don't get shit for sitting at your bar all night so I can make sure Explicit Xio keeps her strap away from my girlfriend's ass."

"Are you sure?" Echo asked after thinking about it for a full minute.

"You have been taking care of me since I was sixteen years old," Parker said. "When I got out, you took me home even though Simone hated me. When I was rationing ramen, you made sure I had electricity and food. You're my sister."

"Which makes you my sister," Lyra added. "And I like you way more than Evie and Sadie. Plus, Parker and I don't need a place that size."

As Echo made plans with her family, Victoria sipped her drink contemplating the rooms in her townhouse. She blamed the soreness of her throat on the alcohol instead of the guilt that refused to go down with the booze. Her stomach was tied into a full-blown knot.

She wondered what Sarah was doing right now. If she was comfortable at Dr. Monica Rose's. If she had a room of her own or if she was sharing with her daughter again; she wouldn't have to share if she came to stay.

Victoria's mind connected the ifs until they shifted to a fantasy that was bigger than any she'd ever considered before. A life where the house wasn't filled with the ticking away of moments that would never be lived.

"I wondered if I would run into you here again," interrupted Victoria's wishful thinking.

Victoria looked up from the drink she'd been unconsciously swirling in her hand to find the dance partner she'd never texted.

"Oh... Hey," Victoria said, standing up from her hunched position.

"You never texted me," Tanya stated.

Victoria looked at Parker for unspoken advice. Parker didn't blink an eye, just tapped her eyebrow and smiled.

Getting the hint, Victoria raised her single brow and smiled into the drink that she rose to her lips. Before the glass made it, she said, "You didn't text me, either."

Tanya's lips parted, and then the lower became trapped between her teeth. And Victoria liked the way the dark eyes ran down her body.

"I..." Tanya swallowed. "You're right. Let's try this again."

Victoria took a sip of her drink.

Tanya rested her hand on Victoria's bicep. "It's great to see you again. Sorry, I didn't text you, but would you like to dance."

"That would be nice," Victoria said. She allowed Tanya to tug her toward the dance floor.

"What about the game?" Echo cried out.

Victoria turned to find Echo sucking down a foaming beer as Parker chastised her for running clitoference. She cataloged the new vocabulary word into her lesbian dictionary while Tanya began to talk about her work.

After several turns around the dance floor, Victoria's daydream of Sarah and Tris living with her had moved into a closet in the back of her mind. Her attention focused on leading the dance. She appreciated how Tanya laughed each time she fumbled and matched her uncoordinated movements. At the end of the dance, Victoria agreed to dinner on Saturday, just the two of them.

Her first date.

25

The flashing lights from the television combined with the periodic slap and smack of the cartoon playing was just enough to pull Sarah from an already uncomfortable sleep. Her neck hurt from sleeping on the overly thick throw pillow, and her arm was being pricked by pins from inside because Monica's couch had no give to it. Just as she opened her eyes the blinds shifted with the fan, flashing her with the early morning sunlight.

It took a few moments for the spots to fade, but she was officially awake. She took a breath, trying to hold in the laughter at being concerned with Officer Evie Greyson learning she hadn't made any substantial progress in life. At least in her apartment, she didn't have to listen to Tris snoring. Also, her couch didn't leave half of her body numb by morning.

She reminded herself that Monica's was safe though. Tris may be sleeping on the chaise lounge beside her, but no one would kick in Monica's front door.

Tris lay sprawled across the grey leather lounge, twisted within the pink unicorn comforter that Sarah brought from their apartment. From the top hole of the burrito Tris had turned herself into, Sarah could see the collar of the girl's maroon polo peeking out.

The kid was dressed and the dried milk on her chin said she'd eaten. That alone gave Sarah a few extra minutes to lay on the cold, comfortless couch. The daily list of tasks she had to accomplish had one less thing on it, which was appreciated since it felt like the list only got longer each day since they'd become homeless again.

Sarah pulled herself up from the couch as the sun peeked through the blinds once more in an attempt to blind her. She hoped the only bra that still had two underwires in it managed to dry after she remembered at midnight it had to be washed. Going to work without a bra on really wasn't an option, but wearing the one with the busted wire was equally not an option. There was no way she could survive sitting in the weekly staff meeting with Maria and Victoria with the wire trying to poke a hole through her again.

"Morning," she whispered, feeling the tiniest scratch in her throat.

Take an allergy pill was added to her list. Then she remembered that today she needed to make another trip to the apartment. There wasn't much left in the space, but she still needed to move the rest out before the end of the week into the newly secured storage unit.

Relief washed over Sarah at the upturned lips of the child who'd cried for the past several days when their attempt to find the terrorist cat had been unsuccessful. Sarah had searched the sides and back of every dumpster. She'd even resorted to scanning the apartment complex's parking lot for any signs the cat had been hit by a car. She'd go back today and see if Tina made it home. If she was lucky, maybe the food Sarah left out brought the feline back to the patio.

That thought was abandoned when she passed the kitchen where Monica leaned against the counter. Finding the cat would probably not be lucky since the therapist only hated dogs more than she hated cats. Since Sarah would need at least a month to raise the funds to move them again, she knew it was better to give up the search than try to ask for more from the woman who owed her nothing.

Sarah skipped brushing her teeth, choosing to follow the smell of coffee after relieving herself. Walking into the kitchen was like walking into a freezer. She tried to move through the space silently as TikTok videos were flipped through more rapidly than she thought was possible.

Monica hadn't looked up from her phone, which wasn't unusual. The years of friendship had provided them with the comfort of silence without awkwardness. It also provided Sarah with the ability to read Monica's more subtle cues of annoyance. Like the fact that she was flipping through the videos just to play enough sound to agitate Sarah.

Sarah held the cup to her nose, inhaling the promise of energy and clarity in her head. As she sipped the warm liquid, the chill tingling her skin became unbearable.

Monica broke her silence without looking up from her phone. "So, did they fix your door yet?"

The question spiraled Sarah back to their confrontation in Monica's office and the anger of being called to the school to pick up Tris. Her best friend was sick of her problems and wanted her life back.

"Yeah. I... thought when you said to come stay here... I just thought you meant to come stay here."

Monica closed her phone and raised her cup to her lips. The sharp blue eyes said what Monica's lips did not. She didn't need to say that she wanted her house back. She didn't need to say that she was fed up with Sarah's life being thrust on her. Sarah knew Monica would never say those things. She didn't need to because Sarah wasn't stupid.

Stupid was a privilege Sarah never had. And by the way, Monica's eyes studied her she'd be stupid to expect to stay there much longer. Not if she planned to keep the only support person in her life.

Sarah set the cup down. Her finger traced the rim. Last week, she'd been worried that Zoe wouldn't want to date her because her smile wasn't perfect. Internally she laughed at the superficiality of the idea that she would have the luxury of worrying about a girl not liking her smile. No, the lawyer hadn't called since their fake date, but Sarah was sleeping on a couch that wasn't sat on often enough to be comfortable.

"So, do you have a plan?" Monica asked.

Sarah chewed on the chapped skin of her lip until she tasted blood. As she bit into it harder, she traced the tiles of the backslash. Each had been placed by hand in the model-like home she'd never be able to give to the kid.

"It's in the works," she finally choked out. Her eyes didn't move from the tiles as she attempted to construct different patterns in her head with the colors. Her eyes kept returning to the dullest gray of the bunch.

"I need some referrals," Sarah stated once more. "If I get some new clients, then I should have enough for a deposit and the first month."

Sarah looked back at the coffee. "I know you're sick of always having to be there when my sister turns my life upside down. I just don't have anyone else."

"I know," Monica whispered. The breath the woman took was long and the exhale was harsh, almost a hiss.

"I'm sorry," Sarah whispered, and she meant it.

"Look, there are some things that I need to say to you because the last time we talked...." There was another sharp inhale. "Look, Sarah. I need you to know that when I referred Victoria to you, it was honestly just a normal referral. I didn't hand her your pamphlet only to laugh when she left at how this was going to just fix everything. I just knew she had the money to pay you and you'd be safe with her."

Sarah nodded to show she was listening. However, she knew Monica was right as well. Victoria was a different type of danger that Monica couldn't have predicted.

"After she called you though, I met with her, and I wondered what would happen if you two clicked. And then you called, and she was working with you, and I thought of star-crossed lovers and all, and it is like meant to be." Monica's chest quaked in a soft chuckle. "The gay version of Romeo and Juliet, you know? But there wasn't, like, this ulterior motive to just pass you off on some lesbian."

"I get it," Sarah said.

"Good." Monica sat back in her chair. Her eyes rose to meet Sarah's. "I do feel the need to say, though, that Victoria is a fucking rockstar. Like, there is nothing that stops that woman when she sets her mind on something, and while I know work has been rough with her, you can't say that she isn't a damn good human."

Sarah glanced down at her coffee, then back up to find Monica waiting for her to probably agree. She couldn't though because she had stopped focusing as she considered if she misunderstood the concept of being star-crossed lovers.

Her head tilted as she considered if she didn't get it. Then she asked, "You know that star-crossed lovers mean that they are destined for tragedy, right?"

"What?" Monica picked up her phone and tapped against the screen. "It's like when two people are meant to be together... and it ends in tragedy."

She set the phone down. The color on her face was a little less vibrant.

Sarah nodded her head as she chuckled. "I mean, if you think about it... you were kinda right. Kinda in the whole tragedy thing, but I'm not sure about the meant-to-be thing. I mean, my life is, like, a constant tragedy."

"It really is... and mine isn't," Monica stated. She looked around the kitchen. "Look, I went to school to be a counselor, but I didn't have the life you did. I.... You know, I want to help people, but really I just wanted to make a lot of money for not doing a lot of work. I knew it could happen because my mom was a therapist, and my grandfather too. It was just like okay cool it's in our genes. And then we got assigned to the same dorm room, and at first, it was just like damn. Like, you were smart and caring, and so fucking cautious about everything. And so gay, and I thought this could be great. I mean, we were roommates and what I did to you was so fucked—like so fucked. But you were still cool after. I mean, no one else would have forgiven me, but you did. And I just thought we would finish school together, open a practice, and be best friends for the rest of our lives."

"Well, you got part of that," Sarah offered with a slight shrug.

"Yeah, I did." Monica chewed on her lip before she found a second wind. "But I got a whole lot more as well. And I love you. I love you and I love the crotch goblin, and you know that. It's just... this isn't the life I wanted. I started the whole referral thing for you because I knew you needed the money, and I figured that it would get you on better footing so that you could settle into your own life."

"If it wasn't for you, we would have ended up back at the shelter," Sarah admitted.

"Yeah. But it's been nine years, Sarah." Monica closed her eyes. "Nine years later, and I feel like you are just in a deeper hole. I mean, you are working more than I think is even possible, but you just give your money to them. You just give your mom and your sister everything you need to get out of that hole. And now you're both in my living room because your crackhead sister broke into your house."

Monica's voice lowered when the commercial on the TV ended and the volume of the show was clearly lower than before.

"I know I don't have that sense of obligation because it's just not how I was raised. But I feel like I am trapped in this friendship with you. Like, I wasn't the one who got pregnant. You weren't even the one who got pregnant, and I wasn't even in a relationship with you when you decided to leave school because she called you to come get her kid from the hospital." Monica's gaze rose to the ceiling. "And yet, I spend five nights a week cooking dinner for a human that likes nothing, told me my ass is getting fat, and I have to go to fucking Girl Scouts and playdates."

Monica rubbed the wrinkle on her forehead, then looked at Sarah. "I never even wanted kids, Sarah. You know this. It's why we kissed in college because we were two women that wanted to take on the world without adding to the population. But here I am, and I'm a shitty mom."

"I'm the shitty mom," Sarah whispered. Then she looked at Monica once more. "And we kissed in college because you were testing a theory, not because you liked me."

"You were never supposed to be a mom, but you are one. You made your choice. But I gotta make mine too."

Monica set her cup on the counter as Sarah counted the tiles of the backsplash.

"I'm a crutch for you."

Thirty-two charcoal grays. Fourteen small; and eighteen large.

"I know we said that if we were both single, we would get married but honestly, Sarah, I don't want to marry you."

White tiles. Twenty-eight. Biggest which is why it looked like there were more.

"I don't want this to be my life. And I am worried if I let you two stay much longer..."

Two shades of brown. Dark like Victoria's eyes when they were in her room. The forest along the edge. Sixteen forest brown. Eight earthy clay. Arizona clay that looked baked under the sun.

"If you stay, you're just that much closer to being in my bed."

Sarah's eyes shot up to the one person in her life who'd never questioned their non-existent sexual relationship. Who'd never made her feel like a girl whose function in life would be to lay beside her on a mattress. It was what she'd done for Victoria.

That was the problem with Victoria and her pillow-top mattress. Sarah knew that she was like the ground while Victoria might as well live in a sky castle. The ground had no reason to pretend like it belonged in the clouds where it wasn't hard to breathe.

"Monica, I have never slept in a bed besides the three months at NU and the shelter," Sarah snapped. "I didn't even get to sleep with Simone in a bed."

She watched the wheels turning in the woman's head. Waited for her to understand something she'd never told her.

Slowly, Monica asked, "Never?"

"The only bed in my shitty trailer, my mom used for her customers. We slept on the floor in the closet until Sierra took the couch with the men my mom forgot she brought home."

She studied the imaginary knife she'd lodged in Monica's chest. Watched the woman try to breathe, but the blade had possibly punctured her lung.

"That's why the closet this summer wasn't anything new. Wasn't something to talk about." Sarah pictured the imaginary dagger digging deeper. "When I was eight, Sierra tied a lamp cord around the handles so no one could get in and I couldn't get out."

Sarah tapped her fists on the counter. "So, the one thing you never had to worry about was me trying to be in bed with you. But I get it. I'm not your problem and you shouldn't have to be there for me all the time."

Monica's trapped breath fell from her lips. She was searching for an explanation to not have to think about what Sarah shared. It was the same panic Monica had when she saw the scar across Sarah's back and started fumbling for some way to change the subject.

"I'm... I didn't mean that.... I just.... I'm actually seeing someone. I want to see her when I want to. I want to be able to have sex in my kitchen if I want to."

"I just need some time," Sarah said, realizing she'd already said too much.

"How long?" Monica asked.

"Look, I'll keep the kid with me at the library, and I'll see if Leticia would be willing to babysit on the other nights." Sarah closed her eyes and tried to think of who else she could call. "Tris has a friend named Madi. I've met her mom, Xio. She might.... I'll see if she can sleep over at her house on the other nights."

"How long?"

Sarah mentally counted the cash she had and the money from the appointments she'd scheduled. It wasn't enough but she'd have to find a way to stretch it. Maybe the clothing closet at work would have some pants for Tris and she could just wash them every other day.

"A month," Sarah said, knowing it would have to take less time. "I need a month and some referrals."

"What happened to all your money?" Monica asked.

Sarah ran her finger over the rim of the coffee mug, she hadn't refilled yet. "She found my cash."

"Cash?" Monica's shoulders rose and fell. "You kept all your money in cash instead of in a bank. Jesus, Sarah. This is what I am talking about. Like, what type of adult keeps that much cash in a ghetto apartment?"

The hit landed on its target. Sarah's chest leaked air from the knife being thrown back at her.

She didn't need to tell Monica what type of adult she was. They'd taken the psych classes together. Monica had even used every piece of trauma Sarah had shared to publish articles in psychology journals.

"Just tell me how much you need," Monica said, digging through her purse. The checkbook smacked against the counter as the click of the pen provided further mockery.

"I don't know, but I won't take your money," Sarah said. "I'll figure it out."

"Sarah." Monica took a step towards her but stopped as Sarah's hands raised weakly in front of her. "You don't have to do it all—"

"Yes, I do," Sarah stated. "I always have. And if there's any hope of saving this friendship, then I have to stop pretending we're family. We're friends. Not future wives. Not sisters. And friends should have boundaries."

She set her shoulders and raised her chin. The plan for the day was trashed, but she'd figure it out.

"Tris, put your stuff in the car," Sarah called into the living room.

The child didn't groan or respond. Only bare feet hit the ground quickly as the girl followed instructions. Belongings were hefted into duffle bags. Legos were stuffed in the flimsy plastic trash bag that they'd been brought over in, each collapsing the carefully recreated structures.

Monica's jaw ground while she stared at the blank check for an account that Sarah had helped fill. But this was Sarah's life. She'd pulled herself up from every stumble and she'd do it again and again.

26

The fifth graders were the most squirrely after their lunch. They moved about the lines as they waited for the teachers to descend the stairs. After recent complaints of bullying, Victoria kept watch over the start of the three lines and Sarah moved around the rear end.

Mrs. Faulkner was always last to collect her class, and Victoria grew more impatient each day the woman failed to show up on time. The short brunette apologized for the fourth time that week as she waved her kids through the side door that led up the stairs to the second floor of the school.

Sarah moved with the tail end of the line, speaking to the newest member of Mrs. Faulkner's English language learning class.

"I need to send a letter home to your parents. Can you tell me what language your mother speaks?"

"Ah... we speak Kinyarwanda but she does not read. She tells me learn English in school in Rwanda, but I only go for a year before the school closed." The boy gestured to himself. "You tell me what you want to write. I tell her."

Sarah gave the boy a smile she reserved for the students. "Does she pick you up after school?"

"No. I walk," he explained. He held up his hand. "It a short walk, Miss. Don't worry. You tell me and I will tell her. I tell her all the things the angel workers need her to know."

Victoria could see the gears in Sarah's head turning. The small wrinkle between the woman's eyebrows appeared as she repeated, "Angel workers?"

"Yes yes." The boy gestured to Sarah. "The ones like you. They bring the boxes with the food and the clothes. Emama calls them the angel workers."

"That is very sweet. If I call your Emama—"

The boy's laughter stopped Sarah mid-sentence. Victoria took a step forward but stopped, not wanting this to be another time she screwed something up.

"Did I say it wrong?" Sarah asked.

"In your words, you say my mother, but she is not your mother. It is funny."

Sarah laughed with the child. "That is funny."

He nodded and repeated, "You call and I will tell her what you say."

The small boy wrapped his arms around Sarah. She hugged him back and said, "Thank you,"

"Goodbye, Angel Worker O'Keeffe," he called from his spot at the end of his class's line.

"Bye." Sarah waved with a smile that spread all the way to her eyes.

Victoria stepped alongside Sarah while the teachers and kids all moved from within the room.

"He's a cute kid," Victoria offered. "We have a lot of refugee families it seems."

Sarah nodded. She wrapped her hair up into a messy bun atop her head.

"Yeah. There's a refugee support center a few blocks away. They rent out buildings of the apartment complex on 31st Ave. so that the people coming have community connections." Sarah toed the ground. "I noticed his pants are getting short. He is finally hitting that fifth-grade growth spurt. I have some uniform pants for him and his little brother that Maria allowed me to purchase with the Winter's Readiness Grant we were awarded. I need to talk to his mother to see if they need a Thanksgiving box this year, though."

"Thanksgiving box?" Victoria asked.

"Yeah," Sarah said. She tugged the sleeves of her sweater down her arms. "So, I run a food drive at the library I work at. And I try to get the staff to chip in. Tris and I pack boxes for a Thanksgiving dinner for our refugee families. Last year, we were able to provide twenty-three families dinner."

Victoria studied the woman who looked like she needed her own food box donation. The bags under Sarah's eyes were heavier than normal and her shoulders seemed as though they were actively trying to meet in the center of her slouched posture.

"I didn't know that we did that," Victoria whispered.

Back home the church had always held food drives, and the missionaries dropped off boxes in areas of high need. They used it as a recruiting tool, promising more aid to people willing to join the community and pay their tithe. If Sarah lived in Salt Lake, Victoria would have been one of the people packing up the food to send to her home with a young man in a white shirt and black tie.

"You'll hear about it when we start hitting up the teachers for donations," Sarah said. She nudged Victoria gently. "You can use that big admin salary to pitch in for some turkeys if you want."

"Count me in."

Victoria watched the last of the tables being pushed into their folded position by the janitorial staff. "I can't believe Thanksgiving is almost here."

"I know, it feels like every year the days move a little quicker." Sarah let out a heavy sigh. "Tris's birthday falls on Thanksgiving weekend this year."

"She's going to be ten?" Victoria asked.

"Yeah. Double digits. She wants this hundred-dollar Lego set, so I guess I'm moving into the phase of expensive gifts."

They moved from the lunchroom to the playground. Afternoon recesses were just beginning and the shortage of support staff left them on playground duty.

"Do you have plans for Thanksgiving?" Sarah asked.

Victoria pulled the sunglasses from atop her head.

"Uh, not really. It's just me."

Sarah shifted her weight from side to side as she wrapped her arms around the thin sweater hanging off her. The November air was bitey, but Victoria couldn't call it cold.

"What about you?" Victoria probed. "Do you and Tris go see family... or friends?"

"No, it's just us." Sarah stepped from the shade to the sun. Her arms ran up and down her arms. "Monica goes to her parents in Oregon for holidays and since she is our only human connection, we just stay home."

With a soft chuckle, Sarah added, "We tried to cook a turkey last year, but we didn't realize there were all the organs in a bag on the inside."

"Oh no," Victoria said.

"Yeah, we cooked the bird and melted the plastic bag inside." Sarah's bun flopped side to side when she shook her head. "I think this year we will binge-watch movies as we go through the Black Friday ads. Probably just make some spaghetti since it's, like, the only thing the kid likes to eat. Except sushi. She has this new fascination with wanting to eat raw fish."

"If you want, you both could join me," Victoria offered. Tapping her chest, she said, "I have been part of the Thanksgiving dinner team since I was Tris's age. And it would be nice not to be alone."

Sarah tucked her bangs behind her ear and looked at the ground.

Victoria reinforced her chest with steel in preparation for another no from Sarah.

"That would be nice," Sarah said. Her eyes narrowed as she watched the first graders sprint across the sand to the patchy grass. They gathered in a circle around one of the gopher mounds.

Victoria choked out, "Really?"

"What?" Sarah said, turning back to her.

"You didn't argue," Victoria stated. "Or bring up the c-word."

"The c—" Sarah stopped. With a roll of her eyes, she said, "Don't make it weird."

"No, no weirdness," Victoria promised. "I am actually excited. I haven't gotten to cook for anyone besides myself since I left Salt Lake. Well besides lunch but... well that didn't last."

"Victoria," Sarah warned. "Don't. Make. It. Weird."

Children laughed and squealed. Their bodies darted away from the field and back to the play structure.

"You want me to bring anything?"

"No."

Victoria worried she'd responded too fast. However, there was no way she could ask Sarah to bring something when she knew the woman was working every minute of every day to make ends meet.

"If you wanted to come early, you two could help and I can show you how to cook the turkey," Victoria proposed.

"I am a lost cause on the cooking front, but I think Tris would like that. She loves to watch those baking reality shows."

Victoria tapped her chest. "I love to bake. I once thought about opening a cupcake shop."

"Why didn't you?"

Victoria chewed on her lower lip. She hadn't thought about Victoria's Cupcakes since she was in high school home ec. It was a dream that didn't fit the plan.

"My mother was a teacher," Victoria said with a shrug. "Then my sisters became teachers and got married. I'm the youngest of seven, so by the time I was finishing high school.... Well, they were starting to work at the high school I was going to. And... it was just all planned out for me. I met Michael in English class our senior year, and our families approved of each other. So, I went to BYU and studied education while Michael was on his mission, and I followed in their footsteps."

Sarah licked her lips. "Wow."

"Yeah."

The younger children wandered in packs. They darted around each other. Sand kicked up at their heels but watching them play was nice. A part of Victoria wanted to pull Sarah out there to run with them because playing would at least warm the woman up some.

"Are you ever sorry you left?" Sarah asked. She began to bounce slightly when a breeze cut between them.

"No. I couldn't pretend to be a good sister when I knew I was, like, living a lie."

"Well, I'm glad you're here." Sarah's eyes ran over Victoria's face. "I wish we would have met here instead of through Monica. I still wouldn't have dated you, but... maybe it wouldn't have been so awkward."

Victoria smiled at the progress they'd made. She didn't regret the awkwardness though. If it hadn't been there, then she wouldn't be where she was now.

"So, I wanted to ask you something," Victoria said just loud enough for their bubble.

Sarah gave her a side-eye glance. "You're going to be awkward now, huh?"

With a chortle, Victoria affirmed, "Probably."

Sarah's mask of indifference fell over her face. "Hit me."

"I... well, I actually have a date tomorrow and I was wondering if you have any advice for me."

The mask fell from Sarah's face when she laughed. Laughed out loud, loudly.

Waving her hand in the air as Victoria's smile fell, she said, "Sorry. I am not laughing that you have a date."

Shaking her head, she started with, "Just that you think I..."

Sarah choked on the air as she held her still-laughing chest.

"You think I..." Sarah leaned forward and held the laughter in her mouth.

Her hand tapped her chest as her fingers split open just enough for the words to begin to tumble out. "You are asking me... think I have any advice to give you."

The whistles blew for the first graders to line up. It gave Sarah a few moments to collect herself, before she said, "You realize that I am a workaholic with no life, right? I mean, the closest thing to a date I have been on in a long time was the fake date and she ghosted me. I guess, I should have expected that, I mean most people don't want to date a woman with a kid that isn't even her kid let alone one that works every damn day."

"Wait." Victoria held up her hand. "Tris isn't your daughter?"

Sarah's laughter vanished. She seemed to be trying to see through Victoria's sunglasses.

"No, she's my sister's. My twin sister."

"I thought you said you didn't have family." Victoria ran through their conversations until she realized her foolishness. "Oh my god, I'm so sorry. I didn't realize."

Victoria reached out and took Sarah's hand. "When did she pass?"

Sarah looked at the hand holding hers. She didn't let go, but she also didn't hold Victoria's hand back. Instead, her eyes wandered over the lines of ant-like children marching back into the school as older kids burst through the doors.

"The whole break-in," Sarah whispered. "That was my sister searching for drug money."

Victoria's eyes widened. "Oh."

A group of girls gathered momentarily around them causing Victoria to drop Sarah's hand. The serious woman melted as the little girls around her jabbered about how their day was going.

By the time they left, Victoria had so many questions that started to fall out of her mouth.

"So, are you a foster parent? Is that why you were so worried?"

"No," Sarah said, stopping Victoria's interrogation. "I'm Tris's legal guardian as long as I can come up with enough money to buy my sister's signature."

Victoria chewed on the inside of her lip. "Does Tris know?"

"Yes. Well, the part about the fact that I didn't give birth to her. Not about the money thing." Sarah didn't look at Victoria. Instead, she changed the subject. "Look, about the date. Where are you going?"

"Dinner in old town Scottsdale, then a walk through the art gallery."

Sarah hummed to herself for a moment. Her fingers tapped against her leg.

"Don't order anything with garlic or onions unless she does," Sarah said. "And don't assume she's going to pay the bill. In fact, show off your fancy admin salary and buy her dinner."

Victoria opened her mouth, but Sarah held up her hand.

"And don't interrupt her when she talks, but also don't sit there silently."

Sarah looked at the window where Victoria's assistant sat, still hating her job. "Oh, and treat the server like a human. Speaking of which, do the same for Leticia. She's like the most awesome human and you haven't been very nice to her."

"I've been trying to work on that, but she doesn't seem to want to talk to me," Victoria admitted.

"You know, when we first met at work, I didn't like you and I know I set your entire day on tilt," Sarah said.

She wrapped her arms around herself once more, and the sweater clung around the body Victoria swore had shrunk even more since Sunday night.

Sarah sighed. "I'm sorry. I do see how you make changes when someone points out when you are being narrow-minded."

"Thanks," Victoria whispered. "I saw you... and thought that, you know, we had, like, chemistry. It wasn't until I met Tris that I realized what you meant by you had stuff to lose. I guess I understand that even more now. I was raised in a world that is not the world. And I appreciate that you tell me when I'm wrong, even if I hate the way you do it."

Sarah looked at the sky, then scrunched up her lips. "I wasn't exactly taught how to do things nicely. I have been trying to be better for Tris. Be the parent I never had. I never thought I would have a kid."

"I was thinking about becoming a foster parent," Victoria said. Instantly she regretted the comment, though. Sarah was sharing her story and Victoria had hijacked it.

"Was?" Sarah probed.

Victoria pushed her hair back from her face as a breeze bit through her body. She watched Sarah's arms tighten around herself, and the brunette's mind wandered to the six outfits the woman had in the linen closet. She'd seen the same rotation of sweaters every three days, and it dawned on Victoria that Sarah didn't own a sweatshirt or a jacket.

She made a note to shift the schedule so Sarah wouldn't have to be outside in the cold anymore. Especially since next week, they were finally supposed to get some rain.

When she looked at Sarah, she realized the woman was still waiting for her answer. "Uh...Yeah. I started the classes and everything but then..."

"What changed?" Sarah probed as the last whistle blew, signaling they could make their way inside.

"Well... okay. I am not saying this to change things, and I probably shouldn't after you told me all about your last job and everything. Look, if you and Tris need a place to stay, I have the space."

Sarah's mouth closed and her eyes studied Victoria. The woman felt like a question Sarah wasn't expecting to show up on the final exam.

She prayed Sarah would understand her offer wasn't made out of pity. She tried to come up with a way to tell her that the two moving in would make her life feel less like she'd made a mistake and more like the community she'd grown up in.

But she didn't get the chance when the green eyes looked away as the chapped lips whispered, "We're fine. I'm... uh... I'm looking at a new place today."

Victoria studied the way Sarah's cheeks turned a slight shade of pink. Sadly, she hoped Sarah was embarrassed and not lying.

"Okay." Victoria held the door to the office open. "Thanks for the advice about the date."

"You're welcome."

They stopped in front of Sarah's office. Victoria hated the tiny space, and decided to search the school for someplace more spacious for the woman.

"The girl that ghosted you is an idiot," she said before she realized it came out.

"I think..." Sarah took a deep breath. "I think it's better this way, honestly. I mean, at least she realized before it got complicated and she learned that I just don't have time for a relationship."

Tucking her bangs behind her ear, Sarah said, "She was like you. Not in the new to the world sense, but in the powerful and stable sort of way. Like she'll meet someone that can take her out to dinner and shower her with homemade meals."

Sarah looked up. "You didn't meet her on a dating app, did you?"

Victoria shook her head. "No, I met her at the bar I was telling you about."

Sarah visibly breathed. "I was just like, oh my god, what if she is going out with Zoe and I just gave her advice on how to pick up the girl I was out with last week."

"Zoe?" Victoria asked.

"Yeah. She's a lawyer. I think she is, like, a District Attorney. Something to do with murders."

Victoria held her hand just below her eyebrows. "About this tall. Super athletic?"

"Yeah."

Victoria's eyes narrowed. "I know Zoe's ex-girlfriend. Well, I think I do. I mean, she comes to the bar and is best friends with her ex's sister. Apparently, she is, like, head over heels still in love with Echo's little sister, and it was, like, a bad situation. I guess Zoe told Echo's sister that she was trailer trash and broke up with her in a parking lot because she was a stripper in college. But Zoe still comes to the bar to see Parker and I watched her staring at Parker all night."

Sarah looked to the floor. Her bangs fell in her face as she shook her head. When she raised her eyes, she shrugged slightly.

"See. It's better she ghosted me. I mean, at least she didn't ask for another date when she's still trying to hook up with your friend's sister." Sarah licked her lips. "Yeah... it's good she ghosted me."

Victoria couldn't help but feel like it wasn't good though. The woman clearly would have hurt Sarah. But with everything going on, maybe the woman would have given Sarah just a little bit of a distraction from everything else weighing down her life.

"I'll see you later," Sarah said before she closed the door to her office.

Victoria didn't have to lean against the door to hear the sound of Sarah's tears. She wondered how many times the woman flooded the space while holding up the sky for everyone else to live.

"Diego's in your office," Leticia told her when she stepped away from the door she just wanted to break down. "Ms. Branche called for an escort because he was disrupting class."

"How was he disrupting class?" Victoria asked, looking at the grinning boy within.

"Apparently, he had a backpack full of pencils and was walking down the aisles of desks handing them out while she was trying to get them settled to take a test."

Victoria's head fell to the side. She looked at Leticia, whose eyes were firmly fixed on the keyboard in front of her.

"I'm sorry for being your Ms. Branche," Victoria said. She waited until Leticia's eyes rose. "I can't do this job without you, and not once should I have spoken to you in a way that made you feel like you were less important than me."

"Thank you, Ms. Brenten," Leticia whispered. The eyes that had held nothing but disdain for her welled with tears.

"I'm Victoria. Just Victoria, please. First name basis because we are in this together."

"Yes, Ms.—" Leticia swallowed. "Victoria."

27

Twenty minutes before work was done. Sarah still hadn't had a chance to ask Leticia if Tris could stay with her tonight because Victoria had evidently taken her request to be nice to Leticia as an immediate command.

After she'd finally stopped crying, Sarah tried to reenter the work world. She found an alternate universe on the other side of the door. She watched from her office as the two across the hall seemed to bury their strife. Watching the ease they seemed to speak to one another comforted Sarah enough to close her door once more and tackle her next big hurdle. Finding them a new place to live.

If Tris stayed with Leticia for tonight, Sarah could just sleep in the car without anyone knowing. She clicked through the Zillow rentals, swallowing how bad of a time it was to move.

The door to Sarah's office didn't even fully open before Ms. Doesn't-Know-How-to-Knock Victoria was in Sarah's space asking, "You busy or do you have a minute?"

Sarah choked on the scream she barely managed to swallow. Victoria kicked the door closed when she looked at Sarah's laptop. Sarah didn't have time to close the computer because she was too busy holding the flesh bulging out of her chest and trying to shove her heart back through her now-busted calcium cage.

"Whatcha doing?" Victoria asked, looking at the muddy brown apartment with the patch of barren earth in front of it.

Sarah slapped the screen shut, scrunched up her lips, and sighed. "I already told you. I have an appointment to see an apartment this afternoon."

"I think your cheeks turn pink when you lie," Victoria stated. She folded her arms over her chest and stared down playfully. "And Leticia said your embarrassed face is more of a tomato, so pretty sure you're telling me a story."

Apparently, making up with her assistant had brought Victoria a new level of comfort. Comfort Sarah didn't have time for.

She gave Victoria a sideways once over and watched the woman try to hide the smile.

"When Tris was younger, I told her that her tongue turned green when she lied. Then I caught her in the bathroom telling the mirror lies and sticking out her tongue."

Victoria moved to the other side of Sarah's desk, making avoiding the woman's direct eye contact practically impossible in the closet-sized room.

"What's the long-term plan?" Victoria asked.

Sarah rubbed her hands down her face. "Book as many clients as I can. I called the officer to get my police report. When I spoke with her on Tuesday, she said that the apartment complex will have to let me out of my lease, so at least I will have my next paycheck to try and get another place."

Humming to herself, Victoria studied everything around Sarah's head but didn't look at her.

"What do you want?" Sarah asked without trying to hide her annoyance.

Victoria's eyes landed back on Sarah. Her head tilted and she looked as though she was searching for what she'd initially barged in to talk about. "Can I ask you a question?"

Sarah rolled her eyes. Unamused, she said, "You just did."

Victoria raised that blasted eyebrow, earning her another roll of the eyes and a huff of displeasure.

Sarah waved her hand in the air. "Go ahead."

"So, this isn't what I came to ask you but—"

Sarah stopped her. "Then maybe you should just ask what you came here to ask."

"You said I could ask a question." When Sarah didn't respond, Victoria spit her question out. "Where did you sleep before?"

"As in before I had that apartment or... when?" Sarah asked. She leaned back in her chair, opening herself up like she would gladly share anything Victoria wanted to know. And she willed her cheeks not to turn pink again.

"At your apartment," Victoria clarified.

Sarah shrugged, hoping to seem light-hearted. "Couch."

Victoria looked at Sarah's desk. Her eyes fell on the picture of Sarah and Tris the woman kept under the plastic cover. Sarah shifted the papers to cover the face of the girl she was letting down.

"So, what do you—" Sarah started, but Victoria cut her off.

"Why do you sleep on the couch?"

Sarah waited for Victoria to look at her. Victoria used the eyebrow on her, but she knew Victoria's weakness. She purposefully placed the smirk the brunette couldn't resist on her face and said, "Because we don't all make an admin's salary."

Not once in all of the time that Sarah had worked with Victoria had she ever seen the woman roll her eyes. However, the force in which it happened made Sarah wonder if Victoria had caused damage to her cornea.

When Victoria looked Sarah in the eyes once more, she said, "Okay. And what about the truth?"

Sarah reached for the apartment applications that she had begun filling out. She hit them against the desk until all the pages were aligned.

Victoria sighed. "Look, I know we are just at the early stage of friends. But, you work three jobs. Two of which I know pay you well. So, why don't you have your own room?"

Sarah searched for a reason not to answer the question. When she couldn't find one, she searched for an escape route, but Victoria's chair was partially blocking the exit.

She slid the applications into a folder and put the folder in her purse.

"My mom lives on disability, and it doesn't cover her meds so I pay for the pills. And I already told you...my sister is a drug addict." Sarah held up her hand before Victoria could even think about interrupting her. "And before you lecture me about feeding her habit, it's how I keep her out of Tris's life."

"So, you don't have custody?"

Sarah wondered if Victoria had been listening to anything she said when they were on the playground. Then she wondered if the exhaustion had officially set in and the conversation she thought she had wasn't real but a dream. Maybe she'd fallen asleep at her desk again and didn't even realize it.

"I told you it's guardianship. It has to be renewed every six months, and if she doesn't sign the paperwork, then DCS will step in."

Victoria nodded silently. She reached over and opened the computer screen. Her eyes dropped momentarily to the application.

"Sariah O'Keeffe?" Victoria asked, looking up at her. "Why didn't I know your name is Sariah?"

"Because I go by Sarah," Sarah snapped, feeling the spiders crawling up her spine at the use of her government name.

Sarah's shoulders fell a little more with every click as Victoria went through the pictures of the one-bedroom apartment that might as well occupy space in another dimension from the woman's Scottsdale townhouse.

"At Dr. Rose's, do you have a bed or a couch?" Victoria asked.

Sarah sucked her teeth. "We are staying in the living room."

Victoria's eyebrow rose. "Both of you?"

"Growing up, I always slept on the couch so it's not like I'm downgrading." Sarah prayed her face didn't change color.

"You've never had a bed of your own?"

She hated the way Victoria looked at her when she met the other woman's eyes.

"I grew up in a shitty trailer. I had a dorm room when I started college but then my sister brought me Tris and staying there wasn't an option, so I worked with the school counselor. She got me into a shelter for teenagers and young mothers. Then, I went into public housing while I finished school, and then after I got a real job, I lost that housing, and I could only afford a one-bedroom apartment. I didn't want Tris to ever live like I did, so she got the room, and I slept on the couch." Sarah wrapped her arms around herself. "You happy or do you need every nitty gritty detail of my life?"

Victoria turned the computer back to Sarah. She leaned back in the chair with her lips turned up in contemplation. "You and Tris should come live with me."

Sarah's mouth opened. She closed it, attempted to swallow her words, and then spit out, "I already told you we're fine and I have the apartment tour today so it will be fine."

With a shrug of her shoulders, Victoria explained, "Well... I have two rooms with two beds that are completely vacant, and no one visits me. I said before you and Tris can come stay with me, but I think I should be more clear. I want you and Tris to come live with me. Live, not just stay for a month or a week. But actually move in and live with me."

"No," Sarah said, even though a part of her wanted to say yes. She reminded herself and Victoria, "We signed a contract."

Victoria held up a finger. Then she leaned forward. She ran her finger over a single wood grain along the laminate top of the desk.

"So... I read that contract after the whole break in and nowhere in it did it mention sleeping arrangements."

Sarah scoffed and then ran her hands over her face. "I can't bring the kid and all of my things to your house."

That eyebrow slowly rose in a challenge. "You can't or you won't?"

Sarah folded her arms over her chest. "Both."

Victoria hummed. She leaned back in the chair. "Okay."

Studying the cocky stare of indifference coming from Victoria, Sarah felt small. So, Sarah echoed, "Okay."

Her eyes then fell to the shabby kitchen with the whole two cabinets of storage. She hated this place, but with the ever-rising rent, this was the only thing she could afford.

"I'll think about it," Sarah whispered.

Victoria turned her attention back to Sarah. "About... what?"

Sarah narrowed her eyes on Victoria. "Renting your rooms."

"I didn't say anything about rent," Victoria stated.

Choosing to ignore the ridiculousness of not charging her rent, Sarah looked at the apartment with the $1700 a month price tag. Three years ago this place was $600 a month and Sarah had refused to live there because it was too scary. Funny how time changes things.

"I said I would think about it."

"Okay," Victoria bounced as she continued to occupy half the space in Sarah's office. "But I'm not going to charge you rent."

Sarah's head fell to the desk with a thump. She hit it a few times before she looked up at the bewildered woman.

"You get that you not wanting me to pay for my kid and me to take up residence in your home doesn't make me thinking about it any more comfortable. It makes me feel like a... you know."

"It's a three-bedroom house, not two," Victoria stated. "I would respect your space and expect you to respect mine. We can even make it a rule that no one is allowed in the other's bedroom."

"Why can't you just let me pay you?" Sarah asked.

Victoria folded her arms over her chest this time. "Why wouldn't you take my money for our sessions?"

"Ugh!" Sarah licked her lips. Her ribs hadn't even begun to reinforce the cage around her heart that was flinging itself wildly within her. "It was only the first session. And the second one you paid me for both and probably more. And you know it's because I crossed a professional boundary by touching you the way that I did when I knew you were sexually attracted to me."

"Well, I can't charge you rent because I am sexually attracted to you," Victoria deadpanned.

Sarah's arms shot up in the air, then landed on her head. She pulled at the roots of her brown locks.

"That literally makes no fucking sense," she growled at the ceiling. "And you have a fucking date tomorrow!"

Victoria laughed. Laughed at Sarah's frustration and her situation, making everything that much worse. But she laughed as she said, "Yeah. I know."

Sarah's chin jutted out as her mouth hung open. She couldn't reason with the woman. She couldn't make sense of what Victoria hoped to achieve from this arrangement.

"How am I supposed to move in with you when you just flat-out said you have the hots for me?" Sarah asked.

Victoria leaned into the desk again. "Where are you going to live that people don't have the hots for you?"

"Monica's," Sarah stated, leaning back in her chair. But she felt the heat rise in her cheeks.

Shaking her head, Sarah reminded herself that Victoria and her couldn't work. Just like it never would have worked with Zoe. Plus, Victoria was her boss. And she'd already played a game like this with a boss who promised her a home and a life. Then the switch to the trap door under her feet was flipped, sending her free-falling back to her reality.

Victoria's eye roll was less dramatic, but Sarah caught a glimpse of the baby of the family attitude. With a wicked laugh, Victoria said, "You cannot tell me that Dr. Monica Rose, with all her life advice, does not have the hots for you."

"Yes. I can." Sarah stated. If she hadn't known before, she knew after the blow-up that morning. "It's possible for two lesbians to just be friends."

Chestnut eyes narrowed at Sarah. A warm brown like the tiles of the house she wouldn't go back to.

"So, you're going to tell me," Victoria stood up and leaned over the desk, "that you and she have no romantic history?"

Sarah searched Victoria's face for the information that had to be buried there somewhere. Something that Monica had said in one of their sessions maybe. Or when she was trying to play matchmaker with the babygay standing over her now.

"Okay. There was that one time in college we kissed, but that was it," Sarah admitted only to not be made into a liar if Monica had said something.

"Well, there was this one time in my bedroom that you held my hand because I was scared," Victoria stated.

Sarah stood up and put her hand on the surface of the desk. Inches from the brunette's nose, she wondered if the pheromone lotion from the night before was still working.

Then she said softly, "While you masturbated to the thought of me. That's an important bit to leave out."

Victoria glanced down at Sarah's lips, then she stared into her eyes. "And since then? Have we crossed any boundaries?"

Sarah reached over and tucked away a stray hair waving in front of Victoria's eye. "This conversation."

Victoria raised her eyebrow and the corners of her lips curled upward.

"Stop looking at me like that," Sarah said.

"Like what?" practically purred from the woman.

"With your fucking sexy eyebrow." Sarah closed her eyes, for the first time wishing she had the power to freeze time and collect the vibrations of words that shouldn't be said and dispose of them before they were ever heard.

But it was too late.

"Eyebrows can be sexy?"

Way too late.

She stood up to full height, removing herself from the other woman's space.

"Yours are sexy eyebrows." Sarah fixed her face. "Which is why I can't live with you, let alone bring the kid to live with you."

"I love kids," Victoria said, sitting back down.

Sarah had to laugh. Really laugh with all of the energy she felt she had left. It rumbled through the office.

When she looked at Victoria, she stated, "You don't even like kids."

"Eh." Victoria offered Sarah a slight shrug. "I could learn to like your kid."

"I'm going to find a new apartment," Sarah declared.

The bell to end the day rang, and Victoria checked her watch. Sarah and Victoria were supposed to be outside, but she'd received an updated schedule taking her off outside duty.

Victoria pushed up from the chair. Her fingers pressed against the desk as she cast a look down at the shit-colored building. "And you're going to think about moving in with me,"

"I will think about renting your spare rooms." Sarah shook her head again. "I have to pay you."

"Why? I have that big admin salary." Victoria blew on her fingers playfully, checked them, and then rubbed them on the shoulder of her blouse.

"You're incredibly frustrating," Sarah said. She opened the computer, appreciating for a moment she didn't have to go back out and stand in the cold.

Victoria raised her eyebrow again. "I have this coach that taught me how to unfrustrate people."

Sarah slapped the screen closed and stood back up. She leaned over the desk and looked directly into the cocky-faced administrator. Barely louder than a whisper, Sarah growled, "Babygay, we both know that I would dominate the fuck out of you."

Victoria leaned over the desk inches from Sarah's face. "My new friend taught me a new vocabulary word this week. She said any woman that claims to be dominant is really just a pillow princess."

Sarah scoffed.

"I teach sex ed as a side hustle. You really think I would be a pillow princess?"

Victoria stood up. She smiled, but her fingers played with the hem of her blouse. "I guess, we'll never know since you made me sign a contract."

"For both our protection," Sarah stated.

Victoria tilted her head to the side. Slowly, she raised a single finger and pointed at Sarah. "For your protection."

Plopping back down in her chair, Sarah sighed. "Okay, fine. It was for my protection because I know I'm not a psycho that will ruin you."

"Am I a psycho?" Victoria asked, gesturing up and down her body.

"No," Sarah snapped.

"Then what's the problem?"

"It's unethical."

Victoria smiled. "What is?"

"Going on a date with you!"

The single brow didn't raise this time. Both did. Victoria's eyes were wide as they searched Sarah much more seriously.

"I didn't say anything about a date. I asked you to move in."

Sarah tried to rub the red from her face. And the worst part was she couldn't figure out if she was embarrassed for assuming that Victoria was trying to get her to date her or if Victoria saw her as something to be pitied.

"U-hauling with a client is also unethical," she tried next.

"We can get you a Penskie," Victoria offered.

Sarah looked up. "A what?"

Victoria shrugged once more. "Well, you are worrying about me U-Hauling you so I was saying I could rent a Penskie to move your stuff. It's not U-hauling then." Then she paused and held up a finger. "But can we go back to the date thing because I didn't ask you on a date. Do you want me to?"

"I'm not going on a date with you. You have a date, remember?"

"That isn't an answer to my question."

"Victoria. Please." Sarah pleaded with her. "You are my boss. You were my client. Now you want to be my landlord. It's just a lot. A lot of boundaries that I was already not comfortable with, and now they are just so fucking fuzzy."

"Sarah, I'm not offering any of those things. I said come sleep in a bed in a vacant room in my house. And you said date, girlfriend, and U-Haul."

Sarah's phone beeped. She looked at a message from Monica asking her to talk. She tossed it on the desk.

"Okay," she said.

"Okay?" Victoria asked.

"I'll rent your spare rooms."

Victoria looked at the phone and then back at Sarah. "I thought you were going to think about it."

"I did." Sarah sighed. "And I know I can't afford this place even though it's shit."

The door to the office opened before Victoria could comment. Sarah tried not to laugh when Victoria was wacked in the ass by the door handle as Tris pushed into the room.

"Hi," Tris said in a quiet greeting to Victoria as she opened the door the rest of the way. The smaller green eyes looked between Victoria and Sarah. "What are you guys doing in here?"

Sarah tucked her hair behind her head. "We were... Ms. Brenten and I... we were just talking about her house. She has a couple of rooms that she is willing to rent us."

"Did Aunt Monica kick us out because of me?" Tris asked quietly.

Sarah got up from the desk. She couldn't help but press her body against Victoria's as she tried to get to the girl.

She held the child's face. "Monica loves you, okay? You shouldn't have heard our conversation this morning, but everything that is going on is my fault. Not yours."

The girl looked up at Victoria's confused face. She stared at the woman.

"Aunt Monica doesn't want us to be family anymore. And she said she didn't want to marry my mom anymore because she never wanted kids. She said you and Mom should realize your star-crossed lovers though."

Victoria glanced at Sarah, whose chest rose like a balloon attached to a helium tank.

"If she is star-crossed to love you, does that mean you have to love me too?" Tris asked. And before Sarah could stop her, "Or are you just going to be a wicked stepmother? You know Disney doesn't make those princess movies now because they know little girls can change the world so don't think I'm going to let you hurt my mom."

Victoria swallowed when Sarah turned the honey-badger-looking child away from their new landlord.

"Victoria is dating a woman who is not me. So put your knives away and live to fight another day," Sarah said.

When Sarah turned back to Victoria, she looked everywhere but at the woman before she asked, "Are you sure?"

Victoria swallowed once more when Tris pointed two fingers toward her eyes and then moved them toward Victoria.

"Yeah, it will be great." Victoria tugged at the back of her neck, and then asked, "Doesn't star crossed mean like tragedy? Like Romeo and Juliet."

Sarah laughed softly as she tilted the child's chin to face her. "Yes, star-crossed means tragedy. Like untimely death. So maybe don't suggest two people are star-crossed."

Tris shrugged. "I'm nine and sometimes it's hard to break your and Aunt Monica's code."

"Come over whenever you're ready," Victoria said before pulling the door closed.

Tris glanced at the door, then at Sarah. "How do you already know where she lives? And why does she want to live with you, you're a slob?"

Tris took a breath as Sarah tried to slap away questions that didn't stop.

With folded arms, Tris stated. "She is always making you grumpy. Does this mean you're going to be grumpy every day or are you grumpy because you love her, and she is going out with someone else like stupid Voldermort's sister?"

Tris rolled her eyes.

"Is that why Aunt Monica doesn't want us anymore? She was talking about you the other night with some girl on the phone and she said that you and your boss would be a cute couple if you just stopped being so stubborn. But she's gonna date some other girl even though she is always making heart eyes at you during pick-up."

The kid tossed herself in the chair Victoria had challenged Sarah in. The mother didn't know if the girl would pick up on how much she and her boss had in common, but she had.

"Tris," Sarah said as a complete sentence.

"Are you even going to answer one of my questions?" the child asked, adding another to the pile with the rest.

"Victoria and I are just friends."

Tris's eyes rolled, then she dug her novel out of her backpack. Before she started reading, she added, "If anyone drove up to kidnap me and told me they were your friend, I would know they were a kidnapper because you don't have friends. But if they had a puppy, I'm not going to lie I would get into the van. Or some candy, as long as it was like good candy and not like a ring pop."

Sarah shook her head and sorted the papers on her desk as she waited until it was her designated time to leave. She tried to answer all of Tris's questions internally, becoming very stuck on how Victoria could go on a date tomorrow when it was clear she still wanted Sarah to give her a romantic chance.

She stopped thinking about it though. There was no point. Victoria only learned through experience. So, she was going to see first-hand how little Sarah was home and how damaged she truly was.

28

Without any hint of when Sarah would arrive, Victoria broke many speed limits to get home. The cleaning caddie was ready for her, and she didn't bother to strip out of her work clothes before she attacked the spare rooms. Fresh sheets were put on each bed, and crisp vacuum lines lay on the carpet. She repeatedly checked her watch like it would tell her when to expect her new roommates.

Victoria cleaned with the same fervor as if her mother had called to tell Victoria she was fifteen minutes away. The rest of the house had already been cleaned, including the spiderweb Victoria noticed last week. Still, Victoria found herself noticing things like the slight grime on the garage door from where she pushed it open and the streak on the microwave door. The baseboards of the laundry also looked just shameful, so those were tackled, and the lint trap was vacuumed to keep the house from catching fire while Tris was there.

As she moved in a circle, looking for something else to clean, she realized the house now smelt like a hospital thanks to all the disinfectants. She hoped the smell of lemon Pledge and April Fresh Tide would fade from the soon-to-be-occupied rooms, but Victoria needed the rest of the house to smell like home.

She searched the entry table for the new Scentsy Cubes she'd picked up. It was fall, and most people liked the smell of manufactured fall leaves and apples. However, fall didn't smell like home. Turning to the living room, Victoria's gaze fell on the black candles Sarah had left last time she was here. They would make the room feel like home, so Victoria lit them with a vow to promise Sarah to replace them tomorrow.

She thought about tomorrow. It would be the first Saturday in almost a year that she would have someone to talk to. Maybe they would trade the newspaper, like in one of those old movies. She tried to think about what section Sarah would like to read through.

Victoria immediately chuckled to herself. There wasn't a newspaper service scheduled for her house because she'd hated the paper in Salt Lake. Finding the same accessibility, she spent her mornings staring at her phone. She didn't want that to be Tris's normal though, which felt weird the second she thought about it.

She bottled those types of thoughts up really fast as her eyes wandered up the stairs. For weeks she'd been considering what her life would be like when she finalized her foster care license. As she watched old sitcoms, she considered what values she'd grown up with she'd like to keep, and which needed to be redrafted. Now, she realized that the plan and dream of motherhood— even foster motherhood— was gone.

Tris wasn't a foster kid, just like Sarah didn't want to be anything more to Victoria than a fantasy. She probably didn't even want to be that, yet she hadn't said that. Except she had. On that first inner-office phone call, there'd been an explicit directive to stop picturing her naked.

Victoria took a deep breath, realizing her routine of unwinding while saying the woman's name over and over and over again would need to be much quieter since they shared a wall now. She couldn't just stop imagining Sarah's lips moving over her breasts to her clit because she'd tried and failed. No, she would have to still perform some self-maintenance to ease the cord of frustration that tightened to the point of madness after she spent a day working beside Sarah.

The sudden realization that Sarah would be constantly nearby, with her perfume that smelled like ecstasy, hit Victoria like a sack of potatoes to the chest. How was she supposed to function every day in a constant state of gay panic? She attempted to locate a time she wasn't completely flustered by Sarah's proximity, and she found nothing. Not even in the weekly meetings with Maria had Victoria left without being uncomfortably wet.

It was impossible not to get turned on when Sarah chewed on the tip of her pen, thinking about seventeen different possible implications or challenges that would be faced for one shift in student routines. The woman had a completely underrated brilliance, leaving Victoria in awe when she wasn't clutching the meeting agenda like a shield. And in those meetings, Sarah was clothed from neck to toe.

Those weekly meetings were about to be nightly dinners and morning breakfasts. Victoria had only her memory of Sarah's wardrobe in the apartment linen closet to prepare her for the sexual frustration attached to Sarah in baggy t-shirts and pajama shorts that would be so, so short. Not to mention, she'd now have weekends of conversations and sitting on the couch that would probably require Victoria to switch to a men's deodorant from all the sweating she'd be doing.

"Ask her to move in, you moron," Victoria growled to herself as she made her way to the kitchen.

Checking her watch again, she realized she'd been cleaning for nearly two hours. Her stomach grumbled, and the next O'Keeffe need Victoria was going to meet came to her mind.

She focused on making dinner for three instead of one. While planning a meal had always felt like a chore, tonight it was a challenge. One she had to win if she hoped to start on good footing with Tris. With so many nieces and nephews, Victoria knew kids judged an adult by two things: the food the adult forces them to eat and the awesomeness of the first birthday present they remember.

The sun was just beginning to set when the doorbell chimed. Victoria quickly pulled off her apron and made her way to the door. She prepared a whole speech for Sarah about not needing to ring the bell, only Sarah wasn't on the doorstep.

With a thin white trash bag hefted over her shoulder, Tris cautiously entered the house. The O'Keeffe eyes did a quick scan of the hallway and living room. The contents of the bag crunched after each step. Then something inside sounded like it shattered within the plastic confines when she dropped the bag on the floor. Before Victoria could ask what was inside, the child bent down and unveiled the busted Lego creations.

The sigh that came from Tris hit Victoria like the first gust of a hurricane. A purple and white airplane lay at the top of the bag. It was missing a wing, and parts were falling off of it as she gingerly lifted it from within. Underneath the plane looked like pieces of a zoo were in three separate chunks. Those crumbling structures lay atop hundreds of other pieces. Tiny Lego girls were buried in the rubble of Tris's metropolis like a bomb had gone off earlier that morning.

"Aunt Monica and Mom were mad at each other and Mom told me to get all my stuff," Tris explained. She let the Legos fall between her fingers and back into the bag. "I thought that if I kept them all together at least I would be able to put them back, but Mom already took the books to storage."

Sarah carried two large duffle bags and the child's backpack up the walk and through the still open door. She did some special bodily contortion to make it by the girl as she said, "Tris, I told you I would find the books so you can put them back together."

"But you said you put them in storage, so it's going to take you forever to find them," Tris whined.

Sarah's arms quivered under the weight of their belongings, but she held everything close to her chest. "I tried to find them tonight, but we ran out of time. And I told you, I'll go back tomorrow to look again."

"You said you have to work tomorrow night, so I know your tongue is green," Tris said, the scowl deepening in her brow. Her eyes fell to the bag of Legos as she muttered, "All you do is work."

"Look, I'm doing the best I can, okay?" Sarah snapped. "Now, can you please help me get the rest of your stuff from the back seat because I don't have time to have this fight again."

The girl tied the top of the bag together tightly and pushed it against the wall by the entry table. The soles of her shoes scraped against the concrete with each step like all the hopes and dreams for the Lego girls in the bag was weighing her down.

"I could probably find the instructions online," Victoria offered as she took both bags from Sarah's arms. "Maybe we could get at least one back together before she has to go to bed."

Sarah glanced toward the kitchen where Victoria had already set the table. Her shoulders curled inward, and her hand rested against her stomach. "I... uh... I have to go... I mean, I have to work tonight at the library until nine."

She fixed her gaze on the street where just the rear of Sarah's car was visible. Victoria could see that the lights were on and now heard the motor was still running.

"I... uh... I just needed to drop off our stuff." Sarah wrapped her hair in a messy bun before she thumbed back at the car. "I didn't want to be rude and show up super late, but don't worry. Tris goes with me when I work at the library, so it's not... I wasn't expecting you to babysit. And we won't be back until, like, ten, so I wanted to make sure her blanket and pillow are here, so when we get back.... Uh.... She usually falls asleep on our way home, and this way I can just tuck her into bed."

Victoria nodded because it was polite. She swallowed the disappointment before she said, "Oh, okay."

Sarah glanced back at the table, and her arms wrapped around herself. "I... uh... we won't.... I promise we'll be very, very quiet when we get back. And we'll make ourselves scarce. I'm gonna see if she can spend the night at her friend's house tomorrow. Diego... uh... his little sister and Tris are friends. Their mom, Xio, lets Tris stay the night sometimes when she doesn't have to work, so I will call her about tomorrow."

Victoria glanced back to the kitchen where she'd spent the afternoon preparing a new recipe for homemade marinara. She hadn't boiled the spaghetti noodles thankfully. Altering her plan, she decided to jar it after they left.

"Yeah." Victoria nodded once more. She shifted with the bags still in her hands. "Uh, don't worry about waking me up. I usually don't go to bed early, and you... you live here. It's your home now too, so don't feel like you.... You don't have to stay away."

Tris came back with another bag, her eyes looking at the stairs. "Do I put my stuff in the hall closet like at Aunt Monica's?"

Victoria shook her head, then slung one of the bags over her shoulder. "Let me you show the rooms."

Tris's eyebrows scrunched together. "We don't have to share?"

"No," Sarah said, but her eyes wandered to the living room. "Pick the one you like the best. I will put my stuff in the other one."

Tris examined each room carefully. The mattresses were tested for bounciness and the view from each window was looked out. Lastly, she asked where Victoria slept, and then she chose the room farthest away from Victoria's.

Sarah brought up two pillows for Tris and two more trash bags filled with stuffed animals and books. Everything was placed in the room closest to the top of the stairs except the lightest duffle bag that Sarah dropped in the closet of the smallest bedroom with the least amount of natural light.

With a soft, "Thanks," and another, "I promise to be quiet when we get back," the O'Keeffes left.

The ticking of the clock and sloshing of the sauce pouring into the quart-sized Ball jars were the only sounds when the house was free from Sarah's fast-spoken instructions and Tris's grumbles. If Victoria hadn't opened the front door to the head of curls, she would have no reason to believe either Sarah or Tris had ever arrived.

Homework occupied an hour of Victoria's evening and the list for Thanksgiving dinner in two weeks took up another. However, the house was just as quiet as any other day. She'd settled in front of the television like most nights. An occasional sigh as her gaze wandered to the trash bag of Legos that was left by the table added to the dramatic dialogue from the show.

Victoria was slightly nodding off when the house began to stir back to life. The front door creaked when Sarah came into the house weighed down by the child asleep in her arms. There was no way Sarah should have been able to pick the kid up, but she carried her nonetheless.

With a quiet, "Fuck," and the drop of her keys, Sarah managed to click the door closed without jarring the artwork on the walls.

She nodded quietly to Victoria on the couch before she set Tris on the ground by the stairs. The child blinked several times, her head leaning against the wall.

"I can't carry you up the stairs," Sarah whispered.

Tris groaned, but she moved upwards like she was doing a bear crawl with Sarah just behind her. The door to the room Tris claimed was opened. Whispered goodnights snuck through the banister rails, and Victoria hoped there would come a time she could say goodnight to the women without it being weird.

Without changing her clothes or showering, Sarah returned to the living room and took up position on the corner of the couch she'd been so fond of the last time she was there. She stretched, and the thin sweater rose just enough to show off a sliver of pale skin on the woman's stomach. The yawn that pulled Sarah's mouth open wide was infectious, and they shared a soft laugh.

"At least I know you're not a sociopath," Sarah whispered, tucking her legs under her.

Victoria wondered if the woman noticed the candles, she'd left last week, were still on the end table. She'd lit the wicks to fill the space with childhood memories. Sarah just stared at the television though.

"I'm going to head to bed," Victoria said, not sure what else to do. Before she could get up, Sarah reached across the center cushion. Her hand was so cold that Victoria couldn't help but cup it between her own to warm Sarah up.

"Thank you," Sarah breathed out softly. "We... Monica and I.... Things were said that can't be taken back. I spent all day trying to figure everything out, and I was going to end up having to get a motel room if Leticia was too busy to keep Tris for the night."

She softly squeezed Sarah's hand and then she tugged gently until the woman crossed the cushion. Victoria's arm wrapped over Sarah's shoulder, tucking her into a side hug. Holding her close, Victoria whispered, "Don't make it weird."

Sarah took a deep breath but didn't move much more than a wiggle. That wiggle was just enough for a bank envelope to be pulled from her pocket and tossed on the coffee table. Without looking at Victoria, she echoed, "Don't make it weird."

Both rested against each other stiffly for half an episode of The Fosters. Their bodies slowly began to relax into a comfortable silence where neither talked through the show. Sarah's head came to rest on Victoria's shoulder like a pillow and the throw blanket was pulled from the back of the couch to be shared like they were friends.

When the show ended, Victoria offered Sarah the remote, expecting Sarah to move away. Instead, Sarah's body curled into a ball still under Victoria's arm as she leaned her head against Sarah's chest. She changed the show to an episode of Gilmore Girls, quietly sharing, "I had a crush on Loralie once upon a time."

Victoria thought about high school, searching for a character she would have considered having a crush on. Television was a new fascination for her though. With six older sisters, the television was rarely open for her to choose a show to watch.

"I didn't watch much television when I was younger," she finally admitted.

Sarah's chest shook a little. "Did you have a TV?"

"Who doesn't have a television?" Victoria asked.

"When I came the first time, you said, 'I have a TV,' like it was strange, and

I didn't know if that was, like, a rule. I don't know much about Mormons."

Victoria closed her eyes, but she too laughed. "Yeah, that was just me freaking out about having someone in my house who was going to talk about s-e-x."

"The fact that you just spelled it."

The slim face turned into Victoria for a moment, and the sound of a deep inhale had Victoria's feelings moving around her insides.

"You smell like a pizza shop," Sarah said, turning her attention back to the television.

"I made spaghetti for dinner." Victoria's fingers strummed lightly over Sarah's arm, but she stopped once she realized she was doing it. "Technically, I just made sauce, and I jarred it."

"One day, I want to learn how to make sauce," Sarah said, but another yawn ripped through her. "I'm so glad tomorrow is Saturday."

Victoria rested her head against her hand on the arm of the couch. She wasn't sure if she agreed with Sarah or not. Her thoughts moved around what would come tomorrow until the sound of the mother and daughter bantering on the screen faded like the soft glow into blackness.

It was the sound of her own snoring that pulled her back from sleep. She wasn't sure how long she'd been out, but Sarah had shifted to the other side of the couch.

She rubbed the sleeping dust from her eyes.

"I'm really going to bed this time," Victoria said, rubbing her hands against her legs. "I... uh... put clean sheets on the bed upstairs for you."

Sarah hummed lightly in response, then promised she would be going to bed soon, too. However, the throw blanket was tugged up to her chin, and she was curled back up in the spot Victoria deemed henceforth as Sarah's.

"See you in the morning," Victoria said softly.

"Good night," Sarah answered before Victoria disappeared on her way up the stairs.

When Saturday morning came, each of Victoria's footfalls echoed against the floor of the empty upstairs corridor. The doors to the bedrooms were left open to spaces where at least the child had left her belongings. Any indication of Sarah's residence was non-existent as far as Victoria could see from the doorway of the other bedroom, and Victoria felt like there was no way the bed in the room had been touched.

As she made her way downstairs, she searched again for any hint of life. And she again was left wanting when her eyes landed on the index card in the center of the table.

Victoria, I forgot to tell you last night that I will be at work all day Saturday and Sunday. I hope your date tonight is magical. Please let me know if you want the house to yourself tonight and Tris and I can find somewhere else to be. - Sarah

A fingertip ran over the print-cursive hybrid Sarah used to communicate. It was messy and rushed, like the woman who wrote it. She tapped the card against the table, before fishing for the phone from her housecoat pocket. She started to text Sarah but stopped.

It wasn't her business if the woman still wanted to work a hundred hours a week. They were roommates, not lovers so her opinion of Sarah's choices didn't matter. Plus, she had bigger problems to solve.

The first was the trash bag of Legos still lying in the corner of the entryway. She picked up the bag, feeling the guilt rise in her throat as she remembered the video she'd watched about making sure a foster child never left a home with their belongings in trash bags. She wondered if Sarah had seen the video or if belongings in trash bags were just Sarah's normal.

Carefully, Victoria pulled the plane from within the bag. The plane's other wing collapsed when Victoria set it on the table.

"Damn it," she hissed.

She studied it in an attempt to figure out how to reassemble it. Legos were toys for boys with the future in building things when she was a child though. And her nieces were raised by the same women who'd prioritized the finer arts of tea parties and choreographed dance routines.

Coming to terms with her inability to correct the wing, Victoria set the pieces together and attempted another retrieval. The zoo was in worse shape than the plane, and Victoria realized it wasn't a whole zoo but one attraction for a zoo. That helped her sort the zoo-like structures into separate areas as the table transformed into a miniature Lego city.

Only when she'd managed to differentiate seven different smaller sets, did she focus on the mixture of the individual blocks. Pouring them onto the other half of the dining room table was an immediate disaster, and Victoria found herself scooping individual handfuls of pink, blue, purple, green, white, and black pieces.

The tiny characters and animals intermixed with the blocks gave her greater insight into the different sets the Tris had. She didn't dare to try to rebuild any of the sets, knowing the fun came from the construction.

With careful online searches, Victoria was able to identify and locate the instruction manuals for each of the sets that had survived the earthquake in Tris's life. She downloaded the manuals to a USB drive and decided a trip to FedEx Print and Go wouldn't interfere with the time she'd allocated to start getting ready to meet Tanya.

While FedEx printed the manuals, Victoria found herself in the coffee shop next door. The coffee shop was cozy but bustling, a small haven from the building storm. The air smelled rich, with hints of espresso and warmed pastries, mixing into a comforting aroma that seemed to thicken the moment she'd walked through the door.

Victoria could hear the low hum of indie music mingling with the soft hiss of the espresso machine. She sat by the window, the green tea latte cooling beside her, as she watched the first dark clouds churn. Thunder rippled low in the distance, soft but insistent, drawing the storm closer. The rain would come soon, she knew, and she should have been thrilled, should have been counting the minutes until she'd meet Tanya at the restaurant. But the thought of meeting Tanya tonight felt as restless as the sky.

Her fingers traced the plastic lid of her cup absently. Her mind tugged back to Tris, wondering if the girl would look at the manuals as skeptically as Sarah did everything Victoria offered. The dark clouds had Victoria thinking of Sarah shivering yesterday. A mental note was made to lay out a jacket for Sarah to borrow tomorrow because the storm expected next week was coming now.

A faint draft from the window whispered against her arm as she sat, carrying the earthy scent of wet pavement. Outside, the clouds darkened, casting a dusky light over the room, giving the space more of a gloomy feel to it.

She closed her eyes briefly, listening to the rain begin to tap against the window. There would be nothing to do when she got home beyond getting ready. The outfit she was planning on wearing had already been approved by Parker and Echo. She would need to shower and do her make-up.

Her stomach began to twist in knots. She'd asked Sarah about what to do, but the answer had been vague. Tanya liked to talk, so maybe she could get away with just being a good listener. It wasn't that she wasn't a good listener, she just didn't want to give up her voice again in a relationship.

Beside her, a group of students laughed. Their voices spilled over the hum, and somewhere near the counter, a child's laughter rang out, bright and clear. It made her think of Tris putting together the Legos. She took a deep breath, saying a prayer to a God she couldn't understand anymore that the girl would see the manuals and prove Victoria cared.

A pitcher of milk screamed at the same time her phone buzzed on the table. Slowly she released a breath of relief as she read, *"Hey, I'm going to have to cancel our date tonight. I am not sure if I have the flu or covid, but my head feels like someone hit me upside it with a board."*

Victoria regretted her initial excitement at the cancellation. However, after the morning of preparing the Lego sets for the city planner to come on-site and start the rebuilding phase, Victoria wanted nothing more than to be on the construction crew wrapped in her comfy pants and sweatshirt.

The message wishing Tanya a swift recovery was easier than it probably should be. Feelings of inadequacy were nonexistent as she smiled into the cup. Checking the time, she made her way back to the copy shop.

The color prints equaled almost a full ream of paper. Thus, the cost was greater than Victoria had initially anticipated, but the memory of Tris' face when she showed Victoria the only toy she'd carried into the house made it worth it.

While she drove home thinking about putting all the Legos together, she wondered if she might get to watch another episode of Gilmore Girls. Then a fear crept up her spine as she thought about the note Sarah had left her. If Sarah thought she was going out, there was a chance Sarah wouldn't come back tonight with Tris.

She pulled into the driveway and parked. Without getting out of the car, Victoria had her phone out. The message was drafted, read, and redrafted. She worked on the it until she couldn't find a less awkward way of begging Sarah to come home.

"I hope your day is going well. Since my date was canceled, I wondered what time you and Tris anticipated being home so I could order a pizza. I am sure you're hungry after working all day and it would be nice to sit down and just be in this house and not like alone. Plus I got the manuals to the Legos and I really want to build them with Tris because I was never allowed to play with Legos when I was a kid."

29

Lego bricks snapped together in careful configurations as the piles of individual bricks were sorted through to find the correct pieces for each step. Initially, Tris had hovered over the manuals, reconstructing the jet plane in silence as the pizza cooled and Victoria stared enviously at the child's task. However, Tris slowly began to engage Victoria in the process. First asking the woman to locate pieces in the multicolored pile, then having her hold together already constructed sections while she secured them together.

It was the grumbling of Tris's stomach that shifted the workload. While the girl ate the pizza from crust to tip, the woman beside her followed instructions on what piece went where.

With the pizza slice dangling over the plate, Sarah watched each drop of grease hit the paper. She grumbled briefly about never being allowed to participate in any task beyond page turner, but Tris had waved her words away.

"There is a school set that is like our school," Tris shared. "It's called the international school and it has all the characters that aren't peach, which is cool because usually they only put in like one not peach character."

"Is that really a thing?" Victoria asked, looking at Sarah.

With a nod, Sarah finished her bite of pineapple pizza Victoria had purchased just for her after she'd shared Tris would only eat cheese. It had taken a full ten messages before Sarah realized Victoria wasn't going to stop bugging her until the woman knew what kind of pizza she personally preferred.

"Mom started working at the library because they didn't have any chapter books with brown kids," Tris said. "She's not a real librarian but they let her set up displays and stuff and she always makes sure that they put out the books with brown kids. I wish there were more brown kids in *Diary of a Wimpy Kid*, but I still like them."

Tris pointed to the page. "We need the green arch, and it goes off the tree here with the leaf part at the end."

"Is that your favorite book?" Victoria probed. She searched through the pile until she found the arch with the leaf already attached to it.

"Not so much the first one, but vacation was really funny," Tris said. "I don't really like that Greg is a bully, but I like that he always gets in trouble for being a bully and has to not be so mean at the end."

Sarah got up from the counter and looked at the half of the pizza still in the box. Victoria had purchased the pizza just for her, so she'd be rude to not finish it. Her stomach was overfilled though and the thought of one more slice made her wish she'd left her favorite a secret. Then they would have finished the cheese, and she wouldn't have to eat the rest of the other by herself.

Picking up another slice, she stared at it hatefully. Not eating food someone gave her was wrong, she reminded herself.

"Why are you glaring at the pizza?" Victoria asked.

Sarah turned to find the chestnut eyes locked on her.

"Did they not make it right?" Victoria got up and moved from the table. "I can take it back and get you another one."

"She can't eat a whole pizza by herself," Tris stated. "You got her her own so she has to eat it because we don't turn down food people give us, just drinks."

Victoria looked at the girl, the pizza box, Sarah and then back again.

"It's great," Sarah promised. "Pineapple perfection. Thank you for getting it."

Victoria nodded, and watched as Sarah took another bite of the pizza. Her stomach twisted in protest, but she chewed slowly to not allow the food to make any noise while in her mouth.

"Are you full?" Victoria asked.

"Yeah, but you bought her a whole pizza, so she has to eat it," the child called out.

Victoria's eyebrows cinched in the middle. "You don't have to do anything."

"She will anyways," Tris said.

"Really, kid?!" Sarah snapped. "Can you just shut it?"

"What?" Tris looked up from the manual she'd been staring at. "She should know that she can't buy you a whole pizza without you getting sick from trying to eat the whole thing. She does the same thing with dinner too. Even if she doesn't like something someone gives her, she's going to eat it."

"Why?" Victoria asked.

There had been a number of lunches Victoria delivered Sarah had no interest in consuming. While she wouldn't consider herself a picky eater, she had a decent sized list of foods she detested and some of them were clearly a staple in Victoria's cuisine.

"We didn't..." Sarah stuffed another bite of pizza into her mouth and willed her stomach not to send it back up again. Pointing to her mouth, she chewed silently as she tried to come up with a way to explain to the woman why she had to finish the pizza.

Victoria closed the box of pineapple and ham pizza, before she moved around the island and fished out a gallon sized ziplock bag

"I wouldn't do that if I were you," Tris said.

Victoria looked from the bag to the box.

With a heavy sigh, Tris said, "She also doesn't eat leftovers unless there is nothing left in the fridge. It's just going to sit there for days and days and days."

Sarah narrowed her eyes at the overly observant child. Forcing what was in her mouth down her throat, Sarah closed her eyes.

"We never knew when there would be anything to eat," Sarah said quietly. "So, when someone shared their food, you ate it because it was the greatest gift they could offer you."

Victoria held up the baggy, and Sarah knew she wanted more.

"When something is saved, it's saved for the long haul. You didn't take it from the refrigerator unless there was nothing left. And you don't throw it away for when there is nothing left."

Setting the bag down, Victoria opened the box again. She took out a piece of pizza and bit into it. Three bites in, the brunette gagged as she reached her first pineapple. The gagging turned to hacking until the woman put her face in the trash can and spit out the pizza.

"That is so gross," Victoria whispered.

"Only heathens eat pineapple on pizza," Tris stated.

Sarah knew Monica had taught her that to ensure the younger O'Keeffe would never want to share Sarah's favorite pie. Monica had meant well at the time, but she'd not realized it meant Sarah would never again order the pizza for herself since whatever Tris didn't finish off the cheese, she'd feel compelled to eat.

Victoria stared at the two pieces in the box. Shaking her head, she said, "I can't do it."

"It's fine," Sarah whispered. "I'm sure I'll be hungry again soon."

"Please don't make yourself sick," Victoria whispered. "Like I get it... but...."

Sarah chewed on her lip. She nodded towards the table. "The Legos are waiting for you."

Victoria looked down at the box and closed the lid. She took it with her, setting it on the chair on the other side of the table.

While Tris and Victoria continued with their rehabilitation mission, Sarah walked up the stairs to the room she hadn't slept in the night before. She'd tried to go up after Victoria had left her on the couch, but the empty room was something she couldn't bring herself to accept as a reality.

Across the bed with boxed corners lay a black jacket. From the doorway, it looked like a thick black pea coat someone in New York would wear to trap out the winter breeze. It drew her into the room as two different laughs raced up the stairs to see who could tell Sarah first about the joy being shared below.

Picking up the coat, Sarah was surprised by its lightness. She caressed the dense sweatshirt material used to create a lighter version of the normally woolen coat. Lifting it to her nose, Sarah inhaled the name-brand detergent Victoria used.

She held the material to her chest, then she measured the sleeve against the length of her arm. It would be a perfect fit. Maybe a little baggy, but still better than any sweatshirt she'd ever owned. Hugging the material, she closed her eyes and silently thanked the woman. She couldn't just keep the jacket though.

Once the jacket was hung on the empty hanger beside her three work sweaters, Sarah shifted through her t-shirts. Victoria's bust was bigger than Sarah's, so it left her with only two shirts to choose from to offer in exchange for the jacket.

Holding up the concert shirt from Jimmy Eat World and the faded navy Lumberjack T-shirts, Sarah debated which Victoria would like. She didn't seem like someone who followed the early 2000s punk bands but the woman had graduated from BYU, so wearing another college's shirt may be a no-no. Deciding that the band shirt was a group of former Mormons, Sarah considered it the better option of the two.

She made her way back down the stairs. Two of the Lego sets had been completely rehabilitated and set alongside each other so the pandas could play with the turtles.

Sarah studied the Roman numeral clock above the downturned heads. She wasn't sure what the letters were supposed to mean or how to translate them. But she knew where the number should be, and the hands told her it was past Tris's bedtime.

"Hey, finish up the page you're on and then it's time for bed," Sarah said.

She wasn't surprised by the groan that came from the girl. The whine from the woman though pulled Sarah's head practically to her shoulder as she stared at the brunette in disbelief.

"Sorry," Victoria whispered, dropping her gaze to the table.

Sarah hung the t-shirt across the back of one of the dining room chairs.

"What's that?" Victoria asked.

Sarah shrugged and pointed to Victoria. "For you. For the jacket."

Victoria looked to Tris and commanded, "Translate."

With another roll of her eyes, Tris asked, "Did you give her something?"

Victoria swallowed, then nodded.

"She don't like presents," Tris stated.

The girl set a Lego on the open page. As she made her way around the table, the curly head leaned over the chair and looked at the shirt.

"Musta been a good present because that's her favorite shirt."

"No more translating," Sarah snipped. She pushed the girl slightly to the stairs. "Teeth brushed and bonnet on all the way."

Victoria leaned over the table and pulled the shirt from the chair. She studied the screen printing.

"I wasn't allowed to listen to their music once they officially announced they were leaving the church," Victoria said.

She looked up at Sarah. "Their song... the one that starts out with 'Don't write yourself off yet."

Victoria hummed the tune to the song that had played on repeat in the stolen headphones Sarah used to block out the reality of her life throughout high school in the figurative and literal closet.

"Just try your best," Victoria sang. "Try everything you can."

Sarah smiled. "You sing well."

A blush crept up Victoria's face as the corners of her eyes crinkled. She peeked back at the shirt.

"Did you see them in concert?" Victoria probed as she flipped the shirt over to see the tour dates printed on the back.

With a shake of her head, Sarah shrugged her shoulders. "I found it at a Salvation Army in Flagstaff when I was in college. Anyways, thanks for the sweatshirt."

Victoria got up and held the shirt out to Sarah. "It's your favorite. You should keep it."

Sarah ran her finger over the top of the pizza box where the two slices waited for her to finish. She chewed on different compilations of words to help Victoria understand she needed to keep the shirt.

When she found some that didn't crumble dryly between her molars, she said. "It's not a piece of pineapple pizza. It won't make you gag, so just keep it and put me back on the outside supervision schedule. Everybody wins and the teacher's union won't try to string you up for making faculty supervise recess."

Victoria didn't argue with her. And to her surprise, the child went to bed quickly with the promise that Sarah would try to get off early the next day. Victoria had stuck her head in the room to say goodnight and made her own promise to have her homework done so she could build more Legos before Tris had to get her hair washed and detangled for school on Monday.

Sarah was already sprawled across the couch when Victoria returned from changing into her nightclothes.

With a shake of her head, Sarah said, "I know you wear fancy satin nightgowns to bed, not band shirts."

"No. No. No." Victoria waggled her finger in the air as she made her way to the couch. "I bought that red thing just for our session because I thought you'd judge my boxers and t-shirts. I tried sleeping in it once and woke up sweatier than a lesbian during testimony. And I should know because I was a lesbian at a testimony."

Sarah paused the first episode of Gilmore Girls in the middle of the theme song.

"Were you on trial for something?" Sarah asked.

"No," Victoria said with a laugh.

Sarah pulled her feet in to give Victoria room on the couch. Once the woman was cradled in the smooshy cushion on the other side of the sofa, she pulled Sarah's sock-covered feet into her lap

"So, testimony is, I think, like when you go into the box thing at church and tell the priest all your sins."

"Confession," Sarah whispered. Her eyes closed as the thumbs applied circular pressure to the ball of the thin foot before working their way down the arch.

"Yeah, except there isn't a box. It's in the open, and you have to stand before all the brothers and sisters and give testimony to your sins and ask for forgiveness from God and the community."

Sarah breathed out as her head lolled from side to side. It took a moment to process Victoria's explanation but when the words aligned within her head, her eyes popped open.

"Wait! You had to stand in front of everyone and tell them you were gay?"

Victoria chuckled lightly. With a gentle nod, she said, "Yes. I confessed to having adulterous thoughts for women and that those thoughts had led me to file for a divorce that afternoon. I hadn't told my parents or my sisters beforehand, because I didn't want them to try and talk me out of it. So, I made my announcement knowing they would put an asterisk next to my name in the records book and my family would forever be seen as tainted. That night I drove away from the only town I had ever lived in and came here where I hit a woman's car in the parking lot outside of Trader Joe's. She was my first friend here and after hearing my story, she recommended me to a therapist she'd seen after her divorce. A Dr. Monica Green."

Sarah's foot was set down in Victoria's lap and the other was picked up. The massage was thoughtful and well executed, leaving Sarah to wonder if this very activity had been a part of Victoria's daily expectations as a wife in a community Sarah didn't understand.

"That is one hell of a coming out story," Sarah whispered.

Victoria hummed in response. "Was your coming out story eventful?"

Sarah licked her lips, hoping the truth would scare Victoria away.

"I never came out." she swallowed the desire to keep the shameful secret and spit it out. "My mom's a prostitute. She... she is the most Evangelical prostitute you would ever meet. So, I never told her or my sister or anyone because I didn't want her to try to fix me with one of her Johns."

The thumbs pressing against the pads of her toes stalled momentarily. Victoria shook her head and looked down at Sarah.

"Well, we never have to worry about Tris giving testimony or being fixed."

And Sarah wasn't sure if she should be happy that Victoria thought of the different life Tris would be offered or worried at how fast Victoria had stepped into a pseudo-parenting mindset.

"What's the deal with the asterisks?" Sarah asked.

Victoria's fingers stopped once more. She barely breathed for a moment.

"The asterisks means gay or mentally unstable," Victoria explained. "It's basically a blacklist from working with kids in any capacity. It used to be if you went to conversion therapy and you completed several years for probation with a deacon, then they would remove the mark, but that changed when major new media started reporting that conversion therapy didn't work."

"So... if you'd stayed—"

"I would have lost my job," Victoria stated. "I wouldn't have been allowed to teach in any school again because most, if not all, of them are run by members of the church."

"There are no gay teachers in Utah?" Sarah asked in disbelief.

"Oh, there are, but they probably didn't stand up in testimony and announce it."

Victoria leaned over Sarah's body and took the remote lying by her side. She held it angled at the TV and allowed the gentle theme song to fill the silence of the room.

It was a somewhat passive-aggressive way to end the conversation, but Sarah understood enough about running away from home to know Victoria had shared her fill for the night.

30

Every Wednesday ended with a late afternoon meeting. Victoria had to sit in the cramped conference room while her boss and the rest of the team rambled on and on about different technological tools they could purchase with the Winter's Education Grant they received. After twenty minutes of arguing over which tool would be the most effective Band-Aid for the bullet hole wound in their students' lack of success on the latest state test, Victoria was over it.

She didn't have an opinion while the blonde bitch, Ms. Branche, sat at the end of the meeting table. The anger radiating from her had raised her blood temperature to 214 degrees. Even the sound of the air coming from the teacher's wide-open mouth pissed her off.

Victoria snapped, providing her own suggestion when the woman claimed purchasing a new computer program would solve the problem of students' low reading scores.

"Why don't we invest the money in pencils and notebooks for all kids, so they aren't made to feel terrible if their parents can't afford to get them one?" Victoria leaned back in her chair as she waited for Ms. Branche's response.

The teacher sat up straighter. She played with the pencil probably stolen from Diego's personal stash. Then she said, "Well, the program would make it so students wouldn't need a pencil or paper."

"Just a computer, right?" Victoria pushed.

"Well, yes," Ms. Branche answered.

Victoria tapped her fingers on the table. "And how many students this week have been sent to my office because they didn't have their computer, so you wrote them a referral for insubordination?"

The blonde swallowed audibly. Victoria hoped the taste of vomit still coating the inside of her venomous mouth. She shifted in her seat when the rest of the team turned to look at her.

"So... the computer program will probably help the kids who technology is already helping, but the ones with an M-Power box beeping to let them know that the power is going to turn off in a day, or maybe two, are being sent to my office because their computer not working has made them a discipline issue." Victoria pushed the hair back from her face. "The problem with scores isn't whether they have a new reading or math game to make it so instruction doesn't have to take place in the classroom. The issue with scores is that the kids that need the instruction are being forced out of the classroom for petty non-issues to force compliance over success."

Several sets of eyes stared widely at her as she got up from the table. "You want to improve academics, stop sending kids to sit outside of my office and actually teach them."

She walked out of the room without a dismissal and made her way immediately to her car. Her day was done, and she was emotionally tapped after the little pieces of Sarah and Tris had begun to eat at her. Like the breakfast dishes that had been layered atop the dinner dishes. The same ones Sarah had promised to clean but fell asleep on the couch instead.

Victoria walked into the house and immediately tripped over a pair of size three sneakers lying in the middle of the hallway. She'd sworn when she left for work that morning the house was clean, including the dishes Sarah had ignored. But after she cleared the shoes, she had to step over the backpack, spilling out onto the rug.

It would be one thing if it was just the child, but Sarah's jacket lay on the floor along with her sex coach ballet flats.

When Victoria looked into the living room, she found the slacks Sarah had worn the night before she'd gone to meet with a new couple thrown across the coffee table and two bras hanging off the arm of the chair. Why none of these things had made it to Sarah's room was beyond her. It was like the woman lived in the living room, always falling asleep on the couch when Victoria had given her a room. Gave her a home.

And she just trashed it, teaching Tris to do the same.

She felt it growing again. The grumbling in her head turned to a glare as she moved to the back of the house. The table she'd cleared and cleaned that morning was sprinkled with cinnamon toast crunch particles and spilled milk had dried from Tris's afternoon snack on the glossy surface.

The sink was filled with dishes once more, while the counters were covered in something sticky and water that had shot food particles from the dirty dishes.

The O'Keeffe women leaned over a pan on the stove as another boiled over the edges.

"I don't think it's supposed to look like that," Sarah said.

"It looks disgusting," Tris added as she pushed herself up to sit on the counter. Victoria's counter had been butt-germ-free, but like everything else in her house was dirty.

Victoria tried to calm the rage building, but when Sarah looked up and smiled at her it was too much. It would be one thing if Sarah felt bad for destroying her home but to not even care sent her spiraling

The glaring shifted to growling as each word clawed at her throat as she tried to swallow them. But the words won the battle and four made it out.

"What the hell happened?"

The smile on Sarah's face fell. Her eyes ran over the kitchen and the dishes.

Tris tucked herself behind Sarah. With one hand Sarah held Tris behind her, and the other she picked up one of the dishes on the counter. She held it between herself and the red-faced homeowner moving toward them.

"I... we were just cooking dinner," Sarah tried to explain in a voice an octave higher than normal. "I just...I will clean it up. I'll clean it up now."

"Like you did the dishes last night?" Victoria spat, picking up the pot she'd just washed that morning.

"I didn't realize..." Sarah's eyes ran over the kitchen. The small frying pan in her hand shook as she still held it out. "I'm sorry. I will take care of it all now."

"Don't bother. I'll do it." Victoria turned the burner off from under the overcooked noodles. "I'll just add maid to my list of hats to wear since apparently asking you to live here made me your damn servant."

"We just wanted to cook you dinner!" Tris cried as she peeked out from behind Sarah.

Victoria looked at the stove now smoking because of her rant. She ripped the ruined pan from the stove and shoved it under the tap. Oil and water screamed in protest as they were forced to mix.

She didn't notice the way Sarah had twisted around so the woman's back was to her. She only noticed after the way Sarah encircled the head of the child and ducked her own face over the girl.

A bucket of ice had fallen over the room. The smoke detector above them screamed to life and Sarah's rigid body curled tighter around the girl whose fingers dug into the baggy blue shirt hanging off the mother.

"I'm sorry," Victoria said, hoping to be heard over the alarm. She reached out and touched Sarah's arm that immediately rose to cover her face as the child was pressed against the counter.

"I'm so sorry," Victoria said again. She turned from the kitchen and stepped as quickly as she could without leaving any loud footfalls.

The keys were in her work purse, but she didn't care. She'd dig them out when she got to the gym. She just needed to get away as the alarm warned the two she'd promise some place safe to stay that there was no such thing.

Victoria yanked the handles of the rowing machine, a task normally easy. The anger replaced with regret made her limbs heavy and every pull didn't take her as far as normal.

"You been on that machine forever," Echo called over from the deadlift bar.

"I'm getting there," Victoria wasped as she pulled again. Only eighteen more meters.

"Bad day at work?" Echo asked.

"Nnnnoooo!" Victoria growled with another pull.

Echo bent at the knees, wrapped her fingers around the bar, and exhaled slowly. She didn't move her arms as she pushed up from the ground, defying gravity until her legs had nowhere else to go. She breathed twice before letting the bar go and the coated weights hit the ground with several thuds. The gym echoed with the same sound as the other participants of the circuit were steadily tackling and finishing the stage Victoria had yet to reach.

"So, what's up?" Echo squirted water from the bottle into her open mouth.

Three more pulls and Victoria was finished. She used the towel wrapped around her neck to wipe the sweat from her face.

"I asked Sarah and her kid to move in with me."

The stream of water from the bottle ceased as Echo choked and then sputtered, "You what?"

When Victoria didn't immediately answer, Echo asked, "Who the fuck is Sarah?"

With a slap to her forehead, she then yelled, "Please tell me you didn't U-Haul that girl from my bar!"

"No." Victoria shook her head. "Worse."

Echo snorted, then asked, "How can it be worse?"

"It's this woman I work with. Her and her kid's apartment got broken into and I offered them a place to stay."

Echo squatted down next to her weight bar and started to disassemble her weights.

"Things not going well?" Echo asked.

Victoria ran her hands over her face, trying to push away the image of Sarah clinging protectively to Tris.

With a deep breath, she explained, "As much as I hated it, I think I got used to living alone. Not cleaning up after other people. And they are like a tornado."

Echo chuckled. "Kids do that."

"Honestly, the kid seems to keep her stuff in her room. But Sarah.... She has a room, but I think she is sleeping on my couch."

"Maybe the bed sucks," Echo offered with a shrug.

"No, I think... like it's more than that." Victoria got up from the rowing machine. "Like, when I went to help her when the house got broken into, she didn't have a room. They lived in this one-bedroom apartment and she apparently wanted her daughter to have a life she never did so she always slept on the couch."

"Wow." Echo looked up at the ceiling. "Sounds like a good woman."

Victoria sighed before admitting, "She is."

"Did you all have the boundaries talk?"

Victoria's eyebrow rose. "The what?"

Weights banged into the others on the rack as Echo returned them to their resting space. The rest of the people in their group had already finished, leaving them alone in the warehouse gym.

"When Olivia came to live with Simone and me, Parker had us sit down and talk about the boundaries. Not really rules but just set guidelines for what we all needed. Maybe you guys need to talk about common areas of the house, you know?"

"Olivia is the oldest right? The new girl. A teenager."

"Yeah."

Victoria picked up her water bottle and looked over the bar and weights still waiting for her.

"Was she like traumatized when she came to you? Like, shrink away if you moved too fast?"

Echo studied Victoria's face like she'd just seen the woman for the first time.

"Olivia's story is not mine to tell. But we did have to adjust to how we used our bodies and the tone we spoke in. You know?"

Tucking a hair behind her ear, Victoria asked, "Was it hard?"

"All habits are hard to break." Echo took another drink of water. She wiped the spillage away with her shirt. "You doing it for the kid or the girl?"

"Sarah... I lost my cool and I was yelling, and she grabbed Tris and was like using her body as a shield so the kid wouldn't get hurt." Just the words coming out burned her throat. Her stomach twisted and she felt the bile rising add to the burn.

"Yeah, so no yelling. Not to mention, not cool, dude." Echo shook her head. "She's an adult... No adult, traumatized or not, should be getting yelled at by the person they live with."

Echo pushed the hair from her face. "I mean, if you yelled at my kids, I would fuck you up. But Simone yelled at me a lot and it just made me feel like a piece of trash."

Shaking her head, Echo added, "Look, I can tell you like this girl. Way more than the bitch who's been to my bar too many times this week flirting with other chicks. So, you gotta treat her with more respect than you would ever show another person. Like that girl clearly puts her kid before herself and that's someone that is special. My bitch of an ex literally kicked her kids out of her house and didn't care where we went."

"I know," Victoria whispered. "It's all just... I mean, with Michael it was easy because I knew what to expect. I don't know why but I expected Sarah to be...

cleaner."

"Girls can be messy." Echo gestured to the mostly empty gym. "Put that shit away and just go home and talk to her. And also hope she's still there because she sounds like someone that's lived through hell like Parker. And when Parker runs, it's really hard to catch her, so get your ass there before she's gone for good with your chance to apologize."

31

Tris looked up from the drying towel to where Sarah was scrubbing the tile backsplash grout. The pan they'd ruined had protested the oil and basil mixture by spraying it as far as possible, and Sarah was determined to correct it before Victoria returned home.

She'd drafted the silent to-do list while she held the child in the air so Tris could wave a towel and clear away the smoke. Unsure of how long Victoria would be gone, she focused on the primary goal: Fix the kitchen.

With the sink clear and the counters streak-free, she scrubbed away the evidence of their vandalism. They couldn't risk ruining anything else, so Sarah sent Tris to the bedroom where the empty hangers still swung from having their garments torn from them, so they were ready to leave once they were done. The girl retrieved two packets of ramen from Sarah's bag in the closet

Holding them up as she descended the stairs, Tris asked, "You want orange or pink?"

"Whichever you don't want."

Weighing the packets in her hands, Tris decided on pink. Without a glance at the woman kneeling on the counter with her head in the range hood, she asked, "Crushed or long?"

Sarah peeked from under the hood with her lips scrunched together. "Tough choice... I think go with crushed so there will be less splatter."

Tris held up a finger, "Crushed is good but also I'm thinking drain the water so there's really no splash."

"Good thinking," Sarah praised.

She stuck her head back in the hood to get the last of their presto pesto fiasco cleaned away. The packets of ramen were beaten against the counter and the noodles obliterated into tiny bits by the child's fist.

Sarah held the wall until the smashing had finished. She controlled her breathing, feeling the fear wash through her once more. Her resolve to find a new place for them solidified in her gut.

Initially, she'd moved from the kitchen with the alarm still screaming to check that Victoria had driven away. Her belongings were gathered quickly as the girl went to her own room. Simultaneously, they'd pulled the clothes from the hangers and stuffed them into the duffel bags still lying in wait within the closets.

But the kitchen had been ruined and the guilt of causing Victoria distress caught up with her. It steadied her shaking limbs and sent her back to the scene of the crime to wipe away any evidence of their presence.

When the microwave opened, Sarah said, "Make sure you check the bowl says microwave safe."

"Okay."

Sarah hopped down from the counter. The digital panel beeped, and the machine whirred to life while the time until Victoria would walk back into the house ticked down with each click from the wall clock.

"Why did we come to live here?" Tris asked when the microwave announced the completion of its task. She wrapped her drying towel around the bowl and pulled the bowl of ramen noodles from the glass tray.

Sarah placed the second bowl atop the first and drained the liquid from still slightly crunchy noodles. Using a fork, she scooped a third of the ramen into the second bowl and handed the larger portion to Tris who shook the seasoning packet in the air.

Tris looked at her bowl, then peered over the rim of Sarah's. With her fork, she tried to even out the portions.

"Stop it," Sarah said, pulling her bowl away, so the girl couldn't split it evenly.

"You didn't take enough," Tris countered. She moved the remaining noodles around with her fork. "Aunt Monica was right."

"She usually is," Sarah grumbled. "But what is she right about this time?"

"You're going to die too early because you don't take care of yourself and I'm going to end up all alone."

The air in Sarah's lungs leaked through the hole between her ribs. The knife she'd pulled from her chest had been discarded but she hadn't managed to heal since she and Monica stopped talking. She made a mental note to call the woman tomorrow and apologize again for not being the friend she was supposed to be.

"You didn't answer my question either," Tris snapped.

The powder sprinkled over the girl's noodles, creating a dingy-looking pasta mush.

"What question?"

"Why did we come to live here?"

Noodles gnashed around in Tris's open mouth. The crooked front teeth caused the wound in Sarah's chest to widen. She'd planned to use the money Victoria refused to take from the coffee table to get the girl braces.

It would have been enough to keep Tris from growing up ashamed of her genetically imposed imperfect smile. Another thing she'd ruined by getting comfortable. For the last forty minutes she'd been thinking about all the boundaries she shouldn't have let been crossed, starting that first night on the couch, followed by the jacket that had been hung in the hall closet instead of packed in the ready to flee bag.

Sarah sighed and put her seasoning in the more equalized portion of the familiar dinner. "I told you. We couldn't go back to the apartment."

"But why couldn't we go back?" Tris pushed.

"Because someone broke in."

"Why would they break into our house? We don't have nothing to steal."

"Anything to steal," Sarah corrected.

Tris didn't say anything. She scooped a spoon of noodles and let it drop back into the bowl.

Sarah sighed again. She swirled her dinner around until it matched the same disappointing color as the child's. As she took in the faucet still covered in food chunks, she made a mental note to correct that after she finished her noodle mush.

"It wasn't safe."

Tris looked up at Sarah. Her mouth opened and closed a few times before Sarah said, "Just say it,"

"It was you sister, wasn't it?"

Sarah searched the child's face. It was her turn to try to find words. However, some leaked out before she decided they weren't the right ones. "Why would you...? How do you...?"

"Your mom called," Tris confessed. "I answered because you were in the shower. She said... she said that she needed our address so that she could send you a birthday present. I got excited because I didn't know it was your birthday... and I gave it to her."

Sarah licked her lips. "My birthday is in March."

Green eyes fell on the bowl still filled. Tris's shoulders hunched forward, her arms coming to rest around the bowl protectively. She didn't look up when she asked, "Then why did she say it was your birthday?"

Sarah whispered, "She wants me to let your mom come live with us."

"Why?"

Sarah had avoided the conversation of Sierra for so long. She knew at some point she would have to tell Tris the truth, but tonight had already been so much for the girl.

"You don't have to keep trying to protect me," Tris said. "I know. I heard Aunt Monica say she's a crackhead. And that means she's on drugs."

Sarah would not be calling Monica after all.

Licking her lips, Sarah said, "Your mom is addicted to expensive drugs but you can't force someone to stop using. And... your mom...she needed money, and I told her I didn't have any when I saw her. She didn't believe me, and she broke into our house. That's why we can't just go back. She would come back again, and it's not safe."

The spoon froze mid-stir, and Tris looked up. "You saw her?"

"Yeah." Sarah pushed away the bowl. The food had nowhere to go anymore with the lump that had formed in her throat. "I see her every six months so that she will sign the papers for me to be able to keep you in school and take you to the doctor."

"Was she still... on drugs?"

"Yes."

Tris nodded and pushed her bowl away as well. Quietly, she asked, "Do you think I will ever be able to meet her?"

"I hope so."

The clock ticked and then it tocked. Neither picked up their utensils as the younger O'Keeffe processed and the older O'Keeffe sent out a silent prayer that somewhere Sierra was still breathing.

"What does she look like?"

Sarah half smiled and waved her hand over her face. "Exactly like me. We're twins."

"Oh." Tris chewed on the information briefly and then said, "Then I don't need to meet her."

Her bowl returned in front of her as Tris devoured the rest of her ramen.

With a cinched brow, Sarah asked, "What changed?"

"I just wanted to see if I looked like her," Tris explained. "It's not like she's my real mom. I just wondered if she looked... like me."

"Did I never tell you we're twins?"

"No."

When Tris finished, Sarah scooted her bowl over to the girl. Tris shook her head and pushed the food back at Sarah.

"There's no pictures. We never have any pictures," Tris stated.

Sarah looked at the girl. "I don't have any pictures of your mom and me, but I bet I could find a digital version of our high school yearbook."

"I'm sorry your mom sucked," Tris whispered.

"Me too."

They sat quietly. The house didn't move as Sarah ate.

"Can we print a picture of you and me and put it in a frame so that one day I can show someone?" Tris asked.

"Of course." Sarah looked at the stupid Roman numerals on the clock. She replaced the letters with numbers as she counted around the circle. "It's late, you should head to bed. I'll finish."

"I thought we had to go."

Glancing back at the door, she realized running away wasn't fair to Victoria. The woman was owed an apology, a real one. Plus, Sarah needed to give the woman the key back, along with the rent money. It would make working next to Victoria easier, and then tomorrow she could start the apartment search again.

"Tomorrow," Sarah whispered. "I'll find us a place to go tomorrow that isn't Monica's."

"What about Mrs. Greyson?" Tris asked. "Could we go back to our first house?"

Sarah thought about Evie being the new owner of their first house. Then she remembered Zoe telling her Evie was renting it out already. That wasn't an option though. She couldn't just go back after what had happened with Simone. There was no way that Simone hadn't told Dilynn Greyson's partner about Sarah being forced to resign after being accused of prostitution.

"Mrs. Greyson doesn't own our old house anymore, but it will be okay. I will find us a new apartment."

Tris didn't argue. She headed up the stairs and tucked herself into bed.

Sarah walked through the lower part of the house looking for anything she missed. Any hint of their existence. When she found nothing, she retrieved the sex supply case from her car and brought it inside. She'd forgotten the first time she'd used the case with Victoria, she'd never cleaned out the wax.

The wax from the candles had spread over the interior and most of the toys. The straps and interior of the time from when she'd last met with Victoria also needed to be cleaned.

She sighed at the time it would take. She had a client tomorrow and she needed to remember to talk to Leticia in the morning. Otherwise, she'd have to actually call Monica. The wax could wait for another day, but the toys would need to be sanitized and organized for use.

As she retrieved them from the bag, she heard the garage. She looked down at the line of dongs on the coffee table and then up at the garage door that had begun to open.

Sarah reached for the dildos and gathered them into her lap when Victoria's footsteps stopped just outside the entrance to the living room.

Sarah kept her head bowed to avoid seeing the rage from the chestnut eyes once more. Hastily she explained, "I'm sorry. I just... I'm sorry. I have to see a client tomorrow so... I'm sorry. I just need to Lysol them, and I will get them out of here."

Victoria set her purse and gym bag down. "Can we talk while you clean them?"

"Yeah," Sarah choked out. "I can... I mean, I'll just keep them on the floor because I know you don't like them. I promise not to bring them out anymore, also."

She knew that wasn't really a problem because tomorrow they wouldn't be here. The words for the apology had been drafted so many times that Sarah couldn't figure out which one wasn't terrible. She scanned the table as though there were notecards with pieces of what she needed to say, but she got nothing.

"Sarah."

The green eyes vanished behind her lids. She counted to five, pleading with her body to relax from flight mode.

"You don't have to.... I'm sorry," Victoria said.

Sarah couldn't help but notice how Victoria's arms glistened in the living room light when she opened her eyes. She'd known the woman actively worked out but the realization that she worked out enough to break a sweat made Sarah's fear of the woman increase.

Victoria sat in a chair caddy corner to Sarah. Sarah pulled a Lysol wipe from the container and picked up the first dick. She checked the silicon for lint and hair before she wrapped her wipe-covered hand around the shaft and ran it up and down.

Neither of them said anything right away. Sarah made it through two penises before she gathered the courage to start.

"I'm sorry about the mess. There's really no excuse or reason, other than we were careless and forgot that we were guests here."

Her eyes watched Victoria's fingers as she spoke. She searched for any sign the woman was ready for a fight. The black candle she'd missed lay within reach and she recognized it as the most likely projectile if she messed up her apology.

The tips of the manicured nails tapped against the beige suede.

Victoria sighed before she said, "You don't owe me an apology. If anyone needs to apologize it's me."

"It's my fault," Sarah said it a little differently so Victoria would know she understood she deserved the lashing she was given.

"No. I shouldn't have yelled at you. I especially shouldn't have yelled at you in front of Tris. I don't know why I snapped."

Victoria's second heavy sigh reverberated through Sarah. The thin hand wrapped around the dick moved quicker but sloppier.

"That's a lie," Victoria confessed. "I know why I snapped, and it had nothing to do with you and everything to do with me."

Victoria's head fell back against the cushion. "My whole adult life, I have always been expected to maintain a clean house. Like my entire life I was taught the house's tidiness was linked directly to my fitness as a wife, and I came home, and it was like I failed."

"You keep a perfect home," Sarah stated. "It's the type of home that I put together in my imagination that I could someday give Tris. And you don't have any wifely duties to me."

She set the toy alongside the others.

"We're guests in your home," Sarah explained. "I shoulda been... I mean, you won't let me pay you so I shoulda been making sure you had to do less. I should be cooking dinner for you and making sure it's like we're not here. I thought...." Sarah squeezed the silicon between her hands. "I thought by staying away as much as possible we wouldn't intrude on your life. I forgot though that we need to make sure our stuff is out of sight."

Victoria tapped her hands against the armrest and her leg bounced so fast that the board under her foot creaked painfully.

"I don't want you to feel like a guest here. This whole living together thing is going to take getting used to for both of us. A friend of mine said we need to set boundaries."

"I just need a few weeks, and I'll get us out of your hair," Sarah promised. It would be easier with the extra time. She would be able to pay Victoria and save some for the deposit.

"I don't want you to leave," Victoria choked.

Sarah dared to look at the bloodshot chestnut eyes staring at her. The earthy irises were covered with a growing tsunami. Sarah held her breath as the wave crashed over the surf-colored skin and rushed down Victoria's face.

"I never meant to upset you," Sarah whispered.

"I messed up," Victoria said, patting her chest. "The dishes. The clothes. None of that should have ever mattered enough to make you so scared of me that you felt like you had to protect Tris from me."

"That's not a you problem," Sarah explained. "It's a me problem. I'm... I'm broken."

"You aren't broken," Victoria breathed out. It was her truth and Sarah knew Victoria's truth was based on the reality she'd constructed of Sarah being a worthwhile investment of her energy.

But Sarah's truth was different, and it wasn't wrong. She knew through all her trauma training that she was the problem. Her whole life was structured in a way to ensure no relationship she'd ever attempt to hold, whether friendship or romantic, wouldn't be tested and come up short.

Every coping strategy she possessed impeded her ability to function in a manner that wouldn't displease the person she wanted nothing more than to see smile. She'd ruin Victoria's smiles until the woman realized, just like Simone, there were better options out there.

"Can we just... I don't know, like, lock away your running shoes?" Victoria asked.

Sarah's brows scrunched in the middle and the wrinkle between them deepened. "I only own two pairs of shoes and neither of them are running shoes. One is held together with actual black duct tape, so even if I wanted to run in it... I couldn't."

"Sariah," Victoria said.

"I hate you found out my government name, so please don't call me that." Sarah's shoulders slumped together. "My mother called me Sariah every time she was high. She would manage to get out my whole name and she'd just point to her cigarettes or a bottle of booze for me to get."

"I can respect that boundary," Victoria stated.

Sarah huffed out an unamused laugh.

"What does that mean? That *humph?*"

Sarah wrapped a new Lysol wipe around the head of the dildo.

"You have literally respected zero boundaries I have asked for," she admitted.

Waves of energy rolled off Victoria's being and crashed against Sarah's chest. The thoughts in the other woman's head seemed to produce enough steam to raise the temperature of the room and create a fog so dense Sarah felt herself struggling to breathe well.

"What do you mean?" Victoria asked.

Sarah looked over at the woman.

"I asked you to keep our relationship limited to work and yet you prodded and probed me every chance you got for personal information that you used to convince me that moving here was a good idea."

Sarah's fear seemed to dissipate as her brain threw more examples forward.

"I blatantly told you I was not in a place to consider a romantic relationship, but you continued to attempt to court me."

She took a breath.

"I told you I needed you to let me pay you rent so I wouldn't feel like a whore, and you told me to basically piss off and my feelings were unjustified even though we met under the condition that I would provide you sexual expertise for payment."

She studied the way Victoria's eyes scanned her face to see if she was lying. But Sarah knew there was no way in hell her cheeks were pink because she had said no to Victoria repeatedly and Victoria had acted like every man she'd ever met.

"I have more examples but those are the most relevant." Sarah shook her head. "So, it's like asking you to do something small like don't use my government name leads to a promise of respect but I don't know how to trust anyone. I mean, anyone, and I just feel... I feel like it doesn't matter what I want or need when it comes to you because you already have decided for me."

"I..." Victoria swallowed. "You're right. I should have respected your boundaries, and you were very, very upfront with me."

"I can't move out for at least two weeks," Sarah said. "I know you wanted to talk about house rules so let's do that. Let's set up the rules and maybe then I can show you that you don't have to expect to take care of everyone and you can show me that you understand what a boundary actually is. Then we can be like actual friends because I could really use a friend. Not a girlfriend. A real friend."

Victoria didn't move. She stared at the table where the cleaned dicks lay in a line.

"Can we split up the work?" Sarah offered. "I mean, if you tell me what needs to be done, then we all can do those things."

Victoria nodded. "I would like that."

Sarah ran her hand over the head of a dildo repeatedly. She chewed on her lip. "How about whoever cooks dinner doesn't have to do the dishes?" she suggested.

"I usually cook," Victoria said. "And I heard from the snitch that your cooking could potentially kill me."

Sarah knew it was a joke. It probably was even funny, but her life had been put on display for a woman who didn't understand her or respect her. So, the playful banter hit like a punch to the gut.

"So, Tris and I will do the dishes," Sarah stated. "Tris and I can take the trash cans out on trash day too."

"I am kind of crazy about vacuuming and the lines, so I will vacuum," Victoria said.

"Okay. I will sweep the kitchen and the dining room floors. How often do you want that done?" Sarah asked. She carefully logged each of the new tasks into her brain. "It's a good job for me to do since it's something that I can do when I get home, even if it's late."

"I usually do it once or twice a week. We will probably need twice now because of the playground sand."

"Okay." Sarah moved on to the next penis. "I can't promise what day I will do it because it will depend on when I meet with clients. Speaking of which, I will be gone tomorrow night. I will talk to Leticia tomorrow to see if she can babysit, and if not, Monica will do it. So, I will take Tris over there for the night and that means you don't have to worry about dinner."

"She can stay here with me," Victoria offered. "She shouldn't have to sleep over at Monica's on a school night."

"You don't have to do that," Sarah said.

"I don't mind honestly," Victoria promised. "I usually play darts with my friend on Thursday nights but tomorrow the team we're playing already canceled. Can you make your appointments not fall on Thursday moving forward? Then Tris doesn't have to go anywhere."

"Yeah. I can do that." Sarah didn't like the idea, but it would mean she was home sooner. "Thank you."

"Of course."

The wipe coming out of the container was the only sound. She moved on to the next toy.

"Would you mind if I put up a picture on the table over there?" Sarah pointed to the entry table. "We have never actually had a framed picture before, and Tris asked about it tonight. I would just like it to be somewhere she can see it. I'll make sure it's the only one that's out."

Victoria nodded quickly. "Absolutely. I would really like to have pictures up again."

"Thank you." Sarah finished the last toy. She gathered all the wet wipes into a ball and scrunched them in her fist. Then she said, "If you don't like something... if you could just tell me. I will fix it. I promise."

Victoria didn't promise. Instead, she asked, "Can I ask why all your stuff was in the living room?"

Sarah felt the cushion of the couch hug her body as she leaned back.

"I fall asleep watching TV a lot. I just don't make it to bed."

If Victoria knew she was lying, the woman didn't point it out this time.

"I'll make sure I don't leave my clothes down here anymore, though."

"It's okay. It really isn't a big deal. It's not like we are the only people here or anything."

Sarah knew it was meant to be a joke again, but this time Victoria was poking fun at herself. And Sarah still didn't have it in her to laugh.

"I'm sure you don't want to be trying to watch TV with my bras hanging over your chair," Sarah said.

Victoria laughed and raised her eyebrow. "I don't mind your bras."

Sarah didn't need to point out to Victoria this was another example of when the brunette made a pass at Sarah. The blush in Victoria's face and drop of her chin told Sarah the woman understood.

"Okay, well I'm going to head to bed," Victoria said to the silent room.

Sarah nodded and gestured to the toys across the table. "I will get this stuff finished up and then I'm going to sleep soon too."

"How'd you go from Sariah to Sarah?" Victoria asked when she made it to the living room threshold. "I know it's random, but when I saw your actual name, I just wondered."

With a simple shake of her head, Sarah provided a piece of her story. "Uh... my first-grade teacher said Sarah on the first day of school. Just plain Sarah. My sister is Sierra and I'm Sariah. I mean, at least I think I am. I sometimes wonder if my mother mixed us up when we were young, but I guess it doesn't really matter. She never spoke to us individually so it's not like we ever really knew who was who."

Sarah forced a smile onto her face.

"I've been Sarah since our first-grade teacher pointed at me and called me Sarah. But if my sister ever committed a crime, it wouldn't matter what my name was because it would still be our DNA at the scene. It's crazy to think about sometimes."

She breathed for a moment, then looked at Victoria. "That was more than you asked for but earlier Tris told me she didn't care if she ever met my sister because she learned we're twins and all I could think about is she really is genetically half me, so she could totally be my biological daughter and if my sister had just used my name instead of her own at the hospital... I never would have had to give her anything because I never would have needed a signature on a piece of paper to prove that I have the right to raise her."

Victoria's head tilted slightly. Her lower lip disappeared between her teeth until it popped out with a simple sentence.

"You're a great mom to your daughter."

32

Babysitting Tris was like sitting at home alone. In the four nights Sarah had left the girl home with Victoria, the child's bedroom door had remained closed and only the sound of rushing water from a flush of the upstairs toilet demonstrated any form of life.

Victoria had hoped for Lego time or maybe a movie night the Friday before. Her hopes were just that, and the girl's chilly demeanor from their first interaction was Victoria's new normal. She'd been unable to provide more than a simple apology to the child before she'd disappeared behind the bedroom door moments following Sarah's departure the first night.

At least she had plenty of time to complete the final week of her course. Her paper on identifying struggling student populations was mocking her. The cursor blinked but the rhythm was off. Victoria felt like each blink took slightly longer than the last as though the computer had grown bored with the reality she'd run out of words three pages into the ten due on Friday.

Kernels of corn rattled and popped in the microwave. The scent of artificial butter and empty carbs covered the lavender candle she'd lit, then blew out when her sinus cavity threatened to collapse.

From Victoria's position at the counter, she was able to catch sight of the recluse when the door upstairs opened. A gangly hand ran its way over the banister, but the floor didn't creak when the ninja-like child stole from her room to the bathroom.

With the week-long Thanksgiving break beginning in two days, Victoria wondered if the three days she'd committed to Sarah as a babysitter had been a good idea. Neither Tris nor herself had told Sarah their evenings together were a bust, but three real days of the kid sitting in her room couldn't be good for her.

She called up the stairs, in another attempt to pull the child into the living space, "Tris, I made popcorn!"

Her fingers burned along with her face from the steam escaping the crack in the expanded trifold bag. She yanked at the corners, then allowed the bag to fall to the counter. Sucking the digits in her mouth, she listened for any hint of life.

The air rushed from her lips when the door to the bedroom shut without so much as a "No."

Victoria's mind accepted a new truth. The O'Keeffe women were the most reclusive and silently stubborn humans she'd ever met.

The computer beeped in displeasure at her triple assault on the shift key. Its anger was so loud she'd missed the soft shudder of the stairs under the girl's weight. Only when the second to the bottom stair groaned did Victoria feel the ninja's presence.

Victoria pushed the bag of popcorn toward the kid, who scrunched her nose at the off-white puffs within.

"Why does it look like that?" Tris asked.

Victoria flipped the bag around and stared at the opening. Pulling a piece out, she checked it for charring. Then she wondered how the child made it to nine, not knowing this was what popcorn was supposed to look like.

"Where's the Tajín?" Tris asked when Victoria popped the piece into her mouth.

Victoria swallowed. "The what?"

Tris's eyebrows scrunched together. "You don't put Tajín on your popcorn?"

"What's Tajín?"

The head full of curls fell backward as if the question had offended her. "The red stuff that Mom always puts on it. It's in the cabinet."

"It has butter on it," Victoria said, hoping to probe the child into more words.

"But Tajín gives it flavor," Tris whined.

"Butter is a flavor," Victoria argued with a smile splayed across her lips

Tris rolled her eyes. "White people."

"What?" Victoria asked, a hand held to her heart.

Tris climbed on the counter and pulled the Tajín out. She grabbed a plate and moved back to the table. Pouring out a handful of popcorn, she made certain not a single kernel touched the table. Then she added a heavy amount of chili limon seasoning atop.

She wiggled the plate, then held it up to Victoria. Victoria stared at the abomination, but since this was the least amount of contempt-filled glares the child had dished her way, she took a piece with just a little and popped it in her mouth.

At first, the brunette's nose crinkled at the shift from the normal. She allowed the kernel to rest on her tongue, rolling it over in preparation for the burn associated with the red flecks. But it never came.

Instead, the tang of lime pleasantly tingled her tastebuds until a smile rose on her lips. She reached for another, but the child pulled the plate back.

Tris pushed the plastic jar toward Victoria as she said, "Just be careful. The lady that owns the table hates messes."

"Owner sounds like a jerk," Victoria stated. She didn't add quite as much

Tajín as the girl had. "This really is good."

"Mmhmm."

Tris plopped pieces of popcorn in her mouth with one hand and scratched her scalp with the other. Initially, Victoria just thought she heard the sound of Tris chewing until she realized it was more of a sprinkling. A sprinkling after every scratch.

She studied the way the girl alternated between eating a piece of popcorn and scratching her head. A vision of barely visible white egg sacks and tiny beige bugs crept into Victoria's mind. Her head began itching behind her ears.

"What's wrong with your head?" Victoria asked, pulling her hand from her hair.

Tris's fingers withdrew from her hair. "Nothing."

She pulled her feet to her chest, but the need to scratch brought her hand back up.

Victoria moved around the table, pushing the curls to the side so she could see what Tris was digging at.

"Hasn't anyone ever told you that you don't touch a Black girl's crown?" Tris growled, trying to pull her head away from the fingers trying to create a part through the 3C curls.

"Just hold still," Victoria wasped. "I need to see if you have lice."

She stared down at the roots of her hair. The scalp was unseeable through rocky sand. Unable to believe her eyes, she pinched the sand between her fingers and let it fall to the floor Sarah had swept and mopped after returning home at 11 the night before.

"What happened?" Victoria asked.

"Nothing."

Victoria pulled Tris's head back, so the girl had to look at her "Your hair is full of sand. That's something, not nothing."

Tris pulled out of Victoria's grip. "I know."

"If you know, then what happened?"

"You're not my mom, so I don't have to tell you anything." The girl dropped her chin. "You're just the lady that wants to date my mom so you're just pretending to care."

Victoria sat in the chair alongside Tris. The green eyes stared at the plate of popcorn.

"I *am* the lady that wants to date your mom," Victoria confessed. She stared at the chair Sarah had silently claimed at the table but never seemed to be home to sit in.

"But I do care," she whispered. Her finger ran over the grain of the wood, tracing it a few inches. "The truth is your mom and me... she just doesn't want me, and I have to accept that. But you should know... I didn't... there isn't like this rule that says just because I have to pretend not to have feelings for her that I should pretend I don't care about you."

Victoria reached over and took the kid's hand as they both stared at the popcorn. With so little conversation between them, Victoria didn't know what she could share with Tris. With her nieces, she'd always used honesty and bribery, but their lives were stable, while Tris seemed to be trying to carry a corner of Sarah's trauma whenever the mother wasn't looking.

"I never could... I just couldn't have kids. It's not that I didn't want them or didn't like them."

The girl studied Victoria out of the corner of her eye.

"Look, since me and your mom are just going to be friends... that just means... then maybe, if you want me to, I could be like your cool aunt."

"I have an aunt," Tris said. "But I don't think she's as cool as I thought she was. She really hurt Mom's feelings but you, like, yelled at her and she was really scared and it's, like, she stopped smiling again."

Victoria could feel the wrinkle indented on her forehead deepening.

"I messed up," Victoria admitted again.

"She's never cooked dinner for anyone besides stupid Voldemort's sister."

"Who is Voldemort?" Victoria asked, hoping the kid wouldn't be able to tell she was lying.

Tris's eyes widened and her head turned slowly to Victoria's forced face of confusion. With a heavy gulp, Tris whispered, "You had those kinda adults?"

Victoria did have those types of adults growing up, but she'd been introduced to the wizard in the cupboard under the stairs by a girl on the playground. They'd kept their spell casting a secret as they tore through the books in a cement tube, hidden from the teacher's glare.

"Well, who is she?"

"He," Tris corrected. "He is an old white dude, but he doesn't have a nose, but he just wants to—"

Victoria held up her hand. "You're saying your mom's ex-girlfriend doesn't have a nose?"

Tris rolled her eyes and popped a piece of popcorn in her mouth. "She had a nose. And she wasn't ugly. Probably ugly enough to go to prison for at least a little while."

Unsure what ugliness had to do with prison, Victoria waved her hand in a circle. "So, Voldemort is this dude that doesn't have a nose, and he is probably an old white guy. Do we not like old white guys?"

Tris snorted and shoveled a handful of popcorn into her mouth. As she chewed, she explained her view on old white men.

"They aren't all bad but..."

Kernels crunched between the child's molars.

"... just got to be careful about what you say around them..."

A piece of smooshed popcorn flew out of the girl's mouth.

"...they get their feelings hurt really easy when they think you don't think that they are like soooo special..."

Victoria decided listening to the story was equal to watching the first grader consume a booger.

"... so Voldemort is like those guys. Just wants people to think he's so special and he wants everyone to be like him."

Tris swallowed at the same time her master's thesis on Voldemort's ideological similarities to old white men ended. And then she scratched her head again.

"So, Monica and I have sucked at being the cool aunt. And I am worse than her because I messed up dinner like Voldemort's sister," Victoria summarized.

Tris's lips scrunched together. She sent another sprinkle of sand to the floor while the wheels in her head turned with the eyes that moved around the room.

"She doesn't like *like* Aunt Monica," Tris said. "And Aunt Monica breaks Mom's rules all the time but she also always tells on me. So, if you want to be my cool aunt, then you can't be a snitch. Because snitches get stitches."

Tris crushed a piece of popcorn between her fingers and dropped it back to the plate. Then she asked, "What are stitches?"

Victoria pulled her phone out of her pocket and ran a Google image search. Holding up the device, she showed the girl a sutured cut across a finger.

"Doctors just like..." The child visibly swallowed. "They just sew you up. Like they push a needle through your skin and sew you together and tie it like a shoelace?"

"Basically, yes." Victoria shrugged, then added, "They give you a shot first so you can't feel it when they are sewing."

"Wait!" Tris held up her hand as she closed her eyes. She took several deep breaths before she slowly said, "So, you're telling me that they put a needle in you to make it so you can't feel the other needle they are going to put in you? That sounds sus. Like no cap?"

Victoria looked the girl over. The perfect English attached to the older woman's attitude had morphed into nonsense.

"Yes?" Victoria answered.

Tris shook her head. Her finger dug at the rocks until Victoria decided she couldn't stall anymore.

"I'll make you a deal." She guided the girl's gaze to her gently with her finger on the child's chin. "I won't tell your mom, if... you tell me what happened.

The whole truth, though."

With a few blinks, Tris started to spill the story she'd forced into a bottle to tuck away within herself.

"I was at recess, and we were playing don't touch the lava. I was winning and most of the boys were out. It was only me and Caleb left. He...he got a water bottle from the ground that was filled with sand, and he poured it on me. Said I touched the lava, so I was dead."

"He did what?!" Victoria snapped.

Green eyes fell to the table and her shoulders scrunched over her knees. She mumbled incoherent words into her pajama pants.

"Wait," Victoria requested. She took a deep breath. "I'm sorry. I heard you. You don't have to say it again."

"You can't tell my mom now," Tris said. "She just got my hair washed at the salon and so we can't go back yet."

"Well, she's going to know when she sees you scratching your head or even your bed. You can't sleep in a bed filled with sand."

Tris scratched again.

"How about you go upstairs, take a shower and wash your hair?" Victoria said.

Tris stared at her. Then she shook her head.

"Why not?"

The thin fingers played with the skeleton bone printed on her pants. Quietly, she said, "I don't know how to wash my hair."

"You're nine," Victoria stated. "How do you not know how to wash your hair?"

"Because I'm not white," the girl snapped. Tears fell from her eyes as she rushed out of the room and ran up the stairs, slamming her bedroom door behind her.

Victoria sat at the table, her chest beating wildly as the artwork on the wall settled on their hooks. She wasn't an expert on children, but she could distinctly remember knowing how to wash her own hair by the time she was nine.

Victoria picked up her phone and went to the stairs. She dialed Jen because Jen had an older kid. As it rang, Victoria decided her next phone call would be to Echo. She was pretty sure her little girl had curly hair too.

Jen answered though. Her voice covered the squeal of laughter in the background.

"I was beginning to think you forgot about me since you U-Hauled the sex lady."

Victoria whispered, "I need your advice. It's a kid thing. And don't call her that ever again and we didn't U-Haul. And we won't ever be because she wants a friend like you said"

"Mmmmhmmm," Jen said. *"So, what's the kid problem? Did candy bars not work as bribes this time?"*

"So, Tris's hair is filled with sand."

"Oh shit," Jen said. *"That's going to take hours to get out."*

"Well, I told her to go take a shower and wash it out and she got upset and said she didn't know how to wash her hair because she's not white."

Jen hummed briefly then added, *"Makes sense."*

Victoria balked. She turned from the stairs to the computer with the unfinished essay. She could Google it but that was wasting time.

"What do you mean it makes sense?" she hissed.

"Look I'm not Black, so I don't know everything to do but I dated this girl in college that is Black and she said that girls don't learn to wash their own hair until they are in middle school or high school. It's a big cultural thing which is why many women go to a salon to get it done. Where's Sarah?"

"She is out and I'm babysitting." Victoria gave Jen time to laugh at her expense and get in some jabs about being pussy whipped before she asked, "So... what do I do?"

"You have to help her wash it. Just like you would help Jackie."

"Like in the bathtub?" Victoria swallowed. "She's not a little kid and I'm a lesbian. That's like asking to go to prison."

"Well maybe you're just lesbian enough to let loose in prison," Jen snickered. *"But no, just do it in the kitchen sink. The girl I dated always did her sister's hair in the sink."*

Victoria looked at the kitchen island. She'd axed the hair in the sink last weekend when she'd come home from the gym to find Sarah scrubbing Tris's head in the same place she washed their vegetables.

"I kinda already said that's a no-go in this house."

"Well then do it in the tub, just get to work. It's literally going to take forever."

"'Kay." Victoria swallowed her own frustration. "Thanks."

The path up the stairs took less time than Victoria's brain could come up with another solution. She rapped gently on the door that opened under the pressure.

Tris was lying in her bed. Her tears absorbed into the pillow cradled in her arms.

"Can I help you wash your hair?" Victoria asked.

Tris looked up skeptically. "Do you know how to do it? Like the stuff you put in it."

"No," Victoria admitted. "But if you help me, I'm sure I can figure it out.

Then we don't have to tell your mom."

Tris didn't respond with more than a sucking back of her own snot. She followed Victoria to the hall bathroom the mother and daughter shared.

"How does your mom do it?" Victoria asked.

"I sit there." Tris pointed to the tub. "Then mom has to help me stay up so I can put my head under there."

Victoria looked at the glass shower doors blocking off half of the tub and the fixed faucets. To help the child, she would have to sit on the toilet and the kid would have to hold her head under the tap while leaning back in the tub.

She glanced at the five inches of curls atop the girl's head. Bile rose in her throat at how petty and stupid she'd been when she'd calmly, but ignorantly, chastised the pair for washing the child's hair in the sink where the nozzle was detachable, and the kid could just lay on the counter without having to hold herself up.

"Does going to the salon cost a lot?" Victoria asked, wondering if that would be a better option.

"It's $45 for washing and Mom tipped the lady a lot on Tuesday so the lady would stop sucking her teeth at Mom so much," Tris explained.

"Sucking her teeth?"

"Yeah. It's not nice." Tris wrapped her arms tighter around herself. "The lady don't think I should live with Mom because she don't think she knows how to take care of my hair."

"But I have seen her do all the braids and stuff in your hair."

"Yeah, but moms are supposed to wash your hair, not take you to get it washed. They said she has to take me in every week."

The guilt tasted rancid as it coated Victoria's tongue. She tried to scrape it off with her teeth, but it didn't change the uncomfortable position she'd put the O'Keeffe women in.

"Let's go downstairs."

"But you said you were going to help me get the sand out," Tris protested.

"I am," Victoria promised. "In the sink."

"But the rules. You said there were rules and it was disgusting to wash hair in the sink."

"I was wrong." Victoria ran her hands up and down her face. "I'm sorry I said that."

With a huff, Tris gathered a bottle and several containers.

"What's all that?" Victoria asked.

Tris set the containers down and organized them in the line. She pointed to the first container. "This is cowash. I just got my hair washed so we use cowash until we go back to get it washed again."

She pointed to the next container. "This is a leave-in conditioner and it goes on after we wash with the co-wash. Then the oil." She pointed to the bottle. Lastly, she pointed to another container. "Then we use this one and it is the cream. LOC."

"LOC?"

"Leave in. Oil. Cream."

Victoria picked up the containers, studying the products. Holding up two of them, she asked, "All of this goes in your hair?"

"Yes. Or it gets dry, and it breaks off."

With a nod, she said, "Okay, do we need a brush."

Tris shook her head. "No. Brushes break. We use a comb, and you use your fingers to get the knots out."

"Your mom does this every time?"

"Yeah. She watched a bunch of YouTube videos and she had me watch them too."

Victoria made a mental note to later this evening look up LOC and watch how to do things right. She gathered the containers, then nodded to the towel rack. "Grab a towel and the comb."

"Okay."

After an hour and a half, the girl was sand-free and her curls were secured under her satin bonnet, which Victoria had learned to secure after two Youtube videos. Tris barely had time to get the products back up the stairs when they heard Sarah's key at the front door.

The keys hit the table, and the woman dragged her bare feet quietly down the hall. The forest eyes were dull from exhaustion, and her shoulders seemed barely able to support her neck.

"Hey," Victoria said. She glanced up the stairs to see the child slip quietly into her room and the bedroom light flick off.

"Hey. How'd it go?" Sarah asked.

"Good," Victoria called as she took a seat in her corner of the couch. "We ate popcorn. Listened to music. Nothing eventful."

Victoria listened as Sarah let out a heavy sigh. The laundry door opened, and Victoria immediately realized she'd forgotten to sweep the kitchen floor. She started to get up but heard the bristles already running over the floor along with several swear words aimed at the school's cheap playground.

"Why does it smell like curling cream?" Sarah called out.

"Oh... uhhh... Tris was showing me the cream. I... uh... I asked her why she always smelled so good."

A cabinet door opened, and the dustpan tapped against the rim of the trashcan. When the woman returned from around the corner, her tired eyes studied Victoria, the room, and then shook her head.

With a wave of her hand in Victoria's direction, Sarah said, "I am just going to tell you that you are a terrible liar, but I am too tired to care what you are lying about."

Victoria pressed the power button on the TV remote and handed it over to the woman already curling into the corner of the couch. The body melted into the cushion as Sarah sighed heavily. Her eyes were already drooping.

She didn't want Sarah to think she was a liar, but she'd promised the kid. So instead, she silently apologized by reaching for the foot of the woman who'd been all over campus, then worked a shift at the library, only to follow it with a two-hour coaching session.

Thumbs pressed into the clammy arches, then the ball. She didn't even care about the moisture as the woman sighed and rolled to give her access to both feet.

Even though Victoria was clumsily kneading her fingers into the flesh, Sarah's heavy eyelids drooped further.

"I don't know how to sleep in the bed," Sarah mumbled under her breath as sleep began to overtake her.

"You can sleep here then," Victoria promised. However, sadness filled within her like steam that was looking for an exit.

A bed had always been an expectation for her, and for Sarah, it was a privilege that she couldn't seem to bring herself to get used to. She wondered what other things Sarah had missed out on in her life, and then wondered if the woman would let her help her experience them. Even if it was just as a friend.

Sarah fell asleep with Victoria sitting under the woman's legs before Loralie Gilmore had her first cup of coffee. She didn't move in fear of waking the brunette who gave to everyone else and did nothing for herself. She wanted nothing more than to give until she had nothing left to give so Sarah could for once be taken care of, but then she remembered that wasn't her place.

She sighed and rested her head against the back of the couch.

Rest didn't come easy, but Victoria clung to the woman of her dreams in the world that she was allowed to. Not realizing as she slept, she'd secured the shattered soul flush against her safe and steady body. Unaware that as she softly snored a serene song, a shaken Sarah lay acutely awake and aware of the arms around her abdomen and the mumbled confessions of adoration.

33

Steam coated the glass encasement surrounding the shallow tub. The faucet streamed out scalding water, turning the flesh under its assault scarlet. Sarah's head barely cleared the low nozzle as her hand provided the service she so desperately needed. If she'd been brave enough to not give Victoria her two-week move-out promise, she'd have asked the woman if she could install a detachable nozzle. But bravery wasn't logical, it was emotional.

There wasn't a time when Sarah wasn't actively trying to bottle her emotions. Every emotion felt toxic, even those people would describe as happiness. It wasn't that she didn't want to be happy, because she yearned for it. Her issue with happiness was directly linked to the guaranteed disappointment soon to follow. Which was why she found herself shoving that particular emotion away quicker and with more aggression than any of the others.

She'd spent her entire known life trying to perfect the art of capturing and securing every single feeling before it could be felt. Which was the true problem with living at Victoria's house. A space without chaos or any threat left her time to dust off the bottles when they rolled around in her head. She was able to read over the label that pinpointed the event, which would cause the feeling within to try an escape.

Just that morning there'd been a calm breakfast and gentle laughter. When the calendar alert announced she needed to pay the cellphone bill, she didn't have to request a payment plan. There was more than enough money in her account to pay it, just like she'd been able to stop at Walmart the day before and pick up a jacket and new uniform pants for Tris.

Having studied Maslow's Hierarchy of Needs, Sarah understood what was happening. She knew that Victoria did what Monica said was possible, made living instead of surviving a reality. Her trauma response chased her from the warm air of the kitchen at a practical run to the shower where she thought she was going to break into a million pieces because the emotions trapped within her needed an exit.

The exit she'd anticipated would wash away with the water as though the tracks of tears had never fallen. However, the thinly constructed wall between the upstairs bathrooms brought a different release when the shower on the other side of the wall came to life.

It was the sound of her name whispered through the wall. The gravelly groan of gratitude reminded Sarah of the few graciously given moments in college when Lyra Greyson slipped out of her mother's house under the guise of playing video games. Lyra understood the trauma associated with being the child of a prostitute, and her walls were as sturdy as Sarah's. That was why sex with Lyra had been easy. They expected nothing but heartbreak from the other, so they never offered up their hearts for examination to find they were unworthy.

Victoria didn't come from pain like that. She apologized without Sarah needing to be broken, and she gave without asking for anything in return. It was the true reason Sarah couldn't take what Victoria offered. But through the wall, when they showered at the same time, Sarah took Victoria's moans and thanks without feeling obligated to reciprocate.

"Please, Sarah," was her favorite thing to hear because it made Sarah feel like she had something to give Victoria.

Sarah's digits worked their way up to a comfortable pressure, easing the tension twisted within her while her ear rested against the plastic shower encasement. She didn't need to hear the way Victoria's hand moved; her memory provided her with the details, including the richness of Victoria's aroused scent as she bit into the back of her hand to keep the interaction one-sided.

This wasn't the first time they'd showered at the same time. Nor would it be the first time the babygay came apart on the other side of the wall after beginning with several bangs of her head. The guilt-dipped words snuck through the surface as Victoria admonished herself for being unable to come apart without visualizing the woman just as guilty on the other side. Those were always followed by: "This is the last time."

Sarah's hand moved on autopilot, knowing the sequence necessary to achieve release in such a calculated manner that it eliminated the need for intimacy. But with each utterance of her name, her fingers slipped from their normal routine, and she imagined the babygay pressed against her flesh as the water cascaded over them.

Picking up the pace, she sought to finish with Victoria. Felt sparks catching when Victoria told her, "Just like that." She imagined the woman's fingers digging into her shoulders as she thrust deeper. Her mind pictured pink lips parting until they formed the "o" that began the, "Oh God!" as Sarah felt within the depths of her own velvety passage.

Sarah shifted the fantasy. Gave Victoria over control as her back turned to the wall. Tried to feel the talented fingers of the woman buried just as deep, reaching the spot within Sarah that her finger just couldn't quite reach on her own. She fell apart with the woman's strangled cry of release on the other side.

As her breathing normalized, Sarah watched the droplets of water wander down uncharted paths. She traced a still sex-coated digit down a track, the tears finally falling as her body released the last of her energy. Her legs gave with a slow tremble, until she cried directly over the drain. Let the pain from self-destruction wash away so that she could reuse the bottles for whatever kind thing Victoria would offer next that she would have to put away before that toxic hope sent her spiraling into the never-ending whirlpool of not being loveable.

She sucked back the snot when a soft rap played on the door to the bathroom. From the hall, Victoria called out, "Hey, Sarah."

Sarah wiped away the tears and let the water wash them from her arm. After a deep breath, she said, "Yeah?"

"Tris and I are going to head out." There was a brief pause, then Victoria asked, "Will we see you for dinner tonight or do you have a full day ahead of you?"

A full day was ahead of her. Every moment of every day of the break had been planned in order to bank as many extra dollars as possible for the shitty one-bedroom in the shittier neighborhood. She'd reminded herself every night since Victoria had promised to love her forever while sleeping practically on top of her that moving was the best thing she could do for Victoria.

"I'll be home for dinner, but I have three appointments after," she shared.

The tap shut off and she wrapped herself in a towel. It was cruel to the woman fantasizing about her to open the door, but she did so anyway. Watched the warm irises meet the pitch-black center that grew into an undeniable desire. Victoria's tongue peeked out between her teeth as though she was biting it to keep the words trapped on the tip Sarah had begged her no longer to say.

"I'll take care of the kitchen and sweep the floor before I leave," Sarah said in a weak attempt to pull Victoria back from reality.

"Okay... well, try to get a nap in," the woman croaked. "It'll be quiet because we're going to be out pretty much all day."

Sarah leaned against the doorjamb. "Where you going?"

"Hair appointment and... uh... then grocery shopping." Victoria stared unblinking at Sarah's forehead. "Oh, and I promised my friend Jen that we would meet her and her daughter for lunch."

"Hair appointment?" Sarah's eyebrows scrunched together as she searched her memory for if Victoria had told her she was getting her hair done.

"Yeah," Victoria whispered, her gaze moving to the stairs. "I scheduled it a few days ago. No big deal."

"I didn't realize you had an appointment. I can take Tris with me to the library, so she doesn't bother you... I'm so sorry for, like, taking advantage of your time. Jesus, this is your break. Of course, you made plans, and I didn't even think." Sarah shook her head. "I'm sorry. I'll just... shit. Tris, I need you to grab your computer and get some stuff to go with me."

With a tightened grip around the towel, Sarah tried to move through the door but Victoria moved at the same time. They did an awkward dance until both gave up and Sarah stayed in the room while Victoria remained posted in the doorway.

"Calm your tits," Victoria practically cried out as the pale hands raised just at breast level.

Her fist tightened on the towel as Sarah repeated, "Calm my tits?"

"Yep. Calm them all the way down." Victoria's confidence was chased away as the dark eyebrows indented just enough to signal a challenge for whatever could come out next. "Not that they are saggy or anything because they are the most perky... shoot."

"Perky?" Sarah rolled her eyes.

Rubbing the back of her neck, Victoria offered a half-smile. "Well, that went downhill fast."

Sarah laughed, though. Her hand crossed her perky pebbled bust as though the laughter would jiggle them free from the tightly wrapped towel.

"So... anywaysss," Victoria started again. "I want Tris to go with me. We made our plans together so don't stress. I just wanted you to know that we're going to be out so you could take a nap and even use a pillow instead of your arm. There's some pretty good ones on your bed."

Victoria's fingers rubbed at the edge of the Jimmy Eat World shirt. "I was hoping.... Look, I know you are, like, hell-bent on moving out but... please reconsider. If you stay, I'll even let you chip in for, like, utilities, and if you really have to, pay part of the mortgage."

Sarah checked the hall to see if Tris was watching. When she heard the cartoons still playing downstairs, she was able to breathe a little easier. Tris and she hadn't spoken about the fact that Sarah was still planning on them moving since the girl had unpacked her stuff once more. Not that she'd seen Tris for more than a couple hours each day with Victoria being adamant that Tris did not need to sit at the library all day when they could hang out and play with Legos.

Victoria's version of hanging out actually meant doing things like going to the movies, and they'd visited the zoo yesterday. Sarah had cried on her lunch break at the pictures of the two of them together. Leaving Victoria's house would be worse than when they left the Greyson's guest house because Tris would go back to not having a best friend with a debit card. One that didn't need to worry about the price of tickets, and let the girl pick something out at the gift shop or play the games in the arcade.

Staying would be good for Tris, but bad for Victoria. Sarah knew she would break Victoria's heart more. She was indebted to Victoria; however, Tris's happiness was what mattered to Sarah, so she asked, "How much are we talking?"

Brown eyes widened along with the woman's mouth. The pink lips almost made the O-shape she'd envisioned but then they slapped back together.

"Uh... I pay $1258 a month," Victoria stated. "So, I want to say like $200 but I know you'd scoff at me and tell me I'm stupid. So, take that number and you decide what makes you uncomfortable. I mean, that's what it will be when you leave."

Supple hips swayed as Victoria seemed to carefully consider the unplanned interest. Sarah wondered if the woman was doing an internal happy dance that her body could not contain.

"You could, like, compare the cost of the places you're looking at and maybe come up with a number that makes you feel maybe slightly... uh..." Victoria lowered her voice to just barely over a whisper to finish with, "fucked."

With a roll of her eyes, Sarah couldn't help the smile. She hoped the flush of her skin was blamable on the hot shower, but her mind wandered over once more fucking the woman better than slightly well.

"Just think about it," Victoria said. She nodded to the stairs. "We have to get going."

And think about it Sarah did. She thought about them living together. Then, she envisioned the idea of getting more than slightly fucked by the woman as she cocked an eyebrow at Sarah. After calling in sick for her shift at the library, Sarah gave herself another orgasm. This time she'd brought herself to a longer finish with her hands in her pants as she gripped the cushion of the couch coated in the floral perfume of a woman who'd wrapped her in comfort.

Sarah woke from her nap to the sound of the doorbell. As a child from chaos, the unfamiliar sound set her entire body on edge as though it may be DCS coming to take her away. Until she remembered she was an adult. The fear then morphed to it being DCS coming to take Tris away.

The bell rang again and then a heavy knock struck three times. Slightly volatile voices argued on the porch, pulling Sarah from her space.

She peeked through the hole to find an older woman holding herself tightly as a younger woman reached forward to knock once more.

"Are you sure you have the right house, Lynlee?" The woman growled. "If we came all this way only to show up at the wrong house, it will ruin everything."

Lynlee's dropped chin tilted just enough to give the woman a sideways glare. "Yes, Gran, I am positive this is her house. I followed her from the school to this house. Maybe she's just not home."

"Well, there's a car in the driveway. Knock again."

Sarah watched as the girl's lips moved but she couldn't hear the grumbles.

When the door banged once more, she choked out a startled cry. Covering her mouth, she tried to collect the evidence of existence. But it was too late.

"I heard someone," the girl said.

The door banged at a different tune and the older woman yelled, "Victoria-Clark Brenton, this is your mother, and I will not tolerate you pretending to not be home. Now you open this door or so help me, I will— "

Sarah threw open the door as the woman's fist tried to knock once more.

"Or you'll what?" Sarah snapped. She locked her elbow to keep the space unenterable as her eyes narrowed at the smaller woman.

"Uh... is Clark here?" Lynlee asked. She tapped her finger on her chest. "I'm Lynny. I'm her niece and we... we're trying to get in touch with her."

"Ever heard of a phone?" Sarah asked. Her hand found her hip as the other readied the door to slam in their faces. "Sorry, I shoulda said text. I know your generation doesn't call people."

"Who are you?" Victoria's mom asked. "And where is my daughter?"

Sarah could have chosen a hundred different paths. She could have said she was a friend, which would have been the truth. She could have said the roommate, which also would have been true. But when faced with a difficult situation, Sarah opted to do what Sarah had been taught to do.

"I'm Victoria's girlfriend, Sarah," she lied. "And Victoria is not here so if you came all this way to try and convince her to go back to Utah, then you should just leave. We're happy. She's happy and she doesn't need any homophobic bullshit interfering with her happiness."

Sarah didn't have the opportunity to hear the woman's response because the silver Volkswagen Atlas pulled into the driveway and a blustered brunette hopped from the driver's seat along with a kid whose hair hung around her face in purple and black box braids.

"Mom? Lynny?" Victoria choked out. "What are you doing here?"

"We came for Thanksgiving. It's your turn to host," Lynny said with a soft smile. She pointed to Tris. "Who's this?"

"I'm Tris," the girl said, making her way to Sarah.

Sarah ran her fingers over the braids and looked at the freshly oiled scalp. "You look beautiful," she said to the girl.

"Well, we've just met your girlfriend," Victoria's mother stated. "She's a beautifully protective woman and I couldn't be happier for you. So, let's just get this out of the way. We never got the chance to accept you. So, we're going to just move forward, and we're not here to try to convince you to come back home."

Victoria's eyebrow raised as the brown eyes flitted between her mother and Sarah.

"Uhhh..." Victoria swallowed. "This is a lot. Just go. Go inside, Mom and... uh... Sarah, um, do you have a second to talk?"

"Vicky-Clark Brenton, you will hug your mother before I burst," the older woman cried out. Her brown eyes welled with tears. She didn't give Victoria a chance to consent when she charged forward and wrapped her arms around her daughter.

"Mom," Victoria whispered as her head was cradled into the woman's side braid.

Taking her daughter's face in her hand, Sarah watched the exchange of tear-filled apologies. Apologies she'd have to provide as well since she'd let her childhood instinct to lie rear its ugly head.

When the brunette was trapped in another hug, Victoria stared at Sarah. She silently mouthed the word, "Girlfriend?"

And Sarah nodded once, hoping the other girl watching didn't take notice as she spoke with Tris about the child's experience at the braider's house.

34

The quiet home the three occupied bustled to life as the six Brenton sisters arrived after Victoria's mother had activated the family phone tree with a celebratory photo confirming Victoria's existence. Women with heart-shaped faces and different shades of brunette waves ushered their offspring through the front door without knocking. Victoria's body had been hugged so many times, she'd lost track of who she'd seen and who she missed. A baby whose name she'd forgotten the moment the squirming infant was placed in her arms and instructed to smile for a photo was snapped for a baby book.

Lynny, the eldest of the third generation of Brentons, worked with Sarah and Tris to unload the groceries from Victoria's SUV. The matriarch of the family, Naomi, sorted through the bags the three placed on the counter, scoffing at the limited items.

"Vicky-Clark," her mother barked. "You barely purchased enough ingredients to feed the three of you once. This is not the type of Thanksgiving feast you were taught to prepare."

Naomi scanned the space. Her fingers wrapped around the neck of a half-full bottle of Merlot. She pulled the cork from the bottle before dramatically draining the wine down the sink.

"Your kitchen is a reflection of you, Vicky-Clark. I understand you are in this whole reinvention state." Naomi tossed the bottle into the trash. "But you know you need to make sure your kitchen shows your commitment to being a good wife and mother. Where is your fruit basket? There should be fruit on the counter for Trissy so she can grow. Speaking of counters, why does yours have crumbs on it? Man or woman, no one wants to live with a slob."

Lynny placed two more bags atop the counter as Sarah scooted past them and found a place to meld into the wall. Naomi pulled the items from the bag.

A small bundle dangled in the air from the older woman's finger. "A single breast? This isn't even a whole turkey. My goodness, Sarah is going to think you were raised without any sense of how a holiday is supposed to be celebrated. It's like you're feeding this poor woman from one of those food boxes the boys take to the trailer park. It's no wonder she's so skinny."

Victoria searched the kitchen until she found Sarah's frozen form hovering against the wall with a canister of crescent rolls clenched between her fingers.

The woman's chin had dropped to her chest and her shoulders gradually drooped inward. The sleep-pressed locks hung alongside her face until she raised her sharp jaw. The bags under her eyes looked almost like war paint and her O'Keeffe family fuck around and find out stare was fixed.

The lithe brunette warrior stood out amongst the busty siblings bustling around the kitchen in their sparkly and speckled tops. Like a raccoon trying to avoid detection, Sarah slinked around the back edge avoiding direct eye contact from the dictator huffing out her displeasure.

"We only cook what we will eat in one setting, Mom," Victoria stated. She hated the way her voice varied in a teenage tantrum timbre.

She steadied her stoic mask as her hands shook at her sides. "And we thought it would just be the three of us, so a single turkey breast was more than adequate."

Her mother shook her head and tsked her tongue as she dropped the turkey breast into the freezer for future use.

"Paper, Vicky-Clark. I need paper to make a proper list." Naomi snapped her fingers as she started shouting out instructions.

Victoria did not retrieve the paper like the obedient daughter she used to be. Lynny took up position along Victoria's side.

"I got this. Go have a moment with your girl," Lynny said. "Gram, I'll make the list on my phone."

"Oh yes, that will work." Naomi smiled for just a moment before barking new commands. "Diana, check your sister's pantry for the staples like flour, sugar, you know. Kathy, look through the pans. You brought your crock pot with you, right?"

The second eldest nodded her head and began rummaging through Victoria's cabinets. "We all brought our crock pots, and Betty and Pandora brought their pans as well because Clark never had enough."

Victoria took her mother's distracted dictating as an opportunity to wrap her fingers around Sarah's bicep and steal her from the room. With children running between the living room where cartoons were blasting to the back patio, Victoria's only option for privacy was the bedroom at the end of the hallway. Quietly they slipped through the crowd and up the stairs.

Sarah was already trampling a path over the crisp vacuum lines with her bare feet when Victoria clicked the door closed.

"I just said it," Sarah spit out. Words projectile vomited from the lips of the overwhelmed woman. "She was standing there and demanding to know where you were, and I just got scared. I was scared that she was here to try and convince you to go back home. I thought... I thought this is how they do it."

The woman spun on her heel and turned back to Victoria. Her fingers dug at the roots of her hair.

"I was just, like, they're here to take you away. And...and they would run, like, an intervention, and they convince you that you can be fixed, and they send you to get, like, electrocuted so you will think you're not gay and I didn't want that for you, so I just lied."

The green eyes were so wide as her hands shot out at Victoria.

"Oh, my fucking god. I fucking told your mother that I was your girlfriend, and her fucking eyebrow raised up on her forehead just like you do when you're like 'Oh really, bitch? Say that shit again,' and I was just like no way. Her eyebrow isn't cute or sexy it's like I'm the boss here and I didn't have a chance to say anything else because you were here, and Tris was here..."

Sarah stopped in front of Victoria.

"And I didn't want you to leave. I didn't go to work today, and I took a nap like you said, and... And I had decided to stay."

Victoria's breath caught in her throat. She couldn't swallow as the bubble grew. Her choked state went unnoticed by the woman.

"I had decided that I wasn't going to run away this time and I was going to stay here with you and so I told her. I told her I was your girlfriend and that you were happy, though I make you fucking miserable, but I can be better. I can be...."

Sarah's eyes begged to be understood.

"I was just scared, you know? And I didn't want them to hurt you so I told them I was your girlfriend because I thought if they were going to try to steal you, then they would have to go through me first."

Victoria took Sarah's hands in her own, stopping the woman waving them around like a waggling water sprinkler toy. But words continued to flow from her lips.

"I'm so sorry and if you want to go back... I get it. I really do because I know what it's like to have nobody." Sarah squeezed Victoria's hands. "I know what it's like to want your family to be okay and to be okay with them... and they're okay with you. They are okay with youbeingwithawoman... andtheyloveyou... andImadeyoulietothemand... I'msosorry. VictoriaIamsosorry."

Victoria's hand cupped the cheeks of the woman talking with words sewn together in cursive letters that failed to leave a finger's space between each one. She couldn't follow the litany of apologies and explanations slapping off the walls and against her. All she knew was Sarah's volume rose with each sentence. So, she did the only thing she could think of to shut Sarah up.

Her lips pressed against the woman's when the words had wrapped around them so tightly Sarah's chest quaked in a sudden need for oxygen. She sought no entrance, nor fitted their lips together in hopes of deepening the kiss. Yet, she felt Sarah's hand on her hip, and the woman's parted lips hug her own.

Victoria didn't dare try to deepen the kiss. She sucked in a sharp breath when she pulled away. The hands holding Sarah's cheeks dropped, and her feet took her a step back, making a path for the woman to rush out the door.

However, Sarah's fingers rose to her lips. The eyes Victoria couldn't stop seeing in her dreams moved over her own, down her nose to her lips where they stayed fixed for a long moment. So long that Victoria found moving them difficult because her brain had short-circuited. Only now that there was space between them did she realize that the kiss had simultaneously felt too real and too fake.

"I'm sorry," Victoria finally whispered with a mouth so dry it hurt. Because she knew she'd just smashed through the barricades Sarah had constructed to reinforce her boundaries. "I just... I needed you to stop talking before... before someone heard you."

"That just—" Sarah cut the sentence off as her chin rose and her head fell back. A hand came to rest on her stomach while each breath was carefully regulated. She was breathing through her panic with the same strategy she had the kids at school use.

Victoria couldn't breathe. The excuses, promises, and pleas she could use to beg Sarah not to hate her all joined in a race to see which would make it to Victoria's tongue first. The simple sentences tried to cut through the complex ones. The compound sentences were folding at the comma, clotheslining the others, and falling from the pressure of the other's momentum, until her tongue was left with a bunch of twisted and garbled subjects and verbs, none of which could be ordered effectively.

"I fucked up," Sarah whispered, pulling Victoria's gaze to the woman's lips. "I lied and I pulled you into a lie. Another lie."

Victoria swallowed the incoherent nonsense as well as the joke that it didn't have to be a lie. She scraped away the request to have a do-over kiss to prove to Sarah that their sexual chemistry was relationship material. Her mind catapulted images of queer versions of Hallmark movie happy endings starting with a lie like this. But the silent tear running down Sarah's cheek wiped away the possible humor of the moment.

"Sariah," Victoria said, hoping the woman's full name would bring her back from the place she'd locked herself within.

When Sarah's eyes rose and narrowed at her, Victoria held up her hands in early surrender. Sarah didn't snap at her, but her gaze dropped once more, seeming to trace a path from where they stood to the door.

"I'm sorry," Victoria whispered, reaching out but not touching Sarah. "I know you hate being called that, and that was another boundary that I just broke. I'm going to say, though, you just learned my mother calls me Vicky-Clark, so when you want my attention, you now know how to get it."

She waited for the fields of green to cast her way once more. When they came, the vibrant irises were surrounded by a fiery red. Like her soul was on fire for a fib.

"I'm not angry with you," Victoria promised. "I'm more terrified that you are going to run out of here barefoot. And I'm going to have to go tell them all my first girlfriend broke up with me because they just showed up."

Sarah licked her lips. With a soft shrug, she said, "I don't even think I can find the door through your family. There are so many of them."

With a roll of her eyes and a snort, Victoria said, "They're Mormon. It's like an expectation to have as many children as possible. Especially boys and since my parents kept making girls... well, there are seven of us. I'm the youngest and my name, well they'd run out of female DC comic aliases, so I was Clark. Well, I am Victoria-Clark since my dad's favorite was always Superman and he was convinced lucky number seven would be the son he'd always wanted."

"I was wondering... about your name. I thought your mom had a thing for English royalty except...." Sarah glanced at the door once more. "Who names their kid Pandora?"

"Yeah. My dad. I'm not sure if he loves hunting or DC comic books more. They used up all the girl names before me, and my Gram had a literal fit apparently that they were going to name me Clark, so I got a hyphen on top of the longest name out of everyone. But seriously, with six other names, you'd think they would have gone for something shorter." Victoria laughed as she added, "Oh, and it was a huge controversy when Pandora married a Marvel fan and named the first male grandsons after the Avengers. Must have been her revenge."

The smile didn't reach Sarah's eyes, but it also didn't fall to the ground either.

"So... we are going to get through the next three days," Victoria said, hoping she sounded more confident than she felt. "We'll pretend to be the happy couple you told them we are, and when they are all gone you and I will talk."

"Three days," Sarah whispered, looking downstairs. "All of them are going to be here for three days?"

"Three days," Victoria echoed. "And you need to talk to Tris. You know how she likes to spill the tea."

"Spill the tea?" Sarah's eyebrows scrunched in the middle.

"You know, tell people's business. Your business in particular."

"I know what 'spill the tea' means, Supergirl," Sarah snipped, giving Victoria a slight shove. "I'm just confused how you know what it means."

"I spent the last two weeks with your child," Victoria stated. "She might not vomit her words out like you do, but she definitely speaks in some strange code that I have been carefully trying to decode."

The soft chuckle eased the stiffness from Sarah's limbs, and Victoria felt like maybe they could pull this off. It really couldn't be that hard since Victoria was incapable of hiding how much she wanted Sarah from anyone. A point that even her assistant decided to point out with their new friendship making things less tense.

"So... that was our first kiss," Sarah said, with a gentle laugh. "It's definitely a story."

Lips curled up Victoria's teeth in a slight grimace. With a shake of her head, she tsked her tongue.

"Nope," she declared. "That was not a kiss. It was a stop talking. And I will not allow you to judge my kissing ability off of that. I might not have a lot of practice, but that was not a kiss. Let's just equate it to me putting my hand over your mouth to keep you quiet because you are really loud."

Thin fingers rose to Sarah's chest. She choked slightly as she said, "I'm loud?"

"Yes. You're loud," Victoria repeated. She doubled down with, "You talk so loudly that anyone walking by your office can hear the string of curse words being chucked like knives at the walls. Shit, *thunk*! Fuck, *thud!*"

Sarah's arms folded over her chest. Green eyes narrowed until Victoria realized she was just about to find out how much she fucked around with her crass example.

"My office isn't the only place with thin walls, Boss."

Victoria didn't get it. Her head tilted to the side when the answer to Sarah's riddle wasn't written across her forehead. She hoped a different angle would provide her with at least a hint, but she still came up empty.

Sarah didn't provide the answer. It was a child singing that caused the brown eyes to grow comically large. A potty song snuck through the shower wall of the bathroom and made it to them standing in the bedroom. She looked at the open door to the bathroom, then to the woman smugly smirking back at her.

"The shower...."

Sarah licked her teeth, then her lips into a cocky smile. One that said so much without words.

"You heard—"

"Ev-Er-Ree-Thing," Sarah finished. "That version of me in your head is very, very good at what she does."

Victoria's eyes closed. She willed the floor of the second story to give out from underneath her. If she didn't die, maybe she'd be lucky enough to slip into a coma.

Sarah's hand tapped Victoria just below her collarbone. Victoria caught the woman's hand though. She held it against her chest, knowing Sarah would be able to feel her heart trying to escape. Her escape route became clear after a moment.

Turning to face the temptress, she said, "You said I'm the loud one."

Sarah nodded, the smile spreading across her face. "I did."

With a raise of a single brow, Victoria asked, "So, does that make you the quiet one?"

Pillowy lips parted and green eyes widened enough to answer without even a whisper. Victoria watched the panic rise in the woman. Heard it come out as Sarah tried to escape, "I have... I have to go talk to Tris."

"So that's a yes," Victoria said, looking down at the fingers held in her hand. She wondered how many times those fingers were doing exactly what Victoria wanted nothing more to do to the woman.

"Stop it," Sarah hissed, pulling her hand away. "Don't you even start your shit."

"You started it," Victoria said, rising to her full height. "And this means, we're even."

Sarah scanned Victoria's face before she cocked her head to the side. "Even?"

"Yep." Victoria pointed to the bed. "Once upon a time, I told you just enough to make you know that I think about you. And you just did the same. You just said just enough, so I know when I am—"

Sarah stepped up so close that Victoria cut her sentence off and waited for the lips to press against her. It was how she would have shut the woman up. But Sarah's breath caressed Victoria's lips instead.

"Don't let this go to your head, babygay."

It didn't. The rush of warmth and desire traveled in the opposite direction. A pulsing need that would go unfulfilled was all she could think about when Sarah didn't kiss her.

Her feet were planted, unable to move. The door to the bedroom opened, but before it could be closed, Victoria whispered just loud enough to stop Sarah in her tracks, "I can't wait to show you how good of a girlfriend I can be for the next three days."

35

Left and right versus right and left, the O'Keeffe women could not fall in step together. When Tris zigged, Sarah zagged, and their arms bumped into each other like little crabs trying to move against their instincts.

Tris snickered when they ran into each other again; the first ounce of forgiveness the child offered after being torn from Victoria's nieces who were about to play with her Legos. A walk through the neighborhood was not welcomed when she'd been alone with one or both adults since the break.

"So, Victoria has a big family," Sarah offered.

The girl twisted the braid between her fingers. Her eyes cataloged the way the strands folded in on each other.

"Yeah," the girl mumbled. "They seem nice."

The sky shifted between the gradual gradients of orange to purple when the sun began its final slide down the other side of the White Tanks Mountains. Half of its hazy glow hung on to the mountain like a toddler refusing to let go, and Sarah wondered if the sun was that orange in Salt Lake where Victoria had mentioned the trees with the leaves that changed.

She missed those shifts in seasons. A reminder of when to start adding another layer or to start scouting out the lost and found for one of the nice coats. The child next to her pulled at the neck of the overlarge hoodie.

"Where'd you get that?" Sarah asked. Tugging at the purple material. The same purple that matched her hair.

Tris's lips spread into a smile.

"When I went to get my hair done... there was this basketball player there. She plays for the NWBA. For the Phoenix Devils. She said she would get Victoria and me tickets for next summer and she told Victoria that they have a basketball camp and that I could go learn how to make a three-pointer." Her hands pulled the sweatshirt out from her chest. "She gave me this sweatshirt. Said she knew it was big, but I would grow into it."

Tucking her chin to her chest, she said, "I was going to tell you when I got home but Gram was already there, and you had your angry eyes on."

Sarah's eyebrows raised, "Gram?"

"Victoria's mom... she said I could call her Gram. She asked me if I was a foster kid, but I told her you are my mom, and she asked if I had a grandma we were going to visit for Thanksgiving." Tris glanced at Sarah. "But I said she is mean to you so we don't ever see her and that I haven't met her ever in my whole life and that we tried to make a turkey last year, but we ended up eating ramen."

Tris scrunched her nose up and pressed her finger to her left eyebrows. "She made this face and then she said that it was a good thing she was here and since you and Victoria were girlfriends it meant that when you got married that she would be my Gram so I should just call her Gram."

Tris licked her lips. "Do you... maybe... do you think Victoria would be mad at me?" There was a brief pause as Tris reconfigured the words. "That she'd be mad that I called her mom my Gran even though you guys told her a lie?"

"I think if you're worried about it, you should ask Victoria," Sarah said. She wasn't sure about a lot of things, but she was pretty certain Victoria would get to the hero and reassure the kid.

Tris wrapped her sweatshirt tighter around herself as they reached the community playground. With no one around, they each took a swing and moved just enough to sway with the evening breeze rustling the palm trees around them.

"You said we always need to tell the truth. So, why didn't you want to tell them the truth?" Tris asked. "Why did you lie?"

A coppery tangy coated Sarah's tongue as she chewed at her bottom lip. She pressed her tongue to the spot bleeding and tried to think of a way to explain that would go better than when she'd tried to explain to Victoria.

"I panicked," she said slowly.

Tris's feet wobbled as she moved her swing side to side.

"Did Victoria ask you to?" she asked.

"No, honestly, we didn't talk about it. It just happened and she chose to cover for me... kinda like she covered for you last week when she signed your reading log even though we both know you already finished the book."

"Shouldn't you tell them the truth?" Tris kicked the wood chips away from her feet. "Like they are going to find out. You two can't be in the same room without you glaring at her."

The kid's words made complete sense, but it was the type of action a parent said to do but didn't really work out for anyone.

"Honestly— "

"You keep saying honestly but you're lying," Tris growled. "And you said... you told me a lie is a snowball and when you throw a snowball it will just keep getting bigger."

"Roll, not throw," Sarah corrected.

"I know that!" Tris snapped.

Sarah leaned forward to look up at the girl. "Lemme see your tongue if you really know."

The almond-shaped eyes narrowed at Sarah. Tris's lip curled up slightly as spit sprayed from her mouth.

"Lemme see your tongue," she spat. "Because I think it's got to have turned green and is probably going to fall out of your mouth and your hair is too brown to be Ariel... and you sing like a cat is being attacked in an alley so it's not like Princess Victoria is going to come to save you."

With a roll of her eyes, Sarah turned to the girl. "First, it's gangrene. Second, rude. I can sing. Third, fairytales are about royalty getting saved and we both know I'm no princess."

"Uld an en er rinses," Tris grumbled under her breath.

Not even turning to look at the girl, Sarah asked, "What was that?"

"Nothin'." But more words were grumbled. "Uln't afta e lone n ore."

Sarah twisted her body around in a circle. She watched the chain bunch as the seat squeezed her hips, and her legs rose from the ground.

"I was scared that they were going to convince Victoria to move back to Utah," Sarah softly confessed.

Tris kicked the ground again. With a huff, she grumbled, "Like you care if she leaves us."

"I do care," Sarah said. She planted her feet to the ground to keep from spinning out.

"What's wrong with us?" Tris asked.

Sarahs fingers gripped the chains. Her knuckles turned paler than her ass as she thought about always knowing she wasn't good enough. Wasn't loveable enough.

"What do you mean?" she asked, and prayed she'd done a better job than her mother.

"Nobody wants us," she whispered. "Aunt Monica. Victoria might leave... Simone."

Sarah swallowed the hate she had for the woman she'd let into their lives.

"Nothing is wrong with us. Well, nothing's wrong with you," Sarah sighed. "We are just different, and Victoria grew up where people are a lot alike."

Sarah tried to swallow the lump in her throat. "Honestly—"

"You're not being honest!" Tris snapped. "You're only ever telling half the truth and you are so scared if anyone knows any little thing about you."

"Look," Sarah threw her head back only to find miles of sky that didn't look like Victoria's eyes for a change. "I know I'm asking a lot, but I need you to pretend Victoria and I are together. We need to keep our crazy in check and no telling people stuff about me."

"Why do you care what they think about you?"

That one was easy. So, Sarah shrugged when she answered, "Because they are important to Victoria."

"You're important to Victoria and you still told her we are moving out," Tris stated.

"Tris, it's not like that," Sarah tried.

"It is," the honest O'Keeffe declared. "She loves you so you hurt her feelings so she would dump you. Why don't you just be her girlfriend? Then you wouldn't have to lie."

Tris glanced at Sarah. "If you asked her, she'd say yes. She'd do anything for you."

"It's not that—"

"Easy?" Tris asked. "But it is. It's easy but you always make things hard. Like working all the time. You are always gone."

Tris wiggled the chains in her hands. "Do you just want to get away from me?"

"Of course not!" Sarah tried to reach the girl, but the tightened chain took advantage of movement and spun her around. The orange and purple sky spun in a whirlwind above her.

Her heart pulsed wildly as she felt the familiar pressure from childhood that calmed the chaos in her body, even for just a moment.

"Is it because Simone dumped you?" Tris asked when Sarah's feet were trying to balance on the ground that had decided to spin out as well. "Did she break up with you because of me?"

Sarah leaned forward trying to steady her brain. She watched the ground tilt as she tried to explain. "Simone didn't leave because of you. She left because she was married and she lied to her wife and to me and when she had to choose, she went back to her uncomplicated life. I'm complicated, Tris. It's me... I'm the problem."

"T Swifty can't save you." Tris's lips moved between her teeth. Slowly she looked up. "They're nothing alike. Her and Victoria."

"What do you mean?"

Tris kicked her feet like she was running in place. "Simone was mean."

Sarah scoffed. "She wasn't mean to you. She spoiled you. The kid she always wanted is what she used to call you."

"So, what. I didn't want her because she was mean to you," Tris said. "She would only stay for a little while and you would get all dressed up and put on your lipstick, but she wouldn't come over."

Sarah stared at the overly mature child she'd created. A girl focused on how others are feeling to determine her situation.

"You were so little. How do you remember this?"

"I was seven not stupid." Tris groaned. "Look, Sarah."

The mother hated being first named. She couldn't accept the title but when the girl first named her it meant a mic drop of wisdom was about to run acapella.

"Victoria likes likes you and she shows you. She doesn't just say it, but she does things only for you She cooks food only you like, and she keeps track of your face when you eat to see if you like it or not since you won't just tell her. She smiles when you walk into the kitchen in the morning even though you look like a Harry Potter troll, not a troll troll. And she stays up late to wait for you when you have to work. I know because she watches tv the whole time and I keep the door open so that I know you're home too. So, she must love you like I love you."

Tris kicked her feet up. Thrusting her legs forward and back, she began to gain momentum.

"I wish you didn't lie," she said as the pendulum hit the center before rising back up.

"Why?"

"Because it's going to hurt Victoria."

Sarah sucked in her lips. "She knows it's pretend."

"Yeah... but when you go back to being mean after you pretended to be nice, it will hurt her feelings."

The kid was right. Victoria had said they would talk, but after three days a lot could happen. She'd promised to be better. She could be. She could quit the library. She could stop taking clients and just pay her share of the bills. She could take her sister to court. It's not like Sierra would show up to fight her. She could look for ways to not add chaos.

She could light the candles Victoria loved and make a romantic dinner. Yeah, no. She could light the candles and order a romantic dinner. If Victoria still...

'Jesus, she knows I got off to her moaning in the shower!' Sarah scolded herself.

Tris scrunched her nose and lips together as she studied Sarah.

"I'll talk to her," Sarah promised.

"You're going to mess it up."

Sarah got off her swing and stood behind the girl. She pushed as Tris came back to help her get higher without having to work for it.

"Thanks for the faith," she growled.

"You always mess it up and then it's just you and me. I don't want Victoria to go away like Simone did. I don't want to have to move again. She likes me and she spends time with me. And I know it's because I didn't mess up her life."

Sarah stepped to the side. She grabbed the chain the fist was holding on to and pulled the swing to a stop.

"You didn't mess up my life," she stated. "Who told you that?"

"Yes, I did. I heard Aunt Monica tell her new girlfriend when she thought I was asleep that she couldn't come over because I was there. That when I came along it messed up hers and your life because she couldn't just tell you no."

Sarah toed the ground. She tried to tell herself the girl had misheard her best friend. But she knew it was just another lie.

"She said that?"

"Yeah." Tris ran the sleeve of her sweatshirt under her nose. "I know she's your friend, but she doesn't want to be our family. Just like you always say you're not my mom."

"But I'm not," Sarah said. "Your mom... she has a lot of problems and I..."

"Why do you always say that?!" Tris yelled.

Holding up her hands, Sarah said, "Because I'm not your mom."

A tear ran down the girl's cheek. "Why don't you want to be my mom?"

"It's complicated," Sarah whispered.

"Then make it simple!" The child shouted. "You can make things simple for everyone else."

"Tris."

The girl jumped from the swing and stood in the woman's bubble.

"She isn't my mom. She doesn't care about me. She left me with you to be my mom."

She choked on the tears before she asked, "Is it because you never wanted me?"

"Honestly?" Sarah asked.

"Yes!" The girl's hands flew up in the air. "Tell the truth!"

Sarah pulled the kid in her arms. Cradling her head, she said, "I am scared if your mom gets clean that you will want her. You'll want your real mom."

The child wrapped her arms tightly around Sarah. She sucked in her snot, choking on the words as they came out. "You are my real mom.... just because... because I came from her doesn't... it doesn't make you not my mom. People can have more than one mom."

Tris' chin rose so she was facing the woman. "Like if you and Victoria got married, she would be my mom too."

Sarah held the kids face from her. "Hit the brakes."

"You should ask her out on a date. She would say yes."

Sarah looked Tris in the eyes. "I will talk to her, but I need you to promise not to tell anyone this week that we lied."

Tris nodded into Sarah's shirt. She whispered. "Okay."

36

Victoria stood in the driveway, waving as the last of her sister's minivans and SUVs drove past the mother and daughter. Sarah held Tris' hand while the streetlights flickered on, lighting their path back to the house.

She was grateful the O'Keeffe women missed the rapid-fire questions about the relationship basics. Sisterly jabs hit their target as they informed the baby of the family that she'd managed to land a woman out of her league. That hadn't been news to Victoria though. News came in the form of learning the man she'd thought they all preferred to her was actually the husband they dreaded attending family events, while the mysterious woman who'd yelled at the matriarch was the one, they looked most forward to interrogating.

Victoria had laughed at the thought of her sisters getting Sarah to say more than three words during their brief visit. She hadn't needed to warn the woman of Sarah's grisly demeanor. Naomi had done that for her, recounting how Sarah held herself like a warrior raised to command an army. She even added the likelihood of Sarah being able to take down Maverix, the burliest of all the sister's husbands who were away on their annual hunting trip with the patriarch of the Brentons.

Victoria shook her head. Sarah was the first significant other ever to attend a Brenton Thanksgiving, and her sisters had been out right giddy at having an outsider to amuse them.

Sarah nudged Tris forward when they made it to the driveway.

"Go ahead," Sarah prodded. "Now is probably the best time to ask her."

The girl tucked her chin into the sweatshirt while her hands hung within the oversized arms by her side. "I was... your mom, she said... I was wondering..." the ends of the girl's sentences were absorbed into the material.

Whatever it was Tris wanted to say wasn't coming out, no matter how long Victoria waited.

"Your mom told her to call her Gram," Sarah stated. "She's worried that you will be upset if she does because we're not family."

Tris's eyes rose to Victoria's tilted head. She felt the wrinkle in her brow deepen. They'd been each other's rock over the last few days, so she couldn't understand why the prospect of being included in her family would make the child think she'd be angry.

"Why do you think that would make me upset?" she asked.

When Tris didn't have anything to say for the second time in her life, Sarah took the reins.

"She didn't say this, but I am pretty sure it's because Monica just wants to be our friend and she's worried you feel the same."

Victoria didn't speak, she moved. She moved into the child's personal bubble and pulled the girl's face to her chest. Her lips pressed against the worried forehead, then she rested her cheek to the carefully crafted rows.

"We are family," Victoria promised. Her eyes rose to the woman hugging herself in the cool air. "I will never not be your family, even if you're mad at me. A friend of mine... she told me that phrase blood is thicker than water. It's, like, actually wrong. It's supposed to mean that the family we choose is more important than anyone we are biologically related to. Does that make sense?"

Tris nodded against her chest.

"Good. So, if she told you to call her Gram and you're comfortable with it, then do it. If you're not okay with it, then tell her you would rather call her something else," Victoria said.

Tris pulled back from the hug. With a crooked grin, she said, "You know, if you guys quit fake dating then we could really be a family."

"Trisaya Monica O'Keeffe," Sarah growled.

A full name had been used. A full name that Victoria was positive she needed know in case she ever had to... that didn't matter though.

Victoria adjusted the girl under her arm. She would tell herself it was to protect the girl, but it was possible she'd use the hold to push the child forward as a sacrifice if it meant being in Sarah's good graces. After all, the kid was the one that said it. Not her.

Tris smiled smugly at the woman though. "You look like you smellin' yourself right now. Did you forget to put on deodorant again?"

Sacrifice. One hundred percent the girl would have to be sacrificed if she opened her mouth again.

"SOOO..." Victoria started. Her grip on the child's arm tightened just enough to fix the O'Keeffe's family smirk. "My sisters and their spawn are gone for the night."

"I thought they were sleeping over," Tris stated.

Victoria smiled. "The girls were sad too, but I wasn't sure how you felt about sharing your room with them tonight so their moms and I agreed that if you were up for it, they could stay tomorrow with you."

"I agree," Tris quickly said.

"Okay good." Victoria tucked her hair behind her ear. "So, my mom and Madi are staying with us. The others have hotel rooms, but I think my mom is worried we will pack up in the middle of the night and disappear again."

Victoria looked at Sarah. "That's not going to happen, right?"

"No. We talked, and we are good. Tris is going to keep her translations to herself, and I am going to be on my best behavior. No grisly, growly troll like behavior."

Shoulders rose as though the promises Sarah had committed to were all being folded to fit within her lithe frame. Breath rushed from her nose, and she shook her head. "I know if anyone is going to mess this up its going to be me. Because... I mean, it's just this is a lot for me. There's a lot of people and they're going to ask a lot of personal questions so I'm going to need both of your help."

"I think," Victoria paused. "Should we get the details sorted? So, you know, no one screws up."

The crickets masked the carefully created construction. A blueprint for a parallel plot with meaningful memories and romantic rendezvouses. Then a timeline of important introductions and quirky quests on their path to the fantasized family in humorous Hallmark fashion. The tremor invoking traumas glossed to glide more palatable for the privileged.

With the devious details smoothed to a shine, the women entered the home. Tris broke away immediately to join the near woman sprawled across Sarah's couch. The home-brought pillow and blanket had been set up for a temporary residence that crashed into Victoria as Sarah's eyes grew wide.

Victoria raised an eyebrow at the flustered woman who'd tried to hide her own sleeping habits by foregoing a pillow for the crook of her own arm and blanket for the cashmere throw now draped across the armchair. She leaned into her fake girlfriend, pulling the woman into another hug she'd longed to give her. Her hand held Sarah's head steady as she whispered just past the perfectly rounded ear, "You gave up your couch for my bed when you told my mother that we're together."

Sarah sighed. Her arms snaked around Victoria's middle. "I mean, I could think of worse things."

With a soft chuckle, Victoria whispered, "You hate beds."

Sarah slapped Victoria playfully. The smile didn't rise to her eyes, telling Victoria this was all part of the ruse. A ruse that would burn them both, but Sarah seemed committed to the role.

With a giggle, she countered, "It's not that I hate them. I just don't have one."

Victoria's eyebrow rose immediately.

"Okay, babe." Sarah cried out and wiggled like she'd been tickled. Then she leaned closer. "I have a bed but if I sleep in it then I may get used to it and if anything happens..."

With a nod, Victoria finished the rest of the sentence. "You don't want to feel like you lost something."

"Yeah."

Victoria released Sarah from her hug. Careful to not project over the movie playing, she said, "Well, I got bad news for you."

"What?"

A smile spread over Victoria's face. "My bed is amazing."

Sarah took Victoria's hand and led her toward the kitchen where Naomi Brenton sat, staring down at a cookbook.

"I remember how amazing your bed is," she whispered. "I remember the way it hugged me as the room became so rich, I could taste it."

Victoria's head fell back, and she spun the woman back into her embrace. Her hand cradled the sharp jaw and eyes flitted to the plush lips she'd pressed against earlier.

"I'm building a pillow wall between us, you vixen," Victoria husked.

Sarah's eyes crinkled in the corners. She pressed a kiss to the flushed cheek before excusing herself to contact her clients. And Victoria couldn't help but feel like Sarah's choice to cancel was a sign of her commitment not for the three days, but for the earlier discussion of paying part of the mortgage, only with just her school salary.

Victoria leaned against the doorway, watching as Sarah kissed the cheek of the already asleep child. The older girl smiled warmly at her as Sarah pulled the blanket over the child passed out in the chair. The sleepover Tris had hoped for was granted by the niece Victoria had missed the most. Tomorrow, she would find time to speak with Lynny. Even if it meant escaping briefly to the store for the item her sisters would undoubtedly forget.

She retreated to the bedroom, leaving Sarah to complete her nightly ritual of ensuring the satin bonnet was still fixed over the girl's head. She eyed Sarah's duffle bag she'd managed to lift from the bedroom Sarah never used just after Sarah stole Tris away.

A part of her had shattered when she found the closet and drawers empty, and then the bag packed with everything Sarah owned. Her mind wandered to a similarly packed bag she'd placed in the trunk of her car before she stood for testimony.

In the weeks they'd lived together, Victoria had learned Sarah's aversion to purchasing things for herself, including pajamas. Always fell asleep in the clothes, she was wearing only to change into whatever job-appropriate costume she would need the next morning.

Carefully, she ran her fingers over the overfilled drawer of articles she only wore to sleep in. Her fingers wrapped around the woman's favorite shirt, but then paused. If she had laid it out for Sarah, would the woman have seen it as a return of the gift? She couldn't chance it, so she withdrew a well-worn BYU shirt. She cradled it in her arms, bidding farewell to her favorite shirt. It had grown a little snug with the increased availability of child-focused snacks. Leaving the shirt and a pair of satin shorts she knew could be tightened around the woman's thin waist, she retreated to the bathroom.

Her eyes narrowed at the apparently paper-thin wall, a flush of embarrassment running through her as she realized Sarah had showered alongside her just that morning. Had heard her call out as the climax rushed through her.

The door to the bedroom clicked shut after Sarah gave Victoria's mother a soft, "Goodnight, Mrs. Brenton."

Pressing against the crow's feet, Victoria swallowed the feelings of inadequacy. As she left the bedroom, the light illuminated the woman's bare back in the midst of changing.

The air became trapped in her lungs. The pale skin across Sarah's spine and down her side was covered in rippled flesh, a battleground once scorched. The tattooed spine, surrounded by a galaxy of scarred tissue, ran from the shoulder blade to the dimples at the base.

The shirt Victoria had left her dangled in her hand, practically touching the ground. Sarah didn't turn around. There wasn't a point when the silhouette of her form stared back at them both from the shade-drawn window.

Thin fingers ran over the edge of the scar as Sarah whispered, "I was seven."

Victoria bit her lip, holding in the rage that filled her.

"My mom had left us again and it had been a few days." She pulled the wavey locks to the side, giving Victoria access to every inch.

"We were making soup in the microwave and my sister had put it in too long. When she went to pick it up, she dropped it, and I was standing too close." Sarah swallowed. "My mom came home the next day and the shirt... it was practically glued to me. The doctors... they said I was lucky."

Without a word, Victoria stepped forward. She took the shirt from Sarah's fingers. Slowly, she raised the material over the woman's head. She pulled it down, her eyes only leaving the woman's face for the moment it took the shirt to come down.

Once step one was complete, Sarah took over the task of finishing the process. "I don't want your pity," she whispered.

"You have nothing but my adoration," Victoria promised. "Well, sometimes my frustration, but never pity."

Sarah gestured towards the bed. "People usually have a specific side."

Victoria nodded. "They do. So, which would you like?"

Sarah glanced back at where Victoria had come from. Victoria followed the green gaze to the closet door.

"How about you take the window?" she suggested softly. "I'll fight off all the shadow monsters for you. Any monster. Ever. I'll fight it."

They didn't say anything else. Each lay on their respective corners of the bed; the pillow wall plan discarded as they lay back-to-back with an ocean-sized space between them. The down comforter raised to fight away the chill creeping through the cracked window.

Sleep didn't come as easy for Victoria as it had for Sarah. The fragile frame finally found rest as it melded into the mattress. Sarah's first dream-induced twist pulled Victoria from almost sleep when her arm began to prickle like snow was falling upon it.

Sarah created a burrito, wrapping the blanket around herself, only to try and kick it away. She didn't thrash with nightmares the way Victoria had feared after seeing another layer of trauma the woman had survived. Instead, Sarah rolled into a roly-poly ball, only to spread out like a starfish. Her toes grazed Victoria's enough to pull her back from another moment of almost sleep. Soft mutterings created a siren's call, but instead of notes leading Victoria to a death-like sleep, they kept her in the land of the living.

As the clock flipped to 1 AM, Victoria lay under Sarah's arm and leg. Her bust replaced the pillow the other woman didn't seem to agree with while Sarah's body provided the warmth she'd been robbed of when the duvet finally made it to the other end of the bed.

She pulled the woman closer, hoping to give Sarah the contact her sleeping form sought. Her fingers strummed along the woman's spine as Sarah's song turned to soft snores and the twitching in her limb finally felt heavy.

37

When the sun rose, the front door to the house opened. Victoria could hear her mother's grumbles through the bedroom door. The doors and cabinets weren't shut quietly, which means the two girls in the living room were also being dragged from sleep when the sun was barely peeking through the blinds.

"Vicky-Clark!" Naomi called up the stairs.

She'd told the woman yesterday that she went by Victoria now. Something that was shared with all her older sisters. They thought it was very proper and equally preposterous. No one seemed to care that she'd renamed herself, which shouldn't have surprised her.

"Vicky-Clark!" Her mother called again. "There are chores to do before your sisters get here."

Victoria peeked out from around the brown locks pressed into her face. She half expected to see her childhood bedroom with the way the older woman was hollering at her. Instead, she found the side of pillowed lips pressed against an upturned thumb as though given the chance Sarah would pop it in her mouth and soothe herself. With her arm already supporting the woman's neck, Victoria lowered her face back to Sarah's hair and breathed deeply.

This was one of the three mornings she would get to wake up with Sarah in her bed. No part of her was stupid enough to believe that in two days the fake relationship would become real. Already she'd received more than she hoped for because Sarah's body was wrapped over half of her, and she had the opportunity to drift back to sleep with Sarah still drooling on her chest.

Another slap from the front door came despite the fact Victoria hadn't come down to complete the chores her mother had yelled about. Voices of the early risers filled the space as the woman in her arms continued to lightly snore.

"Vicky-Clark, do not make me come up there," Naomi cried out again. A threat Victoria knew the woman would follow up on.

Victoria felt Sarah stir next to her and the realization of the ruse they started was just beginning. A part of her wished for the courage to press her lips to the bend between Sarah's neck and shoulder. To ghost her fingers over the soft flesh her hand was already holding.

Sarah rolled toward her. Her arm fell over her face while Victoria's hand rested on the woman's ribs. The half-opened eyes staring at Victoria were angry.

"I don't wanna," Sarah growled.

Victoria pressed her face back into Sarah's hair, not caring she was snuggling through the woman's boundaries. After being used as a pillow, she decided she earned a little contact of her own.

"You can sleep," she offered. "You're the equivalent to the husband with this family so the expectations of you are next to nothing."

"Do they all really always go hunting on Thanksgiving?" Sarah asked.

"Yep," Victoria said with a pop. "They all put in for the hunting tags for the archery deer dates. Most people don't want to go over the holidays, but my dad's family always went then, and when he finally got his sons, he planned within the tradition he understood. Gave each of my sisters' husbands a bow for their engagement."

"Did it ever upset you not having everyone together?"

Victoria snickered. "Like we needed more people to have to feed. Plus, it's the one holiday we weren't expected to wait hand and foot on the men folk."

Sarah's lips pursed. "I feel like your mother may have supported this tradition for ulterior motives."

"We all did!" Victoria said.

Her fingers lightly tickled Sarah's sides.

"VICTORIA-CLARK! You had better not be ignoring me!" Naomi called out again.

"Stay. Sleep in and enjoy being home for a change."

Sarah's leg slapped the mattress. "I can't just sleep in your bed."

Before the woman could pull away Victoria locked her elbow and pinned the other to the bed. "Well, you just did. And it's way more comfortable than the couch."

Sarah hummed for a moment, and then asked, "Is my bed this comfortable?"

Her heart sank because in just two days, when her family left, she'd find herself alone in a comforter that smelled like Sarah once more.

Victoria wanted to say no, but instead said, "I never tried it to be honest."

"I'm going to have to rethink this whole bed thing," Sarah whispered. She twisted under Victoria's grip and wrapped her body over the brunette once more. "I mean, even the pillows were like sleeping in the clouds."

Carding her fingers through the chocolate locks, Victoria fought the urge to run them over the woman's back.

"You slept on my boobs," she said with a smile.

"I always was a boob girl," Sarah said with a giggle. "And you have very, *very* nice boobs. Even better than that thing you do with your eyebrow."

A telling pulse hummed between Victoria's legs as a warm breath waved over her chest. Sarah's leg trapped her thigh, making it impossible for Victoria to squeeze away the want.

"Should we come up with a game plan for today?" Victoria husked out as Sarah's breath caused her nipples to pebble through the thin shirt.

"Can the game plan be avoiding your family, and staying in bed like this?" Sarah's chin rose, and her eyes weren't as green as they were dark. "I mean, I have years of sleep to catch up on and how am I supposed to do it without my pillows?"

"I..." Victoria swallowed. "If we... Your boundaries..."

She couldn't create a sentence if her life depended on it. The woman's weight on her chest lifted and the hollow space left more room for her heart to bounce around.

Sarah leaned on her hand, looking over Victoria. A thin finger traced a slow line down Victoria's chin, grazing over the soft hollow of her throat until her palm found its place on the gentle rise of Victoria's sternum.

"Gay panic?" Sarah asked playfully, barely louder than a breath.

Victoria nodded, her pulse a rapid flutter under Sarah's touch. Her throat moved as she swallowed, lips slightly parted, glistening. She tried to find words, her gaze snagging on Sarah's lips, full and tempting, so close she could feel the warmth radiating from them.

"Words..." Victoria's mind faltered, the words reduced to a murmur. "Words bad."

Victoria's hand slid up, fingers tangling softly at the base of Sarah's neck. Her thumb traced gentle lines, a quiet tether holding Sarah there. Her eyes roamed Sarah's face, from the dark sweep of lashes to the slight curve of her lips, parted just enough to hint at something more. She felt her own lips curl in a whisper of a smile as she pulled Sarah closer.

"Girlfriends are allowed to kiss," Sarah murmured. "Your sisters asked about our first kiss yesterday. And I..."

Her eyes drifted from Victoria's lips to her eyes, a silent question searching for permission. In the pause, the air between them felt electrically charged.

"If I kiss you," Victoria's voice was a bare whisper, "I can't pretend it's just part of this play."

Sarah's gaze dropped to Victoria's mouth again, her own lip catching between her teeth before releasing it.

"If I kiss you..." Sarah began, eyes drifting closed, "I'm scared of what happens when you realize I'm hard to love. That I'm—"

"If this is the only chance I get.... If we just.... Kiss me," Victoria finally requested. "Please. Just once, and if you don't ever want to do it again, then I will have that at least. The memory of that instead of last time."

Sarah's eyes opened, her gaze softer but still uncertain. Her hand rose to cradle Victoria's cheek, fingers brushing against the soft warmth of her skin. Their faces inched closer, noses just grazing, as even the house quieted around them.

The thigh pressed against Victoria's core moved, creating the friction that sent the electrical pulse through Victoria. Her body surged forward with a need to claim the rest of the space between them. But Sarah's body was pulled back like she'd been tied to the door that flew open when the annoyed matriarch marched into the room.

Sarah's face was buried into the sheet that she grabbed to cover herself, but Naomi didn't seem to care that she had interrupted them. "You two had all night to continue your honeymoon," the woman stated. "And as open-minded and curious as they all are, no one, and I repeat, no one wishes to hear your private matters."

The mother's judgmental gaze moved over the room like it had Victoria's entire life. Naomi sighed like a bull and began moving through the space gathering the dirty laundry up in her arms.

"Vicky-Clark, I know I taught you the function of a laundry basket. You move away and it's like you lost all your sense."

She had lost all sense. Every ounce of sense had been stripped of her as Sarah's legs straddled her thigh and the satin shorts offered her no question of the other woman's shared desire.

"Get up, you two," Naomi barked once more before leaving the room with the laundry.

Victoria's fingers held on to Sarah's hip, though. Thumb stroked the protruding bone sticking out and she watched Sarah's breath freeze. Pressing her leg upward, she watched Sarah's eyes grow wide.

"You're playing with fire," Sarah husked out, but she didn't move away.

She moved lower, her leg meeting Victoria's pulsing core. With each shift of Sarah's hips, Victoria was rewarded by the friction.

"Well since we're not getting our morning shower," Victoria whispered. She worked her thigh against the woman. "I can stop if you—"

"VICTORIA-CLARK!!" her mother screamed.

Sarah held the hand on her hip. She squeezed it softly, ceasing the caress. She took several deep breaths and shook her head.

"This... we can't. It's... it's not part of the plan," she whispered. "Tris will.... All of this is.... Everyone is going to get hurt if we do this."

Before Victoria could respond, the bed was empty, and the bathroom door clicked shut. She lay there as her name was screamed again.

"I'M COMING!" she cried out, the frustration within her so tight that she felt like she could burst. Then, she grumbled, "And not the way I want thanks to you, Mother."

Victoria took the first opportunity to escape the lengthy list of chores her mother assigned. She was pretty sure the woman had added cleaning out the trash cans as punishment for running away.

None of it mattered though. With everyone occupied, she nodded to the niece whose eyes rarely left her. They loaded into the SUV and drove to the coffee shop where Victoria planned on purchasing an apology coffee for Sarah, who'd been pulled into the kitchen and squeezed between her sisters as part of the veggie prep crew. Tears streamed down Sarah's face while she chopped onion after onion. A task all the Brenton sisters were more than willing to hand the outsider. She probably should have taken Sarah's place, but that wouldn't have been allowed when Victoria was given every task her father would normally be responsible for.

The drive through the busy streets was quiet. Victoria wasn't sure what she could say to Lynny when she'd just walked away from the girl. Hadn't even sent a late wedding present or a card.

"How are you?" Victoria asked finally. "I saw... uh... the pictures from the wedding. Your dress was beautiful."

Lynny leaned her head against the headrest. Her dark hair twirled between two fingers as she looked out the window. "You didn't come."

"I wouldn't have been allowed in the temple," Victoria reminded her.

The hum of the engine broke up the quiet. Not being permitted in the temple shouldn't have kept her away, and Victoria knew that wasn't the truth. She'd not received an invitation, even though her family knew where she lived, apparently.

"Did you always know?" Lynny asked. "About the gay thing?"

Victoria pulled into a parking space. They stayed in the car, watching people coming and going. In the beginning, Victoria asked herself that question a lot. She searched her memories for clues as though she'd managed her to brainwash herself yet found nothing.

"I need to understand," Lynny whispered. "My husband... he and I don't. We don't mix. But his parents are on the same Level as Mom, so it made sense. But he's... he's always known he... he had no interest in people like me."

Victoria knew that was a thing now. Gay men married because they had to. She felt that boys knew the truth more easily than girls did. That was the conclusion she'd come to when she asked herself why so many times. To be a good sister, like Victoria prided herself for being, girls didn't have any sexual relations before marriage. Kissing was kept to a minimum, and groping was also a no-go.

"Did you know this before you two were married?" Victoria asked.

Lynny's chin dropped. "No one else knows but his boyfriend. I knew before he went on his mission and I figured... you know, everyone gets married because they're supposed to. Mom and Dad hate each other, so it was, like, get married to John or stay at home and continue to play negotiator."

"Lynny," Victoria whispered. "Why didn't you tell me?"

Lynny closed her eyes. "Because you were the worst. Always, 'rules are rules' and quoting the words. I knew... I knew if I said something you'd tell my mom or Gram, and his life would be ruined, and mine...."

With her lower lip trapped between her teeth, Lynny's stare fixated on Starbucks. A barista wearing a pride-colored shirt moved through the space.

"I knew," the nineteen-year-old whispered. "I knew I liked girls when I was in middle school. I wanted... I wanted so badly to fix it, but when I couldn't, I made the deal with John. We'd do what you all expected of us and then we would lead our lives... quietly."

Lynny closed her eyes. "But I met a girl. I met a girl that I wanted to spend my life with and I just... I blew it because I was scared, and she didn't want to be the other woman."

Victoria took the girl's hand between her own. "I'm sorry I contributed to the self-hate you must have felt."

"I had to find you. I had to find you so that... so I could...."

"So, you could see how they would react to me being with a woman," Victoria completed.

Lynny nodded, then raised her thumbnail to her lips. She chewed on the end like the time she'd shot an arrow through her grandparent's car windshield. She wasn't supposed to be touching the boys' bows, they weren't for girls to use. That was why she'd been hiding in the garage, and now she'd been hiding in a closet because Victoria just left.

"Well, they don't seem to be disappointed," Victoria said, thinking about the pack of Brentons back at her house. "I mean, they're my sisters so I know they are talking trash behind my back. But they're here and they have been respectful. That's really all I can hope for."

Lynny finally looked over. Her fingers gathered the baggy jeans in her fist. "So, you think... you think it's possible to divorce a man and be with a woman?"

Victoria smiled and patted the hand she still held. "Sexuality is a spectrum, honey. I say I'm a lesbian. Maybe I am or maybe I'm bi, and I just didn't want to be married to Michael anymore. I don't honestly have an answer for any of that. I do know that whatever label you assign yourself is your choice, and I also know you don't need to spend your life acting as a beard for a gay man."

"It's so weird that you know that word," Lynny snickered. "Like I even heard you say a swear word yesterday."

"Leaving home was the best thing for me," Victoria confessed. "The world there... it's just small and a little too heteronormative."

"The last time I was here... I met... a woman." Lynny's confession came out just over a whisper. Her eyes scanned Victoria as she explained, "She's a little older than me but she's beautiful and she is, like, settled. I just... I keep trying to escape to see her. We... uh... I just want to go see her, but I want to spend time with you and get to know Sarah. Tris is cute too. I never wanted kids with John but maybe... if things were different."

"I'd love to meet her," Victoria said. But her face turned serious. "You have to tell John the truth though. Like the whole wanting a divorce thing."

"I called him yesterday," the girl confessed. "I'm not going to stand and give a testimony or anything but... I was wondering. Maybe after everything is settled, could you talk to Sarah so that maybe I could stay with you guys for a little while. I just... I want to make sure things are right with this girl before we like..."

"No U-Hauling!" Victoria cried out. Her face paled as she realized the girl who'd been stuck in her hand-me-downs wasn't a child anymore. "Lynny, did you already sleep with her?"

A blush crept up Lynny's throat as she turned back to Starbucks.

"Was she... your first?" Victoria choked out. When the girl nodded, Victoria rolled her eyes. "Great! You imprinted on her Lynnly-duck. You are so fucked."

38

The house moaned under Naomi's second day of scrubbing. Floors that had been mopped the morning before were mopped once more, and Sarah found herself trapped on the last stair. She decided watching a floor dry was the equivalent of watching a pot boil.

She sat, scrunching her toes in the taped-together Bobs. The sandy gravel stuck to the tape irritated her little toe just enough that she knew she'd have a blister by the end of the day if she didn't change out the tape.

But the tape was in her bag. The bag in the room that Victoria had hidden on the window side of the bed. To get the tape, she'd risk waking the woman bridging the boundaries of pretend into an actual trial run.

Victoria's arms were around her when they walked through the store with her sisters or took the younger kids to the park. The smile when Victoria spoke just past Sarah's ear had given her pleasant tingles rather than creeper chills. It had turned into a game, and her need to have the upper hand had Sarah playing along until she was leading the rush.

She felt guiltier than after their first lesson or lying to the matriarch. So, she'd snuck out of Victoria's sleeping grip, stuffing a pillow in her place for the woman to cuddle. Because it was all too easy.

Sarah sucked in her lower lip and bit down. The pain reminded her of the truth. If she allowed herself to believe this could be real, then the self-inflicted pain would be only a fraction of what she would go through when the woman understood that she was unlovable.

She'd thought her scar would give Victoria a visual understanding of how imperfect she was. The tattoo artist had grimaced when he saw the canvas she was asking him to detail. She'd been a kid with a fake ID, and she used it to get a tattoo. But Victoria had....

Naomi returned from the garage. Her socked feet left small impressions along the still-damp floor. A soft tune came from parted lips that turned into a low screech when Sarah leaned closer to the wall. She clutched her hand to her chest as her body flew into a dining room chair.

"Sarah," she huffed. "You almost scared me into an early grave."

Sarah looked at her statuesque form. She raised her eyebrows as she took in the woman still trying to catch her breath.

"You're like a ninja."

Sarah's eyebrows tried to join her hairline, but she said nothing. Just forced a smile on her face.

If Naomi questioned whether Sarah wanted to talk to her or not, it was unnoticeable. The wooden legs of the chair glided across the ground, as though the dining set knew better than to talk back to the woman caring so carefully for it.

"I was thinking about making pancakes for the girls this morning," Naomi said as she took a seat across from Sarah.

"Tris likes pancakes."

Rubber gloves slapped against the table and the dingy sock-covered feet lifted to another chair. It was the most at rest Sarah had seen the woman, and it gave her a moment to take in the luggage weighing down the sun-kissed cheeks. Naomi's shoulders hung a little lower, but Sarah appreciated the fact the woman had foregone a bra. Whenever she saw women, even older women, braless Sarah felt a sense of freedom in their presence. Hoped one day she'd be able to let go of her concern for others and break such a solid societal expectation.

"You don't like me, do you?" Naomi asked, but it felt like a statement.

Sarah knew it wasn't a question. She'd given the woman no reason to believe otherwise. Avoided being in the same room with her unless she was forced. Answered questions in simple sentences to ensure the woman wouldn't hear the fact that she wasn't good enough for her daughter.

"I can understand why," Naomi stated, her fingers fumbling with the ties of her sweatpants. "I was so oblivious to my own child's needs that she had to run away to be free."

Naomi glanced toward Sarah. "I would hate me too. I mean, I do... hate myself for making her think I would ever not love her."

Years of training taught Sarah to go against her instincts. She learned in her social worker classes to match body language. To not contribute unless she had to. To not provide any acknowledgment beyond eye contact because most people used uh-huh but weren't really listening.

"You know, I had my own crushes of the female sort," the woman held up her hand. "In my day, we called everyone a girlfriend and you weren't a lesbian unless you had on trousers and cut your hair. So, I never thought of it. But... they said it runs in the family, so she probably got her eye for the ladies from me."

The smile didn't have to be forced this time. It came easy as Sarah thought of how much time Naomi had probably spent questioning her sexuality since Victoria's announcement.

"Tris said your mom... she isn't very nice to you," Naomi stated. "Is it the homosexual thing?"

With a soft laugh and a hang of her head, Sarah tried to imagine the drug and booze-wrinkled woman even considering the possibility of her gayness. She would have needed to remember Sarah even existed so it was unlikely.

"So, not the gay thing," Naomi stated.

Sarah held up her hand as she tried to regain her composure. The woman was looking for a conversation and was more likely to probe for details so Sarah needed to have her wits about her.

"She doesn't even know," Sarah admitted.

"Oh." Naomi studied Sarah for a moment. "So, may I ask why you don't see her?"

Lying got her into this situation. If she hadn't told this woman she was Victoria's girlfriend, then this interrogation would not be possible. Just like if she hadn't tried to run away from the house that morning, she would probably be nose to nose with the woman still in bed. They might have kissed this time. She probably could have gotten off from just the kiss with how sexually frustrated she was. But here she was, trying to sugarcoat the truth for a woman she didn't even want to know.

With a nod towards the stairs, she parsed the explanation down to just a few sentences. "I haven't seen her since Tris was a baby. She... uh... made a joke and we left."

"A joke?"

"Said I musta banged a basketball player for a payday. Said I better force the paternity test to get the paycheck since I ruined my p—" Her mouth snapped shut. She tried to apologize to the G-rated woman with an awkward half-smile.

Naomi didn't seem phased by the almost slip. She waved her hand in the air silently telling her to continue, but the courage Sarah had momentarily found dissolved on her tongue.

Sarah shrugged her shoulders at the same time she sealed her lips. The muscles in her neck twisted into knots until it felt like she couldn't turn without her neck breaking.

"So, you never went back," Victoria's mom whispered. She twisted the floral top between her fingers. "I was scared I wouldn't be able to find Victoria. I just kept thinking about everything I'd ever said about the gays. Searching for any reason she'd have to run away from me, and I came up with nothing. Do you know? Did she say why she just left?"

Sarah chewed over the question and her lower lip. There were parts of the story that she knew, but nothing told her why Victoria didn't just talk to her mom. From what she'd seen thus far, the Brentons acted like a typical family Sarah could find in a Hallmark movie. They argued with each other and laughed with each other. There were a million stories that proved Victoria's life had been just as sheltered and warm as Sarah previously assumed.

"You should ask her." Sarah ran her hands over her thighs and checked to see if the floor was dry yet.

"You don't even have a hint for me?"

Sarah met the mother's gaze. "It's her story to tell so even if I knew it, it would be wrong for me to share."

Naomi nodded. She held out her hand to Sarah. It would be rude not to take it, so Sarah offered over the expected contact. It's not like she'd ever craved a mothering connection.

"May I ask about your story?" Naomi queried.

The wrinkles between the eyebrows deepened when Sarah studied the woman's face.

"I thought you just did," Sarah whispered. "And I told you."

"No, you told me about taking your daughter home and that the woman you don't call Mom assumed your straightness," Naomi explained. "And you said you didn't come out so I would like to know more of your story. You're a mother to a beautiful daughter, but is there a father in the picture or a partner you planned her with?"

"You want the motherhood story, not the gay story," Sarah summarized.

Naomi squeezed Sarah's hand. "The motherhood story is the most important one I have always found. The partners... they are there. They track their muddy boots into the house after you just mopped. Or they bring their mother over to visit and she will tell you all the ways you aren't taking care of her baby well enough."

"I am pretty sure you have been riding Victoria's ass for two days about not being good enough for me." Sarah softly chuckled and shook her head. "Which you should know is not true. If anyone is the slob it's me, and if anyone doesn't know how to feed a human properly it's me."

"So, there is a story," Naomi said, moving to sit beside Sarah on the stairs.

Sarah's chin dropped to her chest. "I never thought I would be a mom. Mine had been so... neglectful is generous. So, I figured... I mean it's not like I would never be able to keep a kid alive or make them, like, stable. And to answer your question it's just me and Tris. No one else but Victoria, which is... still very new."

"Well, you're doing a great job," Naomi waved their connected hands together. "That girl has kindness in her mouth and strength in her heart, and that came from you."

Sarah's lip was swollen from biting it. She released it to whisper, "Thanks."

"Sarah," Naomi said, pulling Sarah's eyes to her. "My daughter loves you. I know this because I have spent my life learning to read the look in her eyes. I knew she never loved her former husband, but when I had given her a way out, she'd buckled down to make her father proud. But she loves you. She loves you out of no obligation or expectation."

Sarah smiled softly. "She's wonderful."

"She is." Naomi squeezed Sarah's hand. "And you are too. But do you love her? Because something tells me you're holding back."

Tris had warned her she'd fuck it up. She'd mess it up because she lacked so many foundational skills. This was the moment that she would say too much without any words. She could fix her face, but stoicism would draw suspicion. So, she looked at the mother and waited.

"You're scared to love her," Naomi answered for her. The weathered hand cupped Sarah's chin. "Child... you've spent your life trying to survive, didn't you?"

Sarah couldn't answer because her eyes welled at feeling what life should have been like. The only woman who'd ever treated her with this kind of understanding was Dilynn Greyson, and Sarah had kept Mrs. Greyson at an arm's distance at all points in time.

"It's not that I don't like you, Mrs. Brenton," Sarah whispered, turning away before the tears fell. She squeezed the woman's hand.

"Please, call me mom."

Sarah shook her head after she wiped away the tears. "I can't do that. What you offered to Tris... letting her call you Gram means so much to her and me. But I can't because I'm not..."

Naomi wrapped her arm around Sarah when the front door opened. The Brenton girls were returning for day two of meal prep.

"You scare me as much as your daughter does. Your open heart... giving nature." Sarah sucked in all the breath she could and exhaled the words. "It's like your family fell from the sky while I've spent my life in a war zone. So, this whole thing... the people and the happiness. It's a lot."

Naomi stood up as the sisters carried in crockpots and boxes of pans from the trunks of their cars. Sarah was pulled down into a hug. Unable to contemplate what else to do she patted the woman on the back while the dining room table became an extension of the cabinets as the tools for the day were organized.

"Escape for today," the woman commanded in a wasped whisper. "Go now before my daughter tries to run away with you."

Cupping Sarah's face between the weathered hands, the woman held Sarah's gaze. "Tomorrow, we cook so there's no running away. Don't worry though. The cooking... it's not a talent, it's a skill that I will teach you because I know you're brilliant, and I know that you love my daughter. You wouldn't be scared if you didn't."

Sarah slipped out of the room by sliding against the wall. She managed to avoid being hit by boxes being sightlessly carried down the hallway. The Brentons didn't seem to notice her retreat. Well, all but one. She glanced back at the kitchen when she heard Victoria asking her mother if she'd seen Sarah.

"Don't you worry yourself about that lovely woman," Naomi stated. The mother waved for Sarah to get out while pushing a hand-scrawled list against Victoria's chest. "Here are your chores for the day. And don't even think about not washing out those trash cans again."

39

Victoria woke with a jump when her mind had realized she'd once again dreamed of Sarah wanting more than the friendship she'd begged for. She'd known the tables had turned when she'd been left with a pillow to cradle. Rushing from the room, she searched for Sarah in the sea of her sisters and their spawn carrying more stuff into her house.

There was no sign of Sarah though. The woman hadn't even left a note or verbal message before disappearing for half the day. She'd always left a note or sent a text, and the lack of communication made breathing a little harder. She'd sent three texts, because something must have happened yesterday.

She thought about the afternoon trip to the grocery store while scrubbing the patio table where the kids would eat tomorrow evening. They'd held hands, fingers intertwining so naturally, which Victoria instigated while moving through the parking lot. That was because Sarah kept crab walking into her though. Every detail of the grocery visit replayed until Victoria moved on the trash bins that her mother was adamant about getting cleaned out.

Victoria had to empty the trash from the bins to clean them. The wrappers from the footlong sandwiches were smashed on top of all the other trash. As she wrestled with the bag, she considered if it was the kiss Victoria pressed to Sarah's neck that made it so the woman needed to flee. But Sarah had kissed her on the nose shortly after they'd stared at each for so long Pandora pointed out that everyone was waiting on them to order.

Maybe it was the lack of television in the bedroom. That would be something she would correct if Sarah didn't want to move back into the living room or the third bedroom, where she only kept her clothes. Watching TV was how Sarah fell asleep usually, so they lay side by side with Victoria's cellphone propped on the comforter between them to watch a few episodes of Gilmore Girls.

Sarah had fallen asleep first, at least Victoria was pretty sure she had. The hose was running as she tried to remember when she put the phone on the charger. It was on the charger when she woke up, however, Sarah could have done that. Which might have been after she woke up and gave Victoria a pillow to hold.

Victoria had moved on from cleaning the trashcans to peeling potatoes when she decided it was the cuddling that sent Sarah running from the house. She must have been cuddling Sarah, otherwise there wouldn't have been a reason to give her a pillow. The woman probably felt like Victoria was trying to suffocate her. That's what Michael always said when Victoria ended up on his side of the bed. She would lean against him, and he felt like she was trying to "steam roll" him. A comment made often enough to send her to the local gym since her body had changed after her hysterectomy. Had the doctor told her the hormone fluctuations could make her gain fifty pounds she might have continued to cry through each crippling monthly cycle.

When Sarah still wasn't back after she'd peeled an entire bag of potatoes, Victoria was past the point of nervous, and on to the point of fear. It made her mother's critical comments concerning her housekeeping dig deeper than the typical topical wound.

She'd been sent to get a broom to sweep the floor once more when a bowl of sugar had been tipped from her sister's hand. The parade of children rushing inside to play hide and seek were the cause of the mess, but it was apparently Victoria's fault.

"I know you don't know what it's like trying to keep up with children always making a mess, but you have to," Naomi stated, snapping the ends off of the green beans. "It took your sisters getting use to as well, but you don't have the learning curve they did. Tris will only grow up to care for her home as well as you care for yours, so you must set a better example. Just yesterday, I pulled out that table by the front door and it looked like a litter box underneath."

The patient portion of her tongue burned with the bile she'd swallowed trying to silence the rage building within her body. Several sets of dark eyes had grown wide when her breaking point was breached.

"Why can't you just get off my ass, Mom?" she snapped. The broom in her hand didn't break under the pressure of her grip, so she used it to point to the door then the table her mother sat at. "You literally fly in here unannounced with your swarm of worker bees buzzing around in a constant hum of passive aggressive comments about me not being good enough."

Victoria's arms shot up, her hand still clutching the broom. "I know I'm not good enough. That's why I left! Because I would never be the daughter you wanted, but seriously you have six others that did exactly what you wanted, and I tried. Okay, I tried to be the woman you wanted but I can't. I just can't."

Vegetables screamed as their structures were softened with the scalding butter in the pan on the stove. An Instapot sputtered until the vent locked into place. But the knife chopping had paused. The footfalls of children previously running came to a screeching halt as the matriarch snapped one green bean at a time into a bowl.

"Are you done?" Naomi asked.

Victoria was done because the mother had managed this meltdown from the hosting daughter yearly. It had become a day before Thanksgiving tradition.

The hive began to buzz again as the smoke of her emotional eruption cleared. Honey-laced words sweetly coated the walls with a new layer of paint and laughter applied a second coat.

Sarah arrived shortly after her explosion. Her arm weighed down with an oversized Walmart bag. She clutched the large box to her chest when Tris moved past her and held up her multi-colored nails for Victoria to see. Sarah bolted up the stairs with the package without an explanation.

"Nat and Lena painted my nails in Avenger colors," the girl stated proudly.

Victoria grabbed the child's hand and held it up to Pandora. "What blasphemy is this? We are a DC family."

The middle sister rolled her eyes dramatically at the preposterous baby of the family. With a wave of her hand, she said, "Sorry I forgot to pack the kryptonite green."

Victoria grabbed a green bean tip from the discard pile and chucked it at the brand traitor. When the woman deflected the first throw, Victoria launched several others.

"You. Will. Not. Teach. My. Kid. My. Fatal. Flaw," Victoria cried out, pelting the woman who batted away half of the projectiles with the whipped-cream-covered spatula.

White speckles flew through the air until a larger chunk launched from the base and splattered across Sarah's nose.

Everyone froze as the stealthy woman, who'd just descended the stairs, narrowed her eyes at the family of clones. Slowly, thin fingers scraped the fluffy pie topping from her face, leaving streaks across her cheeks like warpaint. It sat in a glob atop fingers as Victoria cautiously approached.

Carefully Victoria fished a dish towel still tucked in her apron pocket out, allowing the white flag to wave in surrender. "Mercy," she requested, and then held the towel towards Sarah.

When Sarah moved, she didn't reach for the towel. She simply flicked her hand in the air at Victoria. The dollop of creamy goop missed its target and hit the creator of the clone army still dutifully snapping beans in solidarity.

A single bean pod smashed under the older woman's grip. The beans popped from their encasement and bounced along the floor in search of an escape. Everyone needed an escape as Naomi rose like a queen at a formal dinner. The heads of her subjects dropped until their chins touched the floral printed tops.

Unphased by the matriarch's irritation, Sarah's chin rose. The stoic stare made Victoria's knees weak, and her core pulsated. She'd never get to kiss the woman, at least not while she was alive. Because Naomi Brenton looked set on murder and Sarah didn't seem concerned that she was about to be executed for treason.

The worn hand of the woman, who'd raised seven children without ever succumbing to be a victim of their antics, wiped the watery whipped cream from her face.

"You think you can get away with such a weak attack," Naomi snarled. The corners of her lips rose until her canines were shown. "Well, my dear, you will learn that I don't play fair. I attack at the heart of the issue."

A hand shot forward, and Victoria closed her eyes. Her hair was pulled from her ponytail and her face was coated in the thrice-thrown topping. The sweet-covered finger pulled her bottom lip down so Victoria had no choice but to taste the assault and assess the need for another teaspoon of vanilla.

"Hey!" The second to the foreign warrior cried out and grabbed the spatula from Pandora's hand. "Don't. Touch. My. Adult."

Victoria had enough time to wipe the cream from her eyes before the girl let out a battle cry. The spatula waved wildly as the girl rushed toward the grandmother.

All the eyes in the room grew when Naomi's hands rose in the air. But the girl was struck back. Her body flailing as she was sent backwards into the mother behind her. Their bodies sank to the floor as an uncooked biscuit slapped against the wood.

The spatula clanked alongside the damaged dough. A dark hand gripped into the worn BYU shirt hanging off Sarah's body, stretching the neck out.

"Fire is catching," the girl choked out. Her legs wiggled in fake spasms as she groaned. Tris would never win an Emmy, but she died like a proper martyr.

Sarah's eyes rose as she clung to the child. She bared her teeth. Her finger like a sword swung through the air as she pointed at the nineteen-year-old traitor.

"I trusted you," she growled. She waved the army of children gathered in the hallway. "Attack! Leave none to tell the tale of this act of treason."

As the children rushed into the kitchen, the sky dropped adults fought to save their ammunition. Laughter mixed with battle cries created a memory worth saving. A tale that was told throughout the night as all the Brenton children were tucked into blankets across the living floor for another sleepover that Lynny was charged with leading.

The food for the feast would not be as plentiful, but none of them cared the next morning. Not when the Brenton sisters dragged themselves back to the house at the crack of dawn.

They were woken once more to the sound of life. At some point in the night, the gap between them had been closed, though neither gave the other a chance to question if they should kiss and no jokes were made about missing their daily shower. They simply dressed with their backs to one another, and then made the bed in tandem. The bed that wouldn't be required to be shared after dinner.

When Sarah and Victoria made it downstairs, Victoria found normal. An old normal like the quilt she'd wrap herself up in after finishing the dishes from Thanksgiving dinner. The familiar compression turned suffocatingly hot as her sisters moved around her in their perfected choreography Victoria had forgotten the steps to.

By the time dinner was served, Victoria was exhausted. Her body fell in her chair at the table that had been turned and extended with the other tables in her house to accommodate all her siblings. The children had welcomed the opportunity to eat outside with less formality, but Sarah was smashed between Victoria's sisters Kathy and Diana.

Kathy sat with her overfilled plate, picking through her meal piece by piece. "So, how did you and Sarah meet, Vicky-Clark? Was it love at first sight?"

"Through a friend," Sarah chimed in as the color drained from Victoria's face. "And I don't know about it being love at first sight, but when we first met there was... chemistry."

Victoria drained her glass of water, wishing her mother hadn't located her last bottle of wine. She needed it with the way Sarah savored each bite of the meal she'd helped create at the side of the Brenton matriarch. Victoria vowed to cook with the woman more often, so she could enjoy the sight of Sarah's contentment and pride.

"What about you, Aunt Victoria?" Lynny asked. "Did you know immediately?"

Sarah opened her eyes. They'd not rehearsed more than what she'd just provided. She wasn't the only one staring at Victoria though. Her mother was also watching Victoria carefully from her seat at the head of the table. A look that said she might know more than she was letting on. That all the harassment had been punishment for lying to her, or maybe it was meant to be a reminder that she had to work to get Sarah to love her.

Victoria's fork clinked when she set it against her plate. She swallowed the gravy-drowned mashed potatoes she'd pushed into her mouth.

"The first time we met," she started softly. "Well... I was nervous to say the least. She'd come into my life when I was very unsure of myself. I was terrified of dating and what would happen when someone found out I was... uh... Mormon. And that I'd been married to a man. I actually overheard—"

"Is this going to be long, or can you skip to the good part?" Pandora interjected.

"It's the first time we met so it can't be that long," Victoria growled at the sister who'd been Victoria's biggest bully growing up. "Anywaysss... back to the story."

Victoria ran her finger over the rim of her water glass.

"I had never met anyone quite like Sarah." She glanced up at the woman across from her. "She was confident and held herself so poised. I remember my hand was shaking and I tried to give her a glass of water."

She smiled as she looked at the glass in front of her. Maybe it was the same one.

"Our fingers... they had barely touched, and it was like the clock had stopped ticking each lonely moment away. Well, the clock wasn't ticking because the battery had died, and I had been thinking of changing it."

She looked over when her sister groaned. Pandora's head fell back, and her hands hit the table.

"I know, okay? I know it sounds so cheesy, but it was like... like I was alive for the first time since I don't even know. And I knew that I wanted to know her. The whole her."

When Victoria returned her gaze to Sarah, she found the other woman sitting farther from the table. The occasional blink was the only sign she was alive, because she didn't appear to be breathing.

"I didn't think I would see her again," Victoria whispered. "We had met through a friend, but it wasn't a date. We were supposed to talk about what to expect when I tried to date. And we did that, and that was it. Just a simple, 'Hey, welcome to the life of a lesbian. I'll answer your questions and then I'm done.'"

"That's a thing?" Lynny asked. "Like you get issued, like, a support lesbian so you don't have to figure it out by yourself?"

Victoria chuckled and shook her head. "No. I just knew the right people who knew the right people. And Sarah was the right person."

"So, if she just answered your questions, how did you two end up living together?" the matriarch asked.

"Our paths crossed again at work the next day. And... it was like, we were, like, meant to be in each other's lives. I knew immediately but Super Serious Sarah?" Victoria laughed, and she tapped her fork to her plate. "Well, she wanted nothing to do with me. I was cocky and hell-bent on proving myself to the point that she yelled at me two weeks in for being narrow-minded and... what was it you called me?"

The corners of Sarah's lips rose in a more subtle smirk. She twisted her knife in her hand as she looked over at Victoria.

"Something along the lines of another clueless admin," Sarah stated.

"Admin is clueless," Diana interjected. "The lesbian thing I can deal with, but an admin, really? That's where I draw the line." The eldest sister looked at her daughter. "I mean it, Lynnley. You want to be a lesbian, then fine. But if you even think about becoming one of them, then no more Christmas presents."

The table of teachers offered a chorus of agreement. Lynny's face was a vibrant shade of red, but she looked to Victoria and mouthed a simple "Thank you."

"So, is there more to this story?" Pandora asked. "I mean, what ended up happening that Sarah decided to give you a chance?"

"Well, after that day. I knew... I knew she'd never give me a chance if I didn't do better. So, I went back to school again. I listened and studied how she reached kids. Always meeting them at their level and helping them work through the why and not the what."

She could feel every set of eyes studying her like a living statue in a museum. It made her shift in her chair, and then her eyes fell to her plate.

"Every day I learn something new about her. About her strength. Her bravery. Her kindness." Victoria licked her lips. "It's like every day I wake up and find a new reason to fall in love with her."

"But how did you end up together?" Pandora demanded. "See, you always do this. You turn something that should just be like we met at work, and I asked her out into this—"

"My apartment got broken into," Sarah interjected. Her gaze fell to her plate. "I... I'm not like you all. Tris and I... that's it. We didn't have anywhere to go and I was... I dreaded walking out into that apartment. I had broken down because Tris was at school, and she wasn't there to see... and I was just.... It's hard when there's no family. When it's just you and a kid, and you have to keep it together all the time."

Sarah's head fell back and let out a deep breath. It took her a moment to gather herself, but the Brenton women waited for her.

"I had ignored probably twenty of Victoria's calls. Cried myself to sleep in Tris's bed because it was the only room that didn't look like a warzone. But I had to get up." She looked around the table. "You all know it. You can't just stop being a mom because bad things happen or because you're tired or because this maybe wasn't the life you thought you were going to have because it didn't look like Full House or Family Matters, and you didn't end up in a fancy farmhouse with a wraparound porch like Loralie Gilmore. So, I got up, but it was like FEMA had come in after a tornado. Only it was Victoria."

Their eyes met across the table.

"I walked out to find her in my kitchen with her rubber gloves on. She'd shoved the stuffing back into the couch. Left perfect lines vacuumed into the carpet. Scrubbed the ice cream from the floor, and folded all of my clothes so I didn't have to do it. And then she packed me a bag and one for Tris. And we went to stay with a friend for a few days until Victoria convinced me to move here. And I was scared and I was stubborn because I've spent my whole life just trying to survive. And she asked for nothing. In fact, she refused everything, especially the rent money I tried to give her."

Lynny cleared her throat. "So, what happened next?"

Sarah gestured to Victoria. "We fought about the fact that I'm a slob. And she did something no one in my life had ever done."

"What'd she do?" Naomi asked.

"She apologized even though it wasn't her fault. I was the one who hadn't been considerate, and she'd lost her patience and she... she just apologized." Sarah licked her lips. "That was when things changed. That and the fact that she gives the best foot massages."

Victoria forced a smile on her face. The story was as close to the truth as they could get. It just wasn't the truth because after that Sarah was ready to leave. She'd still be preparing to leave if Victoria's family hadn't shown up. And she'd probably be ready to leave tonight once they were gone because Victoria had said the words that Sarah begged her to hold back.

"Well, we are happy you're here with us, Sarah," Naomi stated. "I am sure us all showing up has been a lot for you, but I can see how happy you make Victoria, which is something I was scared of. Not that she would be happy with a woman, but that she wouldn't. That she left feeling lost and unloved."

Victoria's eyes moved from the woman shrinking into herself to her mother. The person who'd taken yesterday's blow-up in stride and not shared the pain she'd been inflicted by Victoria just leaving.

"When I left, I didn't even know what was possible because nothing had ever felt so real as it does with Sarah and Tris," she explained. She bowed her head slightly to her mother. "I know I hurt you, and I know that even though I left people still talked about the fact that I had let you down. But I can't be sorry."

She paused for a moment. Sent out a prayer that her mother could and would understand that leaving was the best thing for her to do.

"I can't apologize for leaving when it brought me here. To Sarah and to Tris. A life I never imagined was possible."

Victoria turned back to the green eyes searching her face. She may never again get the chance to tell Sarah how she felt, and even if their relationship was a temporary ruse, she had at least taken the opportunity to provide her testimony once more.

Their gaze was only broken by the girlish chatter of first love stories. Victoria stirred her peas and carrots into her mashed potatoes. Even though her stomach grumbled, she couldn't bring the fork to her mouth.

The clock on the wall ticked as her sisters finished the food on their plates. When the food was gone, her family would soon be after. Her mother and Lynny were already packed and ready to return to the hotel with the other Brenton women. And tonight, the bedroom at the end of the hall wouldn't be their room anymore, and the home would again be a house she shared with Sarah and Sarah's daughter. So, she allowed the minutes to stretch into what felt like hours of silence from Sarah. The one person whose voice and touch she craved had melded into just another part of the table, then the wall, as the women of Victoria's past made their way back into her future.

She should be happy. A part of her was. To be loved and accepted was something she'd thought she'd have to give up. The rest of Victoria needed a drink. A strong drink that she'd only find with Parker's heavy pour at Echo's bar. To numb the burn of being in love with a woman who didn't love her back.

40

Exactly ten crepe paper streamers of green, pink, and orange dangled from the door jamb of Tris's bedroom. Birthdays had always been tough. Sarah wasn't able to give Tris parties at trampoline parks or backyard bounce houses when she was little, so she did what she could to celebrate from when the girl woke up to the end of the day. It was supposed to be part of the talk she had with the homeowner once the rest of the Brentons left. Only Victoria left too.

Victoria was gone not long after her niece and mother followed the caravan of minivans away from the house. The promised debrief for the three-day fake relationship was postponed, leaving Sarah on edge. That was at least familiar for her, and the cortisol pumping through her system made her able to function as normal while the bedtime routine took place.

The woman hadn't called after climbing into the car, but it wasn't like Sarah had any intention of answering if she did. She needed quiet and time to tik away. Time to process the tsunami of the Brenton family with their dark eyes all trying to pull her towards an island while Victoria sang her a siren's call. The makeshift raft she'd been paddling was falling apart already as Sarah tried to keep the child away from the world she'd known to be harsh and unyielding, just trying to find them a better place. But sirens were liars. She'd already been trapped by one for two years. So, why would she think Victoria could be any different?

The woman had gone so far as to take ownership of her daughter. Claimed her as her own publicly and ensnared the girl into a fantasy Sarah felt couldn't possibly be real. She wanted it to be real though, that hope she'd tried to stomp out was so alive that hanging the streamers alone had her on the verge of tears.

Sarah had to freeze halfway through hanging up the streamers because the child opened the door in the middle of Sarah's birthday ritual. With eyes barely opened, Tris zombie walked to the bathroom, not casting a glance at Sarah frozen on the step stool holding the streamer meant to cross the door. There would also be ten of those for the girl to burst through in the morning.

Once the door was decorated, she retrieved the giant box of Legos from her side... no, the window side of Victoria's bed. She swallowed the reminder that the ruse had run its course. Being in the room without Victoria was no longer permissible, so she picked up her bag as well.

"Bye, bed," Sarah whispered. Her fingertips grazed over the cloud-like surface. "Thank you for teaching me what I've been missing."

She dropped the bag back into the closet and looked at the mattress she'd been provided. The bed was made with the same box corners as Victoria's but smelled like the wrong Brenton. She'd told herself the first change she would make in her life would be to sleep in the bed. It was meant to show Victoria that she was taking a step forward, but that step would have to come tomorrow. After she was able to ask Victoria which sheets in the linen closet were supposed to be used on that bed.

The present was wrapped with twisted edges because measuring the precise amount of paper was on the same skill level as cooking something in an actual pan. More streamers were hung around the kitchen. She placed the paper plates in the coordinating colors on the table that she'd picked up from the Dollar Store, wishing she could have set some for the younger Brenton girls. It would have been the first birthday party Tris had with guests, but the trip hadn't been planned for an extra day. She wondered if Tris could have a party with the girls present next year. It seemed unlikely after the dinner confession that had Victoria fleeing the house.

With nothing else to do, and Victoria still gone, Sarah curled up into her corner of the couch. It gave her the hug she needed as the familiar voices on the television lulled her to an equally familiar sleep until a thud on the front door ripped Sarah back to reality.

She blinked at the television, briefly wondering how many episodes of *Mike and Molly* had passed. There was another thud at the door, followed by the jiggling of the handle. Her greatest enemy in her head berated her for not setting up the doorbell camera on her phone like Victoria had asked her to.

Sarah glanced up where she knew Tris' decorated door sat. The door was still open. The breath caught in her throat as the handle jiggled again. She contemplated if she could claim defense when it wasn't her house, and Victoria had left immediately after saying goodbye to her relatives. The reality of talking to Sarah had finally been the thing to terrify the woman and send her packing because the excitement of the relationship game with the unlovable woman was done.

But another slap against the wood sent the air rushing from Sarah's lips. She scanned the room for something to stop whatever was on the other end of that door. She fumbled around the floor of the coffee table, her fingers grazing lost Legos and a snapped hair tie until she found what she knew would be there. It lay in wait under the coffee table, the one space the mother of sirens hadn't bothered to search. The sharpest object in the room.

The handle continued to wiggle, and the door protested when something heavy smacked against it again. Sarah peeked around the corner of the living room just as the door burst open. The figure was nothing more than a shadowy demon haloed by the streetlight. White spots peppered Sarah's vision. Her body turned to hide behind the wall while the sluggish feet dragged across the floor.

When the canvases rattled with the closing of the door, Sarah shot out from behind the wall with Victoria's impractical high heel angled at the intruder. Her eyes burned and red and green spots shimmered as the hall light flicked on.

Two sets of wide eyes stared at her. Two bodies that were conjoined at the hip. Victoria's frame was supported entirely by a fit redhead in a corset-cinched top.

Sarah ignored the heat radiating from her skin because she definitely didn't have any feelings for Victoria and her new interest. None would she say were the type of feelings to make her skin crawl because the stranger held Victoria's body protectively in perfectly toned arms. She had absolutely no reason to look the woman up and down and stare at how her bra had lace and was not beige or old. Or notice the way the woman's eyes popped from the smokey shadow perfected probably from ample amounts of time to practice.

Victoria's face fell from a drunken smile when she looked at Sarah. The brown eyes were unable to sustain contact with her and instead wandered up to the space where Tris was hopefully still sleeping.

The other woman smiled at Sarah. She hoisted Victoria further up on her shoulders and walked Victoria forward.

"Hey," the redhead said with her perfectly painted lips. Kind eyes ran over Sarah's face without assumption. The type of confidence only held by someone who knew they were chosen.

Sarah didn't respond. She just dropped the shoe and stood awkwardly in the space as the two made their way past her to the couch. Her couch. Victoria had brought a beautiful woman home to make out and possibly have sex on her couch.

She couldn't say anything as Victoria's drunken form fell into the cushions and the gorgeous woman stood between her legs. Manicured nails pushed the hair from Victoria's face, and Sarah watched like she was with a client. Not looking, but there with her stomach twisted in knots at what her life had become because she'd given up her chance for that first kiss.

"You good?" the satin voice asked.

"Yess. I'm grreaatt," Victoria slurred.

The door to Tris's room was still open. She couldn't let the girl wake to find Victoria losing her gay virginity in the living room.

Sarah moved to leave them but walked into the redhead with the sensational silicone tits. Hands clasped over Sarah's arms, steadying them both.

"Sorry," the redhead whispered. When she released Sarah, she held out a ring of keys with a child-painted lion hanging off them. "She left her car at the bar, but here."

Sarah's eyebrows scrunched in the middle. She looked back at the drunk woman giggling at the television, then at the goddess.

"Aren't you staying?" Sarah asked.

"Uhhh... didn't plan on it." The smokey eyes glanced back at Victoria, and then her eyebrows rose. "Oh! No. No," she said with a shake of her head.

The woman placed a hand on her sparsely covered chest. "I'm Parker." With a wave of her hand between the drunk and herself, Parker said, "And this... not what you think."

Sarah swallowed the bile of her assumptions. The name sounded familiar but she wasn't sure why or from where she'd heard it.

"I'm a bartender. Victoria plays darts with my sister." Parker's head fell back as a gentle chuckle escaped her. "They both had way too many tonight. Something about this one drinking away the memory of a beautiful girl who'd never love her back. And my sister trying to drown the pain of her divorce."

Parker waved her hand in the air. "Anyways, sorry about all the noise. I bet that must have scared the shit out of you. I just had to make sure they both got home okay, and Echo was the most likely to puke in my car, so she got dropped off first." Parker thumbed toward the door. "So, I'm gonna go."

Sarah took the keys from Parker and walked her to the door. She stood outside as the woman made her way to her still-running car. When she was halfway down the driveway, Sarah called out, "Thanks for taking care of her."

"No problem," Parker called back with a wave. "Oh, but tell her she tipped me $100 and I'm not givin' it back since she promised me I wouldn't have to carry her inside."

Sarah waited for Parker to get into her car before she went back inside.

Once the door was shut and locked, Sarah hovered between the stairs and the couch within two different timelines. Her body created a barricade from the woman as her mind flashed over all the men her mother had brought home to drop their drunken forms on the first available seat. The drunker the better to squeeze a few extra dollars out of them, the drugged-out woman had once explained in a tutorial on how to be a prostitute.

The door to the room was still open and within it, a child slept, just as she and Sierra had.

Victoria raised her glossy eyes to Sarah. She bit her lip as she ran her eyes down Sarah, still in the BYU shirt and the satin shorts, she'd been gifted. A NU shirt had been left in the drawer in exchange, but Sarah doubted Victoria had noticed yet.

Sierra wasn't here to be the body that blocked the door. She had sacrificed herself until the pain became too much to bear. Sierra's time was done, and she had passed the torch of protector to Sarah when she placed the infant in Sarah's arms and told her, *"It's your turn."*

Sarah's shoulders rose, her chin held high as she allowed Victoria to stare at her. The woman's pupils were wide in the bright glow of the hallway light.

Victoria leaned back, her legs pressing together. She didn't take her eyes off Sarah. There was no questioning what Victoria wanted. Victoria had never been shy about telling her. She knew she couldn't give Victoria the pleasure she desired because the woman was too far past the point of consent, but Sarah wasn't. Sarah could let Victoria do whatever the woman wanted to her body.

And Sarah knew it was better this way.

Better to be in control and give herself away. At least that was what Sierra had told Sarah when the older twin stopped trying to hide under the blanket of clothes in their closet once their mother forgot she'd brought someone home. When they stopped sleeping until the wee hours of the morning because night was the time when bad things could happen.

With each step, Sarah committed to the path she'd always been meant to walk down. Her legs straddled Victoria's lap. She pushed the strands of hair from Victoria's face and cupped the flushed cheeks, bringing her lips to the woman's.

She kissed Victoria with a gentleness she knew the woman needed. Vodka and harsh barley coated her tongue when Victoria's desired entrance was made known and Sarah allowed it. With no urgency, they explored each other in the moment. Victoria's hand came up to Sarah's neck. Her fingers carded through the hair at the base of Sarah's skull and pulled her closer. Her hold kept them connected at the forehead as she came up for air.

Sarah only gave Victoria a moment before she kissed her again. Kissed her as Victoria's other hand traced the skin between Sarah's shirt and shorts, never breaking the barrier.

A smile played on her lips as she realized Victoria had committed her words to memory, but the smile fell as she realized what it meant. That she would have to give Victoria access if she was to keep the drunk woman away from the door.

She pulled back and looked down at the hungry eyes staring at her breasts.

"You are so beautiful," Victoria stated. Her thumb ghosted over Sarah's hip bone, just above the elastic waistband of her shorts.

Sarah hated that she enjoyed it. She hated how she loved the way Victoria's lips fit hers. She hated that if she hadn't been so stubborn, they would have done this out of desire instead of necessity.

Victoria swallowed. Her hands pulled Sarah closer as her hips pressed upwards.

Sarah didn't get up right away. She allowed the other woman to grind against her sex, giving her pleasure while Victoria could not get the friction she needed.

With a sideways glance, Sarah listened for any indication that Tris was awake. The idea of the girl walking out of her room and finding them like this terrified her. It would be even more confusing than if the redhead stayed.

Pressing another kiss to Victoria's lips, she put her fingers in Victoria's hair and pulled just enough to give herself access to Victoria's neck. She kissed along Victoria's soft skin, tasting the salt. She stopped just below Victoria's ear and whispered, "Take me to your room."

With a nod of agreement, Victoria released Sarah. With the freedom to get up, she stood. She extended her hand and helped the other woman up.

The kiss seemed to have a sobering effect on Victoria. No longer stumbling, she took two steps and wrapped one arm around Sarah pulling her flush with her once more. Their hands still clasped together; Sarah was forced to look into Victoria's adoring gaze.

Victoria initiated the kiss this time. Still careful, but hungrier. Her teeth pulled softly on Sarah's lower lip. Sarah didn't try to fight the moan that escaped. She stopped trying to deny that she enjoyed kissing Victoria. Instead, she allowed herself to release some control to the other woman.

They walked silently up the stairs. The laughter from the television below followed them as they each took a turn stepping over the squeaky step. There was no push and pull down the hallway. Just Victoria's hand guiding Sarah through the dark to the bed they'd already shared.

With the door closed Victoria fell back against the wood. She pulled Sarah against her body. Victoria's hands found Sarah's neck and her waist once more. Her legs parted so Sarah could press against the place that would help her tumble over the edge.

Sarah hadn't expected the cool composure at the opportunity to have what the woman asked for. She anticipated a more eager and desperate attack but was met with gentle ghost-like caresses that never crossed a boundary line.

They didn't move from the door, only broke to breathe. Victoria pressed her forehead to Sarah's. The warm pants washed away Sarah's worries about the girl asleep down the hall and the open door.

"I want this," Victoria whispered. Her eyes were cinched painfully closed. "I want this and you so badly."

"You can have this," Sarah committed.

Victoria's eyes opened. The crinkled crow's feet outlined the worried eyes.

"Not like this," Victoria whispered. "I want to do this right. A real date. Please? And then... if you still want to..."

Sarah stared at her. Her heart was racing, and her mind was swirling. She licked her kiss-swollen lips. And she nodded.

Victoria kissed her again. Kissed her and pushed her back. Created space between them so Victoria could open the door.

She held Sarah's hand as she let Sarah leave.

Sarah stepped out into the hallway. She looked at Victoria, and down the narrow path she had once plotted an escape route through until she stopped at the still-open door.

"I'll see you in the morning," Victoria whispered, then released Sarah's hand.

And Sarah nodded again.

She turned away from the woman who didn't do to her what anyone else would have. Quietly, she moved down the hallway until she heard Victoria's door click shut.

Sarah stopped at Tris's room. She gazed through the streamers. The girl lay sideways across the full-sized mattress, her arm dangling off the edge. Sarah watched the child's chest rise and fall as she snorted a snore.

She reached in and pulled the door closed carefully to not let the latch click loudly into place. Glancing back down the hallway, Sarah found herself flicking her gaze back and forth between the doors.

Her mind returned to the trailer where the doors all looked the same and a drunk human had too easily found her and Sierra behind the wrong one when they were eight. He'd been scared at first. His eyes too looked between the twins and the mother passed out on the bed. The door was closed, but Sierra knew what Sarah knew now. There was no telling if it would be opened again, so Sierra left Sarah in the room.

They never spoke of what happened on the other side of the door. Sarah had heard enough in her life to put together the pieces as she held the clothes over her ears.

This was a life Tris would never know. She would never take a chance that Tris would even consider what happened on the other side of a door where a drunk person forgot the difference between right and wrong.

Silently, Sarah sat against the door. Leaning back, she used her body as another layer of protection in case there was a change of heart in the other room. She eliminated the chance for a mistake to be made and two lives to be ruined.

Her eyes closed, and her chin fell to her chest. Both the floor and the door were hard, but sitting propped against a door to keep a drunk out of a space they weren't welcome in wasn't new to her. She'd spent her childhood preparing for this very situation. And she wouldn't let Sierra down this time.

41

An ax tried to split Victoria's skull in two. The first strike wasn't that hard, but it still hurt enough to make her toss and turn under the blankets. The second hit felt like death was coming for her. Her pleasant dreams spilled from the wound, then the memories from the night before. She pressed at the sides of her head, trying to hold it together. She felt the sweat-soaked bed sheets sticking to her sensitive flesh, and she started to cry because this was terrible.

Every aspect of the morning was trying to kill her or at least drive her insane. She needed to get up and start the pancakes. The pancakes with sugary sprinkles Sarah said she made every year. This year her girl would need ten.

Yes, her girl. Her girl and her woman were down the hall. And Victoria needed to get up from the bed no matter how much her head hurt. She deserved the pain. Deserved the Karma for the anguish she'd seen in the green eyes when Parker had touched her.

It wasn't the plan. Well, not Sarah finally accepting her when she came home. The drunk part... that had been part of the plan. They didn't even have a dart game. But she'd pulled into the bar's parking lot and then sat on a stool.

Echo shared a memory of the woman who'd picked her up as a baby adult just released from juvie. She'd been waiting on a bus, green to the world after spending her life selling drugs and then behind a steel door with a tiny window. Shared the way the woman had made her feel important and offered her a bed instead of a halfway house.

As Echo downed the shot, Victoria spoke of the brunette who'd crawled from the literal gates of hell and taken up residence in Victoria's heart and mind. She cataloged for the bar owner the various smiles the brunette possessed and how she'd foolishly thought one day she'd see one that meant actual happiness.

Then they took another shot together. Parker had chastised them about the bucket of beer, but a broken heart needed booze. At least that's what Echo had shouted along with, "Fight me and I'll fire you."

Parker had apparently not been in a fighting mood. She dropped the bucket in front of them and declared, "I hope the puke comes out your nose later."

Whether Echo was suffering the same fate or not, Victoria had barely made it to the bathroom with her hand pressed over her lips. She'd held her breath as the alcohol and bile cocktail burned away her tastebuds.

The vicious vomit didn't let up until it had brought her to her knees. She prayed to the porcelain god for relief, but her stomach wished to inflict upon her the same torture she'd given it. When the gagging ended, she lowered herself to the floor and allowed the cool tiles to send a chill into her bones.

As she lay on the floor, she pressed her fingers to the still puke-tainted lips. At least she hadn't vomited on Sarah. She'd held herself together and she'd done the right thing. She'd convinced Sarah to give her a chance. A chance without the ruse hanging over their head.

Today was Tris's birthday. Her Tris was turning double digits and she'd be up soon. Celebrating the now ten-year-old would come first, and she would celebrate a chance with Sarah tomorrow.

Pushing herself from the floor, Victoria flipped on the tap and washed away the green from her face. She pinched her cheeks to pull back the color she'd undoubtedly lost with the contents of her stomach.

The pancakes were what needed to happen, but not until her teeth were brushed. They needed to be clean and her palate free of puke, in case Sarah kissed her again.

Sarah had kissed her. She'd straddled her lap and kissed her better than any dream Victoria had ever had. Her first real kiss, because anything prior had been a just out of obligation.

The shirt she'd been wearing had not escaped her body's attack. She ran through her more casual options until she stopped at the one she hadn't purchased. A faded navy tee. As she held it up, she thought of Sarah still in the BYU shirt. Sarah had left her a trade. A favorite for a favorite.

Raising it to her nose, Victoria filled her lungs with the scent of the woman. The bargain brand detergent mixed with old canvas from being kept in the bag prepared for flight.

Sarah hadn't run. She'd had the chance, and she'd promised not to.

Pulling the material over her head, she wrapped herself in the wrong school colors. It felt right. Fit like it had been made for her to wear. A symbol of the woman's claim on her.

The house was still sleeping when she opened the bedroom door. The light from the second-story window had just begun to brighten the space.

Her gaze landed on the woman propped against the door. Crepe paper dangled over the hung head.

Victoria figured Sarah was sitting in wait for the child to burst into her new year at life. But the chest of the woman rose and fell evenly. The green eyes didn't rise as she stepped into the hallway.

Sarah was asleep.

Victoria didn't understand why the woman would sleep against the door. She'd been home every night, so she shouldn't be too tired to sit and wait.

Her stomach fell when the punch landed in her gut. The pieces of the horrific puzzle came together as to why the woman had propped herself against her girl's door.

Because Tris wasn't her girl.

Tris was Sarah's girl.

And Victoria... was a threat.

A threat who needed placating with phony promises. The kisses were a distraction to keep her drunken self diverted from something so devious Victoria's skin crawled.

Sarah was afraid of her. Sarah was afraid that she would try to hurt Tris.

And she hated it. She hated it and herself. And then she hated Sarah.

Hated Sarah for thinking that she would ever hurt the child. Because for once in her life she actually loved a child, and now it was twisted from something that was wonderful into something sinister.

Victoria released the breath she hadn't known she was holding. Her fingernails dug into the flesh of her palms to keep her fists from shaking.

The blood in her veins boiled until the substance turned black with sepsis.

The molars in her mouth silently screamed. Her hand shot out, shutting her bedroom door. The room she'd done the right thing and needed to be protected from the impure thoughts polluting the air of the house.

It was enough to pull Sarah awake. The green eyes blinking in the sunlit hallway. The valley of death blinked twice then looked at Victoria unapologetically.

Neither spoke for a moment. Sarah's eyes stoically studied Victoria. Probably weighing the damage she could cause, just like the first time the woman had walked into the house.

Sarah looked up at the ceiling. She wet her lips as her legs stretched out from their position.

"I'm surprised you're up," she whispered. "Do you want me to get you some Motrin?"

"Do you really think that I could..." Victoria started. She couldn't say it though. She couldn't associate herself with something so heinous.

"When you lived the life, I have..." Sarah paused. She shook her head. "Look, you'll never get it. You'll never understand but I would rather you hate me, than me hate myself more than I already do."

"What does that even mean?" Victoria growled.

Sarah didn't get to answer. She fell back through the bottom two streamers. Her head smacked against the carpet, and she cried out in pain.

Tris stooped over Sarah. Her eyebrows scrunched in the middle.

"Why are you on the floor?" The girl asked.

42

Blue sugar-filled silver dollar pancakes lay stacked in a golden-brown tower. The 1 and 0 candles were placed at the top with another layer of sprinkles added.

The woman, who'd kept the pancakes from being served burnt for the first time in the girl's life, moved through the motions of the O'Keeffe family birthday traditions. She kept a smile in place, even though Sarah could tell she was nursing one hell of a hangover.

Sarah silently offered to clean the kitchen by taking the pan from Victoria's hand and nodding to the living room. She felt it was a success, making it through breakfast and celebrating the child with smiles on their faces.

By the afternoon, the pain etched into Victoria's face had dimmed and the closeness in which they all operated felt to Sarah like Victoria was still expecting her family to walk back through the door.

Sarah lounged in the armchair, while Victoria cradled her head and flipped the page to the Lego manual. Tris's attention was fixed on getting the set built, thus tying her tongue from any type of troubling questions.

The Maps app hadn't helped Sarah narrow down where they were going for dinner. With a double-digit birthday, Sarah had promised anything the kid wanted instead of adding the caveat of her being able to make it herself.

Tris had requested to try sushi. A food type Sarah successfully avoided her entire life and one she was sure the kid would not enjoy since she didn't even like mushrooms.

The problem lay in Sarah not knowing the first thing about where to get sushi, what to order when she got there, or how to make two stupid sticks work together to pick the food up. She had also become so distracted with The Great Brenton Takeover that she hadn't spent the time researching. To her relief, Victoria seemed just as dumbfounded and for once they were clueless together.

It felt pleasantly real to for once not be inferior or superior to the other woman. This could be the one thing they would get the chance to fumble through together. Like an adventure all of their own.

Sarah got up from the chair to retrieve her phone charger. She had less than two hours to find someplace she could afford the bill, and she was falling short.

Victoria dragged her slippered feet into the kitchen. She steadied herself against the counter and seemed to be trying to breathe without vomiting.

"You gonna make it?" Sarah asked.

Even though she had no right, Sarah moved to Victoria's side. With the flat of her hand, she ran her palm in circles over the woman's back.

"Feels like a gorilla is using my head like a drum," Victoria whispered. She pressed her fingertips to her eyes. "I... I wanted to talk to you about–"

Sarah held up her hand. "Look, I'm sorry I hurt you. You... this you, there is never a question in my mind whether you would hurt her. But you were so drunk, and I don't know who drunk you is."

Shaking her head, she lowered her voice to barely above a whisper. "When... When I was in high school my mom brought home a customer. She didn't know. She didn't know who he was... but he was my high school counselor. The person who helped me fill out my college applications, checked in with me about my grades. All over a super nice guy. But he was drunk. He was drunk and my mom passed out."

She shook her head as the clock ticked and music from the Encanto rolled down the halls.

Tris sang out with the song, *"I take what I'm handed, I break what's demanded, but...."*

"You don't have to..." Victoria whispered.

"No. You need to know. You need to know, so you can maybe understand a little."

Sarah tried to swallow the lump in her throat, but her mouth had gone dry.

"My sister dropped out of school when she was fourteen, but she was home that night. She was home and she did what she always did to keep me safe. But he didn't know her... he thought she was me. And I heard him. The person I thought cared about me. I heard him calling my name out and I heard him hit her over and over again. And the next morning she was gone. She'd hitched a ride to Phoenix because she couldn't do it anymore."

"... your sister's stronger... See if she can hang on a little longer!" Tris sang.

She pushed the hair behind her ears and held her lip between her teeth. "I promised... I promised Sierra when she handed me Tris that I would never let what happened to us happen to her. And last night you were sooo drunk it just took me back there... and I'm sorry. I'm sorry that I am broken, and I can't just be what you want."

Sarah wiped her face before any tears could create tracks down her cheeks.

"Watch as she buckles and bends but never breaks."

"I'm damaged, Victoria," Sarah confessed. "I couldn't explain that to you during the sessions when you decided to love me. But, when you're with me... it's like my mind forgets to guard the doors that I keep my past in. But I've piled so much into those closets that if I don't keep holding them shut, they just pop open... and all the fear and hurt and guilt comes spilling out and I can't just push it back in because the closets are like a hoarder's apartment and... and... and you are wonderful, but I don't deserve you."

Victoria stared at her. The hurt and anger returned to the lines in her face. She stepped closer into Sarah's bubble. The pale hand cupped her cheek.

"Just please, please pretend for a little bit longer. Pretend for Tris and I will find a way to tell her we can't be here. I'll find a place for us to go. I'll find a new school to work at so you can move on," Sarah pleaded.

Wetting her lips, Victoria's gaze softened. She didn't yell or smile. But she punctuated every word: "I. Don't. Want. You. To. Leave."

The thumb of her hand stroked over Sarah's cheek. "I thought I made that clear in front of my entire family. I don't ever want you to leave."

Sarah stared at her, searching for the lie that had to be there. There was no way it could be real when Victoria had been so hurt just that morning.

Dropping her hand, Victoria inhaled heavily. A weak smile spread across her face as she held her fist to her head. Smacking it against her forehead, Victoria tried to put herself back together.

"I wanted... you don't have to look," Victoria swallowed and hit herself in the head again. "Just needed to tell you... I uh...I invited my friend Jen and her kid to dinner tonight. She knows this sushi place and actually eats the stuff. She said she knows of the perfect place for Tris's first sushi experience."

Sarah's eyes widened, "Oh."

She nodded and fixed her face. "That's great."

Victoria took Sarah's hand as she continued to lean against the counter. She squeezed lightly as though the ruse was still in play.

"We need to talk," Victoria stated. "I just ... I need like time to think about everything and for this headache to go away."

Sarah didn't respond. She acted by taking her hand back and rummaging through the purse Victoria hung up for her. She pulled out a tiny change purse and emptied it into her hand.

"The orange ones are Motrin," Sarah said, holding the selection out to Victoria. "Probably take four. Or the blue and red are Tylenol. Not sure how well those will help a hangover."

Blue eyes squinted at the pills in her palm. Victoria fished four orange tablets out. Then she slowly lowered her body to the stool at the counter.

With a shake of her head, Sarah retrieved a glass of water for the woman. "How many drinks did you have last night?"

"Honestly?" Victoria took the glass from Sarah. The exchange was slower as Sarah's finger locked with Victoria's for just a moment. "I don't know. I think... maybe a half a dozen shots. One tasted like cinnamon candy. That was the last one. Then we drank beer that tasted what I think ass would taste like."

Sarah chuckled and wondered if it would be inappropriate to ask her next ass-licking client if ass had a similar flavor to beer.

"I don't even know why I drank the beer," Victoria continued. "I don't even like beer."

Sarah tapped the table quietly. With a hum she offered a simple piece of advice, "Never mix your liquors."

"Huh?" Chestnut eyebrows scrunched together, along with lips. Victoria's processing time was significantly delayed from the normal rapid fire they conversed in. Her eyebrows slowly returned to normal as her eyes stayed squinted. "Oh, I get it."

"So, I'll go get ready then. Drink that water and then like five more," Sarah said. Then she looked down at the shirt she was wearing. She swallowed the guilt and put her mask back on.

"Do you know..." Sarah started but stopped when she saw the woman grimace. Lowing her voice, she tried again. "I don't own anything fancy. I shoulda asked before but I know sushi is, like, upscale. I mean, should I go get something more appropriate to wear?"

Victoria ran her hands over her face like she could just press the poison from her pores. "Uhhh... jeans and t-shirt... sorry I checked before I agreed with Jen. It's not... fancy."

"Okay, thanks." She took two steps up the stairs before she turned around. "So... this is going to be really awkward because I am going to take a shower, but you should take one too."

Victoria's single eyebrow cocked in Sarah's direction, then the brown eyes glanced down the hallway to where a movie played loudly. She choked trying to make words. "Wi... with you?"

Sarah smiled but shook her head. "Not with the real me. A... uh... loud shower though... will help with the headache... kinda increases flow of blood to the whole body."

Victoria swallowed. Her eyebrow rose once more, and she wet her lips. With a slight smile, she asked, "Are you going to take a loud shower?"

With a wave, Sarah scoffed, "You must still be drunk. I'm so quiet. Like, ninja quiet which makes it easier to hear the song being sung on the other side of the wall."

Sarah left the woman at the table. She would not be taking a loud shower. Nor would she be taking a quiet one. She would be planning a way to make it up to Victoria. To be better, like she promised.

The outside of KiKu's Sushi restaurant was smaller than Sarah expected, while Jen was louder and touchier. The woman arrived like a storm with an overfilled bag of birthday presents for a child she'd never even met.

The presents were opened outside the restaurant. Small trinkets and some packs of child-sized jewelry were handed off to Sarah. Then the big one came out of the bag. Tris was instantly in love with the giant sushi stuffy. She squeezed it tightly to her chest thanking the stranger.

Sarah tried to act normal, but her stomach twisted the way Jen navigated between Victoria and her. With the woman's arm wrapped through Victoria's, Sarah felt like a third wheel on a date.

"Feel like I haven't seen you in weeks," Jen whined. Her dark head rested on Victoria's shoulder looking up at the woman as they continued to hover outside the entrance.

Victoria rolled her eyes dramatically. "It's been two weeks... max."

"Still, we used to go out every week." Jen's eyes scanned over Sarah. "You make a new *friend* and it's like I don't exist anymore."

The smile on Victoria's face was apologetic. She shrugged slightly as she explained, "Sorry I canceled lunch on Monday. My family came in and it was pretty crazy."

"I can't wait to hear all about it." Jen leaned into Victoria even closer, giving Sarah no space but to walk around the handicap sign while the others took the opposite side.

"And I'm so excited you are finally willing to try sushi." Jen turned to Sarah. "I have been trying to get this one to come here with me for months."

"Tris is very excited." Sarah placed her hand on Tris's shoulder. "You ready, kid?"

"Yes!" the birthday girl called out. The sushi squish was held above her head in celebration.

Music hit Sarah in the chest when they walked into the dimly lit dining room. She checked Victoria's face for any sign of distress but the silent shower the woman had taken seemed to do the trick.

A tiny silver conveyor belt ran along a U-shaped track that was lined with booths and a few bar seats. Sarah watched the small saucers of multicolored rolls being removed by other guests. Ordering appeared unnecessary; however, the sushi looked nothing less than slimy seaweed suicide. Tris had been right; she was never built to be a mermaid let alone Ariel.

As she watched Jen hang off Victoria, she decided she was better to be cast as Ursula.

"Dr. Jen!" a woman called out from behind the sushi prep area. The dark-haired server moved toward them in her solid black outfit with a small apron tied to her waist. "I saved you a booth up front."

Jen flashed Victoria a smile and a shrug. Then she guided Tris to the server.

"Suzy, this is our birthday girl."

Sarah felt a whip smack across her. The sting spread over her chest as this woman, someone she'd never met, claimed her kid. It was one thing to go about the day like a normal family with Victoria, but for this stranger— with her going out to dinner weekly money and buying stupidly expensive presents— to stake a claim made Sarah pause as the others moved toward the table.

A pause to collect herself.

A pause to remember this was Victoria's friend.

A pause to gather the ability to keep a cool face.

However, the pause made her the last person to get to the table. While Tris leaned with her nose practically to the plastic-covered plates on one side of the table, Jen sat across from her talking animatedly about each and every item. Jen's daughter had pressed in close to Tris, the younger girl enamored with the older. And Victoria had placed herself next to her friend.

Sarah was left with a choice. Sit alongside Victoria and miss out on 90% of the adult conversation or next to the child she didn't know. Standing awkwardly was also not really an option, so she chose the seat by the little blonde girl. At least that would give Victoria space to spend time with her friend.

The K-pop music videos played on the large TV next to her. Images flashed every three seconds continuously playing with her periphery.

"Are there menus?" she asked Victoria.

The woman hadn't heard her though. The brown eyes were focused on the ramblings of the woman on her right. Sarah watched the way Victoria followed every move Jen made with her and the way their hands moved together as Jen taught her how to use chopsticks. A skill that Victoria picked up easily.

Sarah's mind congratulated herself on teaching Victoria to use her hands on things more intimate and important than squeezing the wooden sticks together, but the thought turned ugly as an image flashed in her head of the long fingers practicing Sarah's lessons on the boobs Sarah was certain were purchased and not grown. It's not that she had anything against women with implants, just that Victoria seemed to favor them. And if there was one area Sarah wasn't endowed it was her chest.

"You want to try anything?" Jen called over to her.

Sarah looked at the plate that had been plucked from the conveyor belt. She didn't like fish, let alone uncooked fish.

"Uh, I think I'm just going to order some fried rice."

Jen shook her head and slid a plate in front of Sarah. The thin layer of rice lined the ring of deep green filled with creamy pink stuff and what she thought must be avocado.

"Try that. It's simply basic."

Sarah raised her eyes from the plate to the woman next to Victoria. Jen raised a piece of sushi with what looked like a nipple atop it toward Victoria's waiting mouth from the plate in between the two women.

Her chest filled with toxic gas at how coupley the two acted when Sarah knew that Jen wasn't Victoria's girlfriend. She was Victoria's fake girlfriend, and whoever this crazy woman truly was didn't matter because Sarah was anything but basic.

She reached over with a single stick and stabbed the booby-designed sushi piece. She picked it up and put the whole roll in her mouth. She hadn't thought it through though because the moment it touched her tongue the silky fish slid toward her throat and the red nipple sauce burned the roof of her mouth. She tried to quickly swallow, but the lump of rice, seaweed, and innards didn't slide.

Face red from the heat, Sarah tried to solve her problem as the other two women stared at her. She had to chew to swallow but the salmon squished when the rest of the roll smooshed. All of her confidence fell out of her mouth into her napkin as she gagged.

Victoria handed Sarah another napkin as she sucked up half the water in her cup. She knew the water would not stop the burning, but at least it washed away the slime.

"Are you okay?" Victoria asked.

"Fine," Sarah said with a flip of her hand.

Sarah tried to avoid looking at the infiltrator who was staring her down but failed like everything else in the last 24 hours.

Jen moved her chopsticks between Victoria and herself. "We are just friends."

Sarah smiled. "Yeah. Yeah of course. So are we."

Jen tilted her head, "Uh huh."

Victoria let out a heavy exhale. "Jen."

"I'm good if she wants to live in the land of delusion."

"What is that supposed to mean?" Sarah sat as still as possible. Her mouth was still watering uncomfortably as her stomach churned.

"It means that if you want to cognitively occupy a delusional space where you do not have some real feelings for my best friend, then I'm good with it."

"Jen," Victoria warned, the octave of her gravelly voice dropping a level.

With hands still waving in the air, the woman continued as though her best friend hadn't tried to stop her.

"I'm just saying that if she wants to not be in a relationship with you, then she can't be getting jealous of someone she thinks is interested in you."

Sarah snapped, "I am not jealous."

With a roll of her eyes, Jen gestured to the rolls. "So, why torture yourself on the sushi roll?"

"I thought you were calling me basic."

Red lips spread into a smile as Jen confirmed, "Oh I was."

"I'm not basic."

"Oh, I know," Jen stated. She put her one boobie piece into her mouth. Unphased by the heat, she wiped her lips with a napkin.

"Who is this crazy person?" Sarah asked Victoria.

A chopstick pointed to her chest as Jen stated, "I'm the best friend."

"Why are you the way you are?" Victoria grumbled.

"Because I want to like her." Jen waved her sticks in the air. "And I want to know if she gives a damn about you or if you really did imprint on her like a little baby duck."

Victoria's eyes grew wide. The table shifted as though someone had kicked the pedestal.

"Jen, please," Victoria pleaded.

But the color drained from Sarah's face. The apologies and fixes she'd tried to come up with didn't matter. Not when everything was compromised. The way she'd warned Victoria would happen.

"You told her," she said.

Brown eyes didn't rise from the table. Her hands had disappeared, probably to play with her shirt. And the woman's ears were redder than they'd ever been before.

Jen swallowed another roll and rolled her eyes.

"Of course, she told me." The blonde woman clearly found the situation amusing. "I'm her best friend. She told me about how comfortable you made her and then gave her the cold shoulder, and then the middle finger all within 24 hours."

"Stop it," Tris yelled. Her eyebrows scrunched together as she glared at the woman across from her. "You're being mean to my mom, and you owe her an apology. Calling someone basic is taking away everything that makes them special, and my mom is special. But you... You're just a bully! So, apologize!"

Jen's smile fell as she looked at the clearly upset birthday girl. She wiped her face with her napkin once more and sucked in her lips. When she looked back up, the smugness had vanished.

"You're right, Tris. What I just said was not kind and not fair." Jen turned to Sarah. "I'm sorry. I was a bit extra because... look, while I am not in love with this fool, I do love her. I am invested in protecting her and I am also a bit of a bitch."

"You owe me a dollar!" the littlest diner called out. Her body bounced on her knees in the chair.

Jen rolled her eyes once more and fished a dollar out of her purse before handing it to the girl. "There. Now eat your sushi."

Sarah nodded her head to Jen at the apology, but the anger fuming within her had little to nothing to do with the woman. No, it was Victoria who had broken the contract. Victoria who had promised her verbally and in writing. But it had all been a lie. And if she lied about that, then she'd lied about other things. That's how it worked, since she too broke the contract the morning after they met.

That reality didn't change the anger for being blindsided by the blonde self-proclaimed bitch. Anger and hurt, but as the deadly potion brewed within her, Sarah felt the fear rise with the steam. The planned talk wouldn't be simple because she would have to tell Victoria that she'd been lying about holding up her end of the contract all these months. It was the only way to handle this situation because Victoria would apologize for telling her busty best friend, and that wasn't fair.

"Sarah," Victoria whispered. "Could we...?"

Sarah couldn't soothe Victoria's anxiety right now. There was no way in hell she was going to admit in front of Jealousy-Inducing Jen that she was the one you hid behind the contact. Not with Tris settling back into her seat and trying a piece of each roll on the table. No, tonight was for the kid who didn't get special events like this.

She wet her lips and fixed her face. She'd been playing pretend all day. She could keep it up for at least another five hours.

"What did you think of the boobie roll?" Sarah asked like she was at work. But before Victoria could answer, she turned to Jen. "Is there something a little less squishy and a little more savory? I am not a fan of spicy."

43

The glass of wine on the counter stared at Victoria. She didn't need a drink, but it had become part of her nightly routine once the girl was in bed. Once she'd poured it, she knew it was a mistake.

Sushi on a hangover stomach had already been a mistake. She felt like the slivers of fish had possibly been an amphibian, and she could swear the food was attempting to regrow limbs within her stomach.

Tris's voice animatedly reverberated down the stairs. The timbres changed with the dialogue as she read aloud to Sarah. A nightly tradition between the two that she'd been privileged to be a part of normally.

However, tonight she needed a moment alone.

When she closed her eyes, she could see Sarah's body against the door. The creature in her stomach twisted again. She'd never hurt a child or a woman or anyone. Never. Not drunk or sober. But tears welled behind her lids as she swallowed the reality of the woman she loved. The woman who didn't know bad things happened because she worked with kids or studied it in a textbook. A woman who'd grown up in a literal closet with the bad things happening on the other side of the door. She'd heard it happen. She'd seen the aftermath. And survived whatever other countless horrors, she'd been too ashamed or scared to share with Victoria yet.

'Damaged,' Sarah had whispered. 'Broken.'

'Not good enough.'

All words Victoria used to justify running away. She'd known what it was like to flee. But Victoria also knew she left with half the sale price of the house and half the bank account. She'd left with a degree and freedom from obligation. She'd had the opportunity to explore herself and seek help when she was ready to.

Seeking help had cost Victoria $89 a session with a $3.99 debit card processing fee. She attended sessions every week to explore her feelings of fleeing. Therapeutic help was, to put it simply, a paid privilege. And Sarah, a social worker, couldn't afford the time or the fee.

Sarah knew better than most the importance of counseling. She worked with the programs to ensure their students had access to the services they needed. Those services weren't available to her though. Victoria knew this. She knew that seeking help took time and energy. Neither of which Sarah had enough of in a day.

Victoria's fingers ran over the rim of the glass. The second break from her known world. She'd found comfort in the spicy juice, allowing its potent powers to soothe away the stress. She'd never downed a bottle in isolation, never sought to drown away her guilt or self-hatred.

Water ran through the pipe in the wall. The hum of the electric toothbrushes ran together as the girl giggled.

Tris. A child born in chaos. The girl understood loss almost as well as the mother, but Sarah was her shield. A hardened warrior who'd survived by crawling through warzones that left few around her standing. A fierce figure for the girl to look up to, never fully knowing what the woman was willing to do for the child.

Or who.

Victoria had thought Sarah's walls had come down the night before. She'd congratulated herself on finally freeing the woman of her fears.

Her fingers pulled at the roots of her hair. She'd been so stupid. It was the only word fitting when she'd seen the shaken frame still smiling for the family she didn't belong to.

Yes, the lie had been Sarah's fault. Victoria knew she could have confessed. Told her mother the truth, that her friend was trying to protect her. They would have laughed about it. Naomi would have praised the woman even. She'd seen it happen with her sisters. Honestly, she was convinced that Naomi knew by the time she'd left. Had held her face and made her promise to take her time with Sarah because women like Sarah didn't know how to be loved.

Victoria had wanted it to be true though. The lie had offered her an opportunity to show Sarah a world where she didn't have to tread water. Forced the woman to sleep alongside her to keep the ruse going. And Victoria began to understand the truth of good and evil. The boundaries people set to decide who is the victim and who is the predator.

The creature in her belly tried to crawl up her throat but the rock stuck in her esophagus blocked its escape. She closed her eyes again and willed the acid within her to kill the parasite before it tore through her chest.

And she saw the green eyes looking back at her from the floor.

'You'll never understand but I would rather you hate me, than me hate myself more than I already do.'

The buckling in her knees when she understood the woman's purpose at the door had been due to an earthquake in Sarah's reality. A reality where good and evil were divided by distinctive lines, and she knew the difference. Because she'd only ever known the good in people. Only ever seen a pained world through a computer screen. Crime and poverty were real. Abuse and assault were real for others.

She'd thought by running away she'd entered the world of hurt. Understood the depth of isolation. The ill-bred thoughts elicited from the lonely ticks of a clock in a home where laughter and joy were shared on the screen by straight people with children who also only experienced pain through the proxy of others. How easily she'd connected to the Tanner sisters or the seven siblings in Seventh Heaven. Where people like her understood unconditional utopia, where people passed but the presence of parental support suspended sinister shadows with supreme safety.

Like a character on the screen, her family had searched for her whereabouts. Arrived in a caravan to shower her in grace she'd never felt she deserved.

'Not good enough.'

She's said the same words to the mother who'd walked back into her life. The mother who'd traveled across state lines to ensure her safety and set her home right. Which is why woeful wonderings of Sarah walking away was something she couldn't stand for.

Sarah's heart had to be as scarred as her body. Her mind was as fragile as her sense of safety. She lived to sustain life but never experienced it. How could she live when her stomach still searched for basic sustenance? her body never known the comfort of a bed? her eyes constantly searching for the dangers in the eyes of strangers?

The drain of the sink drank the wine willingly. The glass was left for the morning and the television was turned to the station of familiar funnies.

Sarah wouldn't laugh tonight, she knew this. The smile she'd worn for the sisters and mother was the same she'd walked in with on night one. It was real, just like every other part of Sarah was real. Only it was reserved for times of self-preservation.

The living room with the couch the woman promised to buy herself someday was a space Sarah hadn't had to preserve herself in. Not since she'd brought in the duffle bag with everything she owned.

Victoria had lived out of a suitcase for a total of forty-eight hours before purchasing herself a new wardrobe, then a house with three closets to hold her seasonal wear in a place with two seasons, hot and hotter.

With the room illuminated in the soft glow of chortling characters, she noticed it. A hand-painted wooden frame that clashed with everything in the room. A single picture of the child smooshed between Sarah and Victoria. Sarah had snapped it when they'd finished the Thanksgiving box delivery. She hadn't noticed its appearance until now. The image angled to the place the woman had laid without a pillow or blanket. Another element of comfort Sarh denied herself to keep up appearances around even those she lived with.

Victoria paced the living room floor. Her toes pressing into the rug she knew would never be pulled out from under her. Her life never in question and her survival not dependent on anything or anyone besides herself.

But her happiness was in question.

Her control of what came next was non-existent. She'd begged the woman to stay with her. Confessed her love. Offered her stability.

But she'd broken the contract before those things. She hadn't shared a secret held for years when Sarah felt secure enough to share in the amusement of their initial encounter.

No, she'd learned about it from Jen, in a half-hearted protective rambling, creating a new crack for Sarah to teeter on the edge of.

'I have everything to lose,' she'd said.

And now so did Victoria.

Everything she'd never known to want was wrapped in a complicated package walking down the stairs.

And Victoria was angry again. The temperature of the room rose with each step closer Sarah came. She would try to run away with Tris. A promise she'd made just that afternoon, as had been made the week prior, and the week before that. It's what she knew how to do.

Victoria had let her push and push and push. With each push, Victoria made the woman another promise. Another promise that led to Sarah pushing again. Constantly testing Victoria to see if she would push back or give up.

Those were the choices tonight.

Push back.

Give up.

Fight.

Flight.

...

Freeze.

44

The lights in the kitchen were off, but the living room glowed from the television. Roseanne, the TV mom for people like her, yelled at a daughter whose tone would have lost her a tooth if she ever tried it. Studio laughter filled the space and Sarah tried to remember if she'd turned it on before taking Tris upstairs. But Victoria's need for order would never allow the television to be left on in an unattended room.

The promised talk must be awaiting her. She stood at the bottom of the stairs listening for Victoria's position. Tried to hear if the wine glass was being set on the table. Craned her ears to hear if a fist was popping against a palm. Concentrated on whether the woman was crying.

She cursed the well-constructed home that didn't creak under the pacing assistant principal. The body turned to her so suddenly she froze. The lights of the screen illuminated Victoria's face, the shadows deepening the areas around her eyes that looked almost yellow in the glow. A lion well adapted to her environment.

But Victoria's steady hands seemed to strike. The hands that had held her were wringing an imaginary dishcloth before her. A sound couldn't be heard but it told Sarah that Victoria was done.

Sarah didn't move forward as Victoria's eyes begged her. She didn't know what they were begging for, just that the crinkles in the corners and the circles under darkened when the woman wanted her. She wanted something from Sarah, but so many of her asks were things Sarah couldn't give.

The words across the dinner table winded down the whirlpool in her head and mixed with the betrayal of trust Sarah had placed in Victoria. She allowed the paragraphs to be broken down into long strings of sentences until the single words clunked around the funnel, disappearing into a darkness she couldn't understand.

The truth slid slowly past her lips. "I trusted you when you promised not to break the contract."

The statement summed up the entirety of their relationship and her life. Sarah had little by little trusted Victoria with pieces of herself.

"Because I told my best friend about my crush, you—"

Sarah raised her hand in the air. She stepped into the space securing her sense of self.

"Please, just... let me," Sarah said.

Victoria crossed the canyon of cyan carpet. Her body met with the hand on her chest, holding her heart within.

"You told her about the contract. It was literally a contract to specifically stop you from talking about us," Sarah whispered. "Which terrifies me because it makes me feel like I need to study every single person to figure out who else knows."

Victoria stared back at her. Her hand rose, resting on Sarah's hip as though it could keep her from running away.

"I can't forgive you for this. I can't—"

"She got me drunk first... no one—" Victoria's lips sealed shut when Sarah shook her head.

"It doesn't matter. I voided the contract before you."

Fingers wrapped around Sarah's tightly. The brown eyes studied her green ones as though they would play scenes from a show no one would ever want to watch. Triggering tales enough to inflict secondary trauma.

"I told Monica the day you showed up at the school. I called her and I told her I have fucked up and I had laid with you and held you and not taken your money," she confessed. "At the restaurant... with your friend. I wasn't mad until after I was afraid. I can't be scared and strong, so I was angry with you because I couldn't trust you."

Sarah's lips opened to tell the woman she couldn't trust her because she loved her. Loved her with every fiber of her being like she loved the mother in the trailer and the sister on the street. Loved her with the fierceness she felt for the girl asleep in the bed.

But her words dissolved on her tongue as Victoria finally broke.

"You are the liar."

Spittle hit her in the face.

"You bring nothing but chaos."

The fingers wrapped around her hand tighten.

"You hide and you manipulate me."

She can't pull away. She'd pushed too far. Found the line Victoria couldn't come back from.

"You pretend to care yet offer kindness only to those that treat you like trash."

She closed her eyes, waiting for the other hand to strike once the whipping words weren't enough. Willed herself to relax so the impact wouldn't hurt more.

"You frustrate me and wind me up only to take literal pleasure in knowing that I can't get you out of my mind."

Her face was so close Sarah could feel the bile burning her skin as it hit her.

Unable to run away until the woman gave her what she deserved.

"You are the one that can't be trusted."

She felt the tear fall. A single tear slid down her spit-speckled face. Past the corner of her lip to the tip of her downturned chin.

"And I love you."

The blood pulsing in her ears must have caused her to miss the can't. It had to be there. The sentence didn't make sense without it.

"Loving you is possibly the most painful thing I can do, but I can't turn it off, because there is nothing that you can do that would make me stop loving you, Sarah."

She wet her lips with the tears now streaming because her mouth had become as dry as Arizona in July.

"You can't love me." she choked. "I'm unlovable."

She flinched when the hand touched her face. The slap she knew would come didn't sting though, it soothed. It carefully caressed her cheek.

"I know your life has been filled with chaos and disappointment, so you seek it out. I know... I know the only people who have ever said those words have let you down. Used them to manipulate you so you don't think you are worth loving so you push it away. From Tris. From me."

Victoria cupped Sarah's face in her hand. "But you can't stop us from loving you. And you can't keep pretending that there isn't something here."

Sarah's lips crashed into Victoria's. Her arms wrapped around the taller woman who lifted her from the floor threatening to swallow her whole. A starved kiss that satisfied a hunger Sarah had denied for so long.

She savored the flavor of Victoria's lips on her own. Stroking the soft tongue that had soothed away the edges of the words to make them hurt less.

Victoria's fingers kept gravity from pulling her to the hard ground. They lifted her to a space where she could breathe in the oxygen the other woman gave her. Victoria backed them into the wall and allowed the home she'd created for Sarah to aid in her support.

Frightened fingers pulled Victoria closer as they learned to breathe each other instead of air.

Victoria's digits danced on the skin of her back and her sides. It wasn't enough for Sarah. She needed more. More of Victoria's touch, more of Victoria's skin. So, she pushed the woman back. She pushed her back until Victoria lowered her to the ground.

"Take me to our bed," Sarah said.

Victoria swallowed. "Are you sure?"

"Yes."

"And tomorrow you will let me take you out. No games this time."

"No games," Sarah whispered. "Just please... please don't hurt me."

Victoria searched Sarah's face, then took her hand. She led the way up the stairs. Sarah didn't search for an escape route this time. She didn't plan a way to stay awake the whole night or worry about the child asleep in her bed.

She followed the patient woman to the bed of nightmareless rest. She stood at the edge after the door had been shut and the light on the nightstand switched on so they could see one another.

Sarah placed her finger under the edge of the shirt that smelled of the best friend with the fake boobs.

"This smells like *her*," she said with a crinkled nose. "May I...take this off?"

Victoria nodded.

Sarah slowly pulled up, only looking away from Victoria's hungry eyes when the shirt was momentarily over the woman's head. She let it drop to the ground as she licked, then bit her lower lip. Her eyes wandered over the creamy skin of Victoria's throat to the bra-clad breasts and down the length of her torso. She reached out to run her fingers from the bra's front clasp down to the woman's navel and stopped at the top of her jeans.

Victoria breathed, her head falling back. Only coming back when Sarah's touch disappeared.

Sarah had pulled off her top and stood before the woman bare-chested.

The breath in Victoria's chest ceased moving. Her hand reached out. Sarah expected her to touch her breast, but instead, the hand took hold of her waist and pulled her forward.

Their bodies melted together as they kissed once more. Slowly this time, their mouths explored each other until Sarah needed to breathe.

With her head leaned back, Victoria took the opportunity to trail kisses down her neck. Fingers ghosted up and down her spine, until Victoria lowered herself to her knees and kissed each of Sarah's ribs to her navel.

Victoria's fingers hooked into Sarah's stretchy pants and pulled them down. Leaving a trail of hot kisses on Sarah's hip bone and down her thighs. She stepped out of the pants when Victoria picked up each of her feet.

Fully bare before the woman, Sarah looked down to find Victoria sitting on her heels looking over her sun-deprived skin. Victoria's fingers reached forward, caressing the tally-marked scars on Sarah's thigh where she'd made the pain real in high school. Victoria leaned forward and kissed each of them. One at a time, she provided long overdue care.

Afraid of the questions that would come later, she pulled at Victoria until the woman complied.

Once on her feet, Sarah made quick work of unbuttoning Victoria's jeans. Without the patience of the other woman, she pushed them down as well as the woman's panties. With Victoria's help, they were soon dropped alongside the other clothes, and all that stood between Sarah and Victoria's bodies was that blasted bra. A front latch designed not for another to easily undo.

Victoria reached between her breasts and unclasped the pale beige. The weight of her bosom burst forward as her breasts were freed from their keeper. They hung with perfect rosy nipples that hardened in the cool air before Sarah's eyes.

Sarah ran her thumb over the perked flesh as Victoria's hand reached for Sarah's ass. Lifting her once more and holding the woman's slick core to Victoria's stomach, their tongues danced against each other again, broken up by teeth nipping at lips until Victoria's resolve shattered and she carried Sarah to the bed.

Sarah crawled back, her body spread, waiting for Victoria to join her. Victoria pulled herself up and kissed her way up Sarah's legs, stopping to breathe in the spicy tang of the woman she'd dreamed of. She placed a kiss over the patch of short curls before making her way up to the breasts heaving toward her face.

Sarah's nipples stood at attention for her. Her tongue came out to tease the perked bud in circles before she wrapped her lips around it and sucked until her chest hummed in pleasure at the feeling of it in her mouth. She released it with a pop before moving to the other side.

A slick core pressed against Victoria's abdomen, Sarah's clit pulsing as her body searched for the friction to ignite the dynamite within her. Victoria's fingers played with her other nipple while her tongue explored the rigid uncharted territory on the other side.

Shamelessly, Sarah ground against Victoria. She held Victoria's hair in her grip as sparks ran like a fuse from her knees and fingers until it ignited a firecracker within her, shooting up until it exploded behind the lids of her eyes. Red, then gold, then blue sparkles flashed in the darkness.

She cried out at the show until her tongue was ice cold, and her heart hammered against her chest.

She didn't know when Victoria had moved but the woman was no longer atop her but behind her, cradling her still-shaking body. Warm air tickled her shoulder and back, cooling the sweat that clung to her skin. Two fingers ghosted soothing circles across Sarah's chest and abdomen.

When her muscles finally found rest, Victoria's hands did not push her away. They pulled her closer even though there was no space left between them. Sarah wondered if the electrons of their atoms had entwined them, bonding them together.

Sarah held the woman's hand against her still-beating heart as she calculated all the ways she'd been wrong. All the years she'd spent with the wrong person.

The baby gay had defied the expectations Sarah had for intimacy. She hadn't taken Sarah to the edge and left her wanting, nor had she pushed her over the edge to fall until reality smacked her in the face. There was no edge to be wary of or a drop to tumble off because Victoria never left her.

The room wasn't spinning, because like Victoria protected the floor from swallowing Sarah downstairs, she kept Sarah pressed against Victoria's breasts on the pillow-top mattress. Deft fingers soothed away any thought of being abandoned. They caressed Sarah's side, over the raised scar, and down the slight curve of her thigh before returning to her navel.

Never returning to the same spot, Victoria explored Sarah's body like a map to a treasure. Her hand glided over the fiery skin leaving trails of pebbled paths. She seemed to be memorizing the details of her body.

The realization hit Sarah in the chest that her body wasn't Victoria's map, it was her treasure. Her being was the treasure that Victoria caressed with adoration.

Tears fell at having never known such care.

Victoria whispered, "You're safe."

And Sarah knew it to be true. Knew she was safe for the first time in her life. So, she cried for the 29 years that she'd had to be strong.

45

Cabinets closing and a cast of characters pulled Victoria from sleep. She glanced at the door now cracked open. Horror filled her as she realized the child had peeked into the room, possibly traumatized from seeing her mother naked in bed with Victoria.

The covers once again had been ripped to the other side where no one lay. Victoria's foot had managed to trap the sheet in place keeping their naked bodies from being bitten by the cool morning air. With her body wrapped around Sarah like a sleeping bag though, it made sense to Victoria why the comforter was treated like a villain. However, she wouldn't have to clutch to the feisty furnace if the woman would stop stealing it.

When Victoria tried to move, the woman beside her groaned. The growly girl gripped her like a cavewoman, tightly grasping her arm against the rising and falling chest.

"Last Saturday of break," Sarah whined. "Wanna sleep on the cloud with you, sky girl."

Chuckles shook Victoria's chest. Pressing her face into the bed-smooshed hair, she inhaled even though the stray strands tickled her nose. She'd love nothing more than to lay in bed with Sarah, but Tris was awake, and Victoria wasn't quiet.

"Sleep," she softly whispered to the woman. "I am going to go get you coffee and when you're ready we'll go to brunch."

Sarah pressed her ass back into Victoria. The subtle moan with soft pressure was just enough to stimulate Victoria. The temptation was almost enough to coax the woman from sleep to sin. With the sun peeking through the shades, she considered running her finger over the woman's nipple once more to see if she could recreate the shaky moans that had erupted into waves of wonder before her eyes.

"You know," Victoria whispered. "Nowhere in your lessons did you mention that I could do that with just your nipples."

A huff of sleep annoyance allowed Victoria a little space to move more freely. Her finger grazing the underside of the breast she wished to knead once more.

"Told you... every woman different. To explore," Sarah growled, and rolled over a little more to the side of the bed with the comforter. "Now shut it, Moana. I'm trying to sleep."

A mental note was logged in Victoria's mind. Don't wake the woman in the morning if she doesn't want to lose a hand.

Victoria got up from the bed only when the woman's soft snores began to serenade the room once more. She grabbed a pair of jeans from the laundry basket and the Jimmy Eat World T-shirt. Pulling them on in the bathroom, she stared at the woman in the mirror.

Kissing Sarah hadn't eased the age from her face. Her limbs even still felt like they needed a level of grease to move smoother. But she didn't feel empty. Her chest was alive, and she secretly hoped it wasn't due to the creature she consumed the night before. However, a chest full of flutters wasn't necessarily new.

Now, a mind not filled with ifs. That was new. The effect of thens became to foci of her fascination.

She smiled as she whispered once she looked over the sleeping warrior, "and then they lived happily ever after."

But she silently snorted at that one. It wasn't like the story was over. It had seriously been one night, and the only thing that changed was Sarah's claim on a side of her... no, their bed.

She walked down the stairs and peeked into the living room. Tris sat before the completed Lego sets moving the figurines through the miniature rooms as a movie played loudly on the television. The green eyes rose from the play set when Victoria hit the squeaky stair.

"Hey," the woman said with a soft smile.

"Are we still playing pretend?" Tris asked without returning the smile. Her gaze had returned to her toys, but her lips were set in a hard line.

Victoria pushed the hair behind her ears. She hadn't considered coming down and having to answer questions.

"We...I think your mom would probably like to be a part of this conversation."

She sat in the chair. Her eyes pulled to SpongeBob flipping crabby paddies. Her lip curled over her teeth as the scene shifted through a hole in the yellow figure's head to a flea-like creature moving gears and tapping together wires.

"You guys slept in bed together again," the girl stated. "She's never slept in a bed. Not even with Voldemort's sister."

Pointing out Sarah had been in her bed all week wasn't going to supply any clarification for the girl. Wiping the sleep from her eyes, Victoria considered what she could say. It was still morning, and she was still waking up so thinking was slow.

"Is she going to get up and make us pack again?" Tris asked. The brunette figurine tightly held one hand and the Black girl with braids was scrunched in the other. Victoria looked at the play set and found the other brunette girl sitting at a table.

Victoria tried to follow the same fear she was holding back behind a door in her mind. Carefully, she said, "I don't think so."

"You were naked."

Victoria swallowed, unprepared for what morning would bring. They'd not talked about how they'd tell Tris. Not considered that the girl would wake up before them or come into the room.

'Reroute,' she begged the GPS in her brain. The mapped-out lines for the morning shifted, and multiple paths were highlighted. She selected the scenic route.

"I want to do something special for her." She tapped her fingers on the jean-covered knees. "Would you like to go with me?"

"Then she'll make us leave," Tris whispered.

Victoria heard her but it didn't compute immediately. This was not on the map still and she couldn't seem to get away.

Deep breath in. A reminder the girl had always been her wingman. Deep breath out.

"She said I could take her on a date today."

Deep breath in. Deep breath out.

Tris's fingers paused their play. The figurine stood in the second story of the school as the girl chewed on her words. The jaw worked over some pretty complex ideas before she looked at Victoria.

"You got to play by the rules, so she doesn't act weird."

Victoria's brows crinkled in the middle. She'd never heard about the dating rules before.

"Translate," she commanded.

The sharp-jawed chin dropped to her chest. Words ground together as though the crank sending them forward needed some morning oil.

"I'm not supposed to translate anymore."

Victoria held her hand to her chest, feigning hurt. "But... I thought. You said I could be the cool aunt, and we didn't have to tell her everything."

Tris's eyes looked up without her face moving. The narrowed glare was equally terrifying to the woman still sleeping. She sucked her teeth next. And a tiny part of Victoria remembered that not being a good thing.

The girl grimaced at the other figurine and shoved her into the monkey zoo attraction. "You can't be my aunt and take her on a date."

"Are you mad?" Victoria asked in a suede-like timbre. "About the date."

"I don't want to move again."

Victoria nodded. It made perfect sense. She sighed at Tris' truth. "You think if we go on a date she'll make you guys leave."

"She's going to mess it up with her things and you... you don't understand the rules," she snipped.

"Can you tell me what they are?" Victoria asked.

Toys shuttered as the girl's patience snapped. She spat, "I already did."

Victoria tried to make sense of it. "Do you mean the food rules? Like, don't order too much?"

"That's one," the girl whispered. She seemed to be coming back around. "But the present one is the big one. You said you wanted to do something special for her and that means you want to get her a present, but she doesn't have anything left to give you back."

Victoria hadn't thought about that. She would have messed it up without the conversation.

"What if I took her to do something?" she tried instead.

Tris seemed to consider it. Then she nodded. "That could work... but if she wants to pay for it just let her."

"Okay... I can do that." Victoria could do that. She wouldn't like it, but she could do it. "Could you help me think of something she'd like to do?"

Eyes wandered over Lego sets. Her attention settled on a decent-sized tree house. She wet her lips.

"When I made her profile for the date site... she said she likes to hike. I still think that's a lie."

Her eyes widened as Victoria tapped her chest. "I love to hike. I could take her on a hike today."

But Tris shook her head.

"Won't work. She won't go because she doesn't have shoes to go. That's why she didn't go to my Girl Scout hike."

Victoria raised a single eyebrow. With a devious smile, she said, "We could go get her shoes."

"That's a present." The girl rolled her eyes and had a gorilla jump on the toy. "See it's doomed."

Victoria rescued the Lego version of herself. "Ummmm, maybe not kill me, 'kay? Because I have an idea."

"That sounds dangerous."

Victoria's eyebrows scrunched together. She was as much of a fan of morning Tris as she was morning Sarah.

"Did you wake up in the double digits and decide you're a teenager?"

"No." Tris's chin dropped. "I woke up and she was gone."

Victoria looked at the empty couch behind the girl. They hadn't... Sarah was always on the couch for the girl to wake up to in the morning. The normal in her chaotic life.

"I came to get you... to tell you she'd left, and I saw you... and her."

"Does it make you upset? Her and me?" Victoria asked, trying to prepare for the girl's potential rejection.

"No. I just don't want to move, and you don't know the rules."

"Okay... well let's play by the rules." It was simple. The rules made the kid feel safe. And Tris was the only person Sarah would never run away from. "Just come with me. Hear out my plan, and then... then you can help me play by the rules."

"You're not going to leave right?" Tris asked.

"Never."

The green eyes studied her. "Stick out your tongue."

Victoria's chin twisted to the side as she searched the preposterous child's face for a clue. "Why?"

"I need to see if your tongue is green."

Victoria's nose scrunched but she played along.

Tris's neck careened as she looked at the organ. "It's not green but I am not sure it really works."

Shoulders rose in a shrug as Victoria smiled. "Well, I passed the test. No changing the rules."

Tris hummed, putting the Victoria-assigned figurine back in the Lego tree house with the other two.

"Did you mean it?" Tris asked.

"Mean what?"

"When you called me your kid?" Tris gathered the three together, holding them like a family picture was being taken with the child's eyes. "You told your sister that I was your kid."

"I did," Victoria confessed. "At least... I want it to be true."

"Do you want kids?"

Victoria smiled at the thought of the three of them. She had accepted so long ago that there would never be one, then she thought maybe she could foster two. But now that she had one, she decided her mother was crazy for creating seven.

"I want you. Others... seem a little excessive. Like where would we put them?"

Tris got up from the floor. She padded her way around the table and pushed herself onto Victoria's lap. She leaned into the hug and wrapped her arms around Victoria's neck.

"Let's go do your plan and you can take her hiking."

Victoria moved a braid behind Tris's ear. "Would you like to go hiking with us today?"

"I don't like to hike... but I want to go. To make sure you don't mess it up."

Sarah was already up when Victoria and Tris came back. Her growly morning body was hanging over the table. Green eyes rose and landed on the bags.

Victoria's smile was too big. She slid the milky beverage to the raccoon-like figure staring her down. Then the bags were placed on the floor and Sarah stared at them skeptically.

"Where did you guys go?" Sarah growled. The coffee on her lips only eased her glare slightly. "You said brunch and coffee and it's been hours."

Victoria nudged the girl. "Go get the stuff."

Tris shook her head. With a wave of her finger and a twist of her neck, she declined. "I don't want to touch them. They're gross."

Sarah's brows furrowed. She set the cup down. "What stuff?"

Victoria ignored the question. Tapping her chest, she explained, "I have to keep her from getting in the bags."

"I can do that?" Tris said with an eye roll. "You go get the stuff."

"She'd break you," Victoria said skeptically.

"I'm strong." Little biceps rose to the challenge "I can stop her."

"I'm right here!" Sarah cried out.

Tris rolled her eyes when they continued to stand over the bags. "Fine. I'll go because she's feisty."

Sarah's head fell back. "What is wrong with you two?"

"Nothing," they said together. The girl went to the sink and pulled out a trash bag. She dramatically slapped the air with it until it opened. Then she walked out of the house.

Sarah followed the girl with her eyes. "Where's she going?"

"To your car ta get sumthings out of it," Victoria said.

"There's nothing in there besides trash and my..." Sarah's face fell, and she looked back at the hallway. She whispered, "Sex case."

With a wave of her hand, Victoria swiped away the worried words. "She knows what she's looking for."

Victoria's body bounced lightly on her toes.

With a curious wrinkle across her forehead, Sarah asked, "What's wrong with you?"

"I... uh... I had duh Frappuccino."

Sarah's eyes grew. "And it made you bounce?"

"You love coffee soooomuch. I just thought like like I was missing outta something. So, I ordered oneforme andoneforher—"

Sarah's eyes narrowed and her voice raised an octave. "You gave her coffee? Victoria, you can't—"

"No! No!" Victoria slapped away the start of the statement. "I'm not stupid. She got chocolate and I got coffeechocolate a... uhhhh...theycalled it... itjavasomething and it am jus... jussss reallyreallyexcited."

Sarah laughed. "You are shaking like you're on crack."

"Crackcoffee... it's hasssaring tosit."

"Oh my god, sit down." Sarah sighed. "You're going to crash soon, just FYI."

Victoria sat as commanded. The table shook with her leg to the point the ice in Sarah's cup clinked around as they waited for the girl to come back.

The bag was full, and the duct-taped shoes were held out an arm's distance from the girl.

"What are you doing with my shoes?" Sarah asked.

"You'll see," Tris said.

Victoria retrieved the bags from the floor. Having something to focus on seemed to set aside the java jitters. Starting with the orange Nike bag, Victoria pulled out the shoe box.

"Tris showed me your dating profile."

She smiled as Sarah's face turned paler than an albino monkey's fur.

"I do agree with her. You're too pretty for prison."

With a roll of her eyes, Sarah waved her hand to hurry up.

"Soo... she said when she asked you what you like to do, you told her hiking."

Sarah wrapped her lips around her straw. She chewed the tip lightly before she confirmed, "I do like hiking."

"Well, for our first family date, we are going hiking."

"Ohhkayyy." Sarah looked at her shoes on the floor. "So, you bought me shoes to go hiking in?"

"I did." Victoria bounced again. "And in exchange for those shoes, I am claiming those living creatures right there." She pointed to the taped-together shoes with a crack across the sole.

Sarah shook her head. "I need those shoes for work."

Victoria raised a finger. "I knew you would say that, so I got you these."

Another box of shoes was retrieved from the bag. They were similarly ugly but had been a safe choice.

Folding her arms over her chest, Sarah leaned back in her chair. "And what am I exchanging for those?"

"Good question." Victoria looked at Tris. "What's she exchanging for the shoes?"

Tris rummaged through the bag and pulled out a half-empty box of tampons.

Victoria's face lit up. "Thank God. These things are like $11 a box with inflation."

"I need those," Sarah stated.

Victoria waved her finger around the nasty shoes. "You need to bury those more."

"Rude." Sarah leaned over the table and snatched the new shoe box. She ran her finger over the untaped Bob, then pulled a Nike from the box.

Her whisper was barely audible, but Victoria's caffeinated ears caught it. "I've never had a new pair of shoes before."

Victoria bit her lip. She studied the woman's face to see if she'd gone too far.

After putting the shoes gingerly back in the box, Sarah careened her neck to peek at the other bags. "What else is for trade at this black market?"

The plan was working. Victoria haggled like a champ, getting three half-filled disposable water bottles filled with child-spit floaties for the price of a camelback hiking backpack. A box of kind bars to tide Sarah over until brunch was bargained over and Victoria was thrilled to trash three tupperware of month-old spaghetti and fungi. A North Face hoodie was fought over until Sarah agreed to part with her coffee straw wrapper collection.

But the real kicker was the stretchy pants with pockets Sarah paid for with a song because she was unwilling to part with the French fry and chicken nugget science fair experiment. Apparently, the budding biologist had been studying the lack of decomposition for potentially three or more years. Sarah had promised to check her data journals and get back to Victoria on the exact date the experiment began, but she was certain it had started with the bite-mark-riddled nuggie.

Belting out a true classic, Sarah's voice carried throughout the house. Shaking the windows and scaring the neighbor's dogs, Sarah finished the final lyric to the Gilmore Girl's theme song and erupted into her best Roseanne cackle.

Tris didn't appreciate Sarah's vocal range as much as Victoria. The woman practically was moved to tears as she checked her ears for blood.

The transactions were finalized with a G-rated kiss and a gagged, "Gross!"

The gagging continued when the girl left the adults to cuddle in the single dining room chair.

"You didn't have to do all of this," Sarah whispered from her seat in Victoria's lap.

Victoria laid her head against Sarah's shoulder. She inhaled deeply, catching the slightest hint of the woman's arousal. A smile spread over her face, considering the comfort she'd been able to provide the woman at the same time as cleaning out the clunking car.

"How about you go get changed so we can go on this date you promised me?" But she didn't let Sarah go. "I hope you don't mind... I... I, like, invited Tris to go with us. It's still our first date but I'm not really just dating you. I'm dating her too because you two are a package deal and I want to make sure you both know that I want to spend time with both of you."

She felt the woman freeze in her arms. Her cheek was no longer rising and falling with Sarah's breasts.

She looked up and tried to explain, "I didn't mean... not like dating her in like—"

Sarah pressed her finger to Victoria's lips. "I understand. It just... it means a lot to me that you would even think to... you know?"

Victoria hadn't known. She hadn't realized it would be something that would bring a new smile to the woman's face. One she'd never seen before. So, she memorized it, filing it away in her head as the smile to strive for.

46

When Sarah told Victoria the child didn't like to hike, there was no iota of a lie. The kid didn't just dislike hiking, she loathed it. Her feet kicked up rocks with every step. When there were no rocks to kick, she tripped on air, flailing around until a ghost caught her before she fell. Sarah knew the spirits traveled with Tris when the girl tried to walk. If an insect flew within a foot of her, Tris spun around flinging her arms to the side like she'd been temporarily possessed by a demon wearing tap shoes.

"The sun is eating me," she whined, after twirling in a circle and shuffling her feet.

Victoria's idea to bring Tris was thoughtful; however, prolonged the trek along the single-person path. They reached the summit of the five-mile path with more stops than it felt like steps. For Sarah though, it was a blessing in disguise. After years of playing the roles of single mom and workaholic, her hiking muscles had lost their fitness. She still managed to move through the trails, but her legs felt wobbly when she found rest atop a large rock with only a sprinkling of shade.

South Mountain didn't offer her the towering trees of her childhood. The ponderosa pines of Flagstaff reached for the sky, refusing to allow the elements the satisfaction of dictating their growth. Standing under one of the mesquite trees capable of surviving near the Phoenix metro area was more like stopping under an angry bush. The spirits of knife-clad warriors lived within the trees, ready to stab any they deemed unworthy.

Sarah rubbed her fingers over the leaf of the creosote alongside her. Bringing them to her nose, she inhaled the scent of July monsoons.

"What's that?" Victoria asked after a long drink.

"Creosote," Sarah quietly said. She rubbed a different leaf, letting the oil coat the pads of her fingers once more. Then she held it up to the woman. "It's the smell of rain."

Victoria held Sarah's hand in her own. Sniffing it, then turning it over so she could press a kiss to the back.

"I always thought rain smelled like asphalt."

Sarah's brow furrowed. "Like the road?"

The woman nodded, taking a seat alongside Sarah on the rock overlooking the city below them.

Shaking away the idea that rain smelled like something as unnatural as a road, she said, "That's so weird."

Victoria's fingers intertwined with Sarah's when Tris caught another dancing ghost. Thin brown arms flailed over her head and then her fists wiped across her face. She stomped her feet and moved in a circle, but whatever was within her did not call for rain. In fact, the few clouds in the sky split open to cast a warm ray over the three of them.

"How can anyone like hiking?!" the girl spat between pants from her performance. "Like it's bad enough we walked all the way up here. Now we have to go all the way back down."

"Down is the easy part," Victoria reminded the child.

Tris followed a lizard whose push-up had caught her attention.

"Careful of the jumping cactus," Sarah called when the child took a few steps off the path.

The size three feet froze, and a braided head twisted side to side. There were three different spiny assassins near her. Not having been raised in the open forest or the desert, she had no idea which was going to jump at her.

Victoria leaned closer to Sarah. Brown eyes were comically large as she animatedly swallowed. "Jumping cactus?"

Sarah nodded, then pointed to the furriest of the unfriendlies.

"That's a cholla. It's really a static electricity thing but basically, when you get too close to it, it flies through the air and..." her fingers shot out and pinched Victoria's thigh.

The woman jumped as the child slowly backed away from the lizard working on its upper body.

"What sort of sick joke is this?" Victoria asked as she pressed her finger to her temples. "Like they already have spines, but they jump too!"

"Does your head hurt?" Sarah asked.

Victoria's jittering java-induced high had long since faded but the aftershocks of withdrawals still quivered in the woman's limbs.

"Yeah." She rubbed the back of her neck. "It's like my eyes and my neck are sore. And I feel like a truck hit me."

"Caffeine withdrawal," Sarah said simply. "Remember when you asked me why I always have a coffee in my hand while I'm at work?"

Victoria shook her head. "Yeah, no more coffee. This may be worse than beer."

The waves of their laughter danced around each other, moving out into the world as they sat side by side. Leaning into one another, Sarah savored this moment. She loved being away from the city and wondered if she could get Victoria to agree to head north during the spring so they could hike in places where the view wasn't over the urban sprawl below them.

"I think we missed brunch," Sarah said. "And if the way up was any hint as to how down will go, I think we can consider ourselves lucky if we don't end up at the ER covered in cholla. I never realized how uncoordinated she was."

"I can hear you," Tris growled.

Sarah looked over the dusty shoes covering Victoria's feet. She'd never seen the woman go for an actual hike, but she had mentioned it once in a session.

"Do you hike often?" Sarah asked, hoping she hadn't robbed Victoria's time to do so over the past few weeks.

Victoria followed Sarah's gaze to her shoes. With a smile, she explained, "When I got here, I met Jen. Like literally the day I arrived, I backed into her car at the grocery store. So, my car was fine minus a small dent, but Jen's was a little worse. The front bumper had dented into her wheel well."

Tris groaned. "Hiking. She asked about hiking."

Victoria shoved the kid a little. "I'm getting there."

"I'm going to be old before you do," Tris snipped. She grabbed the hose of Sarah's camelback and tried to drink from it.

"That's mine!" The woman protested. "And you still haven't learned how to drink without spitting."

"But I'm out," the girl whined.

Sarah held her hand over the mouthpiece and turned the backpack around. She rummaged through the bag and pulled out a bottle of water she'd brought for this exact reason. As she handed it to the girl, she looked at Victoria. "So, accident. Jen's car no bueno."

"You speak Spanish?" Victoria asked in awe.

"I can say no bueno." Sarah took a drink. "So, you going to tell this story or is Tris really going to go gray before the end?"

"Oh yeah. So, Jen was actually headed to Sedona to this like all-girls retreat where women, like, meet other women." Victoria wet her lips and glanced at Tris. "She was ranting about having wasted money on a three-day babysitter, so I offered to drive her."

Tris's head fell back. She called out to the spirits, "She asked about hiking, but she is still talking about other stuff."

"Anyways, we drove up together and it was like... so overwhelming. Like, there were so many women there and they had this, like, singles hike, so I went. I loved the rocks, and it was so pretty."

Sarah watched as Victoria scanned over the city below. She realized she'd never had the time to just listen to Victoria talk. She'd shared so much with Victoria, and every time she needed Victoria to understand that she didn't want to be the way she is.

"I would love to go back to Sedona again. I don't think I ever told you this and I don't know if you've seen it in the garage, but I have a little pop-up trailer." Victoria turned to Sarah. "Maybe in spring, we could take it up to Sedona or Prescott. I hear there's a lake that we could go fishing."

"I bet you're great at fishing," Sarah said. "I've never been."

"Me either," Victoria whispered. She dropped her eyes to the toes digging in the dirt. "It wasn't a thing girls were supposed to do. My dad was so happy when my sisters started getting married. He finally had the sons that could do those things."

When Victoria didn't seem to have anything else to say, Sarah leaned against her.

"I grew up next to a heavily wooded area. The trailer... it was at the edge of the park and the fastest way to school was through the woods. They had built the nice new houses just a street over, but the school was zoned for the rich kids that lived there."

Tris' groaning had ceased. She sat still as a rock, but Sarah knew she was listening to the story she'd never heard before.

"The highway ran through the woods and the school was on the other side. So, my sister, me, and the other kids, we would walk to the highway. There was a bridge for the deer to go under the highway, and it was about a quarter mile out of the way, but it was safer than running across the highway. We used to joke... say the city knew when they put it there it wasn't for the deer but the Parkies."

Sarah shook her head. "We were less than a mile from the school so they wouldn't send a bus even though we had to cross the highway."

Victoria's face scrunched up. "That's terrible."

The woods in every story Sarah had read as a child were supposed to be dark and scary. They were where monsters waited, and witches cast their curses. Not Sarah's woods though.

"I love the woods." She tucked Tris under her arms. "They offered ample coverage for wars between the ice kids and those of us who were prepared to survive the apocalypse."

"Ice kids?" Tris asked.

"Their parents bought these cabins and only came up for winter or summer break. We called them ice kids because summers they spent at the lake, so we never saw them. But winter they came on their snow blowers and always wanted a war." Sarah squeezed Tris. "We kicked their ass every winter. Climbing a ponderosa pine is no joke but we could disappear if we needed to."

"Do you ever want to go back there?" Victoria asked.

Sarah wet her lips.

"No."

She hoped Victoria would understand that even though she loved the forest, Flagstaff offered her nothing but a trip down nightmare lane.

As though Tris knew story time was over, her momentary pause from whining ended. Her legs kicked out and dust flew up around her feet.

"I'm hungry," she bellowed.

On the walk down, Victoria and Sarah took every opportunity provided to walk together. They were halfway down when Tris looked back at Sarah and Victoria moving hand in hand.

"Are angels dead people?" the girl asked.

Sarah practically tripped over a twig. Or at least she was going to blame it on the twig. Luckily, Victoria saved her from tumbling into a prickly pear cactus and a trip to the ER she forecasted.

"Some people believe that," Victoria offered as she held Sarah's arm, ensuring she was good.

Tris chewed on the answer for a moment. Then she asked another zinger: "So, does that mean angels are zombies?"

"Uhhh..." Victoria shoved the water tube in her mouth. She seemed to be chugging the remainder of her pack as though she needed time to reach Tris' level of logic.

Sarah just laughed. She didn't answer because she knew Tris wasn't done.

"But if angels are on Earth but we don't have zombies on Earth then does that mean the zombies are in Heaven?"

Victoria choked on the water. She hacked as Sarah patted her on the back forcefully to keep from laughing.

"But then why do people want to go to Heaven if it's where the zombies live?" Tris shook her head. "I have no interest in Heavenly zombies. Or being a zombie. When I die, make sure they do that thing in the back of the head. You know, so I don't become a zombie."

"When did you watch The Walking Dead?" Sarah hissed.

"I didn't." Tris smiled at Victoria. "Lynny and I watched The Last of Us on her phone during our sleepover."

Victoria's eyes watered. Her voice cracked as she asked, "How do you make it stop?"

Sarah waved a finger in the air as though she were casting a spell. Quickly she said the magic words, "Ask Monica tonight when she picks you up to go to the movies."

Questions about the existence of zombies in the afterlife ceased and the girl picked up her pace. Mentioning the missing aunt and movies seemed to cause the child to grow wings on her feet.

"So, Tris is going to the movies with Monica tonight," Sarah said. "For her birthday."

"That's sweet of her. I was wondering if you two were back to talking again."

Air rushed from Sarah as her shoulders fell inward. "There's been a lot to absorb," she admitted. "A lot to forgive, and let's be honest, I'm not a big forgive-and-forget type of person."

"I don't know her like you do," Victoria said. She took Sarah's hand in hers. "But... she is the reason this was possible."

Sarah's eyes narrowed. "You still would have been my boss. We would have met just a few days later than we first did."

"But..." Victoria raised her eyebrow. "You never would have given me a chance and I never would have had the courage to ask if you were gay."

"I'm not gay," Sarah quipped.

"I'm sorry." Victoria raised Sarah's hand to her lips. "If you were a lesbian."

They took a few more steps in silence. Tris practically ran to the car within sight, leaving the adults to fend for themselves.

"So, what happened on that Sedona trip that ended you up on Monica's couch?" Sarah stopped. "I'm so sorry. I just... You don't have to tell me."

"I'm surprised your friend didn't tell you," Victoria almost growled.

"I swear we only ever talked about the fact that I fucked up your first session and... then how much I hated you were my boss and how irritatingly hot you are."

Victoria's lips twisted, but then she smiled. "When did you first tell her you thought I was hot?"

"Will you tell me what happened in Sedona?"

Victoria nodded, but Sarah checked to make sure her fingers weren't crossed.

"I slept over her place after your meet and greet. The subject of your hotness came up then, then again on our first day back to work."

Sarah shoved Victoria with her shoulder. "Stop gloating. Sedona and all the lesbians. Spill it."

Victoria's steps slowed. They took their time as people passed them by.

"So, there were sooo many women and they were all so like comfortable with who they were. I saw my first Drag King show. It was so much and I had just come out literally four days earlier and I was there with Jen being Jen only drunk and she was also a stranger who didn't know me."

Sarah's eyes narrowed at Victoria.

"Someone hit on you, didn't they?"

Victoria sucked her teeth and crinkled her nose. With a nod, she glanced at Sarah.

"She was nice at first. Offered me a drink and when I told her I didn't drink she started probing with the questions until she made a joke about me being an escaped Mormon. When my face turned red, she told me to come to her tent so she could 'fuck the brainwashing out of me.'"

Victoria's chin fell but she looked up with big eyes. "I just... I was so freaked out and I turned her down. Later that night she was pointing at me and telling her friends how the event wasn't even good enough to find real lesbians. And I wasn't even sure if I'm a lesbian or bi or what. So... I got back and I set up an appointment with Dr. Rose to help me figure me out."

They left the trail but stopped outside of the car where Tris was already nose-deep in a book. Holding on to one another, Sarah studied a cactus that wasn't too far off from the one she'd seen with Zoe at the botanical gardens.

"I have a lot of shit," she whispered. "I know me and Tris need, like, professional help. And I need help learning to set boundaries with my mom and my sister. I never had the time to do it before but maybe... since we are doing this, I could cut back on clients and do that. Like, see someone to help me not let myself go back to the trailer in my head, you know?"

Victoria wrapped her arm over Sarah. She pressed a kiss on Sarah's head. "I one hundred percent support this."

Tris popped the door open and got out of the car. She put a hand on each of them and began to push. "Food people!"

"Food," Victoria promised.

Victoria drove as Sarah dictated directions until they found themselves outside LoLo's Chicken n' Waffles. With the car in park, Victoria looked at Sarah.

"Since Tris is going to be gone, how about we get dinner and then we can go dancing? I have that friend who owns a bar. It's a gay bar so it will be comfortable, and you can get some enjoyment out of her and her sister making fun of me and my dancing."

Sarah looked at the phone buzzing in her hand. Scam rolled across the screen, but it wasn't her car warranty calling. She ignored the call for the fourth time that week.

"Yeah. Sounds great," Sarah said.

47

Tris threw open the front door when the Navigator chirped outside. The handle hit the wall and the vase on the entry table shook under the aftershock of the attack. Sarah moved quickly from the living room to steady it before something in Victoria's house was destroyed.

The child's brow furrowed at Monica's quiet ascent up to the walk. Hair no longer blonde, the honeyed brown dangled in waves around her face. She smiled softly at Tris, opening her arms for the girl to run into.

There was no running into the woman's open arms. The girl folded her arms across her chest like an angry mother. She sucked her teeth before a hand shot out in front of her. "You've been away forever! You don't call. Did you forget that I am your best friend?"

Monica's patient eyes waited for the child to finish her rant.

"You don't even know that Victoria's whole family showed up for Thanksgiving and there were so many people, but Gram made the turkey, and it was like a real Thanksgiving."

Blue eyes shifted from the narrating girl to the mother leaning against the door behind her.

"And everyone was so loud, and everyone looked alike, but Victoria called me her kid. Like *her* kid and did you know she was named after Superman because she was supposed to be a boy?" Tris barely took a breath before her foot stamped into the ground as though she was capable of shaking the ground below them with her own superhuman strength. "AND you missed it. Lynny hit me with a biscuit and killed me because Mom waged an entire war with Gram over getting creamed in the face by Victoria and..."

Monica's eyebrows rose, and her lips parted. A devious smile spread across her face as the previously slumped shoulders rose.

With a single finger wand, Sarah stilled any commentary from exiting her mouth. She watched as the angled jaw ground away the pokes and prods. Unable to create words, Monica nodded to the car and pushed the keys into the kid's hand.

Unphased by the quiet adults, Tris grabbed the zipper-busting backpack from the ground. She held it up to Monica and proudly announced, "I packed enough stuff if you wanted me to stay the night."

Two sets of eyes rose to Sarah's watchful gaze. In ten years, Tris going to Monica's had never been a question asked because it was the way of their family. However, Monica's desire to not be family changed things.

She tucked her hair behind her ear. "Tris, go get in the car and let Aun—" she cut the word off with the snap of her teeth. Recalibrating to the woman's wishes, she said, "Just let us talk."

The girl lifted the bag over her shoulder. Her purple sweatshirt dangled from her hand as she trudged to the car. Sarah silently agreed with the kid it was better to be prepared than be left without a change of underwear.

"So, I'm not even her aunt anymore?" Monica's shoulders had lowered as though a whip had been snapped across her back.

Sarah's tongue poked around her mouth as she let out a heavy breath. Her mind flipped through the images of Tris and Monica throughout the years. The two possibly spent more time together than Sarah had in the last few years as she tried to right the world that had flipped upside down on her when Simone texted.

Shaking her head, she remembered the child's retelling. The tales of a world she'd never known from Monica until it had been slung in her face like sand during a sword fight.

"I forced that title on you when apparently I ruined my life and yours," Sarah stated. She offered a simple shrug to distract from the tremor in her hands. "And I wasn't sure you still wanted it."

Crinkles gathered in the corners of the eyes studying her. She suddenly felt like a piece of gum stuck to the woman's shoe. A sudden annoyance that would cause her to stop from her prearranged plan that always seemed to work out for her.

"Why would you say you ruined my life?" Monica asked.

"She heard you talking to your girlfriend."

Monica's head snapped back to the girl sitting patiently in the backseat, spine straight with a face set on good behavior. With her ear turned to the car, Sarah wondered if Tris was working on learning how to hear things through barricades, like car doors.

"That wasn't what I meant," Monica whispered. She rubbed the back of her neck and shook her head again. "Jesus, Sarah. You should know better than anyone that—"

"Well, that's what she heard. And... I mean, you basically said the same thing to me before we left, so... you want to be her aunt, then you get the choice this time. But she's listening to you because you're the one with the life she wants. You're the one she worships."

She tapped her fingers against her forehead. Morse Code to her mind. Begging for it to find neutral and reroute the message to her heart trying to burst through her chest.

"Is this why you stopped answering my calls and texts?" Monica's head fell back. "Like, I thought we had a fight and then it was, like, you were fucking gone. And not just, like, stormed out for coffee or something but gone. Like, I know you're capable of."

"You wanted me gone."

Sarah's arms wrapped around her body. The hug she'd needed from Monica when her stability had been stolen from her once more.

"I wanted you off my couch, not out of my life." Monica shook her head. The brown tendrils waving effortlessly, like the rest of the woman's existence. "And even then, I didn't want you off my couch, I wanted a plan for you to get off my couch but I was bleeding and pissy and the girl I was seeing was being a douche about you living with me because she saw a picture of you and was suddenly so insecure about you and all your attractiveness in my face. She was convinced that you being on my couch would end up with you in my bed."

"You said that same thing," Sarah snapped. "You told me staying there was one step toward crawling into bed with you. That you didn't want me to need you. That you didn't want me to be your life."

Monica's hand waved in the air to the house behind Sarah. "That was me just being mean. I didn't mean it. I wanted you to get up because you had hit the ground again and being sweet and caring never works on you. It's always the same broody exchange game. Like the cash I found with the spare key you left on the counter."

The throat clearing behind Sarah caused her bones to try and separate from her muscles as her skeleton made a run for it, but her flesh sank to the door. Unable to divide, her insides felt wobbly at best and to add to it "Scam" scrolled across her phone once more. She hit ignore as Victoria stepped up to the door.

"Dr. Rose, would you like to come in?" Victoria asked. "Maybe not, like, yell at each other while Tris is watching in the car or for the neighbors to hear."

Sarah wondered if this was one of those normal people hospitality things, but she couldn't help but feel the lower timbre of the woman's voice casting a protective bubble around her. Like Monica coming in wasn't a threat but proof Sarah had improved her situation.

But it didn't feel like an improvement at the moment. She'd moved from one couch to another, then into the couch owner's bed. A little piece of herself seemed to fall to the ground and shatter. A statue with a protection charm that still managed to crumble.

"I should... I should just go." Monica nodded back to the car. "Tris is waiting, and the movie starts in thirty."

The frustration in Monica's tone had fizzled to their new reality. "Can I keep her tonight? She packed her stuff already and I think her and I need to have a talk talk. Clear some shit up because we are family. No matter what I said. We'll always be family."

Sarah nodded and leaned into Victoria. She felt the woman's arm wrap around her back and hand come to rest on her hip.

"She'd love that... and maybe if your girlfriend is up to it..." Sarah gestured between Victoria and herself, "We could go on a double date. I mean, then she won't feel so threatened by my attractiveness in your face. That is if you're done bleeding and being so pissy."

A smile crept up to Monica's eyes. They flicked between the women on the other side of the threshold. She tapped her hand to her chest.

"I'm just going to say that I..."

Sarah used her magic finger wand and flipped the silencing spell back in effect. Then for good measure, she said, "Your niece wants to know if Heaven is filled with zombies. Have fun with that."

Monica's mouth dropped open, then her head fell back. "I finally got her to stop asking if people we pass are ugly enough for prison."

She looked at the ground, trying to see what piece had fallen off her. Maybe if she was careful, she would be able to tape it back on and cheat her truth.

"Sucks being the favorite aunt," Sarah said with a laugh that didn't shake her chest. Just enough to put away the anger.

Sarah checked her phone for the hundredth time. The notifications for texts from Scam had reached sixteen by the time they'd gotten into the car. They would go unread at least for the rest of the night.

She tapped out a text of gratitude to Monica before holding the phone up to show Victoria the Lego set that out did the combination of all their birthday presents.

Victoria's lip curled over her teeth and a subtle growl rumbled her words. "It's like she's trying to show us up."

Little bulbs of cotton caught Sarah's attention. She twisted each between her fingers as she dropped them to the side of her. Her tone barely shifted as she explained, "Oh she is. And you can bet it will be even worse after tomorrow because she's groveling now."

Victoria pulled the SUV into the gravel parking lot. Once the car was in park, she turned in her seat while still holding the wheel.

"We didn't really get a chance to talk about how you were feeling." Victoria bit her lip. "You two seemed to be starting to... talk about... like things."

Sarah's head fell back into the headrest. She rolled it to the side, admiring bar-ready Victoria. Her brown eyes were softer with the brown shaded accents. The normal formal shirt was replaced with a tank top and a flannel, Sarah had never seen before. But then she thought of the closet overflowing with clothes the woman owned. Probably had enough outfits to dress for a month and never repeat an article.

"You interjected at a good point," Sarah admitted.

Victoria tucked a curl behind her ear. Her chin dropped but her eyes wandered over Sarah's body before rising in a childish innocence.

"I heard her talking about how attractive you are... and I was like..." Victoria wet her lips. "Like nope."

"Nope?" Sarah asked. Her brows scrunched in the middle as her mind tried to translate what nope meant.

"Your best friend... she is very beautiful and at one point you two apparently agreed to a marriage pact." Victoria searched Sarah's eyes, moving between both as though she could see the memories of her and Monica together.

"We were drunk," Sarah explained. She pointed at the door to the bar. "Actually, drunk in this very bar on my twenty-first birthday. She'd just been played... badly. And I was me... a constant tragic mess. So... we agreed we would get married so that no one else could make our medical decisions if we were still single when forty was knocking on the door."

"Medical decisions?"

Sarah hummed in acknowledgement. She cast a warm smile to Victoria. "Never in my life have I had any romantic intentions with Monica. Never."

Victoria's eyebrow rose in challenge. "You said you two kissed in college."

Sarah wet her lips. She had to explain, but no matter what words came out it wasn't going to paint her in a good light. And Monica in a worse one. But she knew it wasn't the way things were. It was just something that happened.

"You don't have to tell me," Victoria offered.

"I just... I mean... just give me a minute to make it make sense in, like, normal people world."

She wrapped her fingers through Victoria's. Felt her hand raise to the pink painted lips. The patient kiss Victoria offered her throughout the day whenever the conversation got real. Like she could kiss away the rough edges of Sarah's armor.

"So... I need you to know that I don't know how to do things. Like never saw a healthy relationship in my entire life."

Victoria nodded, but Sarah knew she couldn't understand.

"Before Tris, Monica was my roommate. My annoyingly perceptive roommate and she... she liked to practice her psychology textbook readings on me. I mean, she would read something and try to apply it to me because she could tell I was guarded and to her that was something new."

Another ball of cotton twisted off the worn shirt. She'd have to replace it soon because it was one of her favorites to wear to work.

"So, one time..." Sarah took a breath. If she just said it all fast, then it would be done. But her mouth opened and closed as words gathered in formations ready to rush into battle.

She scraped the soldiers from her tongue with her teeth and breathed them out. "She read that women without a stable family would likely fall into bed with anyone who showed the slightest care for them. So, she pretended to care. Kept a logbook about my behavior after she did something that would be in a sense... providing for me. And... well her readings had been correct. I didn't like her, but I felt like I owed her. So, when she waited up for me when I stayed too late at the library, I hugged her. When she took time to teach me how to braid my hair, I wore it that way for days. But when she bought me dinner and I thought it was a date... I kissed her. I thought it was what she expected so I kissed her, and she kissed me and when I was half naked... she saw my scar and she panicked."

Without any more cotton balls to twist away, Sarah turned to her cuticles. Pushing back the overgrowth, then picking at the skin until tiny cuts lay alongside the nails.

The wave rolling off Victoria, caused Sarah's eyes to shift just enough to fully take in the woman in her periphery.

"Why did she panic?" Victoria finally asked.

Sarah turned to the window. Her finger traced over the handle. An escape route she could take right now.

A bus rolled to a stop along the road, and a brunette in a short skirt staggered off. Sarah squinted at the figure hunched over, trying to light a cigarette. The lighter shook in the woman's hands a few times, then a flame emerged. She studied the woman, waiting to see her own reflection.

"Sarah."

Her name. A complete sentence. Just like the no Monica had given her. A stop to what she was going to do. The first time a woman had seen her naked and decided she was too damaged.

She looked back at the woman swaying her hips to the silent siren's song. A call to the drivers passing by. But the face was oval when she turned. The nose wide and the breasts too big be an O'Keeffe.

She swallowed the hope tinged with fear. Satan hadn't popped up on her screen. Just Scam. Two sides of the same coin with the same desire.

The explanation fell from her lips after the woman waltzed across the street to the dimly lit Food City. The escape to the conversation would be the truth.

"The trauma... it became real for her. She'd thought it was daddy issues. A fun experiment until she had a visual cue of what hell could look like." Sarah swallowed. "I'll tell you... that's when I stopped accepting things without a trade. Because where I come from, you gave sex for things like food, clothes, a place to sleep. I didn't... I didn't want to be my mother or my sister, so I just made sure that when I got something... I didn't have to give that."

When she turned, she found Victoria staring out the windshield. Her hand on the steering wheel was paler than the whites of her eyes.

It was her turn to pull the woman back. She squeezed the fingers in her hand until she watched the glassy brown eyes blink several times.

"How could you be friends... after?" Victoria asked.

Sarah smiled but turned to find Victoria still angry. The foundation on her cheeks wasn't thick enough to hide the boiling blood in her face.

"Simple. I told her it was fine because kissing her was like kissing my sister. And the next day when Tris was born and I was called to Phoenix, she used her mommy's money to drive me down here. Took me to Walmart and bought formula, clothes, and a car seat. Her world turned upside down and rather than be a dick, she cradled Tris in her arms and told her she was her auntie and that she would never leave her side. I mean, she stayed in Flagstaff for the rest of the year, but she transferred to State U and finished school with me."

She squeezed the woman's hand again. "It wasn't a gift to me. She cared about Tris, and I needed someone to care about her because I was scared and angry and... and it was like everything I'd done to get where I was a waste. But she made it possible for it not to be a waste. Like you did when you showed up after the break in. And when you barged in after mine and her fight. I was so fucking angry, and you both stepped into the space that I pushed you from and you said no. No, I couldn't let the ground swallow me. I couldn't give up."

Music from the bar found a crack in the car to sneak through. The door opened, then flapped closed as a group of women exited. Their loud laughter lifted Sarah, reminding her of the heart-eyed beauty.

"You ready for our first dance?" Sarah asked.

Victoria groaned through her grinding teeth. She held up a hand, and said, "I promise to cover any expense that may result from a broken toe."

"That bad?" Sarah asked.

The keys were pulled from the console and the door pushed open. She turned just enough to cast Sarah a smile.

"Maybe we just stick to slow songs."

"Middle school style. Turn in a circle. I can do that," Sarah promised.

But she swallowed as Victoria led her through the doors to a table already surrounded by women. To the masc with dark hair and dark eyes holding out a beer for Victoria. Marissa was what Simone called her, but she'd met Echo at the Greyson house a few times. Sarah had looked at the photo often to not to know who Echo was, even when the photo on the desk that had been turned face down as Simone took what Simone wanted from her.

"Well if it isn't Babygay Brenton. Your heart seems to be healed." Echo raised her hand in the air and pointed to the bare finger. "I took the step and took it off."

Sarah walked a step behind Victoria. She hung back as Victoria was wrapped into a burly hug.

"Hey, Echo. This is Sarah," Victoria said, tugging Sarah to her side.

Echo held the bottle of her beer to her lips. She scanned over Sarah before tilting the bottle in her direction.

"I don't know why, but you seem familiar." The bottle raised to Echo's lips. She swallowed a few sips before she set it on the table. "Did you used to work at Cactus High School?"

48

The high-top tables were filled with patrons. Laughing lesbians, flashing flamers, and amused allies filled the space in a gentle roar that rolled with the hip hop hammering into Victoria's chest. She'd left Sarah momentarily, making her way to the bar where Parker leaned with a tray in hand.

When the redhead turned, Victoria gestured to her frame. "Fix me," she begged. Then, she glanced back at the table were her friend and girlfriend were speaking.

"She finally give you a chance?" Parker asked. Her hands pushed Victoria's breasts together and Victoria pulled her boobs up. Why she'd forgotten that trick was beyond her, but she'd remember so Sarah wouldn't have to worry about another woman touching her.

Standing back, the redhead admired her work on Victoria's chest. Her eyes ran down to her shoes, and a smile crept up the woman's face.

"Steve Maddens are always a good choice in winter. You have a survivor of an apocalypse vibe going. Edgy but hot," Parker stated.

They looked back to the table where Echo's bottle was angled at Sarah. A flush had risen up Echo's neck and settled in her cheeks. She set the bottle to the table. Her finger rubbing her ear lobe.

"Something's wrong," Parker stated. She held her tray in her hands like a shield, then she walked toward the battleground.

Victoria followed at her heels, eyes flicking back and forth between her friend and Sarah.

They finally settled on Sarah. Searching for any sign of distress. Long finger she'd held minutes prior were pulling at the hem of her shirt. The material stretching to cover more of her, when it already sagged off her lithe frame.

"When did it start?" Spittle flew from Echo's mouth as she leaned against the table. The dark bottle rolled against the table as Echo twisted it with her fingers. The always smiling eyes had fallen to the mouth of the beer.

Sarah's shoulders caved inward. Her shirt no longer able to be stretched without her body giving some. She lowered her eyes to the bottle, and Victoria followed her gaze.

There was no way Echo would hurt Sarah. She couldn't. But Victoria understood the way Sarah watched it carefully. Every action the woman took was out of self-preservation learned from experience.

She placed her body between Sarah and Echo. Her mind reeling through what could have happened between them walking in and her getting her tits lifted.

As the song shifted into something slower, Sarah's voice rolled over her shoulder. "Three years ago."

The hand rolling the bottle gripped the neck. The glass didn't give the way a throat would, but there was no doubt in Victoria's mind that Echo was capable in a fight.

Three years ago, she'd been sitting at home. She'd been waiting for the men in her family to come back with tales of adventures in the woods she'd never been allowed to see. Sarah was here three years ago. A mother taking care of her daughter. Working with a boss who'd taken advantage of her. And the pieces clicked into place.

"She said she was going through a divorce," Sarah explained. "She had a place. A condo. Said I could come stay there with my kid."

Pieces to the puzzle Sarah had been too ashamed to share. Victoria had known about boss, but never the offer. The same offer she'd made. The offer Sarah had been backed into a corner to take.

Echo's head fell forward. A fist smacked against her skull. Her lips were licked, then licked again but the chapped flesh still cracked as a wicked smile spread.

"The bar was finally turning a profit," she said. "Big promotion. Lots of late nights at games. Weekend events. It was all a lie."

"I didn't take the offer," Sarah said. She moved around Victoria. Her body knocking into the chair beside the table. She fumbled with it as she tried to right it.

"How long?" Echo asked. "How long were you fucking my wife?"

Sarah looked to Victoria. The green had shifted into something more vibrant. The grass of a cemetery stared back at her as though she accepted this as the death of whatever there was.

"Two years. We were seeing each other for two years and then last year she sent me a text and said she was going to keep her promise to you."

Echo's chin rose slowly. Her biceps flexed and she pushed up from the table.

"Did you know about me in those two years?" Echo's battle worn hand slapped against her chest. "Did you find out she was coming home to me during that time?"

"At her birthday. That first year. I mean, I knew about you. I used to live with the Greysons. But she'd said you two were getting divorced, and I thought she'd moved out."

Victoria reached down and took Sarah's hand in her own. She leaned in and whispered, "We should go."

But Sarah shook her head. "She deserves to have her questions answered."

Parker's hand rested on Echo's bicep. Pulling her back from the possible battle into a moment with her sister.

"Simone was a terrible human," Parker whispered. "She preyed on you when you were a kid. By the sound of it, she did the same thing to her. She pulls her power from manipulating people who are in tough spots."

"She fucking knew she was married," Echo growled.

Her finger raised in the air at Sarah so quickly Victoria was certain she was trying to strike. She turned her body into the table and wrapped the woman whose head had dropped in preparation for the blow.

"I should knock you out, kick you out. Fuck!" Echo's fingers pulled at the roots of her hair. Curses flowed from her lips, drawing the attention of the tables around her.

"I'm sorry," Sarah said. Her words muffled by the arms wrapped around her protectively. She pulled back, tapping Victoria above her heart. "I'm sorry I didn't tell you. And I'm sorry I didn't reach out to you, Echo."

The nostrils flaring sent out heavy breaths as the woman stilled. Echo studied Sarah, and then sighed. "She had you fired," Echo stated.

Sarah nodded.

"She said she found out you were a prostitute, and she reported you and she had you fired." A sick laugh fell from her lips. "She was so fucking proud of herself. Uncovered a scandal. Made her, like, a badass."

Victoria's body spun on the toe of her boot. Her chest rose and fell.

She clutched Sarah's fingers in her own. Lips curled over her teeth ready to rip through Echo. The pain, the betrayal. It didn't matter to her. The friendship was as fragile as her relationship with Sarah. And she'd choose Sarah.

Victoria's eyes stared into Echo's as she spat, "Don't. You. Ever. Talk. About. Her. Like. That."

Echo shook her head. A sickly smile flew up her face as her hand gestured to the woman being held behind Victoria.

"Simone was a bitch, but she showed me the arrest photo. Showed me that girl's face arrested for whoring around downtown." Echo laughed. "You just mad because the first bitch you fucked is a cheating fucking whore looking for a payday."

Victoria's nails dug into her palm. But Sarah's hand pulled free from Victoria's grip.

"I don't need you to protect me," Sarah stated.

Sarah's chin rose as she met the raging bull before her with a steady stoicism perfected through years of pretending to be okay.

"My sister was arrested for prostitution. She is a whore. Still on the street addicted to probably everything. And we're twins so you did see my face. Just not me."

Echo's eyes searched over Sarah's face. She scanned once, then again.

"Fuck!" Echo's hand pounded against the table. "I just want to fucking hate you. I fucking... I fucking want it to be your fault."

Fingertips popped as Echo pressed them into the table.

"You can't hate me worse than I hate myself," Sarah stated. "But this is not your burden to carry. The blame is not yours. It is hers and it is mine. Not you."

"Not mine," Echo whispered. Her head twisted as she looked at Sarah.

The crowd surrounding them had begun to dissipate. But Victoria's hand still rested on Sarah's hip, ready to move her out of harm's way.

"Why's everyone looking at you all like you about to get in a fight?" a woman's voice asked with a strange sense of authority.

Echo sucked her lips between her teeth. She offered Sarah a nod before putting the bottle of her beer back to her lips. Leaning back, she finished the drink.

Two women approached the table. The one who'd yelled looked

more out of place in a bar as her hand held the pregnant belly peeking out over her pants since the last time Victoria had seen her and the woman attached to her hip.

"What are you doing here, Evie?" Parker bristled.

"Playing wingman for your hopeless ex," Evie snickered. "Zoe needs to get laid and the dating profile her mommy made for her didn't seem to work."

Nudging the other woman alongside her, Zoe's body came into view. Victoria watched the woman raise her smooth hand shyly in Sarah's direction.

"Hey," Zoe offered quietly to the woman holding Victoria's hand against her hip. The simple wave with the simple word set Victoria's teeth on edge.

Parker's eyes widened. She gestured between Zoe and Sarah. "You two know each other?"

"We went on a date." Zoe stated.

"A fake date," Sarah interjected. "Tell your mom the food was great."

Victoria had felt the need to interject when Monica told Sarah she was attractive. Those were just words while the fit, younger woman standing before her might as well be preparing to launch Cupid's arrow into Sarah. Her Sarah. The woman she'd worked so hard to get tonight and the entirety of the lesbian community seemed to be showing up to stop them from happening.

"You get out of your lease? I keep an eye out for your sister but like you said, everything is already gone." Evie admitted tugging on the neck of her shirt.

"Yeah, Tris and I moved." Sarah wet her lips before she said, "How's the twelve-year-old moron who kept asking 'AM or PM?'"

Evie's eyes rolled dramatically. "Uh yeah. I'm on light duty field training until the baby comes. He is one of the most annoying people I have ever met."

"Look, I'm sorry I didn't call you," Zoe spit out. Her hand pulled at the back of her neck. "I really did have fun, and I wanted to call because I really liked—"

"I told her not to," Evie snapped, cutting her friend off. "When she showed me your picture, I told her about the whole break in and that your sister was like a crackhead and that with her running for DA it would just look bad."

"I should have called," Gaia whispered, her head hanging slightly. "Maybe you could give me—"

"Same stuck up, asshole," Parker growled. She waved between the friends. "Jesus. You two individually are barely tolerable but together... you said you changed, Zoe but here you are casting people off like they're disposable."

Sarah pressed herself against Victoria. She waited for Zoe to look at her, and said, "I'm glad you didn't. This is my girlfriend, Victoria."

"Your boss?" Zoe asked.

"I think we should go," Victoria said, leaning into Sarah. "I didn't think... let's just go somewhere else, or home. We can go home."

Echo stepped in the way as they started to leave. She pointed to the patio. "I need a minute, but I want to talk. Can you two like go outside? Parker will get you a drink on me for like losing my shit. I just need to process because look, Sarah, Victoria is my friend. I need to just get my head sorted because all of this... we were the ones that got played. She doesn't get to win. 'Kay?"

Sarah nodded, but Victoria hated it. Tonight was supposed to be fun. Instead, they'd almost been in a fight. The dating site lawyer lady, Zoe, was too pretty to not be annoyingly threatening. But Sarah had agreed so she followed.

The plastic chairs' legs wobbled slightly when they sat. Hot dank air filled the space. The smokers had left but the air was still thick and rolling around the patio cover.

Victoria's fingers fiddled with the cold glass Parker had dropped off. She picked up the napkin and rolled it into a ball.

"That was a lot," Victoria said. She shook her head. "I wouldn't have brought you here if I had known that your ex was Echo's ex."

A slow smile rose up Sarah's face. Her shoulders seemed lighter as she said, "Honestly, I am glad I got to face her. I saw Simone a few weeks ago. She was back to the same games, and I saw through it this time. I'm glad I did."

Sarah's hand reached across the table to pick up the napkin ball Victoria had discarded. She unwrapped it, then pressed its wrinkled form back on the table.

"I kinda feel like the napkin right now," Sarah confessed. "Like I have been carrying that stone on my back. All the guilt for letting Simone convince me that she was the victim in their marriage. But it's like I can just let it unravel."

Victoria stared at the paper. The watermark from her drink had caused the material to give and tear. She wasn't sure if she'd torn it, or Sarah had tried to right it. But it was there along with the creases she'd caused from the pressure. And it was a little too similar to the woman for Victoria's liking. A need to fix it. A guilt for destroying it. A helplessness to do more than stand by while Sarah worked the creases with her fingers.

"So, you and that woman?" Victoria asked.

"That's the one that ghosted me."

Victoria looked through the French doors to the edge of the dancefloor. She was supposed to be dancing with Sarah tonight. Instead, she was waiting for her friend to come to terms with Sarah sleeping with her wife.

She found the woman leaning against the railing. Her eyes were fixed on them and she seemed to be plotting.

"Well, it turns out she didn't intend on ghosting you," Victoria offered hesitantly.

"I prefer where I am now," Sarah stated. She continued to press the napkin to the table. The tear widened but the wrinkles seemed to smooth. Some were barely even noticeable.

Victoria searched Sarah's face for even the slightest hint of pink. Then carefully, she asked, "You mean it?"

"Yes." Sarah's eyes rose. She stuck out her tongue in Victoria's direction. Her eyes crossed when she tried to look at it. With it still sticking out, she said, "Theee ot geen."

Victoria shook her head. "What?"

Sarah rolled her eyes. "Not green."

Victoria brought the glass to her lips as the chuckle rumbled in her chest. She tasted the burn of Parker's heavy hand.

"I'm not trying to rescue you," she said. "I just... like, I need you to know. I heard what happened with Simone in there and I just... had I known I would have gone about things differently."

Sarah sat back in the chair. Her foot pushed her into a slight recline that brought a worry into Victoria's vision.

"You did things differently," Sarah stated. "Simone didn't offer me and Tris a place to stay. She offered me a place in her bed. That's what she wanted. A fuck toy to keep her bed warm. And eventually I would have been replaced with another one, probably more damaged than me. It's one of those lesbians that I didn't warn you about because I didn't need to."

Sarah ran her finger over her glass. The coconut rum had caused the ice to melt and the soda to separate. She hadn't yet taken a drink.

"You know this is going to be hard. We come from different worlds."

"I'm in this," Victoria promised. "As long as you want me."

Sarah's head fell back. She breathed deeply and let the air rush from her. Victoria followed her gaze to the words scrawled across the yellowed roof.

"Today is the first day of the rest of your life," Sarah read aloud.

Victoria scanned through the quotes, searching for the one Sarah had found. In scratched scrawl, the letters bled together as though the author knew someday someone would need those words. Sarah would need those words.

"I guess it is," Victoria whispered.

Echo pushed through the door. In her hands was another round, though the first had yet to be finished.

Victoria pointed to the quotes. "Why are their words written on your ceiling?"

Echo's chin rose and she looked at the patio as though she'd never seen it before. She seemed to be searching for her own message, but then she explained, "Princess Parker decided one night to start writing lessons on the ceiling for people that look up in search of answers. It's grown since then. I randomly get people asking for a sharpie and a ladder and so it's a thing now."

The drinks clinked together, and Echo pushed them on the table. She pulled a sharpie from her pocket and let it roll against the table. "Have something to add?"

"No," Sarah said. She continued to read through the others. "I think I found something I needed."

With a hum of approval, Echo rested her forearms against the table. Her hot breath rolled over the space. She tapped against the plastic with beat with the bass.

"So..." Echo swallowed. "I don't want there to be bad blood between us."

She gestured between Victoria and herself. "We're partners. Dart partners. And you're my partner's partner. I want us to be good."

Victoria watched the crinkles gather at the corners of Sarah's eyes. Softly, the woman said, "I would like that."

"Victoria, says you have a kid," Echo stated.

"Yeah." Sarah tucked her hair behind her ear. "She just turned ten."

"Well, we should all go do something some time," Echo stated. Her hands used the table like a bongo drum. "I have kids. We can have a non-bar night. Maybe bowling."

"That would be nice," Victoria said.

An evil grin spread up Echo's face. She raised a finger to the air. "Plus, when I post it on Insta, Simone will shit her pants."

49

Rain plunked against the metal awning covering the after school pick up zone. Children cried out and toddlers in strollers wailed as the thunder crashed over them. Night was falling quickly with the heavy cloud covering as parents wrapped a blanket or their own sweatshirt over their children's heads.

Sarah turned toward the school as a gust pushed against her. Her arms clasp around her middle, but for once the wind didn't cut through the holes of her thin sweater. Wrapped in her North Face sweatshirt and the light jacket Victoria had traded her, the late November thunderstorm didn't make Sarah's bones ache as much.

As she stood with her plastered smile, an internal war raged within her. She gave a high five to a third grader as her mother approached with a smaller child in tow. Then her eyes wandered back to the assistant principal tapping out a complicated handshake with an eighth grader.

A part of Sarah knew she should be celebrating the success Victoria was having with the kid. One who'd spit in her face the week before the break was now her buddy. But the part of her was frustrated with the pull back from Victoria when it came to their intimacy. And it had set her one edge.

Four days since she'd come apart with the woman's tongue on her nipples and her body pressed against her. Four days of sleeping with cuddling hands instead of caressing hands. Four days of soft kisses that lasted only moments.

And she felt like she was breaking in two. Like Victoria had finally reached a chapter in the story of Sarah's life and realized it wasn't a book worth finishing.

"Bye, Ms. O'Keeffe," a fourth grader from Tris' class called out.

Sarah turned to see the girl following the afternoon staff in a line through the rain to the cafeteria. She raised her hand to wave, but the girl had already turned back to her friend.

The unclaimed children trudged through the water, and she searched for the ones whose pants had grown short, or knees were torn through.

Victoria's fight for basic necessities had won the grant funding, and she had a closet filled with appropriate winter uniforms to hand out.

"Hey," Victoria said, but ducked with the thunder shook the awning above them. Lightning slashed through the sky, spreading its arms wide before the crack hit them.

"We should go inside," Sarah said.

Victoria nodded, putting the umbrella over them. The singular drops of water turned to a fire hose. Asphalt filled with water, and Sarah realized the playground didn't smell like creosote. But something rough and dirty. Like her.

"Are you good with pizza for dinner tonight?" Victoria asked when the door shut out the downpour.

"Sure. but maybe just a large cheese this time," Sarah whispered.

Victoria didn't respond. Their steps didn't align as they walked. Arms nudged into each other as though they couldn't find a way to move through the space together. Sarah finally slowed half a step to give Victoria the space she needed.

"I found a basketball league for Tris. It's a rec league and I could take her to practice during the week; if it's, okay? I know she said she likes basketball so like if you're good with it. I could sign her up."

Sarah nodded, then realized Victoria couldn't see her. "Yeah, I mean if she wants to, that would be great. She'd never gotten to play sports before because of my schedule but..." Sarah chewed on the rest of the sentence.

She'd planned to cancel her clients. Tell Monica she was done. She'd already quit the library, but if Victoria was having second thoughts.

Victoria stopped outside Sarah's door. "But... what?"

The inside of Sarah's lip was raw from the amount of flesh she'd already chewed from it. Her mind constantly tried to figure out why Victoria's dilated pupils had vanished when she looked at her. Why she'd begun to pull away so quickly?

Sarah knew the answer of course. It had been the answer she knew would come. She looked over to where Tris leaned against Leticia's desk. They were examining something on the woman's computer screen.

"Can you..." Sarah pointed to her office. "Can we talk for a minute?"

A wrinkle deepened across Victoria's forehead. Her fingers played with the hem of the floral shirt now visible with the first layer beginning to be shed in the heated office.

"Sure."

Sarah shut the door behind them. Her office was safer to have this conversation than the house. If Victoria was having second thoughts, then she could go back to the house and face reality rather than walk in still believing in fantasy.

"Are you okay?" Victoria asked. Her hand cupped Sarah's face as the woman's chin dipped.

The burrito she'd shared with Victoria at lunch was suddenly not so friendly. Her body felt like it was preparing to reject the spice she wasn't accustomed to, and a fear washed over her that she was either going to puke on the woman she was falling for or gas her into an early grave. Pressing her hand to her stomach, she willed her body to do neither, but her throat still felt bubbly, and her insides were arguing.

"Are we... okay?" she asked when the twisting became too much. Word vomit seemed better than actual vomit, so she let it spill before Victoria had a chance to process the initial question. "I just... you haven't. Since the bar it's, like, you're different. Like, you're changing your mind and I'm sorry I didn't tell you about Echo. I was honestly hoping when we went that she wouldn't know who I was and that I could give you that night of dancing that you were so excited for. I mean, I figured we would come home and pick up where we left off, but then it was like sooo much."

Sarah swallowed the bile burning her throat.

"I just never wanted you to know everything that happened because who would ever want to be with someone that did that. Let alone did it to their friend. And I get it. I know you said you were still in this, but I get if now that you have had time to think about it. But—"

A finger covered her lips. The words coming out were slicing in two and fell to the floor before they could splash against Victoria.

"You're talking so fast. I can't really keep up," Victoria whispered. "But to answer your question, I don't think we are okay because you are like clearly upset."

Sarah squeezed her eyes shut. She held the bubble in her throat until it popped in her mouth, and she blew out. She could taste the peppers from the salsa.

"Is this because we didn't have sex yet?" Victoria asked.

Another bubble rose from the pit of Sarah's twisting tummy, and she held it in. Swallowing repeatedly, Sarah sent it back to where it came from. Then she nodded.

"I know you wanted to," Sarah whispered. "Then the bar... it was like everything changed."

The manicured thumb ran over Sarah's lower lip. She didn't get words to calm her fears. Instead, her lips were sealed with a bruising kiss from the woman pressed against her.

Their head turned and the twisting in her gut lessened. She parted her lips, allowing Victoria's tongue the entrance it requested. The kiss lasted until Victoria rested her forehead against Sarah.

"I needed..." Victoria whispered. "I just needed you to stop doubting me before I tried to explain."

Sarah licked her kiss swollen lips, before biting down on the lower. The thumb brushed over the abused flesh.

"Nothing about how much I want you has changed," Victoria confirmed. "Nothing. I just... after hearing what that horrible woman did to you. What actually happened and not the CliffNotes version you gave me originally, I just felt so guilty. I felt like I took advantage of you when you were vulnerable, and I was ashamed of myself."

"I told you, you didn't," Sarah said.

"I know."

Victoria leaned back. Her butt rested on the edge of Sarah's desk. She held Sarah's hands. The fingernails of the nimble fingers were bit to the quik after days of worrying.

"You say things though to protect yourself. You do things and you say things to make other people feel comfortable. And in that moment... I, like, wasn't sure if you really meant it. So, I didn't... I didn't want to take you home and just have sex with you. Not when you had to relive so much that night. With your ex... and with Monica Rose. And how they made you feel like your worth was in your body."

Victoria met her gaze.

"And the last few nights, I just wanted to hold you. I wanted you to know that you lying beside me wasn't so I could see stars. That just having you in my arms was enough."

"To prove you were different." Sarah stated.

Victoria wet her lips. "To prove I wasn't her. I'm not your boss trying to fuck you. I... I hired you to teach me how to please a woman, but now that I'm here... with you. I don't want to just please you."

Thumbs rubbed gentle circles over the back of Sarah's hands. She raised the red fingertips to her lips and kissed each.

"I hate that I made you worry. Made you think I don't want you, Saraih."

While the gray sky outside continued to storm, the vibrant brown irises searched green valleys for understanding in Sarah's office.

"I come from a world that is different from yours. Sex isn't a commodity. It's sacred. Shared between people committed to one another." Victoria chuckled slightly. "I'm not saying I want to wait to marry you to make love to you. God knows, I can barely manage keeping my hands off you. Like sooo much restraint it took these last few nights."

Sarah leaned into Victoria, letting the woman wrap her arms around her.

Victoria pressed a kiss on Sarah's hair, then tilted her chin up.

"I just want you. You when the day hasn't sucked. When the world doesn't feel like it's against you. When you don't feel like you owe me anything."

"I owe you everything," Sarah whispered.

"Then I guess we both are going to be some pretty sexually frustrated people for a while," Victoria said with a cocked brow. "Because I'm not them. I'll wait for years, decades... hell maybe I will have to wait until we are heavenly zombies. I waited thirty-three years to have an orgasm. But even that doesn't compare to how I feel when I watch the unbridled smile spread across your face when you stand atop of a mountain you just conquered. Or the fierce determination when you rally an army of children to overthrow a seasoned dictator."

Sarah's eyes rolled so hard it was almost painful. "Your mother is not a dictator."

Victoria scoffed. "She didn't yell at you all week and make you clean out the trash bins."

"She did it to break a cycle," Sarah whispered as she pressed her face to Victoria's chest. "She and I spoke, and she basically said she never wanted to be the mother-in-law that alienated her daughters' partners. So, instead of bashing me for my housekeeping abilities or my inability to cook, she focused her attention on you."

"My dad's mom always had something to say about our house. Or if there was a wrinkle in one of our dresses at service," Victoria said. "Okay, dictator is harsh. Can we go with demanding chancellor?"

"Sure."

Victoria hummed before picking up where she'd left off. "Okay, so... comparing the things I love about you to my first orgasm. Oh! How you sing with your whole body. Or the way when you laugh at a joke you actually think is funny it sounds like a witch cackling over a fresh potion of poison."

Sarah smacked Victoria in the chest and fought back the urge to cackle. "Rude."

Victoria pressed her lips to Sarah's head again. She nuzzled her nose against the top of Sarah's head. Her deep inhale could be heard, and it made Sarah melt into her embrace.

"Okay," Sarah whispered. "I will work on the trusting thing."

With a chuckle, Victoria released Sarah from her arms. "Okay you work on the trust thing so that I don't have to be a zombie to try out my Regal Queen harness."

Sarah's mouth went dry while her thong became uncomfortably damp. Her thighs pressed together, and she prayed Victoria didn't have the nose of a hound, because she could already smell herself.

But Victoria's lips pursed together. Her eyes rose to the ceiling as though Sarah also kept answers to life's questions there.

"Do you think they have dildos in heaven?"

Another swat landed against Victoria's chest. Then another caused the woman's breasts to shake.

"Hey!" Victoria hollered in a voice too loud for the tiny office. "Stop hitting my best asset."

"Keep talking nonsense and it's the only action they will be getting," Sarah jeered. Then she swatted Victoria again.

Victoria grabbed Sarah's hands as they moved to attack once more. The sudden motion sent them both backward in the wall with a thump. Sarah's body held to the wall as Victoria's lips grazed her chiseled chin in a chaste caress.

Before Victoria could press her thigh closer to Sarah's core. The door to the office swung open. A handle struck Victoria in the ass and sent her face careening into Sarah's chest.

Both women jumped as Tris crossed her arms over her chest, and Leticia stood behind her with her mouth trying to catch a fly.

Leticia moved to grab the door handle as Sarah held the back of her head that had smacked against the wall.

"Sorry. We heard a bang and..."

"We're fine. Victoria just tripped over the corner of my desk, and I tried to save her but... I mean, small office."

Before Sarah could try to lie again, Tris tsked. Then demanded, "Lemme see your tongue."

50

The third bedroom was emptied of everything but the end tables, dresser, and bed. Victoria's carefully chosen décor was boxed and removed to make room for the newest addition to the household.

"Are you sure you're comfortable with Lynny coming to live here?" Victoria asked.

Sarah hummed in acknowledgment. Her hair pulled up into a loose knot wobbled as she hoisted the bedding from Naomi Brenton's stay.

"Is your sister and mother livid she is leaving right before Christmas? You said they do a massive Christmas celebration." Sarah pushed her way through the doorway. She hoisted the linens over the half-wall and dropped them down to the girl, with a simple, "Incoming!"

Tris cried out as the blanket and sheets rained down on her head. Child-sized eyes stared up once the avalanche had been cleared from her head.

"You're supposed to warn me before you drop them on me!" the girl yelled. "I could've been turned into a zombie or worse an angel that has to stay here and haunt people." Without missing a beat, Tris asked, "Why don't people ever talk about ghosts from, like, now? Why is it always creepy ladies in too many skirts?"

Sarah shrugged, then leaned back into the woman trapping her against the half-wall at the top of the stairs. Pale fingers ghosted under the T-shirt hanging off Sarah's body, while plush lips pressed precious kisses up her neck to just below her ear.

"You know this means you're going to have to learn to be quiet?" Sarah whispered.

Victoria's teeth bit the lobe of Sarah's ear, applying just enough pressure to pull a gasp from the woman trapped in her embrace. Her hand dipped just below the waistband of Sarah's shorts, testing the boundaries still not crossed.

"She can get some headphones," Victoria husked. Her hand reached lower, cupping the curly-covered apex of Sarah's core. "Because when I finally get to taste this. I'm going to make sure you know how much I appreciate the flavor."

Sarah's head fell back as the middle finger ran just over her slick slit.

"Please," Sarah whispered.

"Do you trust me?" Victoria asked.

Sarah's fingers gripped the ledge as the finger made another swipe. Victoria knew she was playing with fire. Teasing the woman had become a part of her everyday list of things to do. Making certain Sarah held no doubts in her devilish desires that still were just fantasies.

"Yes," Sarah whined. "I trust you."

Victoria's lips moved just past the woman's ear. Her fingers pressed just lightly within the folds to the flooded entrance. "Then, you'll let me cook you dinner and do the dishes."

Sarah's chest heaved, the pad of the digit just applying light pressure but not entering.

"Trusting you means letting you clean up the mess you make," Sarah let out a laugh, pushing her ass back into Victoria.

The sudden movement made the woman's hold loosen enough for Sarah to twist free. Her body turned to the surprised woman now pressed against the wall.

Sarah's finger traced the nipple pebbled through the woman's shirt. "You think you can just tease me and get away with it, Ms. Brenton."

A single brow arched in a challenge. Her hand found its way back around the brunette, pulling her body against her once more.

Requiring Sarah to trust her had turned out to be a poorly devised plan on Victoria's part. She'd only realized it when she was unable to come up with any way to measure Sarah's trust in her. When she'd taken the woman shopping at Kohl's and insisted Sarah purchase clothes that were appropriate for winter, it had backfired. Because even though Sarah had reluctantly done as asked, she'd also checked every price tag and refused to look beyond the clearance section. Date nights had gone similarly when Victoria had paid the bill, she couldn't bring the woman home to bed without considering the possibility Sarah saw it as payment for providing her a meal.

Sarah pressed her thigh against Victoria's core, providing fantasy-filled friction. Victoria's body leaned into Sarah, praying for the strength to pull away. Strength, she didn't have as the woman used her leg to wipe away Victoria's ability to process. Heaving breaths and grinding hips left

Victoria a heady mess, and Sarah won another round of who could bring the other to the brink of bliss and pull back.

With clenched eyes and jaw, the heat between her legs was robbed, and Victoria pulled at the woman in an effort to get her back.

"Dinner and dishes are all yours," Sarah stated, dropping a placating kiss to the tip of Victoria's nose. "I think I like this whole trust thing."

"I don't know how much longer I can last," Victoria confessed.

The doorbell rang, then. Bare feet slapped against the floor and the handle hit the wall. As Tris cried out to her new best friend, the vase on the entry table smashed to the ground.

Sarah's face went pale. The shirt fluttered behind her as her feet pounded against the stairs. She cried out, "Don't move!"

Victoria followed the woman also barefooted to the glass-covered floor. She slipped her house shoes on at the last step. When she turned, Sarah was already on her knees gathering the larger pieces of glass in one hand.

Terrified green eyes shifted back to Victoria while apologies fell from her lips. "I'm so sorry, Victoria. I'll replace it and, like, glue it to the table. She just doesn't know that things like this... I can try to glue it back together if it's important. I know it won't be the same, but I... I can try to fix it."

Victoria leaned down alongside Sarah. Careful not to jostle the fragile successes they'd made.

"Hey," Victoria said softly.

Her eyes wandered up to Lynny's raised brow, then the braided head tucked into the older girl's sweatshirt. Lynny held the child against her as she mouthed, "It's just a vase."

Victoria shrugged lightly, turning her attention back to the woman emotionally crashing.

"I will... We can be... fix it. I can fix it."

Sarah held the pieces in her hand. A line of blood dripped from her palm. She used her collecting hand to run the back over her face as her apologies grew quieter and less coherent.

"Won't happen... Not again. Promise."

And the measurement Victoria had been missing was there before her eyes. Blood dripping on the floor as the woman continued to pick up shards of a bargain buy from TJ Maxx.

"Sariah," Victoria said. The full name was always able to draw the woman's eyes to her before. A shift in the norm, like yelling Marco in the store only to hear Sarah call out Polo.

The green eyes didn't rise but the hand stopped collecting. She just knelt over the slivers of blue and green still decorating the floor.

Sarah's chin rose but her shoulders remained hunched over the glass. She peered out her periphery and Victoria understood the woman needed to check.

"You're safe," Victoria whispered as a reminder. "I'm not angry. I just need you to come to me so we can make sure we don't need Jen to stitch up that cut."

"I can't fix it," Sarah said to her hands. "There's just too many pieces... too much damage. I can't even remember what it looked like before... before it was broken."

Lynny stopped the child from moving into the glass-covered space with a swoop of her arm. "Hey, I heard you're going to be playing basketball, and you have your very first game in a week. And I saw the hoop in the driveway. Let's go... uh... shoot some hoops. I played in high school, and it will be fun."

Tris glanced up at Lynny. She smiled with her lips, but her eyes wandered back to her mother still studying the glass covering the entrance to the house like ruins tossed to tell the future.

"Lynny, I'm going to open the garage for you two to come through. Tris can help you get your stuff up to your room." Victoria took a deep breath as the two girls made their way back toward the garage. "Let's get you up, and then I'm going to get a broom."

Guiding Sarah to the kitchen, she heard the woman suck back her snot and watched her wipe her face against her forearm as she tried not to drop the glass or drip blood to the floor.

Sarah held her hand under the faucet while Victoria dug through the first aid kit. She winced when the antiseptic was applied, and the gauze pad pressed to the cut.

"I'm never going to be fixed enough to give you the life you want," Sarah whispered. She wiped away the tear before it fell.

Ego was the problem, Victoria decided. She'd set the conditions of sex on the belief she could fix Sarah like the napkin she'd watched Sarah try repeatedly to make right again. A personal need for Victoria to give the woman an undeniable sense of safety was made unrealistic by a shattered vase slicing through the tender membrane of time Sarah would possibly never not be able to travel between.

"You're not broken," Victoria whispered as she held the gauze against the woman's palm. She peeked at the cut, grateful to find the wound not deep enough to require stitches. "I'm sorry I made you think you needed to be fixed."

Another week passed. With Christmas break barreling toward them, Sarah's nerves were etched into her face as Victoria and Lynny splurged on every gaudy decoration they could find to bring the house they all shared into some semblance of normal for them.

With only two Saturdays left, Victoria found herself waking earlier each week. Her mind raced through the list of things still needed to be done to ensure Sarah and Tris experienced a real Christmas. Plus, the weekly basketball game where Tris was positioning herself to be named MVP.

Sarah's hair tickling her nose was what pulled Victoria away from the alternate universe. Her heart thrummed a chaotic beat as she tried to regain her sense of self. Hot air rushed over her exposed nipple from the breast that escaped from the tank top in the middle of the night.

Light from outside was barely peeking through the windows and she knew she'd awoken at dawn. Victoria adjusted her tank top to tuck her tit within. Sarah's body jostled in the movement, clinging tighter to Victoria's chest. Her lips pouted as though they knew the breast was no longer within their reach.

She ran her fingers along the woman's back, coaxing the frown away. A soft whimper breathed out with a subtle snore behind it. Her fingers moved carefully, tracing the memorized path around rippled flesh across the woman's back.

She smiled as she closed her eyes and replayed Sarah coming apart in her dream. The simple dark nightgown had been dropped to the floor of a candlelit room. Her mouth had ravished Sarah in the other dimension. Broke through the broody persona to feel the woman fall apart in more positions than one, but just as Sarah's mouth had lowered to her chest, she woke drenched in sweat and slick.

Fingers twirled a lock of hair. The cotton material no longer felt extra soft covering her. Every place it touched felt rough and intrusive compared to the soft flesh pressing against her.

Sarah shifted slightly. Her face nuzzled closer. A thigh rose up Victoria's leg and rested against her soaked core.

Biting her lip to silence her moan, Victoria closed her eyes.

Hot breath rolled in gentle waves over her skin. Tiny goosebumps traveled along the path, chasing the warmth in the cold morning air.

"Someone woke up excited." Sarah's gravelly morning voice reminded Victoria of home.

Heat rose in her chest, and she didn't need the light to know she was flushed. She fought the urge to admit she felt this way every time Sarah walked into the room or left her office door open. That making the deal to wait was a mistake because her subconscious was getting more action than she could accomplish during her short silent showers.

Victoria choked back the truth and supplied a colder reality. "I was just thinking about all the things we have to remember for basketball today. We can't be the parents that forget to bring snacks."

Sarah hummed, then pressed her face into the crook of Victoria's throat. She pressed her leg closer to Victoria's center. The cotton shorts rode up Sarah's legs, so her arousal was also painfully apparent.

"Should I be concerned that bringing snacks to a basketball game makes you this wet? Did you get vagina-shaped cake pops or something?"

Victoria swallowed but the lump in her throat did lessen. She strummed her fingers over Sarah's sides, causing the woman to squirm in her arms.

"Okay," Sarah whined. "Okay. I'm sorry."

Victoria clutched the woman to her chest, pulling her closer since the tickling had caused a retreat to the other side of the bed.

"You were dreaming about fucking me again." Sarah's finger grazed over the collarbone just at her eye level. She tapped the center of Victoria's chest lightly as though her fingertips were the woman's personal pacemaker.

Victoria sucked in a breath of air as the beating in her chest returned. "How did you...?"

Sarah pressed a kiss to the tiny freckle peeking out from the twisted tank top.

"You mumble in your sleep," Sarah answered the incomplete question. "You mumble and moan, and when it's a really good dream you move."

"I have to go to the bathroom," Victoria choked out.

Sarah groaned and rolled back to her side of the shared bed. She waved her hand to the bathroom door. "You go first. Because I have to piss like a racehorse."

While Sarah took her turn in the bathroom, Victoria quickly pulled off her sweaty clothes and flipped through her shirts. She needed something that didn't make her look like an evil stepmother. Even though she wasn't a stepmother she'd called herself a parent. A part of her was grateful Sarah hadn't commented on it. Her little slips had come more often, but they'd gone unnoticed thus far.

The simple black wouldn't clash with the kid's highlighter yellow jersey. She needed to remember to take a picture of them after the game for the photobook she'd been putting together for the mother and the daughter.

She shook the shirt some, but the material was forced from her hands to the floor.

"I don't think we need clothes yet," Sarah whispered. She bit lightly at the pale skin on Victoria's shoulders before making her way around.

Victoria blinked. Her eyes moved over the points of the woman's collarbones. Down the subtle curve of the ivory skin to rosy nipples.

Her gaze would have made its way down the expanse of the woman's body if a finger hadn't run its way over her parted lips, pulling the bottom down in an almost pout.

"Do you trust me, Victoria?" Sarah asked. She guided Victoria's hand to her breast, kneading the flesh over Victoria's hand in encouragement.

Victoria nodded silently.

The woman had shown as much trust as she felt possible, and Victoria had no willpower to fight back anymore. Not when the door was closed, and the rest of the house was still asleep.

A smile crept up Sarah's face as her hand dropped to the treasured crevice between the woman's thighs. Leaning into the embrace, Victoria felt the same type of torture she'd dabbled in over the days of teasing the woman. The labia parted with ease and the pads of Sarah's digits grazed the sensitive bead.

Muscles in the woman's thighs and calves shuttered. The wobbling in her knees threatened to give out. But she stayed as silent steady as possible. Willed herself not to give Sarah a reason to pull back from the first time someone had touched her there.

Sarah stroked the pulsing pearl as her other hand worked with Victoria at her still pert breast.

"I trust you to love me," Sarah said, dipping her finger to the entrance. "Please trust me to unravel you and put you back together."

Victoria's lips crashed into Sarah's. A hungry and demanding kiss. Her hand pulled the woman forward by the back of her neck until the only air to breathe was each other's. She didn't have the chance to deepen the kiss before she felt the perfectly positioned finger ease within her entrance. The sudden but gentle protrusion stroked once, then again.

"Please," Victoria moaned against Sarah's lips. "Don't stop. I can't... no more teasing."

Fingers gripped a taut hip as the other clung to the woman's neck, holding on as Sarah's fingers danced softly within her.

"You feel so good," Victoria whispered as their heads came together. Her legs trembled as she prepared for another thrust, but her body protested with the sudden emptiness within her.

Sarah raised her slick fingers to her lips. Her pink tongue ran up the length of them and her eyes closed as she hummed in approval.

"You're evil," Victoria whispered. Her core clenching against nothing, the emptiness with the pulse from her clit made her feel like a fire had just fizzled out. "I asked you not to tease me."

Sarah's head tilted slightly. Her fingers popped from her lips as the last of Victoria's essence was cleaned from them.

"I'm not teasing you," Sarah said. Her damp finger traced over Victoria's chest, circling the rippled areola. "Your body is a work of art and I want to explore it. So, get back in bed."

Victoria didn't think. She didn't have any blood left in her brain to think as the pulsing picked up. She stepped back until her knees hit the edge of the mattress and she crawled back.

Sarah moved alongside her. Her head rested on her hand. The other found a place just under her breast.

"Last time we were in this position, I wasn't allowed to touch you."

Victoria closed her eyes. Remembering the way, she'd stared into

Sarah's eyes. Wished they'd met in a different lifetime.

A smile spread up Victoria's face. "You said you didn't watch."

"I had to tear my eyes away," Sarah admitted. "So, I told you to do what I wanted to. Do you remember?"

She couldn't forget even if she wanted to. The softness in Sarah's voice.

"Touch my breast," Victoria whispered.

Sarah hummed, her finger tracing over Victoria's ribs. Her ghost-like caress ran along the underside of her bust.

"May I touch you this time, Victoria?"

Fingers clenched the sheet as she nodded.

Softly at first, Sarah cupped her breast. The supple flesh spilled from her hand. A thumb grazed over the pink surface before the breath rolled over the already perked peak. Her body jolted upward as Sarah's lips wrapped around her nipple.

"Please," Victoria begged. And the bed shifted. A soaked core rested against her thigh as Sarah's mouth expertly moved over the mounds of ivory rising and falling.

"Twist my nipple," Victoria recalled. A slight twinge sent a wave of pleasure through her body as the fingers twerked her other nipple.

Sarah's lips rose from the perky pebbles up Victoria's neck, and the weight was shifted from her thigh to press against her slick core.

"Kiss me, Victoria."

The lips met but the kiss was broken between soft moans. Sarah dominated the motions, her tongue stroking against Victoria's, then sucking her bottom lip.

"Tell me what you want," Sarah whispered between kisses.

"I want..." Victoria tried as Sarah's lips moved to her jaw, then her throat. She knew what she wanted but she was afraid to ask.

"Yes?" Sarah said before her lip encapsulated the bud of Victoria's breasts once more.

Victoria couldn't help the way her body arched into Sarah's mouth and then recoiled with the cool breeze of Sarah's breath when the nipple popped from her lips.

"Do you want me to touch you here?" she asked. Her fingers moved down to Victoria's dripping cunt.

"Yes," Victoria said.

"With my fingers or my mouth?"

Victoria sucked in her breath and cast all caution to the wind.

"Your mouth. Please." She hated the way it sounded like she was begging. But she was. She would beg and plead for Sarah to dance her tongue over the pulsing pearl between her legs.

Sarah's lips moved from the left to the right, giving each side equal attention now her map had been drawn.

Her fingers continued their menstruation against her nipples as she traveled down the valley to the peak of Victoria's hip. Tracing a lazy circle with her tongue, Victoria canted her chilled sex.

Pressing her hand to Victoria's knee, Sarah spread Victoria's legs. Her kiss turned into sucking and nipping as she worked her mouth over the soaked slit.

Sarah hooked her arm around Victoria's leg. She breathed out over the spread woman, staring up at the sparkling brown eyes watching her.

Victoria swallowed and tried to prepare for the sensation of Sarah's tongue stroking her, but nothing could have done so. Her head fell back with the first slow and steady swipe. Thoughts went fuzzy and the rest of her body became nonexistent because every atom in her being was spinning out of control.

She couldn't hold back the cries to a God she'd thought had abandoned her. The not-so-silent prayers fell from her lips with each caress, until Sarah lapped at that spot just to the left. Hips jumped against Victoria's will, but Sarah's grip pulled Victoria back to the bed.

"There," Victoria cried out. "Please, that... there."

Sarah circled another lap, only to return and press the weight of her tongue against the spot that made sparkles dance around Sarah's grinning green eyes looking up at her from between her thighs.

She spread her thighs wider, giving Sarah room. Her fingers found the back of the woman's head, holding her hair like a lifeline.

With her heart beating wildly in her chest, her pussy pulsed in rhythm with every stroke. She felt the fire building in her too quickly and her hips canted against the woman's face. She wanted to slow it down, but she couldn't stop the desperate need in her. The fire spread under her skin until she felt like she was ready to erupt.

Her world nearly collapsed when Sarah's fingers slipped within her. With each thrust of the woman's hand, her tongue pressed against that special spot on her clit.

Time was of no concern. Her own menstruation were too calculated to measure up to the unknowable pleasures she'd been missing throughout her life. As the fire turned to lava under her skin, she pleaded to the goddess between her thighs to not stop. Her throat became dry and her voice hoarse from the prayers. But she was not forsaken.

Sarah did not stop. She moved quicker and another finger stretched Victoria open in a deliciously devious manner. Plush lips wrapped around her clit and her tongue pressed against the full erect bud.

Victoria gasped for air as the cry broke from her lips. Every inch of her body tickled from the fire blazing within. Whatever imprint she'd had before was replaced with something deeper.

Her whole body became sensitive to every move Sarah made. The silky cavern clamped around Sarah's fingers like a vice grip. Legs locked the woman's head in place. She couldn't stop the waves rushing over her again and again.

Victoria couldn't feel the bed anymore. Her body moved with the waves of pleasure as her muscles moved until she floated to shore once more.

Breath tickled her core. The flesh was so sensitive she could feel the woman smiling without touching her.

When Victoria's legs relaxed enough to release Sarah, the woman moved carefully to Victoria's side. Sarah's icy skin chilled the sweat-soaked body, bringing her back to the bed from where she'd been floating. Her arms welcomed Victoria into a new reality. A reality Victoria would lay down her life to protect.

As she lay in Sarah's arms, she was grateful the tears did not fall like they had their first night together or their second.

Victoria looked at the clock. The numbers were fuzzy as she waited for the rest of her senses to return to her. Slowly the digits made sense, and a new plan was made with the hours she had before Lynny or Tris would be up.

It wasn't even seven yet. The game wasn't until ten. And Tris never woke before eight unless forced, which meant there was still time. And she would take every second of it.

Her hand pulled Sarah closer to her. When the woman pushed at her chest and giggled, Victoria raised the brat slayer and said, "I'm just getting started with you."

With a roll of her eyes, Sarah laughed. "Are you trying to top me?"

Victoria rolled her body over Sarah, pressing the woman into the mattress. She applied the new trick Sarah taught her and pressed against the woman's core with her thigh until the smug smirk of the O'Keeffe family line wiped itself from the woman's face.

"I don't know what topping means, but if it involves hearing you say my name until you cum on my tongue, then yes. I will be topping you, Sarah O'Keeffe."

And she did hear her name as her tongue traced each letter over Sarah's clit. She heard them again a half hour later when she moved her thumb in circles as the woman rode the silicon toy she'd purchased and hid within the nightstand. The vibration of the bullet buried in the base brought Victoria to another climax as Sarah's body bucked against her.

The two were a mess of sweat and tangled limbs when the bathroom next door slammed closed. Sarah had enough time to crawl off the cock still standing proud against Victoria's cunt.

But the handle to the master bedroom door wiggled, and then the door cracked. Victoria's body flew over the bed toward the window, the dangling dong slapping Sarah's sensitive core as Victoria landed on the floor with an "Umph!"

Sarah's body was barely covered by the sheet when the door fully opened to the unamused ten-year-old gawking at her.

"Where's Victoria?" Tris demanded. "She promised to make me pregame pancakes."

With a heavy sigh, Sarah waved at the bathroom. "She's peeing and will be down in a minute."

Tris' nose scrunched up as she looked at the door. "Eww. You and her pee with the door open."

After a brief pause, the girl found a new line of pebble-shaped questions to pelt Sarah with.

"Is that like an adult thing? Like, I'm just supposed to get used to peeing with people in the room?"

Victoria bit her hand from laughing as her body shivered. She pressed against the base of the bed so if the child did make her way over at least the dick strapped to her waist would be hidden."

"Do you only have to pee with people that you share a room with? Or is it like that's why the bathroom stalls have a huge gap?" Tris tapped her lips. "Do the gaps get bigger as you go to different schools so by college you just can pee with anyone there?"

A pillow flew through the air and smacked Tris in the face. When the angry girl glared at her, Sarah yelled, "Those are Aunt Monica questions. All of them. So, get out of my room and go call her on that cell phone she gave you or write them down to ask her after the game. I don't care as long as you get out and close the door."

51

Ice fought against the Gatorade bottles in the cooler in Victoria's arms. A cooler was purchased for the one assigned snack day of the season. There was enough for not only the ten girls on the team but for the siblings of every kid as well.

Sarah carried the box of drawstring backpacks with the basketball Victoria had found on Amazon. She shook her head at the level of extra her girlfriend was. Victoria had gone as far as to buy a cricket machine. Putting the niece to work, the two Brentons individually pressed each kid's name to a bag and filled it with multiple snacks and individually sewn hair ribbons to match their uniforms.

"The other parents are going to hate us," Sarah growled. "It's the first game and you set the snack expectation ridiculously high."

The epic smile plastered on Victoria's face gave absolutely zero fucks. Sarah's legs had barely recovered from the pregame party that morning, but they weakened at the knowledge Victoria didn't care about the petty competitions between helicopter parents. Victoria had done what she did because she wanted Tris's first game to be extra.

A soft wave of sadness stroked her ankles, but she waded through. She'd never been able to give Tris the extras. But as the girl ran to greet her teammates now her focus wasn't on the new hair band tied over her braids or the expensive flamboyant shoes Victoria had put on her feet like the other girls. She was taking a ball from the coach to work on her ball control. Yeah, Sarah hadn't done so bad.

The ice chest slapped to the ground alongside the bleachers. Sarah's brows rose when she found Echo with a toddler in her lap and Parker leaning back in the stands. With a simple chin nod, Echo acknowledged their arrival. Parker's head rolled to the side, then her eyes fell to the crest of Victoria's cleavage.

"Why is your friend's sister staring at your tits?" Sarah growled as the box was taken from her hands.

Victoria's eyes snapped up to Parker. The woman pressed the sides of her boobs together and then flicked Victoria a thumbs up. A blush crept up Victoria's face, earning her a smack against the arm from her girlfriend.

"When I was... she just used to help me figure out how to dress and she's telling me I got my boobs right this time."

Sarah didn't like it. She had nothing against the woman, but she still didn't like it.

"Why are they here?" Sarah asked.

Victoria shrugged. "Thursday, I told them it was Tris's first game and Echo asked for the details. I didn't think they would actually come. Jen said she'd be here though too."

Echo handed off her daughter to a teenager who'd come in and sat alongside them. "Which one's yours?" Echo asked.

"Number 2," Sarah said, pointing to the girl working on field shots.

"Why number 2? Vicky said the kid is like a badass." Echo followed Tris's move across the floor. "I got a friend who plays for the WNBA. She's overseas right now but when she gets back, we should get her to do some one-on-ones. She owes me for starting a fight in my bar a few months ago."

"Or you could ask your fuck buddy Sylvia Winters," Parker said. She waved to the name painted over the scoreboard. "I mean, she owns the gym and the Devils."

Victoria and Sarah both watched as Echo's face grew hot and the hat atop her head was pressed down tightly. "So... uh... the number?" Echo asked after a moment.

"My best friend Monica, she was number 1 when she played ball in college and Tris has always been her second, so she chose number 2." Sarah found a lock of hair that had come loose from her messy bun. She wrapped it around until it disappeared with the rest. "Tris met someone that plays for the Devils when she got her hair done. She's convinced she's going to play for the NWBA someday."

Tris moved through the lay-up line until she accepted the pass and took off toward the basket.

"Thanks for coming," Sarah said.

"No problem. Parker and I kinda have this thing. We never had anyone growing up and Vicky said you were kinda like us... except the whole getting locked up thing for being a criminal." Echo pulled out her phone and snapped a few pictures of Tris mid-layup. "So, we decided we're going to start our own family tradition and Vicky's family whether she knew it or not. And we are going to be the badass aunties that go to every game and every school event. So, we got this game, and then our friend Charleigh's kid plays next. We get it if that's not your thing... I wouldn't expect you to..."

Sarah shook away the possibility of exclusion. She'd always wanted people. "We'll be there. You just tell us when."

"Cool."

"You know she hates being called Vicky?" Sarah shared as Victoria ran after a ball.

"Yep," Echo leaned back. "I told her when she stops snapping the tips off her darts she could be called whatever she wants. Until then, she's Viscous Vicky."

The bench creaked as a set of hurried footsteps made their way to them. A heavy handbag hit the metal, and an older woman landed with an oomph.

"Did I miss anything?" Naomi Brenton huffed out. "I swear Lynny drives like she is 90 years old."

"Mom?" Victoria choked out coming back to the bleachers. "What are you doing here?"

Naomi waved at Victoria as she searched the team chairs for Tris. "It's my granddaughter's first game. You and your sisters were always too uncoordinated for sports, but you couldn't really think I would miss her first game."

Sarah stared at the metal seats filling up around them. Other grandparents were in attendance, but her mother couldn't be bothered to call on the kid's birthday let alone fly from a different state to sit in the stands for 45 minutes.

"Thanks for coming," Sarah said.

Naomi took Sarah's hand in her own as she raised the other to wave at the girl jumping with an ear-to-ear smile.

"You got this!" Naomi shouted across the court. "She's going to be quite the beauty with all those eyelashes. Going to have to beat the boys off with a stick." Naomi's shoulders shrugged and she squeezed Sarah's hand lightly. "Or the girls. Whatever she wants."

With a determined walk, Monica arrived when the girls were taking the court. She raised her foot as she stared at Tris, standing at the back of the center circle to receive the ball, and wiped her hand over the bottom of her shoe. With a nod of her chin, Tris followed suit. Her gangly legs raised so she could wipe at the bottom of her shoes. Monica approved of the action as Tris's shoes squeaked against the floor.

Tossing a pair of new Nike slides in Sarah's lap, Monica said, "She can't wear her shoes outside. It messes up the grip."

With a roll of her eyes, Sarah handed the shoes to Victoria. Victoria studied them looking ashamed that she hadn't known to get some when she'd bought out Dick's sporting goods.

"Can she wear them when she is practicing in the driveway?" the woman asked. "I just put up a new hoop."

"Just have her wear regular sneakers. Court shoes are for the gym only." Monica took a seat in front of Sarah. Her whole body leaned forward on her knees. "We shoulda done this years ago instead of fucking Girl Scouts. Like sports parents are normal. Girl Scout moms are so extra with their need to Circut a damn decal or a name on every little thing!"

Tris took the ball down the court in a fast break. Halfway in the air, a girl in blue shoved Tris back. The girl's body hit the ground but the shot sunk.

"Where's the foul!" Monica was back on her feet, yelling at a kid just trying to earn $20. "Did you swallow your whistle?"

Victoria's eyes grew wide. Sarah leaned into her girlfriend's space and whispered, "This is why I chose Girl Scouts."

Sarah shouldn't have been surprised when Jen raged into the stands, demanding space for herself and her distracted duplicate. She plopped behind Victoria only to notice the broody bartender.

"Yellow or blue?" Jen asked Echo, eyes falling on the chiseled bicep.

Echo glanced over Jen, running her eyes down the woman's body to the blonde kid tapping on a tablet next to her.

"Yellow."

Jen hummed in approval. "Me too."

"Who you here for?" Echo asked. Her toddler had made it back into her lap and was busy pushing the mother's cheeks together.

"Shit. I don't know," Jen tapped Victoria on the top of the head. "What's the kid's number?"

"Two," Monica growled, not giving Victoria a chance to claim her again.

Jen smiled. "Two."

Echo's smile rose to her eyes. "Us too. I'm Mormon Barbie's best friend."

Jen's eyes narrowed. She grabbed the ponytail at the back of Victoria's head and yanked her backward. "What's this bullshit about you having another best friend?"

Victoria whined, trying to get out of Jen's hold. "Babe, help."

Sarah gave the preposterous woman behind them a side-eyed glare. "My hair to pull. Now stop being basic. She has more than one friend."

Victoria's fingers rubbed the roots of her hair when her head was pushed back forward. With a wave of her wrist, she supplied introductions. "Jen. Echo. Echo. Jen."

"Don't mix your gays," Sarah stated.

Victoria's brows furrowed. "Huh?"

Parker leaned forward and stole Echo's Gatorade. She twisted off the cap as she explained, "It means don't mix friend groups. You already got a basic taste of lesbian dating drama but now these two will probably hook up by the way they are sizing each other up, so thanks for that."

"It's true," Monica stated. "The community is small. You can't date someone that someone else hasn't dated. Six degrees of separation is probably more like four in lesboland."

Monica was on her feet again. "Ref, where's your glasses? My girl is fighting just to stand!"

The teen in the bulky black and white uniform let out a heavy sigh and ran back to the other side of the court.

"Is it just the two of you?" Echo asked Jen.

"Yep." Jen nodded to the toddler. "You and her."

Echo nudged the teen buried in a sketchbook behind her. "Three of us."

Monica received a warning at the end of the first quarter. If she opened her mouth again, she'd be asked to leave by a high schooler with a whistle. Echo started taking bets by the quarter and Sarah put $5 on Monica being removed just after halftime. By half time the woman's face was glowing brighter than a stop light but her yelling had turned to angry growls.

"Where's Lynny?" Sarah asked, realizing she was missing as the minutes ticked down.

"She was waiting in the parking lot for her girlfriend," Naomi stated. "Apparently, the woman got lost."

Sarah's question seemed to have beckoned the girl's return. Lynny moved through the standing parents and siblings unable to get a seat due to the crowd Victoria had brought. The girl's fingers were intertwined with another's.

Sarah tapped Victoria's arm until the dark eyes rose and followed Sarah's finger.

"No way," Victoria whispered. The woman's head twisted back to Echo and slapped the woman's leg. Echo in turn hit Parker.

Sarah had no idea who the woman with Lynny was, but it was clear the other three did.

"I can't believe she—" but Parker cut herself off.

Echo narrowed her eyes at the woman looking equally perplexed. "I swear to god she is never allowed back in my bar again."

"Who is she?" Sarah asked. And Naomi had leaned over to participate in the gossip as well.

They missed Tris's basket, but Monica was already on her feet yelling for the girl whose eyes only looked to her first for approval.

"Remember the date..." Victoria swallowed and didn't finish the rest of her sentence.

Victoria put her arm over Sarah who was still watching the scene unfold. The date was overly vague for Sarah. Victoria hadn't been on a date. There was the girl she was supposed to go out with... but... oh.

"Uh... this is Tanya. She and I are..." Lynny's smile had faltered some when she stood before her family. Seeing Victoria and her friends with matching glares, she tucked her hair behind her ear. "We... we met at Echo's Escape. The gay bar in downtown Phoenix."

"Yeah, I know the place." Victoria turned back to Echo. "She's nineteen, how the hell did she get into your bar?"

"Dude, we ID. What more can I do?" Echo's head rolled back to Parker. "You didn't serve her right?"

The redhead shrugged. "Who the hell knows? If they come to the bar, they made it through the door. Maybe it was when Caris was working the door. She sucks."

"She's my baby cousin," Victoria groaned. Her eyes turned to the woman who'd kissed her. "When did you even meet her?"

"I met her... and I canceled our date," Tanya said. "I mean, it's clearly not like you were that interested in me anyway."

Sarah leaned into Victoria, then looked back at Echo. "Could be worse. She coulda showed up with Simone?"

"Fuck that bitch," Monica growled. Her hands shot out, but the words stayed quiet. "Come on, that was totally a foul. That girl is trying to climb up Tris's back."

Victoria's face paled. But Naomi's attention was now torn between the game and the drama.

"Who's Simone?" the mother asked.

Sarah tapped her chest. "My ex."

"And mine," Echo added.

Jen raised a brow. "I was friends with a Simone like four years ago. Psycho pretended to be my friend and then tripped when I wouldn't sleep with her."

Victoria glanced back. "That's the one you told me about."

"That sounds like my ex-wife," Echo growled.

"Sounds like delicious drama for an old woman," Naomi said, squeezing Sarah's hand once more. "Maybe you can share the story before I leave."

Her eyes followed Tris as the kid cut through the key, popping out between the defense to accept the pace.

The shitty human was forgotten as the stands erupted with Tris' two-point field shot. Victoria was up on her feet competing against Monica for who could yell the loudest.

"That's my girl!" Victoria claimed.

"She learned that from her favorite aunt," Monica barked.

Sarah leaned into Naomi's steady frame. Their hands remained clasped as the others jumped from their seats periodically.

"Means a lot that you came," Sarah said to the woman. "Not only to Tris but to me. We... you know."

Naomi patted their conjoined hands. Her smile-weathered eyes didn't search Sarah's face for meaning. She just chuckled lightly.

"Well, I want to be here, but I am also hoping to convince you all to come back for Christmas. Maybe we trade off on the travel."

"I'll talk to Victoria," Sarah promised. Always up for an exchange of favors. "I don't think she would necessarily be against it."

By the end of the game, Sarah couldn't be certain of who was more excited with the first win or the player of the week award: the kid, the girlfriend, or the favorite aunt. It didn't matter though because people were there to give Tris high fives and hugs. Shrouded the girl in a secure bubble of support.

52

The struggle with the zipper to the hoodie was no joke. The teeth were misaligned and no matter how hard it was tugged it didn't want to break free. She yanked it by the sides trying to pull it apart but contrary to her namesake, Victoria possessed no such superhuman strength. The energy and effort weren't worth it when it became clear the sweatshirt was the stronger opponent. So, she ripped the material over her head and dropped it to the floor.

Shoes kicked off, one hitting the wall as it came to rest against the door. The other flew a few feet down the hall, rolling to a stop definitely in the middle of the floor.

The lock was flipped, and the soaked jeans were stripped off. Huffing and puffing, Victoria dropped her shirt next, but the air in the house nipped at her mostly nude form.

"You survived," Sarah said from her seat on the couch. The blanket covering the woman was pulled back to reveal the set of joggers and the BYU shirt.

Victoria's grumble wasn't words, let alone sentences. Just a mixture of grunts and half the syllables of an incoherent thought as she climbed onto Sarah's lap. The blanket did not even get pulled over her freezing form before she pushed the frozen fingers under Sarah's shirt.

"Fuck you off," Sarah cried out, with a knee to the crotch Victoria tumbled half-naked to the floor. She pulled the fuzzy blanket up to her chin and scowled at her lover. "No, ma'am. I am not your personal heater."

The wine in the glass felt heavy because Sarah had yet to learn that wine isn't filled to the brim. She took a sip, ignoring Victoria's roll to her side.

"You kneed me..." Victoria gasped as her head hit the rug, "... in the peeper!"

Sarah almost sprayed the red wine over her favorite coach, the rug, and the woman. She pressed her fingers to her lips, the spicy juice now bubbly as she swallowed more than a sip.

"Peeper?" Sarah choked. "What the hell is a peeper?"

Victoria's fingers covered her aching core.

Sarah's eyebrows rose. "Vagina. Pussy. Cunt. Crotch. All age-appropriate terms. Oh my god! When you were a kid did you have to call it your flower?"

Fingers reached up from the floor. They found the edge of the blanket. With a sharp tug, the material was free from the cruel lover on the couch as Sarah moved to catch her glass.

"Everything okay down there?" Lynny called from the top of the stairs. "I heard a bang."

"Just your aunt bruising her peeper," Sarah called up.

Victoria wrapped the blanket around her body and flopped down on top of Sarah's legs. She wiggled until the other woman gave her space, and then she curled up between Sarah's thighs.

"It's Arizona. Why is it so damn cold?" Victoria asked through the chattering of her teeth.

"You were just complaining you had no use for the seven jackets you bought," Sarah quipped.

"Why do I love you?" Victoria glared up at the woman. But the question only earned her a shrug.

Sarah's fingers pushed the wet hair from Victoria's face. "You didn't have to load the car tonight while it was pouring."

"I had to get the presents hidden," Victoria whined. "We didn't make plans soon enough so only half her presents were able to be shipped directly to my parent's house."

"Real question," Sarah said. But she didn't ask her question, she took another sip of wine. Only once she passed the glass to Victoria, did she seem to remember she started a conversation.

"Oh, yeah. So, there is a Santa, right?"

Victoria sat up. She studied the woman expectantly waiting for her response, then the glass in her hand.

Then it occurred to Victoria that maybe Sarah hadn't been told the truth of Santa. With her life, maybe she genuinely didn't know.

"So, Santa is based on this story. Like, there are hundreds of different versions in various cultures that had a figure who brings gifts to children." Victoria took a sip. She enjoyed the tingling heat it caused in her chest as she swallowed. Then she picked up, "I'm not sure I am one to say Santa is not real, but I don't know how much the whole flying reindeer and toy-making elves can be true. He probably was a person, but you know it sounds more like something a woman would do so I wouldn't be surprised if it was really Satana Clause, but some white guy said I will tell the story and make it more believable by making it a guy."

She turned back to find Sarah's mouth ajar. The wrinkle between her brows had deepened.

Victoria tightened her fingers around the blanket. Her skin prickled as she felt the woman's eyes examining her. Mind running through the possibilities of what other explanation she could have given. They hadn't really had the personal theologies talk, but come on Santa? The woman couldn't believe Santa was real. Like she didn't even want to believe love or chemistry was real when they met.

"Did you just give me a history lesson on Santa Claus?" Sarah asked.

"Yesss?"

Sarah reached over and took back her glass. "You..."

Finger to her chest, Victoria asked, "Me what?"

"You are so weird sometimes."

The dimpled chin jutted forward as Victoria balked at her. "ME?"

"Yes, you." Sarah took another drink.

Tapping her chest again. Victoria snipped, "I answered your weirdo question."

"No, you didn't," Sarah said into the mouth of the glass. "I was asking if you had Santa as a kid."

Victoria's mouth fell open a little wider.

"You look like you're trying to catch flies," Sarah said. She leaned forward and looked into Victoria's mouth. "Also, you have spinach in your teeth. I told you that stuff was out to get us, but you insisted, 'it's healthy and we have to eat it.'"

"Really, the high-pitched voice?" Victoria snapped. "We both know I do not have a high-pitched voice."

Sarah hummed against the rim. The wine's color seemed to seep through Sarah's skin. She smiled as her head rolled against the couch. "So... Santa. Do I have to tell Tris your family are non-believers or are we good to go?"

"Mormons believe in Santa, yes." Victoria snuggled back into Sarah's lap. Her body began to return to normal temperature.

Victoria glanced at the table when Sarah's phone went off again. She read as Scam slinked like a snake across the screen.

"Hey, babe. Do you have like a bill in collections or something?" Victoria asked.

"Nope." Sarah took another drink. "No credit cards. No car payment. No bills in my name. I mean not that I know of, but I have both mine and my sister's paperwork so it's not like she could open something in my name."

Victoria logged that information into her mind for a future conversation. If Sarah had nothing in her name, that meant she had no credit. She could help with that though. Economics was her jam after all.

"So, why does Scam keep calling you?"

Sarah leaned over Victoria. Her breasts pressed against Victoria's face as she picked up the phone and ignored the call.

"It's my mom."

Victoria looked up at Sarah. "You have your mom saved in your phone as Scam?"

"Yeah... We still haven't found the damn TV remote." Sarah used her phone as a TV remote to turn on *The Grinch that Stole Christmas.*

Victoria patiently waited for more details.

With a heavy sigh, Sarah added, "Tris told me she answered my phone when my mom called. She told Tris it was my birthday, and she needed our address so she could send me a card. My sister broke in a few days later... so I changed the name so Tris wouldn't think to answer it again."

There wasn't anything else to say. Victoria could ask why her mother was calling but it would be a really dumb question. If it was an emergency, it was clear Sarah didn't care. If it was about money, it was better for Sarah to not answer. But also, Sarah had no real way of knowing why she was being called unless she answered, and for once she appreciated that Sarah was taking the path of least resistance. Maybe she really was feeling secure enough to cut ties with the people who plagued her.

"I'm going to grab some dry clothes," Victoria said.

"More wine and popcorn when you come back," Sarah requested.

With a towel wrapped around her head, a bag of popcorn, the bottle of wine, and her own glass, Victoria made her way back to the living room where the gas fireplace burned just hot enough to make the ice in her bones melt. Her path was diverted back to the kitchen when her phone threatened to tumble from the table to the floor with the vibration dance it was suddenly partaking in.

"Hey Ech—"

"Turn on channel 5," Echo demanded.

"Channel 5?" Victoria asked, heading back to the living room. "Why? What's happening? Is the world ending?"

"Oh my god! I just... Is Sarah home?"

"Yeah, she's here." Victoria dropped the popcorn on the table and set down the bottle and glass. Then she tossed Sarah's phone at her, "Echo says turn on Channel 5."

Sarah's lower lip protruded into a soft pout. She pointed at the TV, "But the Grinch is about to get ready to be Cheer Master."

Victoria turned her phone on speaker as Echo continued to ramble. *"Do you see? Oh my god, Brenton. Tell me you see this shit."*

With a heavy sigh, Sarah flipped the channel using her phone since the remote was still missing, though Victoria was positive no one had tried to look for it.

A plastic-faced reporter read through the teleprompter as she stood outside the sign for Cactus High School.

"... the student said she had reported being kicked out of her home by her mother. She turned to her school for support and that is when the student claims the assistant principal, Simone Wyatt offered her a place to live in exchange for sexual favors."

The coverage cut from the reporter to a fuzzy-faced teen. The voice had been altered, but it didn't change the account.

"She told me I could come stay with her. I thought it would be better than staying at a homeless shelter and since I was already eighteen, I couldn't go into foster care. But when I got to her house, she took me to the room I was supposed to be sleeping in, but it was her room. And I just keep thinking, like, how many other girls has she done this too?"

Victoria watched as Sarah leaned against her knees. Her jaw ground, as she pointed to the screen. "I know that kid. I just... I know that kid."

"Simone Wyatt has been put on administrative leave, as the matter is investigated. We reached out to Ms. Wyatt; however, she has been unavailable at this time for comment."

Echo continued shouting but her words were lost as Victoria watched

Sarah's hands squeeze the cotton of her pants. Green eyes rose to brown, but neither had a chance to say a word before the doorbell rang.

Victoria looked at the time on her phone. It was past ten. Without a goodbye, Victoria said, "Echo, I have to go," and she hung up the phone.

"Are you expecting someone?" Victoria asked even though Sarah's eyes were staring at the exit to the living. When Sarah didn't move, Victoria tried to come up with a reason someone would be at their door so late. With a shrug, she said, "Probably just Tanya coming to surprise Lynny before we leave tomorrow."

The bell rang again, and when Sarah still didn't move from the couch, Victoria took it as her cue to answer.

She checked the peephole, relieved to at least recognize the woman on the other side of the door. The relief rusted as the oxygen mixed with the rain. Evie's hair was slicked back into a tight bun, and she stood in full uniform on the other side of the threshold.

"Hey Victoria," Evie said. Her nose wasn't held as high, and her hand hung from the top of the vest clasped over her chest. "Is Sarah here?"

Victoria wet her lips. Scanning Lyra looking at the ground beside Evie and the other woman wrapped in an oversized sweater on the other side, the world seemed to tilt just enough to make Victoria grip the door a little tighter.

"Hey Sarah," Evie said.

Victoria turned to find Sarah standing just behind her.

"Is she...?" Sarah stopped talking and Victoria turned back to Evie softly nodding.

"She was found in a motel off 3rd Ave. The M.E. says she definitely passed due to an overdose." Evie tugged at the vest. "Can we come in?"

Victoria didn't hold the door open for them. She moved to the woman who had careened off course as the first words hit Sarah. The woman's knees hit the floor as she cradled Sarah's limp body in her arms. The limbs didn't quiver, and the chest didn't quake. Tears didn't fall as the cemetery grass irises gazed up as though she were trying to search the clouds.

"I forgot to tell her I loved her the last time I saw her," Sarah whimpered. "I told myself to tell her I love her because I never knew... I never..."

She closed her eyes. Her head shook.

"This is my fault. I shoulda gotten her help. I... I did this."

Hands held the lithe frame. Victoria pressed her lips to the hair. She inhaled the blackberry custard of the woman's shampoo, remembering when Sarah had made her house a home. Sarah brought life where she'd found loneliness, and now Victoria would hold the frames of the house up to ensure the roof would still be there when the rain stopped falling.

It took time to get up from the floor. Bones cracked and muscles wobbled. The uninvited women of wary news had made their way into the living room and waited patiently for Sarah.

Victoria walked Sarah to the armchair. Rather than sit, she stood alongside her girlfriend. Because Victoria knew Sarah was like the Titanic and the guests an iceberg. The collision between them had done enough damage to sink the brunette, but Sarah was only taking on the water presently. Still afloat, for now.

"I'm sorry, Sarah," Evie said. She rubbed her stomach. "I... I was the responding officer. I... called my sisters. Sadie, she... uh... she works for DCS."

Victoria's eyes shot up the stairs. The door to the girl's bedroom was thankfully still closed.

"I brought them because... look," Evie pulled at her vest again. "Zoe told me about your kid and how your sister signed you over guardianship. My mom, I mean, we all thought Tris was yours. But, as next of kin—"

Sarah's body jumped from the chair. The wooden legs scraped against the floor. The woman moved to her purse hanging from the hook Victoria had hung just in the spot where she put her bag. She pulled out the papers and held them out to Sadie.

The pages shook with every tremble Sarah couldn't hide. "I have them, and they're notarized and everything. I get them updated every six months. My sister... she never even met Tris. And I have a job. A steady job. I can show you my check stubs. I don't have a lease or anything but Victoria... she owns this house, and we live here. I can show you. I can show you that all of Tris's stuff is here. She has her own room and her own bed. She goes to school. She is enrolled in the school where... I work there. And..."

Lyra held up her hands and got up from the couch. She reached out and took the papers from Sarah, then she took the trembling hand in her own.

"Take a breath, Sarah." Lyra breathed in slowly, then out. "I know you're scared, and I know you think we are here to take away your child."

"You can't take her," Victoria snapped. "No, you can't. Even if... even if you won't give Sarah custody, I'm licensed. I finished my foster care classes, and I submitted all my paperwork, and we can call the after-hours line and I have a single bed approved."

"You said you changed your mind," Sarah whispered. Her eyes studied Victoria. "You said you started the classes but stopped because Tris and I..."

Victoria turned to Sarah. "I was worried when you were working so much. And I just thought, it was another layer of security if I finished the classes, so if something happened to you, then Tris wouldn't have to go into the system. I... I don't want it to be like that but if it has to... I'll do it. I'll do whatever it takes because I love you and I love her and we're going to get through this."

A soft clearing of the throat pulled Sarah and Victoria's eyes to the DCS worker. She offered them both a polite smile and promised, "No one is taking Trisaya away. I'm just here to find out how I can support you, Sarah. There will be a formal hearing in a few days where you can take over permanent custody without any state interference, but tonight I just need to fill out some forms that prove Trisaya is with you and is safe."

"She's asleep," Sarah whispered. "She's a hard sleeper. I don't want to wake her up to tell her. Not like this. But I can open the door so you can see she's here."

Sadie nodded. "That is more than sufficient for tonight."

Sarah's hand was squeezed by Lyra once more. "Sarah, I'm going to represent you at the hearing for custody. I'm a lawyer and normally I represent the state, but this is a personal matter. Don't worry about any fees and it's not like a trial. I just promised Mom that I would stand next to you so if you had any questions, I could answer them for you."

Sarah nodded, then broke her contact with Lyra. Her arms hung at her sides. The subtle rise and fall of her shoulders were the only sign of life in Sarah. The television continued to play in the background and Echo's attention was drawn to the scene.

"Is that Echo's ex?" she asked. "Wait."

Victoria didn't wait. "Yeah. Echo just called before you... It's been a lot tonight."

Victoria wrapped an arm around Sarah's waist. She asked, "When is the hearing?"

"Well since Christmas is on a Wednesday this year, it will be pushed back until Friday," Lyra explained. She looked at the Christmas tree without any presents underneath. "Were you planning a trip?"

"Salt Lake," Victoria croaked. "We are supposed to leave for my parents' house tomorrow."

Lyra's smile dropped. "I'm sorry. But until the hearing, Tris cannot leave the state."

Sarah rubbed her face. "It's okay. You... you and Lynny can go. Should go. We will... we will wait for Santa here. You know. She'll understand and you can bring back her present from Naomi and it will be okay."

Victoria took Sarah's face in her hands. Her thumbs smoothed over the woman's cheeks. "We're staying home. All of us. I'll call my mom, and she'll understand. Trust me, okay?"

"Okay."

Sadie fumbled with the papers in her bag. She withdrew a hefty stack and placed them on the coffee table with a pen atop.

"Let's get these signed so we can give you all the space." Sadie nodded to her sister. "Could you and... Victoria?"

"Yeah," Victoria affirmed. "That's me."

"Okay. Victoria, will you take Evie upstairs so she can peek in on Trisaya while Sarah and I get these all filled out?"

"Tris," Sarah whispered. "Her name is Tris."

Victoria didn't want to leave Sarah's side. Her heart felt as though to walk away would be tearing a part of herself in two. But Tris needed her to go upstairs, and Sarah needed to sign the papers.

"Sure."

Each step seemed to creak under their weight. The house refused the silence it had been accustomed to when Victoria was its only occupant. But the joy and laughter and sometimes screaming had breathed the home into life. So, as the women within pushed through the panic to the pause, the house grieved for them. Protesting every disturbance to their normal.

Victoria opened the door just enough to let the hallway light fall over the girl asleep sideways in the bed. How Tris managed to shift a full ninety degrees was beyond Victoria, but the satin bonnet lay halfway off the girl's head. Her stuffed sushi squished awkwardly under her arm. And her soft snores and snorts sang to the women in the doorway.

When Victoria closed the door, Evie nodded back to the stairs. At the base, Evie pulled a card from her vest. "This is my number. Text me tomorrow and I will have information regarding where Sarah can claim her sister's remains or if she has any other family, then you can give me their information and I'll reach out."

"Thank you," Victoria said. She took the card and ran her finger over the imprint. "Please, thank your sisters also for coming. I doubt this is... normal."

Evie shrugged. "My parents adopted all of us. When I saw... Jesus, at first, I thought it was Sarah. I mean, I didn't know she had a twin. Zoe said she had a sister, but I didn't realize... And I had to call Parker and that girl hates me, so I am pretty sure Lyra wants to kick my ass because I scared the shit out of her girlfriend. She told me Sarah lives with you, so I looked you up in the DMV database and we came here."

Evie tugged at her vest. "I can't stand my sisters most of the time. But losing one. This is going to be hard on her so let me know if you need anything. Anything at all. And uh... expect my mom to show up with her partner because Sarah is important to our family."

"Thank you," Victoria said again. "I just... it's been a long night."

Lyra and Sadie came around the corner. Sadie pushed the papers deeper into her purse.

"You got everything?" Evie asked.

They left without goodbyes. The door slipped closed, and the click of the latch and the lock was drowned out by the Titanic snapping in two. The scream muffled by the shirt Sarah's teeth sunk into as her soul seemed to shatter. Collapsing to the couch to cry, cradling cushions created comfort.

Victoria blazed to the weary woman pounding pillows with fists of fire. Angered anguish spewed septic waste in words of catastrophic curses.

Survivor's guilt tainted the spells and prayers Sarah used to bargain and plead for a different outcome. Nothing she could do would change the events. Because as she'd read to Victoria from the top of the patio:

Today was the first day of Sarah's life. The first day of being untwined from her twin.

53

The marble hallway of the courthouse echoed. The borrowed black heels matched the black dress wrapped around her waist. Sarah had purchased the dress for a different type of date, but it clung modestly enough to her frame to make her more presentable before a judge than in her cigarette-singed button-up.

The elevator didn't move smoothly. It jerked some on the ascent, making Sarah's stomach drop. She felt like was going to be sick, but the child between her and Victoria was on a different rollercoaster of grief than Sarah. There had been tears two days before Christmas, but Tris's grief would be different from Sarah's. She knew this but Parker came over to draw with the girl because it turns out she was the friend Monica wanted Sarah to contact about therapy for Tris before all of this happened.

Parker warned Sarah and Victoria that Tris's grief would come in waves. Said at this point they could expect what would feel like random outbursts that Tris wouldn't be able to identify as grief. She warned them both that even though it would be difficult, they would need to avoid any major changes to Tris's schedule even though she didn't have a relationship with Sierra. That the reality of her mother's death would not set in all at once as it had with Sarah.

The truth of Parker's words was evident in the wide smile plastered on Tris's face. Sarah held tightly to Tris's hand, even though the girl showed no fear when the elevator opened. She led from the middle, pulling Sarah and Victoria forward. They couldn't keep up as she made her way to the courtroom.

Standing beside the bolted-down metal chairs in the lobby, Sarah was surprised to find people once again. There were more people than Sarah had thought to reach out to, causing her to pause even though Tris was trying to tug her forward.

"What's wrong," Tris demanded when she couldn't move as fast as she wanted.

Sarah scanned the lobby outside the courtroom. Victoria's league of lesbians lounged in the metal chairs and leaned into the crevices of the space. Echo and Jen shared a smile. Each held onto their daughters' hands as the kids took turns sticking their tongues out at each other. Monica had found a column to press her foot against like she was posing for a picture. Parker didn't have her hands on her girlfriend's boobs, but she was addressing the placement of Lyra's necklace. Sarah offered Dilynn Greyson a smile, who waved at them from beside her partner. Evie was also there, along with her sister, Sadie. These women had each played a role in Sarah and Victoria's lives, but it still surprised Sarah they'd all come today.

What had Sarah's feet rooted in place though was the Brenton women gathered in a syndicate of sisterhood around the matriarch. The modest skirts hung to the women's knees in a cacophony of floral designs. They'd arrived in a swarm the day after sharing Christmas with their children. The littles were left with their frantic fathers who'd been calling in waves as they learned to demands of the large households the so-called led. The calls were answered as Victoria explained the function of an LDS relief group.

Apparently, Naomi had activated the phone tree before getting on the first flight to Phoenix two days before Christmas. She'd carried and packed as many of the gifts Victoria had shipped directly to Salt Lake, leaving all her clothes behind to get to the house. She knew Naomi was coming with Lynny, but she didn't expect the rest of Victoria's sisters to come.

Sarah smoothed away the wrinkles from her dress when Tris dropped her hand and ran to Monica. She tried to make herself worthy of all the support, but that wasn't a feeling that came naturally to her.

"You're going to do great," Victoria promised, sealing it with a kiss to her temple. "Lyra said all you have to do is agree. They won't ask for proof of anything. You've been her mother her entire life. Now you'll be it on paper."

Sarah nodded because she understood. But it didn't make her hands shake any less. Without Tris to support, she found herself unable to chase away the terror. Her entire body was shivering while the heater had made her pits uncomfortably damp. She tried to remember if she'd put on deodorant, but nothing really seemed to stay in her head since Evie and her sisters had rang the doorbell.

"O'Keeffe," a small woman called out from the courtroom door.

"We're here!" Tris called out. She returned to Sarah's side and took hers and Victoria's hands once more. Her sure feet stopped once inside because no one knew where they were actually supposed to sit. Luckily Emori squeezed by them and gestured to a table on the other side a three-foot railing.

Tris didn't allow Victoria to release her hand, forcing the woman to follow within the area and sit next to her. Sarah and Victoria shared a worried glance but decided not to fight what the girl wanted.

The judge cleared his throat as the quiet room bustled to life with more bodies than there were seats. His eyes widened as the two sides of the family intermingled between both sides of the courtroom. Jen and Echo's littles found rest on the laps of the sisters cooing to them.

"My, this is quite the showing," he said with a warm smile. His eyes dropped to Tris with her hands still holding onto both women. "You must be Trisaya."

"Just Tris, sir. I mean, judge, sir. Or is it sir, judge?" Tris didn't wait for an answer. "Are you a real judge though if this isn't a real trial with a crime?"

The girl's eyes grew, and her hands dropped her adults to wave in the air. "Wait. Are you the person that decides if someone is ugly enough for prison? If so, is my mom really too pretty prison? Because my aunt says she is but like how do you decide because sometimes she doesn't shower for a few days and she smells like the spaghetti tubs she leaves in the car? Can smell make someone ugly enough for prison?"

The courtroom broke out into low rumble as Sarah's mouth dropped open and the blood fled her face. No one laughed harder than the judge, bringing a scowl to Tris' pinched lips.

She leaned over to Sarah. "I don't think he's a real judge."

"Shut it," Sarah growled.

Waving a hand in the air, the crowd calmed before the smile on the man's face became more serious. "I am a judge, Ms. Tris, and I can promise you that I don't use prettiness as a determination for prison time."

Tris looked over her shoulder at Monica, then back to Sarah. "Guess this means you can't kill Aunt Monica for letting me watch SpongeBob."

The rumble of amusement faded quicker this round, and the process moved forward.

"Ms. Tris," the judge began. "Do you understand why we are here today?"

Sarah squeezed the girl's hand as she stood up like Lyra had coached her to do.

"My mom's sister is now a zombie in Heaven. I know she's a zombie because she did a lot of drugs and Mom said she didn't like to wear long skirts so she can't be an angel on Earth haunting some old house. And Ms. Parker said you're going to hit your wood hammer on your desk and make it so my mom is finally my mom. But you should know she's always been my mom so hammering or not won't change that."

The judge nodded. He opened his mouth but didn't get the chance to acknowledge beyond his nod.

"But could you use that hammer thing to make Victoria my other mom?" Tris reached down and held up Victoria's hand. "Mom and Victoria aren't married. But I read kids with two adults have a better chance of going to college and making lots of money. So, if you could use your hammer to make Victoria my other mom... that would make me more likely to not be a zombie in Heaven because I don't like dresses either and big houses are creepy and probably crowded with all the angel ladies scaring people."

Tris took a short breath, then kept going. "And I was searching up stuff on what my mom told my aunt was an inappropriate Christmas gift last year, and I read that kids whose moms did drugs are more likely to do drugs. And I don't think that will be me, but I looked up what things make it so kids don't wanna do drugs and it said having two parents made it not going to happen. So, you should use your hammer today and give me two real moms. I mean, I know that it would mean that I would have three moms, but my mom who died, I never met her, so this would mean I really have two moms. And Victoria is a great mom like my mom is a great mom, so can you do that for, like, a Christmas present. I don't think my mom would call that one inappropriate."

No one laughed this time. Sarah's eyes were locked on Victoria, who was staring at Tris. Her face shifted between fear to adoration and back to fear.

Victoria squeezed Tris's hand. "Hun, that's not... we are not here to... your mom and I need to talk."

Tris's lips crinkled. "You guys take forever to just get to the talking. She loves you and me. I love you and you love me, and you told everyone I was your kid. So, tell him and he can make me your kid with his hammer."

Sarah cleared her throat. With a silent nod, she added her agreement.

"This is what you want?" Victoria asked.

Sarah swallowed the lump in her throat. It dissolved and her ability to speak returned. "I trust you, Victoria."

The judge's clear blue eyes studied Sarah. "If you are sure, then I have no reason to deny the request. There will be some changes to the paperwork, but I am sure your lawyer can have that on my desk by the end of the day."

Lyra stood up and buttoned her jacket. "Yes, your honor. I can get Ms. Brenton's name added and her signature on the documents if she is in agreement."

The room shifted as a whole. All eyes became focused on Victoria as the woman glanced back to her mother. They shared a smile before Victoria rose. Her hand lifted Tris's hand to her lips and she pressed a kiss to the back.

"Nothing would make me happier than to be your other mom, Tris."

Tris had a dozen questions when the judge offered to let her do the hammering. There were so many questions that Sarah had to tell her to just bang the gavel. This led to more questions about if she was the gavel banger, then could she add stipulations to the agreement that she would in fact be allowed to watch Spongebob.

The gavel was finally struck, and Tris posed for a photo with the judge. A photo that Lyra promised to provide a copy of to the judge who'd branded Tris his favorite person of all time.

They left the courtroom through the crowd of cheers. They were the same people they had been when they walked in, but they left with one major change. The girl with braids twisted into a bun nodded her head to each person she walked by and announced. "Hi, I'm Trisaya Monica O'Keeffe-Brenton. Don't worry about being too pretty from prison. The judges don't decide that way."

The steam from the shower left the mirror in a foggy haze. Even when she wiped away the condensation, the reflection staring back was incomplete. The finer details were smudged making it easier to believe it wasn't her looking back.

Avoiding mirrors was a tactic Sarah used most of her adult life. It had started the night after Sierra had left, when her mother had walked by thanking her for taking care of the high school counselor by dropping half the take on the counter. She'd never really considered if her mother could tell her daughters apart. But knowing had changed things. Changed her ability to not see her missing twin staring back at her. Scared to explore the possibility that she was the older twin, and her sister's sacrifice was one she was supposed to give. So, she stopped looking in the mirror when she could avoid it. She wouldn't have to talk to the other version of her. Listen to the whispered doubts of questionable identity.

The mirror called her daily now. Four days and the whispers no longer quietly sought her out. She could swear she heard the woman staring back at her screaming. Watched as her mouth dropped open. The whites of her eyes were pink and bloodshot. She reached out to the other side, but her hand didn't penetrate the reflective surface. It didn't ripple into another reality because there weren't two of her.

It was just her. The hazy surface cleared as the air cooled, and the skin created a cobblestone path to the scar that had separated them. Made them no longer interchangeable. A medical record of their differences that made her Sariah and the other Sierra.

Her fingers traced over the scar tissue. She didn't hate it, but worried about it each time someone saw her. Monica had shuttered, while Simone's face had turned to a grimace. She'd never dared to look at Victoria to see what she could learn from the lips as they reacted.

But the woman now stood behind her. Worry etched into her brow as another version of her stared back at Sarah from the mirror.

"I thought I heard you calling out," Victoria said.

Well, that explained the voice from the mirror. The reflection was a reflection, not a missing piece of herself. She's known that from the beginning... but it was funny knowing things.

Sarah ran her finger down the scar again. She watched Victoria's eyes follow the digit. Watched the woman lick her lips and eyes raise less brown than before.

"You're beautiful," Victoria whispered. She held up a thick housecoat. "Here, I figured you'd be cold."

It was New Year's Eve, and the rain had begun to fall again.

Her mind wandered down the path with her finger along the ridge of her scar. She wondered how the path would have been different had she not denied Victoria's interest to begin with. Would they still be living together? Would they have had sex already? Would her apartment ever have gotten broken into? Would Monica and her still be talking about a marriage of convenience pact?

Victoria was talking, which pulled Sarah back to the present. Away from the reflection and into the fuzzy embrace of the coat.

Sarah looked over the woman, and the questions came swirling back.

"I was just thinking about how different things would have been if I hadn't been so stubborn in the beginning."

"I don't regret it," Victoria admitted. She pressed her body to Sarah's back.

"Really?"

Victoria hummed, kissing her way from Sarah's neck to the back of her ear. She gently explained, "What's happening here is because of the path we took. Any change to the path could have resulted in a different outcome and I don't want a different outcome."

"So, you believe in free will over fate."

Victoria wet her lips and stared at Sarah through the mirror. The alternate universe where they were still together.

"I don't know what I believe, to be honest. I followed what I was told to do for so long that when I finally started making choices for myself it felt like everything I knew was lost. Like I was told gay people didn't belong in my world and then I realized I was gay and in my world. Then I decided I had to leave that world because I didn't belong and that meant leaving everyone behind."

Victoria sighed, and her eyes looked like she was seeing a different world in the mirror. She blinked a few times before Victoria's reflection met Sarah's gaze.

"But then they showed up in the way that Netflix got completely wrong. Circling back though makes me annoyed that I push off responsibility for my life up until coming out. People told me what I should do, yes, but I didn't have to. That was still my choice, and so it was free will. But then I struggle with what if the choices I make along the path are not as important as the big moments, like this. Us being together was fate but the free will was what made the story interesting. There were hundreds of different ways we could have ended up together, but what if the paradox of fate is that we were going to end up but there is not a particular way that it will happen."

Sarah chewed away the already sensitive flesh on her lower lip. She swayed safely between the ideas in the secure arms of the woman she loved.

"So, basically, the major plot points of our lives are predetermined. Like in every story of my life, I would still end up being Tris's mom?"

Victoria's brow furrowed slightly. But she nodded. "Yes, I guess that is what I am saying."

Sarah cocked her head slightly. "But doesn't being Tris's mom involve some element of precision? I mean, the right sperm with the right egg, means my sister would have had to meet whoever she did still when she was eighteen and still get pregnant."

"Well, maybe."

"What do you mean, maybe?" Sarah probed.

Victoria turned Sarah from the mirror. Looking into her eyes as though for once she was trying to give Sarah a glimpse into her soul.

"If we are rewriting the story, then who's to say the egg wouldn't change as well? And you don't know who the guy was, so what if he is a lawyer and your sister met him at work instead of well at work? The years may change, but in the realm of fate then it would work itself out to be the correct egg and sperm at the correct time to make the correct Tris. I mean there's only one Tris. I still can't believe she told the judge your sister is a zombie in Heaven."

Sarah felt like she should laugh or smile with Victoria. But the logical path Victoria had mapped out meant only one thing.

"But that means there would still have to be a tragedy for Tris to become mine," she whispered. "That means no matter what Sierra would still be dead."

"When I was younger, they told us that God gave the hardest challenges to the strongest people," Victoria stated.

"I feel like that is saying what doesn't kill you makes you stronger," Sarah stated. "Which is some fucking shit because I would rather her be alive than be strong."

"I know," Victoria whispered. "But you are strong. You've survived for so long. It's time to live, Sarah. I know you say she sacrificed for you. She made the choice as a child to give you this chance, then gave you a child because she trusted you."

Victoria cradled Sarah's head against her. "It's okay to cry and to miss her, but you can't live in a world of regret because you're not alone anymore. I'm not alone anymore. Your sister gave us both a gift we never thought we wanted, and now we get to live a life we never dreamed possible."

"To live..." Sarah whispered. "It sounds like an adventure."

Acknowledgments

I wish to express my deepest gratitude to the remarkable individuals who have contributed to the creation of this book in various ways. Your support, insight, and understanding have been instrumental in bringing these words to life.

First and foremost, I want to extend my heartfelt thanks to my wife. You have shown incredible patience and an extraordinary capacity for forgiveness during the turbulent journey of writing. Your willingness to endure my moments of creative madness and to let me act out scenes to capture the perfect facial expressions was a priceless gift. Your unwavering support is the cornerstone of my creative endeavors.

To Tara, my friend and confidante, thank you for being a dedicated partner in this creative journey. Your willingness to sit across the lunch table and engage deeply with my characters allowed them to evolve into multifaceted, authentic individuals. Your commitment to reading each chapter after dinner has been a constant source of motivation, and I'm profoundly grateful for your friendship.

I am indebted to Robin, for reading close to several hundred versions of this story. Your constant love for these characters made it possible to bring this story of open doors to fruition.

A special thank you goes to the young women who shared their stories with me. Your willingness to open up and provide insights was instrumental in shaping the narrative. Your bravery and candidness have made this book richer and more meaningful.

To everyone who supported me, whether through sharing experiences, providing guidance, or simply believing in the value of this project, I extend my thanks. This book is as much a product of your generosity and understanding as it is of my creativity. As I send this book out into the world, I do so with gratitude in my heart. I hope that it resonates with readers and serves as a testament to the collaboration and support that brought it to life.

About the Author

Chelsey Blue Spicer is a trailblazing author with a deep commitment to amplifying the voices and experiences of the LGBTQ+ community. Born with a storytelling spirit, Chelsey embarked on her writing journey at the age of twelve, inspired by her mother's own published autobiography. From a young age, she understood the power of words to spark conversations, challenge norms, and create positive change.

Chelsey's novels stand out for their fearless exploration of post-coming out narratives within the LGBTQ+ community. Fueled by a deep-seated passion for representation, she confronts and dismantles harmful stereotypes, particularly the "bury your gays" media trope that has plagued LGBTQ+ storytelling for years. Chelsey's stories break free from the shackles of conventional narratives, showcasing everyday life and celebrating the diverse experiences of LGBTQ+ individuals without resorting to violence or relegating characters to stereotypical roles.

Infuriated by the lack of nuanced representation, Chelsey Blue Spicer writes with a mission—to provide models of life for LGBTQ+ individuals after they come out. Her narratives go beyond the struggles, offering glimpses into the joy, resilience, and triumphs that define the everyday lives of the LGBTQ+ community.

Chelsey is not just an author; she is a voice for those whose stories have often been overlooked or misrepresented. Through her work, she aims to create a literary landscape where everyone can see themselves reflected, celebrated, and understood. Chelsey Blue Spicer invites readers to join her in breaking down barriers, fostering understanding, and embracing the diverse and beautiful spectrum of human experiences within the LGBTQ+ community.

www.chelseybluespicer.com

Turn the page for a preview of Chelsey Blue Spicer's new novel

Available in 2025

Meet Xiomara

Self Love. Each letter was inked into a knuckle. A word for each hand. A message from a younger Xiomara that was difficult to hide. It was a dream she couldn't hate, even though the ink had caused every potential employer to scan their desk for anything missing before promising she'd hear from them shortly. She rarely heard back and today would probably be no different.

The heavy footfalls of Echo's nonslip sneakers reminded Xiomara she wasn't alone. The other woman's presence required Xiomara to fix her face. Her shoulders straightened, and she unfolded the cuffs of her shirt to cover the rest of her colorful self-recreation.

"You think this lady will at least call me to tell me she won't hire me?" Xiomara asked.

She took the suit jacket for Echo, expecting it to be heavy since she knew it was expensive. The wool didn't feel how Xiomara imagined; it was silkier against her fingertips. Xiomara second guessed putting it on because if she snagged it, she would spend the rest of her life in debt to Echo's friend.

"At least try it on." Echo nodded toward jacket. "You don't want to wait until you get there to find it doesn't fit. My friend said not to stress about it getting messed up. You know Dilynn and her credit card."

"I liked her cash more than her card," Xiomara admitted.

"Well, she apparently got Alex five of these suits."

Xiomara felt the power that came with a jacket like this transfer to her being once it was on. The fit was tailored a size too big for Xiomara, and she felt like she was going through her dad's side of the closet again. It hadn't worked when she was a kid, but it was working now.

"Looks good on you," Echo promised. She adjusted the tie's knot at the base of Xiomara's throat. "And I think Ari will call you back to hire you."

"You know, know her?" Xiomara pressed.

"I've met her a few times," Echo said. "I hate her father. And her mother is worse. But Sylvia spoke really good of her. I have a feeling she's letting Ari hire her own paralegal because she is going to promote her soon."

Running her hand over the fresh fade of her undercut, Xiomara began second-guessing the bun on top of her head. Wearing it down would be professional. The type of look the Winters Real Estate Sect would be looking for in a paralegal.

"Stop stressing," Echo instructed. That was easy for Echo to say. She owned a bar. She could wear what she wanted.

Seven interviews, and Xiomara had only managed to secure one lawyer who offered her part-time hours. Part-time didn't pay the bills with two kids at home.

"I just... I want this job." Xiomara licked her lips. Her words were only partially truthful. She wanted the job, yes, but she couldn't tell Echo she needed the job.

"She's going to hire you," Echo said again.

A sinking feeling settled in Xiomara's chest. She'd worked so hard to get her certificate. Earned two pieces of paper with her name on them that said she wasn't a loser anymore.

"You didn't say anything to that rich lady who had her tongue down your throat, right?" Xiomara asked. She pressed the tie down. "I gotta do this on my own. No favors."

The bar wasn't open yet, but Echo made her way around the counter and began wiping glasses. Talking about the not-relationship between the bar owner and the billionaire was supposed to be a no go. She knew Echo had a thing for Sylvia Winter; even felt sorry for Echo because that crush had been almost ten years in the making and Echo was single now. Echo was going to end up hurt when Winters chose someone on her level.

"I didn't say anything to Sylvia about you. And like I said, I only met Ari a few times." Echo studied the glasses that still needed to be pulled out. "Sylvia is, like, hot and cold, and asking for a favor means you'll owe her forever. I don't want to owe her, and I don't want you to owe her, either. Just get the job, but don't take nothing extra."

Xiomara searched the woman to see if time had turned her into a liar. Since juvie, though, Echo had always come through for her when she needed a job. Always found something for Xiomara to do to keep the lights on, especially since DCS had come knocking on her door a few months ago after Xiomara's mom passed.

Echo's Escape was still just a dive bar. It was barely surviving, but Echo was good people, and Xiomara needed good people who knew people with job openings. People who maybe would give a masc covered in tattoos a chance.

She silently rehearsed her responses to the questions from her other interview as Echo went about her pre-opening routine. The job Xiomara had taken at the bar didn't have the types of questions the lawyers asked. No, today, she needed to highlight her skills and experience while she battled Ari Simmons's first impression.

Ari Simmons would see the tattoos and unconventional hairstyle first, so

Xiomara would start as a no. She'd be labeled the butch dyke and probably be assumed a member of the Cartel before she even opened her mouth. Even grown up, she was still the same kid standing before some white lady with a degree who got to decide her future.

As the minutes ticked away, Xiomara's anxiety intensified. She needed a drink, but going in smelling like tequila and tatted was probably a worse impression.

"Xio, your thoughts are so fucking loud," Echo said.

Xiomara hated that Echo knew her as that girl. She'd put her whole name on her resume. Vowed to leave Xio behind on 10th Ave.

Hitting the volume button to the stereo, Echo brought life to the dimly lit space. The music wasn't Xiomara's pre-interview jam. Its beat was a little too slow to make Xiomara feel like a badass. No, this was music for slow kissing and soft grinding bullshit. Also, not Xiomara's style.

Her style was the problem, though.

Xiomara tugged at the sleeve to see if it would cover her knuckles. She needed to stop at CVS to pick up some foundation. She could do that. Cover up the promise to love herself so she could get Diego cleats for baseball tryouts. Maybe she could get Elena that gem-growing kit she kept looking at so she'd do some science instead of practicing how to dance on a pole.

"Look, Xio," Echo waited for Xiomara's gaze to rise to her. She slapped a towel over her shoulder. "Just talk to Ari like a real person because people like her and Via don't need someone else kissing their ass. I mean, don't cuss at her, but shoot her straight."

Echo raised a single finger. A condition. "And don't stare at her tits." The woman's hands pressed against her own decently fitted shirt and pushed her boobs together. "She always wears these low-cut tops, and she is hot as shit, and her wife is Evie's partner. I know you've seen her around"

Xio pressed a finger to her throat. "The one who used to be a dude."

"Yeah. So, don't stare at her tits. She's going to be your boss, not one of your girls."

"Sounds exactly like my kinda girl." Xiomara's chest swelled. She could talk to a lady's lady; she could talk well for that kind of lady. They were her specialty. Especially ones looking for something quiet. Well, she preferred them to be loud, but—

"No," Echo warned. "Leave your strap in the car. You pull that playa shit, and she'll chew you up and shit you out with a harassment lawsuit wrapped around your throat. You want to work for her and not doing that kinda work."

"So, I'm her type," Xiomara said, taking a seat on the empty stool.

Echo's head shook slowly. "Don't shit where you eat."

"I don't shit," Xiomara reminded her old cellmate. "And you're one to talk. I watched you just last week trying to get the billionaire to cum on your thigh after she spilled her drink all over your tits."

"Everyone shits," Echo said, snapping the towel at Xiomara. "I just read that book to Henrie. I'm not looking forward to potty training. Any tips?"

"Naw. Ma took care of that."

Silently, Xiomara said a prayer for her mother. Then, she prayed to her mother, asking her to look out for Leonel in heaven because her son had been a good boy. Not a 1030 like his father, and he'd died because she took too long to get her kids out of reach, which was why Xiomara needed this job. She had to get Diego out of the hood before he was on the wrong side of the road or Elena fell for one of those fast-talking boys who would fuck up her life.

"How's Diego and Elena?"

A smile pulled up Xiomara's lips. Those kids were going to do better than she did because Xio was going to follow Echo's instructions. She was going to get this job. And then, she would get her family out of Maryvale without gang tats or their own kids, so they wouldn't have to worry about job interviews.

"Diego got a citizenship award at school. Said he's gonna be the first Chollo president. My son's got big dreams." She rubbed at the back of her head again.

"What about Elena?" Echo pressed.

Xiomara's head fell back. "That girl has all of Citlaly's attitude. I swear, my bitch of a sister taught Elena to scoff like she's sixteen instead of ten. She told me I needed to take her to get her nails. You know, the fucking claws that will take out an eye. She's ten!"

The laughter from Echo bounced around the space. Xiomara didn't like being laughed at, but she would give Echo a pass this time for borrowing a jacket for her.

"I gotta go," Xiomara said, running her finger over the tats once more. "I want to make sure I'm early. And I need to still stop at CVS."

www.ingramcontent.com/pod-product-compliance
Lightning Source LLC
Chambersburg PA
CBHW070846280626
47161CB00017B/2454